Praise for the Imager Portfolio

"*Rex Regis* is a worthy finale to what's turned out
to be the author's finest complete
fantasy series to date."

—*Tor.com*

"A wholly absorbing entry in this highly
addictive series."

—*Kirkus Reviews* (starred review) on *Antiagon Fire*

"Provides a fascinating picture of imagers at war,
while continuing to explore different styles of
governance in this intriguing world."

—*Locus* on *Antiagon Fire*

"[Modesitt's] ability to ring changes on this classic
has resulted in many a good book,
this one included."

—*Booklist* on *Princeps*

"Modesitt enjoys a following that appreciates
his verisimilitude, versatility, and
storytelling talent."

—*Library Journal* on *Imager's Challenge*

"A fascinating story."

—*Sacramento Book Review* on
Imager's Intrigue

TOR BOOKS BY L. E. MODESITT, JR.

Rex Regis

The Eighth Book of the
Imager Portfolio

L. E. MODESITT, JR.

TOR®
fantasy

A TOM DOHERTY ASSOCIATES BOOK
NEW YORK

This is a work of fiction. All of the characters, organizations, and events portrayed in this novel are either products of the author's imagination or are used fictitiously.

REX REGIS

Map by Jon Lansberg

A Tor Book
Published by Tom Doherty Associates, LLC
175 Fifth Avenue
New York, NY 10010

www.tor-forge.com

Tor® is a registered trademark of Tom Doherty Associates, LLC.

ISBN 978-0-7653-7090-7

Tor books may be purchased for educational, business, or promotional use. For information on bulk purchases, please contact the Macmillan Corporate and Premium Sales Department at 1-800-221-7945, extension 5442, or write to specialmarkets@macmillan.com.

First Edition: January 2014
First Mass Market Edition: January 2015

Printed in the United States of America

0 9 8 7 6 5 4 3

For Kevin and Lani

Characters

Bhayar	Lord of Telaryn and Bovaria
Aelina	Wife of Bhayar
Kharst	Rex of Bovaria [deceased]
Aliaro	Autarch of Antiago [deceased]
Quaeryt	Commander, Imager, and friend of Bhayar
Vaelora	Wife of Quaeryt and youngest sister of Bhayar
Khaern	Subcommander, Eleventh Regiment
Alazyn	Subcommander, Nineteenth Regiment
Zhelan	Major, First Company
Ghaelyn	Undercaptain, First Company
Deucalon	Marshal of Telaryn
Ernyld	Subcommander, Chief of Staff
Myskyl	Submarshal, Northern Army of Telaryn
Skarpa	Submarshal, Southern Army
Fhaen	Subcommander, Third Regiment
Meinyt	Subcommander, Fifth Regiment
Kharllon	Commander, Fourteenth Regiment
Paedn	Subcommander, Fourth Regiment
Dulaek	Subcommander, Sixth Regiment
Fhaasn	Subcommander, Twenty-sixth Regiment
Calkoran	Subcommander, Fifth Battalion, Pharsi
Eslym	Major, First Company, Fifth Battalion
Zhael	Major, Second Company, Fifth Battalion
Arion	Major, Third Company, Fifth Battalion
Voltyr	Imager Undercaptain
Akoryt	Imager Undercaptain [deceased]
Shaelyt	Imager Undercaptain, Pharsi [deceased]
Threkhyl	Imager Undercaptain
Desyrk	Imager Undercaptain
Baelthm	Imager Undercaptain
Khalis	Imager Undercaptain, Pharsi
Lhandor	Imager Undercaptain, Pharsi
Horan	Imager Undercaptain
Smaethyl	Imager Undercaptain
Elsior	Imager trainee, Pharsi

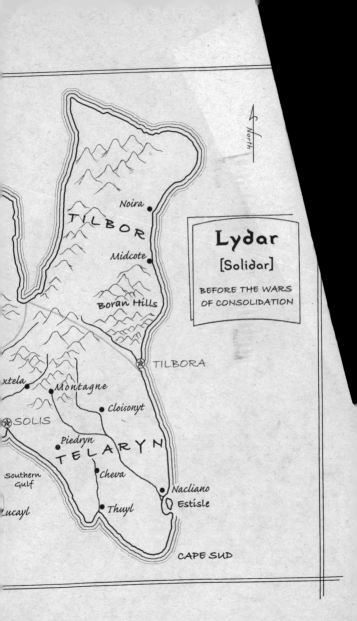

Lydar

[Solidar]

BEFORE THE WARS
OF CONSOLIDATION

North

TILBOR

Noira

Midcote

Boran Hills

TILBORA

xtela

Montagne

Cloisonyt

SOLIS

Piedryn

TELARYN

Southern
Gulf

Cheva

Nacliano

Estisle

Lucayl

Thuyl

CAPE SUD

Rex Regis

1

~~~~~~~~

In the cool air of early spring, on the second Solayi in Maris, the man who wore the uniform of a Telaryn commander stood at the foot of the long stone pier that dominated the south end of the harbor at Kephria. Behind Quaeryt were only ashes and ruins, except for the old stone fort to the immediate south of the pier, and the rising trooper compound more than a mille to the north, situated at the corner of the old fortifications that had once marked the border between Antiago and Bovaria. He looked out onto the Gulf of Khellor, where patches of mist drifted above the dark surface.

Then his eyes dropped to the pier, once the pride of the port city that had been leveled by the late Autarch's cannon and imagers. Most of the stone pillars that supported the pier remained solid—but not all. The stone-paved surface of the long pier was pitted, and many of the gray paving stones were cracked. A few were shattered. Almost every stone showed signs of fire, either in the ashes in the mortared joins between the stones, or in blackened sections of stone. The wooden bollards were all charred—those that remained. One section of the pier, some two hundred yards out from the shore, sagged almost half a yard over a twenty-yard stretch.

The *Zephyr*—the large three-masted schooner that

had brought Quaeryt, his imagers, and first company to Kephria—lay anchored a good half mille out from the pier in the now-quiet waters of the Gulf of Kephria.

Quaeryt took a slow deep breath, then concentrated on the section of the pier where it joined the harbor boulevard to the first charred bollards, roughly fifty yards away.

The briefest flash of light flared across the first section of the pier, and then the gray stone was shrouded in a white and cold fog that drifted seaward with the slightest hint of a land breeze. When the afterimage of the flash subsided, and the fog had dispersed enough for Quaeryt to see, he smiled. He hadn't even felt any strain, and the first fifty yards of the stone pier looked—and were—as strong and as new as when they had been first constructed, centuries before.

He waited a bit for the frost on the gray stone to melt away, then walked carefully to the end of the section he had rebuilt with his imaging. Once there, he concentrated once again, on the next section of the pier. After the second imaging, he did feel a slight twinge across his forehead. Rather than immediately press on, given the length of the pier requiring rebuilding, Quaeryt lifted the water bottle from his jacket pocket, uncorked it, and took a swallow of the watered lager before recorking the bottle and replacing it in his pocket.

"Take your time. You've got all day if you need it." He glanced toward the fort where Vaelora was—he hoped—taking her time in preparing for the day. He tried not to dwell on the events that had caused her to miscarry their daughter . . . but he had seen the darkness behind Vaelora's eyes when she'd thought he wasn't looking.

Then he walked slowly to the end of the second rebuilt section, trying not to think about how much of the pier remained to be reconstructed, a good four hundred yards more extending out into the waters where the River Laar and the Gulf of Khellor met and mixed. He glanced to the west where he could barely make out through the morning mist the low smudge of land that had once held Ephra, before the Autarch's imagers and cannon had destroyed it.

Finally, he concentrated once more, and another section of the pier was renewed. Quaeryt took a slow deep breath. There had been another twinge as he'd imaged, but it hadn't felt any worse than the last one.

"You'll have to keep taking it slow and easy," he murmured as he took another small swallow of watered lager and waited for the mist and frost to clear.

Section by section, over the next three glasses, Quaeryt imaged and rebuilt fifty-yard lengths, although his skull ached slightly more with each effort, and he had to rest longer after each section was completed.

After he had finished the last section, and he walked to the seaward end of the pier, Quaeryt took a deep breath and massaged his forehead. His head definitely ached, and faint flashes of light flickered before his eyes, a sign that—unless he wanted to be laid up and unable to image for days—he was close to his limit for imaging. *For now . . . for now. But if you don't keep working to build up your strength, it won't be there when you need it.* And he had no doubts he would need it on the return trip to Variana, and most likely even more after he reached the capital city of Bovaria, a land totally defeated, yet, almost paradoxically, far from conquered and certainly a land with more problems, the nastiest of which would likely fall to him—and Vaelora—to resolve.

Standing almost at the end of the pier, Quaeryt

gestured, then called, image-projecting his voice toward the *Zephyr* so that Captain Sario could bring the ship back to the pier to tie up. The quick jab across his skull was a definite reminder that he needed to do no more imaging for some time.

He hoped he'd recover in a few glasses, but . . . he'd have to see. Part of the reason he'd worked on the pier was to determine what he could do and how fast he would recover after all his injuries in the battle for Liantiago.

While he waited for the schooner to raise enough sail for headway into the pier, Quaeryt lifted the water bottle from his jacket pocket, uncorked it, and took another swallow of the watered lager before recorking the bottle and replacing it.

Almost half a glass later, the *Zephyr* came to rest at the most seaward position at the pier, with the crew making the schooner fast to the pier, and then doubling up the lines.

Sario looked from his position on the sterncastle to the pier, and then to Quaeryt. "Is it solid?"

"Come onto the pier and see for yourself."

After a moment the Antiagon merchant captain walked forward to midships, then made his way down the gangway that two seamen had extended. Sario stamped his boots on the stone.

"Solid enough, but it was before. It still could be an illusion." His words held the heavy accent of Antiagon Bovarian, almost a separate dialect, and one that Quaeryt still had to strain to understand.

Quaeryt almost said that he didn't do illusions, except that he had. "Run your fingers over the stone or the bollard there. There wasn't one here before. It had rotted out."

The dark-haired captain did so, then walked another few yards toward the foot of the pier and tried again. Finally, he straightened and walked back to Quaeryt, shaking his head. "Why do you not do more like this, instead of destroying men and ships?"

"Because there are few indeed of us, and our greatest value to a ruler is what creates and supports his power. Without the support of a ruler, imagers are killed one by one. That is because few have great power. You saw how my undercaptains collapsed after less than a glass of battle. So we support Lord Bhayar because he has supported us and has pledged to continue to do so. That is the only way in which imagers and their wives and children will ever survive in Lydar . . . or anywhere on Terahnar." The reality was far more complex than that, but Quaeryt wasn't about to go into a long explanation. Instead, he smiled and gestured at the reconstructed pier. "So Kephria has a good pier for ships like the *Zephyr*. Your family might do well to open a small factorage here before others come to understand that Kephria will now serve as the port for both southern Bovaria and northern Antiago."

Sario laughed. "Commander, you have a way of making your point." His face sobered. "Yet . . . I can see the possible truth in what you say. I will talk it over with the others when I return to Westisle."

"You'll have to make a stop in Liantiago to drop off several of my troopers with dispatches."

"I can do that."

"I'd appreciate it." Quaeryt nodded. "You should be able to leave by the end of the week. I've put out word to the towns inland that you have some space for cargo."

"That would be welcome."

"We do what we can, Captain."

"How's your lady, sir?"

"She's much better. Much better, but she needs a few more days before she'll be up to a long ride."

Sario offered a sympathetic smile.

Quaeryt wished he could offer comfort in return, knowing that the captain had lost his beloved wife some years earlier, and still missed her greatly. *You were fortunate that you didn't lose Vaelora to the mistakes you made.* But they had lost more than either had intended. "Until later, Captain."

Sario nodded as Quaeryt turned and walked back toward the foot of the pier . . . and the fort. His head still throbbed, but the pain had been far worse many times before—and he had redone the pier without tariffing the other imagers, who had more than enough to do in dealing with rebuilding the trooper compound from the ruins.

2

~~~

"Now what?" asked Vaelora. She sat on the bed, wearing riding clothes, propped up with pillows, because there was little enough left of furnishings anywhere, let alone in the unruined section of the stone fort that remained the only structure in Kephria to have survived the Antiagon assault of both cannon and Antiagon Fire. In fact, all of the furnishings, except for the bed, had been imaged into being by two of Quaeryt's undercaptains, Khalis and Lhandor, except for one chair that Quaeryt had created.

The small amount of sunlight filtering into the fort on Solayi afternoon was enough for Quaeryt to see that Vaelora had color in her face and that the circles under her eyes were not so deep as they had been when he'd first seen her on Vendrei.

"Well?" prompted Vaelora when Quaeryt did not reply.

"You're feeling better," he replied in the court Bovarian they always used when alone . . . and with a smile.

"I am. You haven't answered the question."

"I think we need to report back to the lord and master of Lydar. In person and with a certain deliberate haste."

"Khel hasn't acknowledged his rule," she pointed out.

"I'm hopeful that in the coming months the High Council will see that discretion in negotiation is better than courage without strength in battle."

"That's possible . . . but you're still worried."

"Why should I be worried? Autarch Aliario has perished, and Antiago lies in the hands of Submarshal Skarpa. Presumably Submarshal Myskyl has used his forces to assure that northern Bovaria has accepted Bhayar's rule. With the fall of Antiago and the destruction of the wall around Kephria and the devastation of Ephra, the River Laar is now open to trade . . . even if there are no warehouses for traders around the harbor or anywhere near." Quaeryt let a sardonic tone creep into his next words. "Of course, our lord and master knows of none of this, and as you pointed out, he will be less than pleased that the High Council of Khel did not crawl on their knees to accept his most magnanimous terms. Seeing as the last two months have been winter, also, I have my doubts about how assiduously the submarshal of the Northern Army has pursued a campaign of persuasion in the north . . ."

In fact, Quaeryt had few doubts that Myskyl had already undertaken yet another effort to undermine and discredit Quaeryt, although Quaeryt had no idea in what form that effort might manifest itself.

Vaelora held up a hand in protest. "Dearest . . . I think you've made your point. When should we leave?"

"Not until three days after you think you're ready."

"Then we'll leave on Jeudi."

Quaeryt shook his head. "No anticipation. You don't feel ready to leave today. We'll see how you feel tomorrow."

"You worry too much."

*No . . . I didn't worry enough about you, and I almost
lost you . . . and we did lose our daughter.*

"Dearest . . ." began Vaelora softly. "You did the best
you could do. If you'd left another regiment or some
imagers, you would have failed in Antiago, especially
in Liantiago in facing Aliaro."

"I should have taken you with me, then."

"With all that riding, the same thing might well have
happened. What might have happened in Liantiago?
Where would I have been safe there?"

Quaeryt had no answers to her questions.

"We both knew that seeking what we want and need
would be dangerous, but unless Bhayar unites all of
Lydar, that cannot be. If Bhayar fails to unite Lydar,"
Vaelora went on, her voice quiet but firm, "sooner or
later all will turn against him for the costs of the wars.
You are the only one who can assure that he is successful."

"No. You and I together are the only ones. Without
your presence in Khel, there would be no chance that
the High Council would even have considered his terms.
Without your counsel, I would have made too many
mistakes." *Even more than I already did.*

"Dearest . . . I've made mistakes as well. Trusting
Grellyana was a terrible mistake."

"I doubt that it made much difference in the end, not
with the mistakes I made," he replied with a soft laugh.

They both smiled, and both smiles were rueful.

"What about Nineteenth Regiment?" asked Vaelora
after several moments. "Will you summon Alazyn to
join us?"

"I think not. Skarpa will need all the troopers he has
in Liantiago. And it would take weeks for Alazyn to

march here, and we don't have the ships to transport a full regiment and its mounts from Liantiago. Also, another regiment won't help us in returning to Variana." *Or after we get there, since resolving any problems we face won't require large battles.* "We still have Eleventh Regiment, and it is almost at full strength. First company is at three-quarters strength."

"Of a normal company."

Quaeryt nodded, acknowledging that first company had set out from Variana with five squads, rather than four, then went on. "I think Calkoran should accompany us, with his first company, so that he can brief Bhayar as well, but Major Zhael and Major Arion and their companies should hold Kephria and Geusyn . . . what's left of them."

"They should encourage the locals to relocate to Kephria," suggested Vaelora. "That's where the traders will come now."

"I'll make certain that they spread the word." *I'll also make certain that they don't allow people to build shanties or the like near the harbor.* He paused. "I had thought we might find a way to use Rex Kharst's canal boat on the return, but the Antiagon imagers destroyed it when they fired all the wooden piers in Geusyn."

"Trying to use it would just have slowed us down." Vaelora shifted her weight in the bed, then swung her feet onto the floor. "I need to walk some more." She leaned forward gingerly and pulled on the low boots.

Quaeryt rose from the chair beside her bed, then extended his right hand. The end two fingers on his left still refused to move, except slightly, and then only when he tried to close the entire hand. It had been almost half a year since the battle of Variana, and he had come to the conclusion that he might never regain the use of those fingers.

Vaelora took his hand, but used it only to steady herself for a moment, before she walked toward the gun port that had been sealed for years. Quaeryt walked beside her. With each step, fine ash swirled around their boots, even though the area had been swept just glasses before.

"It's warm enough. Let's walk over to the pier and out to the *Zephyr*."

"Are you sure?"

"I'm sure. I won't get stronger doing nothing. I'm not bleeding, and my bruises are all healing. Sometimes this happens to women for no reason at all, and they survive. So will I."

Quaeryt wasn't about to argue.

Once they reached the pier, Quaeryt checked his imaging shields, making sure that they covered both Vaelora and himself. He could feel the effort, most likely because of what he had been doing earlier.

"Quaeryt . . ." Vaelora's voice was cool.

"Yes?"

"There are no burn marks left on the stone. There are no cracks or chips. The center section of the pier no longer sags."

"I had the pier repaired," he said blandly.

"That's why you look so tired. Just how much imaging did you do?"

"All of it," he admitted. "It took much of the morning. I did it a section at a time. It took almost three glasses." He held up a hand. "The other imagers are needed to rebuild the trooper compound. I could do this alone. Besides, I need to rebuild my own imaging strength."

"And you want *me* to rest?"

"It's different." *I didn't get hit with a tree and lose a child and nearly get burned alive by Antiagon Fire.*

"I may use those words myself . . . sometime."

Quaeryt kept his wince inside himself. "Shall we walk out on the pier?"

"So I can admire your image-crafting and might?"

"No . . . so that you can regain your strength in order to tell me where I should take care." He offered the words lightly and with a smile.

Vaelora shook her head.

As they walked, Quaeryt again studied the harbor, empty of all vessels except the three-masted schooner that had brought him, the imager undercaptains, and first company back to Kephria. The waters of the Gulf of Khellor lapped placidly at the stone pillars of the rebuilt pier, the sole remaining one, which had survived the efforts of the Antiagon imagers that had destroyed the others only because it had been built of stone generations earlier. The stone boulevard that circled the harbor also remained, but the only trace of the buildings that had stood there less than a month before were rain-flattened ashes and occasional piles of brick or stone, the remnants of chimneys or the infrequent brick or stone-walled shop. Even after the rain of the previous day, the smell of charred wood remained strong.

"It's quiet now," said Vaelora.

"It will be for a time, but it's too good a port not to be rebuilt. It won't ever rival Solis or Liantiago, or even Kherseilles, but it will serve the south of Bovaria and the north of Antiago." Quaeryt glanced ahead to the end of the pier where the *Zephyr* was tied up.

As Vaelora and Quaeryt neared the schooner, Sario, standing by the gangway, inclined his head to Vaelora.

"Lady." Then he turned his eyes to Quaeryt and raised his eyebrows.

"With some fortune, Captain," replied Quaeryt to the unspoken question, "as I said earlier, you should be on your way back to Liantiago within the week. I'll also suggest some additional recompense from Submarshal Skarpa." *Seeing as he has all the paychests, except for the small one he sent with us.*

"That would be appreciated." The dark-haired captain replied in heavily accented Antiagon Bovarian. "Will you have troopers remaining here?"

"We will leave some forces here to keep order while others rebuild, and the remainder of our forces will return to Variana to report to Lord Bhayar . . . and to see where else we may be needed."

"You will always be needed, Commander." Sario inclined his head. "We await your orders."

Vaelora and Quaeryt turned back toward the fort.

When they reached the foot of the pier, Vaelora looked to her husband. "You need to talk to your officers . . . if we're to leave on Jeudi. You can't do any more here."

"More likely Samedi or Solayi," replied Quaeryt. "The one thing Bhayar would not forgive would be more injury to you." *He may not forgive me for what you have already suffered.* He did not tell Vaelora that he had already summoned Khaern, Zhelan, and Calkoran to meet with him at the third glass of the afternoon.

"Although," Vaelora added with a smile, "I'd be surprised if you had not already arranged to meet them this afternoon."

"I did indeed, and how did you know that?"

"I know you, dearest."

Quaeryt escorted her into the old fort, past the pair

of troopers standing guard duty, and into the makeshift quarters area.

Vaelora sat down on the bed. "I'll be fine. Go."

"At your command, my lady." Quaeryt grinned at her.

"Don't be impossible, dearest, or I'll read more about Rholan and quote long passages to you when you return."

"There are worse fates," he quipped.

"Do you want me to find one?"

With another grin, Quaeryt shook his head.

Vaelora gave a soft laugh.

He bent down and kissed her cheek. "I won't be too long."

"Take the time you need."

"I will." He turned and made his way out of the fort and along the stone walk to the stone boulevard that bordered the eastern end of the harbor. As he walked north, he hoped that Vaelora was indeed as strong as she said, although he had to admit that her steps had shown no weakness on the walk up the long pier and back. *And she rode the entire distance from Ferravyl to Variana to save you, hardly pausing even for rest.*

Still . . . he worried. And that wasn't even accounting for the difficulties they were likely to encounter on the ride back across a still-restive Bovaria.

The three officers were waiting outside the structure that had once been a small stone blockhouse at the base of where the wall along the south side of the harbor had joined the wall that had once defined the border between Bovaria and Antiago. Now, it was a much larger building, thanks to the four imager undercaptains.

"Sir," offered Zhelan.

Both Khaern and Calkoran inclined their heads.

"Once the Lady Vaelora is recovered enough to ride,

as I suggested yesterday, we will be returning to Variana to report on the results of the mission to Khel and the conquest of Antiago. I'd like each of you to prepare for departure later this week, possibly as early as Vendrei." Quaeryt paused, wondering if he should mention again that Calkoran and his company would be accompanying them, while Arion and Zhael and their companies would remain to keep order in Kephria. *They already know. Don't repeat yourself.*

Quaeryt turned to Zhelan. "Are there any troopers in first company that should remain here?"

"No, sir. Those with broken arms and legs can accompany us, and there are none injured more seriously."

"What about mounts? Have you found enough between those Calkoran returned with from Khel and the locals?"

"We've obtained some spare mounts locally, and we have enough. We've also acquired some packhorses as well, and two wagons. We thought those might be needed." Zhelan did not smile.

Quaeryt did see a hint of amusement in the major's eyes, but he more than appreciated Zhelan's continual forethought. "Your thoughts were correct, and I appreciate your efforts." He looked at Khaern. "Eleventh Regiment?"

"We're prepared to leave at a day's notice, sir."

"Good. Is there anything I should know?"

"None of the holders whose holds you destroyed have returned, but . . . what if they do?"

"That's something that Major Zhael and Major Arion will have to deal with, one way or another. They won't have that many armsmen. The reports the submarshal sent with me indicated that a number of them lost men at Liantiago, and two of the former High

Holders likely were killed at Barna. Apparently, Aliaro wanted to use them there, and spare his own troops."

"Even were they not," declared Calkoran, "my officers can handle them."

Quaeryt suspected that was not likely even to be a question. "Subcommanders . . . you can go and inform your men. I need some time to go over some first company matters with Major Zhelan."

"Yes, sir."

In moments, Zhelan and Quaeryt were alone outside the building that would be the trooper headquarters in Kephria.

"Do you intend to send a dispatch rider or courier before us?" asked Zhelan.

"I had not thought to," replied Quaeryt. "What are your thoughts on that?"

"What you and Submarshal Skarpa have accomplished might best be reported directly. That way there would be no misunderstanding. There would also be no plans based on information that might not be . . ."

"Accurate?" suggested Quaeryt.

"Yes, sir."

"I think we share the same concerns, Zhelan." *That Myskyl and Marshal Deucalon would use any information against them.* Quaeryt paused. "I do appreciate your forethought."

"Your concerns were with Lady Vaelora, sir."

"Yes, they were. But she is much better. She also feels that we should return to Variana . . . and not for reasons of her health."

"We'll be ready anytime after Mardi, sir."

"Are there any men among the wounded who are especially dependable?"

Zhelan frowned. "Both Wessyl and Ralor. Wessyl's

arm was broken, but not badly. Ralor has his leg splinted."

"I'd like to send them back to Liantiago on the *Zephyr* with dispatches for the submarshal."

"They'd do well, sir."

"If you say so, I'm certain they will."

All in all, Quaeryt spent more than a glass discussing preparations with Zhelan, before he left to walk back to the fort.

3

Just before midmorning on Lundi, as Vaelora and Quaeryt walked northward along the harbor boulevard into a brisk wind under a gray sky, she turned to Quaeryt. "I feel fine."

"That may be," he replied, "but I'd like to see how you feel this afternoon."

"I'll still feel good."

"We'll see," he replied, glancing to the north as he saw two riders in Telaryn uniform greens riding toward them. Each rider was leading a second mount, one leading the black gelding Quaeryt had ridden in Khel, and the other the black mare Vaelora had ridden. Quaeryt had his doubts about the symbolism, but Calkoran had insisted.

"That's Major Zhelan, with another trooper," Vaelora said. "He needs you for something."

"And that means a problem or trouble, if not both." Whatever it might be, it had happened recently, because Zhelan had not mentioned any difficulties at the morning muster. Nor had Khaern or Calkoran. "It has to be something involving the locals."

"Could it be a dispatch rider from Bhayar?"

"It's possible, but not likely this early in the day."

They stopped and waited for Zhelan to reach them.

When the major and the ranker reined up, Quaeryt asked, "What is it?"

"There's a messenger here from a High Holder Basalyt," said Zhelan.

"Basalyt?" Quaeryt frowned. Where had he heard the name? It took him several moments to remember. "One of the southern holders whose hold we leveled because he wouldn't meet with Vaelora and Skarpa? Is that the one?"

"I imagine so. He sent a youth, and the boy's trying not to shake like a leaf in a gale. He's waiting at the blockhouse."

"Did he say what he wanted?"

"He said he was under orders to deliver the message to the submarshal or senior officer in command."

"He sent a youth . . . so we wouldn't kill him?" Quaeryt shook his head. "I'll see him . . . after we escort Lady Vaelora back to the fort. I assume that's why you brought the mounts."

"Yes, sir."

Quaeryt looked to Vaelora, raising his eyebrows.

"Yes . . . I can certainly ride that far," she replied, adding in a much lower voice intended only for his ears, "and much farther, dearest."

She did accept his offer of a leg up, since there was nothing to serve as a mounting block anywhere near.

Then Quaeryt mounted and turned in the saddle to look at her as they rode back south toward the fort. "I'm judging that his master likely wants to beg forgiveness and pay tariffs and be a good High Holder. Either that, or he sent the boy to demand his lands back. What do you think?"

"It wouldn't hurt to allow him to retain his holding . . . if he's begging and requesting. And if he's remotely trustworthy. Under the law, you haven't actually conveyed his lands to Bhayar yet."

"You'll have to meet with the High Holder as well, then," Quaeryt told Vaelora.

"I can do that."

"What do I do if he's not trustworthy or it's an attempt at something else?"

Vaelora smiled sadly.

"I was afraid that would be the answer, not that I disagree with you." Quaeryt shook his head.

Once Quaeryt had left Vaelora at the fort, he and Zhelan rode back toward the blockhouse.

"What do you think of the youth?"

"He's well bred. He's not common. He rode in with two guards."

"The High Holder's son?"

"Might be. Or his nephew. Someone he trusts."

"It's a gamble on his part."

"Is it, really, sir? If he doesn't do something, he's lost everything."

"I can't very well . . ." Quaeryt broke off his words, deciding that saying more before he met the young man would be premature.

When Quaeryt reached the blockhouse, he saw how much progress the imager undercaptains had made in rebuilding the former Antiagon structure. The walls, floors, and roof of the new wing looked to be complete. "They've done well."

"They're trying to complete the quarters and stables for a battalion before we leave."

Quaeryt turned his attention to the full squad of troopers from first company stationed just south of the reconstructed main entrance to the blockhouse. Half were mounted. The others loosely guarded two men in dark blue. Quaeryt dismounted and followed Zhelan inside into the single large room on the ground-floor level.

Standing on one side was a youth, likely close to full grown, almost as tall as Quaeryt, but still thin, if with fairly broad shoulders. His light brown hair was short and well trimmed, and his riding jacket was a dark blue, with a touch of white piping. His trousers were also dark blue, and his dark brown boots, under a thin coat of dust, had been recently polished. His eyes fixed on Quaeryt, and although he said nothing, those eyes widened as they took in Quaeryt's snow-white hair and eyebrows . . . and even the pure white of his fingernails.

Quaeryt nodded to Zhelan.

"This is Commander Quaeryt," stated the major. "He's the one you sought."

"Are you a submarshal, sir?"

"No, I'm not. The submarshal is in Liantiago. I'm a commander and an envoy with credentials that empower me to make decisions for Lord Bhayar. What do you seek?"

"I bear a message from Basalyt, the former High Holder of Bartolan, the hold that the armies of Lord Bhayar leveled this winter."

"We leveled five holds," said Quaeryt. "Bartolan was one of the last. I would have thought that the High Holder would have understood the danger by then."

"His choices were few, sir. Bartolan is the smallest."

Quaeryt wasn't about to point out that Bhayar would have defended Bartolan had it pledged allegiance. Based on what the High Holder had likely experienced under Rex Kharst, he would not have believed Quaeryt, Vaelora, or Skarpa. "And you are?"

"Barlaan, his son and heir."

"His sole surviving son?"

"Yes, sir. My brothers died in the battle of Barna. That was when my sire decided it was best to make peace with Lord Bhayar."

"Were you there?"

"No, sir. My sire was, but he insisted that not all his heirs fight in the same battle."

Quaeryt wasn't certain he would have called the Antiagon attack at Barna a battle, but he merely nodded.

"Begging your pardon, sir . . . are you an ancient?"

"I've been called many things, Baarlan, from a lost one to an ancient. I am who and what I am, and that is a commander serving under Lord Bhayar. I'm Pharsi by birth, and most Pharsi call me a lost one."

"Yes, sir."

"You have a message for me?"

"Yes, sir. You are the commander here?" the youth asked again.

"I am, but any decision I make must also be approved by the Lady Vaelora. She is also here in Kephria."

The youth extended a sealed envelope. Quaeryt stepped forward, took it, and broke the seal. Then he began to read.

To the Submarshal or Commander:

I would most humbly apologize for my failures in not recognizing the rule of Lord Bhayar and in failing to pledge allegiance to him and to you who represent his power and his rule. I would request your forbearance and beseech you to allow me to offer in person such allegiance and any recompense that I can offer. As a token of my earnestness and desire to be a faithful holder of Lord Bhayar, I am sending this missive with my sole living son and heir, Barlaan.

Quaeryt lowered the single sheet and looked at Barlaan. "What orders did your father give you?"

"To deliver the missive, sir, and to return with your reply. To do so honorably."

"To die honorably, if necessary?"

"Yes, sir."

Quaeryt nodded. "We will meet him here at a glass past noon tomorrow. He is to bring no more than a half squad—that's ten—retainers or guards. That's for their safety, not ours. We have close to a regiment and a half of troopers." He paused. "I'll write that out, but it will be on the back of his message. We're a bit short of paper and the like."

It took almost a quint to find a pen and some ink for Quaeryt, and a bit longer for him to write out what he had in mind. Then he handed the missive to Barlaan.

"You and your men are free to leave. You are to accompany your father tomorrow, or we will not meet with him."

Quaeryt could see the apprehension in the young man's eyes. "Barlaan . . . if we wanted to kill you both, we wouldn't go through an elaborate charade to do it. Lord Bhayar is more interested in live and faithful High Holders than dead High Holders. Why your sire's hold was destroyed was because he refused to pledge allegiance. Nothing has happened to any Bovarian High Holder who pledged allegiance." *Not so far as you know . . . and you hope it stays that way.*

"Yes, sir."

"Wouldn't it have been easier for me just to hold you and ask your father to join us?"

"Yes, sir."

"Go . . . and carry both messages to your sire." Quaeryt gestured for the youth to leave the blockhouse.

After waiting a time, Quaeryt walked to the open door and watched as Barlaan and his men mounted and then rode toward the gap in the wall created by the imagers during the initial capture of Kephria.

"Will you allow him to pledge allegiance, sir?" asked Zhelan quietly as his eyes followed the youth and his two guards.

"I'll have to discuss it with the Lady Vaelora, but my inclination is to accept his allegiance, not to take his life, but not allow him to remain as High Holder."

Zhelan nodded. "He should pay some price for his lack of faith."

"Oh . . . it appears that he already has. We just have to make sure that others understand that as well." Quaeryt turned. "We need to go over the arrangements for tomorrow, and your thoughts about what we need to do to be ready to ride out on Vendrei or Samedi."

4

"No!"

Vaelora's cry was so wrenching that Quaeryt, deeply as he was sleeping sometime after midnight, bolted awake instantly. He scrambled up from the pallet on the floor where he slept, less than a yard away from her, to the side of her bed.

"No!"

Even in the dimness of the old stone fort, he could see that she was fully awake, her eyes wide, but focused somewhere well beyond Kephria. He stood, looking down at her, afraid to touch her for fear of interrupting what she might be seeing, yet worried about what she might be experiencing.

Abruptly her eyes focused on Quaeryt, and he bent down. "What was it?" he asked, his arms around her. "A nightmare . . . or a farsight?"

"I wasn't sleeping. I woke up a while ago, maybe a quint or so ago, thinking about how much we have left to do, and worrying about what the Khellan High Council will do . . . and about what has happened in Variana since we left, and how Bhayar was . . . and . . . whether we could . . . you know, dearest."

"I know . . . and I'm sure we can." Quaeryt didn't

want to say more, not since it had been such a short time since Vaelora's injury and miscarriage.

"Then . . . out of nowhere, I had this flash."

"About what?"

"I don't know. Rather . . . I know, but it didn't make any sense at all. It was extremely clear. You were standing in a well-lighted room. I didn't see anyone else. It could have been a High Holder's study, or a library, even a salon. Then, there was total darkness. You were still there. I could sense you, but there was only darkness . . . and the darkness was filled with danger." Vaelora shuddered again. "That was all." After a moment she added, "Maybe I shouldn't have told you at all."

"It wasn't familiar to you?"

"No . . . but that doesn't mean anything."

Quaeryt held her a bit more closely for several moments before he spoke again. "Like the way you didn't recognize the entrance to the Telaryn Palace years before you were actually there?"

He could feel her nod.

"Did I look like I do now . . . or was I older?"

"You looked much like you do now . . . but you'll look the same for at least a few years more."

That doesn't help much.

"Don't ask me more questions. I may have told you too much already."

Quaeryt unfortunately understood. As he and Vaelora had discussed before, she feared that his questions would be based on what he thought and expected and not what her farsight really had shown . . . and too many questions could result in him misleading himself and creating even more problems when whatever she had foreseen did occur.

"Just hold me."

Quaeryt did, shifting his weight slightly on the edge of the bed. He couldn't help wondering what her far-sight portended . . . or when and where those events might occur.

5

~

After morning muster on Mardi, Quaeryt and Vaelora, accompanied by a half squad of troopers from first company, rode through the ruins of Kephria, while Quaeryt, often prompted by Vaelora, took notes—in Bovarian, since Zhael and Arion would need to be able to read them—about what buildings should be allowed where, and where no buildings should be constructed. *Assuming anyone even shows up to build anything,* thought Quaeryt, although he and Zhelan and Calkoran had already put together a rough plan and location for the trooper compound around the buildings the imager undercaptains were already imaging into being.

Then, a quint past noon, after Vaelora had rested for a glass, and Quaeryt managed to avoid asking more questions about her farsight, she and Quaeryt rode over to the "new" trooper headquarters building that the imagers had created from the old blockhouse.

"It's amazing what the four of them have done in four days," said Vaelora, taking in the front courtyard, and the barracks building to the east of the headquarters, a structure that Quaeryt knew was essentially an empty but solid shell that would provide shelter, but would require a great deal of work by Arion's and Zhael's men to make it comfortable.

The two dismounted. Quaeryt tied both mounts to the hitching rail on the west side of the entrance. They walked toward the single heavy oak door.

Vaelora stopped and pointed to the image cut into the flat white stone set into the wall above the door—two troopers riding through a sundered wall toward a paved road. "That's you and Skarpa, I think."

Quaeryt glanced up. "It could be any two officers."

"Yes, dearest," replied Vaelora in the falsely sweet voice that told Quaeryt he was wrong, but that she was being too nice to contradict him in public.

"Thank you, dear Lady," he said, grinning at her.

The two had barely stepped through the door than Baelthm, the oldest of all of the imager undercaptains, stepped forward. "Commander, Lady." He nodded and then said, "I did the tables and chairs just like you ordered, sir, the longer one for you and Lady Vaelora, and the shorter one for the holder and his son."

"And you and Lhandor did the image over the entry?"

"Well . . . sir. We've been in haste, knowing that we needed to do all we could for the Khellan companies before we ride out. So Lhandor, he just drew the image in charcoal on the stone, and every so often I imaged out a piece here and there till it was done."

"It's excellent," said Vaelora.

"We do what we can, Lady Vaelora."

"You do it well."

"Thank you, Lady." Baelthm beamed.

"And thank you for the work on the tables and chairs. I appreciate it, and I'm certain that the Khellans will also after we leave." After seeing—again—what Lhandor and Baelthm had accomplished, Quaeryt wished that he had the artistic skill that they had. *But when have you had time for art?*

That, too, was another reason why he wanted a secure place for imagers—so that imaging did not have
to be entirely about wielding power just to assure the
survival of the few handfuls of imagers born in Lydar
every year.

At roughly a quint before the first glass of the afternoon, Quaeryt walked outside the headquarters building, leaving Vaelora inside, flanked and shielded by
Khalis and Lhandor. A half squad of troopers from first
company, with Undercaptain Ghaelyn in charge,
mounted and then formed up to the south of the entrance, leaving Quaeryt standing alone directly before
the building entry. Before long, Quaeryt caught sight of
a group of riders, twelve in all. They rode through the
gap in the northern wall and along the stone-paved road
that led southward, parallel to the remaining wall that
bordered the Gulf. Then they turned onto the shorter
and more recently imaged pavement leading to the
trooper compound.

As they neared, Quaeryt could see that the ten guards
all wore blue uniforms with white piping, as did Barlaan, who rode at the fore beside an older graying man
with his right arm in a sling. The older man, presumably
former High Holder Basalyt, wore a pale blue shirt and
a dark blue jacket with one arm and shoulder free and
tucked under the sling. Barlaan kept looking at the walls
of the stable, walls that had not been there the day before. Finally, he leaned toward the graying older man,
almost certainly his sire, and said something.

The older man offered a short reply, and Barlaan nodded.

The twelve riders reined up short of Quaeryt and the
troopers.

"Welcome to Kephria," offered Quaeryt politely, but firmly.

From the saddle, Basalyt studied Quaeryt, then inclined his head. "Thank you, Commander. I appreciate your hearing me out." He paused, but briefly, then said, "I can see that there is little left of Kephria, and I have heard that there is less remaining of Geusyn and of Ephra."

"That's largely true," admitted Quaeryt. "Except for Lord Bhayar's forces, of course, and the compound here. That will change before long." *You hope.*

"Is it true that Autarch Aliaro is dead and that Lord Bhayar's forces hold Liantiago?"

"We have to presume that the Autarch is dead, since there is nothing left of that section of the city, and all that were within the palace perished. There are seven full regiments there."

Basalyt nodded slowly.

"I'm not the only one who must hear you. Lady Vaelora awaits us inside." Quaeryt gestured to the door.

Barlaan dismounted, and moved toward his father's mount, but Basalyt dismounted with the ease of long practice. Quaeryt did notice the wince as the holder's boots struck the stone pavement.

"Might I ask her role and position in this?" inquired Basalyt politely.

"She is Lord Bhayar's sister. She was and is his envoy to Khel and was in command here until I returned. Her leadership preserved the regiment and battalion stationed here."

Basalyt frowned, if momentarily, then took several steps toward Quaeryt before stopping.

"Sir . . . I'd not thought I'd ever see an ancient in the

flesh. I see why Lord Bhayar holds Bovaria. But . . . given your power . . ."

"Why is the Lady Vaelora here? For several reasons. First, because Lord Bhayar commanded it. Second, because she was given the authority to deal with High Holders who refused to pledge allegiance to Lord Bhayar. Third, because she sees what I do not." Quaeryt smiled cheerfully. "Shall we enter? Your men can wait here." He turned and walked through the door a ranker opened and into the main room.

Vaelora stood behind the table, still flanked by Khalis and Lhandor.

Quaeryt walked to the table, where he turned and stood beside her.

"You may be seated," said Vaelora.

Quaeryt could sense the aura of command emanating from her. Barlaan was clearly shaken, and Basalyt inclined his head. "Thank you, Lady."

Vaelora and Quaeryt seated themselves simultaneously.

"You requested this meeting," Quaeryt began. "You refused to meet with Lady Vaelora and Submarshal Skarpa, and you did not pledge allegiance to Lord Bhayar. Why should Lord Bhayar accept that allegiance now and restore your lands to you?"

Basalyt looked directly at Vaelora. "Might I ask, Lady . . . if I am dealing with you . . . ?"

"You are not dealing with just me," replied Vaelora. "Lord Bhayar also appointed Commander Quaeryt as envoy. He trusts the commander absolutely. It is also because the commander destroyed the entire Bovarian army. You are dealing with both of us. Is that clear?"

"Yes, Lady. Yes, Commander." Basalyt shifted his weight in the wooden chair. "The answer to your question is simple, Commander. I had no choice. If I had agreed to meet with anyone representing Lord Bhayar, all the neighboring High Holders would have immediately attacked and murdered me and my entire family."

"Why?" Vaelora's voice was as smooth and as cold as liquid ice.

"Because Bartolan was the smallest and weakest holding, and because Chaelaet and Duravyt had sent nearly a hundred armed men to Bartolan. You must have seen Bartolan. Our walls were barely two and a half yards high, and I could not afford more than thirty armsmen. They insisted that we stand together. They asked how a ruler who had not even finished the conquest of Bovaria could possibly force demands on us when Rex Kharst had been unable to do so. I was in no position to argue. So we took what we could and left the rest. We thought we would be able to return once you passed through. None of us ever dreamed that you and your forces could destroy any holding, let alone five, so quickly and so thoroughly."

"We sent messages to the remaining four of you *after* we leveled Chaelaet," Quaeryt pointed out.

"It was too late then. Chaelaet had forced his men upon us."

Vaelora looked to Barlaan. "How did Chaelaet enter your hold? *You* tell me."

Barlaan swallowed. "He rode up with ten men. I think it was ten, and he said he had good news about the Telaryn forces. He often visited, and Challan—he'd paid court to my older sister. That was before she died of the flux. Then, there were scores of men inside the gates, and he told Fa—my sire that he had paid dearly, and so had Duravyt, and that they would not be the only ones who paid."

Quaeryt image-projected both power and a compulsion to tell the truth as he addressed Basalyt. "You had time to respond before Chaelaet stormed your holding. Why did you not appeal for protection?"

Basalyt laughed softly, but bitterly. "Never has a rex of Bovaria protected a High Holder. How was I to know that Lord Bhayar would do so? No High Holder would have dared to make such an appeal to Rex Kharst. If I had done so, I would have lost everything."

Unfortunately, as Quaeryt had already discovered, Basalyt had an excellent point.

"Would it not have been wiser to try?" asked Vaelora.

"I know that now, Lady. But it is far easier to say that one should have avoided the hidden pit on the road after one has fallen in."

"You have yet to answer the question as to why Lord Bhayar should allow you to pledge allegiance now and restore some, or any, of your lands," said Quaeryt.

"I will be a faithful High Holder, now that I know who rules and how. I also have managed well, and Bartolan is prosperous, if smaller than other holdings. I did not spend golds on armsmen, and that cost me dearly. I have but one son remaining, and no daughters. It cannot hurt your lord to retain the one surviving High Holder in the south—"

"Were all of the border holders at Barna?" asked Quaeryt.

"Four of the five were, Commander. Gaaslon was not. He took all his golds and made his way toward Hassyl. He said he could not fight a son of Erion and Lord Bhayar and that he and his family would leave Lydar before submitting to the whelp of a Yaran warlord."

Quaeryt could sense Vaelora stiffening, but he merely smiled politely. "He is welcome to his opinion. He has paid dearly for it." He turned to Vaelora and raised his eyebrows to inquire if she had any more questions.

She shook her head.

"You may leave the chamber and wait to hear what we decide."

Both Basalyt and Baarlan rose and bowed, more to Vaelora than Quaeryt, and left the chamber. So, after a nod from Quaeryt, did Khalis and Lhandor.

Once they were alone, Quaeryt turned to Vaelora. "What do you think?"

"He's sincere . . . or as sincere as any High Holder is likely to be. It wouldn't hurt to keep one of the original High Holders. That would still leave four holdings that Bhayar could bestow. It would also show that he can be merciful . . . to some degree."

"I don't like the idea of his retaining the holding. If he does, that's a precedent—even in one out of five— that Bhayar may regret. What if we insist that the holding go to Barlaan, who can rely on his sire for advice? That way, no one can say that Bhayar can't be merciful to a degree to the family. It would also make the point that Bhayar can remove individual High Holders and replace them with heirs who are more loyal."

"How do you explain that?" Vaelora glanced toward the closed door, then back to Quaeryt. "They took up arms."

"Barlaan didn't fight against us. We don't have to get into the reason why he didn't, and Basalyt isn't going to say anything, not if it means that the family loses everything."

The two talked for another quint before Quaeryt walked to the door and called, "Have Basalyt and Barlaan return!" Then he returned to the table and sat beside Vaelora as the undercaptains and two troopers returned, followed by the former High Holder and his son.

Barlaan kept looking to Quaeryt, while Basalyt's eyes were fixed on Vaelora.

Vaelora waited until the chamber was absolutely still. "As empowered by Lord Bhayar we have heard your appeal. Our decision is this. You, Basalyt, former High Holder of Bartolan, may live out your days on the holding. You will not be High Holder. Ever. From this day forward, your son and heir, Barlaan, will be High Holder, and only his direct heirs may inherit the holding. If there is any failing to meet the obligations of a High Holder to Lord Bhayar, or those acting in his name, or if any deception has been practiced in presenting this appeal, the judgment will be revoked and the holding will revert to Lord Bhayar. So be it."

"Thank you, Lady and Commander," replied Basalyt. "That is a just decision."

Let us hope it's also a wise one, thought Quaeryt. "High Holder Barlaan, you may rebuild a hold house, but it may not have walls or moats or gates, or any form of fortification."

Barlaan nodded.

Quaeryt thought he looked slightly stunned.

Basalyt cleared his throat. "There is one thing you should know, Lady and Commander. Chaellonyt, the son of Chaelaet, has sworn vengeance against the submarshal who destroyed Laetor and slaughtered his father at Barna. He is Chaelaet's surviving son, and he did not go to fight in Liantiago. He has claimed that nothing will stop him. I would not want it said that I knew something and did not reveal it."

"Did he say this to you?" asked Quaeryt.

"No, sir. I heard this from his assistant steward. It was

Loetnyn who told me. He is a most honest man, and I trust him. Loetnyn told me because he felt Chaelaet had treated us ill, and he did not wish more ill to fall on us."

"Is there anything else Lord Bhayar should know?" asked Vaelora.

"Not that I know, Lady." Basalyt inclined his head.

Quaeryt and Vaelora exchanged glances.

"Then this hearing is at an end," she declared. "You may return to Bartolan. You will receive a written record of this judgment shortly, and a copy will also go to Lord Bhayar."

Neither Quaeryt nor Vaelora stood until the two men had left.

Then they rose.

"We'll need to send a message to Skarpa with the other dispatches about this Chaellonyt," said Quaeryt. "Someone who is that angry could be a real danger."

"It's a good thing he has Voltyr and Threkhyl."

"I'd still be happier if Chaellonyt had died in one of the battles."

"You can't do everything, dearest," murmured Vaelora. "Nor do matters ever go as smoothly as we might wish."

"No . . . but . . ." Quaeryt shook his head. He had the feeling that he'd missed or forgotten something, but he honestly couldn't think what it might have been.

6

"How are you feeling?" asked Quaeryt as he sat down on the simple chair beside the bed. Even with the sun seeping into the old fort in late afternoon on Jeudi, the light was dim.

"I'm a little tired now, but that might be because of all the riding," replied Vaelora from where she was sitting on the bed, propped up with pillows, and her feet up. She looked at Quaeryt. "We're not going to leave tomorrow, are we?"

"I'm thinking Samedi or Solayi, depending on how you're doing tomorrow."

"I hate feeling weak."

"You're not weak. You were wounded, just like any trooper. And you sound like most of them when they're told they can't return to duty yet."

Vaelora offered a mock-glare at Quaeryt.

He grinned back at her.

"You're making fun of me," she replied in a doleful voice.

"I didn't say a word."

"You didn't have to."

After several moments of silence, he asked, "What did you think about the meeting with the locals in Geusyn?"

"They weren't happy."

"I can't blame them, but in time things will be much better." *Not that most people who've been devastated want to hear that.*

"Do you think some of the traders in Geusyn will take your advice and relocate to Kephria?"

"Some will right now. Several have ordered lumber from the mills in the hills. The others will as soon as they see that Kephria is a better location. A factor from farther north, Ghaern, in fact, came to see me while you were resting. He's already made plans to open a factorage here." Quaeryt smiled ruefully. "It doesn't hurt that Ghaern wasn't burned to the ground by Aliaro's imagers."

"The local traders and factors won't like that."

"No . . . but I've talked things over with Zhael and Arion. You remember all the goods we removed from Laetor?"

"The ones Khaern had stored in that abandoned shaft? You're going to use them?"

"There are two pieces we're taking back to Bhayar— one is a Cloisonyt vase that's worth close to a hundred golds—but I went over the goods with the majors and wrote out a listing of approximate worth. If they can get that worth, they can use the golds and silvers for provisions, and perhaps to offer a little help to some of the locals. Some of the silver was battered and not worth much more than the metal. I had Khalis and Lhandor image it into silvers that the majors can use immediately. I also left them thirty golds out of what Skarpa sent with me."

"You've been busy."

"I've tried to foresee what they'll need. I've kept the imagers very busy. It does maintain their skills and strength."

"You've been imaging a fair amount, too. Beyond what you did with the pier. I can see it in your eyes."

"I've needed to rebuild my strength as well."

"Did you have to reinforce and refinish the entire pier?"

"A good pier is a necessity, and that's something that would take stone masons weeks, if not months. Sario thinks his family might want to open a factorage here. He likes the pier and the harbor."

Vaelora shook her head.

"While you've been recovering, have you discovered anything of interest in *Rholan and the Nameless*?" Quaeryt leaned forward slightly, shifting his weight on the chair that he'd wished he'd imaged to be a bit more comfortable.

"You're humoring me."

"I am . . . but humor me as well."

After the smallest of sighs, Vaelora picked up the small leatherbound volume that was *Rholan and the Nameless*. For a time, she flipped through the pages. Then she stopped and began to read.

"As with all who think themselves philosophers, Rholan seldom allowed small inconsistencies of fact or of logic to get in the way of powerful words. Whether such inconsistencies were small or not, he always considered them so, as when he insisted in a homily that the Naedarans were 'negligible nabobs of nothingness.' When Chorister Thamus told him that Naedara had rivaled Bovaria in power, Rholan dismissed Thamus's words with the statement that the so-called ancients of Naedara knew nothing of true power. This was despite all the documents and books that mentioned them in the great library of Tela, before it burned. Rholan said that since he'd seen no proof, and what proof there might have been was as smoke, then there was none."

Vaelora slipped her worn leather bookmark into the book, closed it, and looked at Quaeryt.

"Why did you find this so interesting?" he asked.

"There were two things. The writer quoted exact words from Rholan's homily. The writer also knew of the great library and what was in it, including material about Naedara. Naedara wasn't that widely known in the east of Lydar, especially in Rholan's time."

"So you're saying that the writer knew Rholan very well and was also high in position, from a High Holder's family, possibly even a High Holder?"

"I don't see how it could be otherwise."

"And the writer has no compunctions about revealing Rholan's imperfections, regardless of whether he revitalized the worship of the Nameless all across Lydar."

"Except in Khel," Vaelora pointed out.

"That's interesting, given that Rholan didn't like the Naedarans, and there's definitely a link between them and Khel."

"The writer doesn't say he didn't like them."

"If he called them 'negligible nabobs of nothingness' he didn't like them. That's not exactly a favorable description," Quaeryt pointed out.

"It also suggests he might not have been fond of imagers."

"That's true . . . in a way," mused Quaeryt. "The book doesn't ever mention imagers, but does that reflect Rholan or the author . . . or both of them?"

"Both, I'd guess, but it's not likely we'll ever know." Vaelora smiled sardonically. "It does make me wonder just who wrote the book . . . and why."

"There's not even a name at the end, just the letters that look to be a fanciful curlicued version of 'The End.' "

"I've never heard of it, and Father's library was not small."

"There was nothing like it in the scholarium library in Solis, and I've never heard of any chorister who spoke about it, but then, I also haven't asked."

"How about leaving on Samedi?" Vaelora said quietly.

"Have you had another farsight image?"

She shook her head. "The ones I've had have all been . . . well . . . frightening, even the one that turned out well."

"The one about me, you mean?"

She nodded.

"But you're worried about your brother?"

"I'm worried about him when you're not around, and we've been gone long enough for there to be trouble."

"I'll think about leaving on Samedi when I see how you are tomorrow."

"You're stubborn."

"No . . . I'm worried about you."

Quaeryt was relieved that she smiled softly.

7

Quaeryt woke abruptly, not because he had heard something, but because the silence was overpowering. He immediately glanced from the pallet where he lay to the bed where Vaelora slept. In the darkness, he could see nothing. Nor could he hear anything, not even her breathing. Was she breathing?

He started to sit up, but found he could not move, except for his head, as if he were pinned to the pallet by unseen chains. Then the thinnest streams of silver light flowed from the cracks and gaps in the boards covering the gun port of the old Antiagon stone fort and into the makeshift quarters section.

The light formed an archway, and through the archway stepped the figure of a man with hair like flowing silver, standing at the end of a road of reddish silver that stretched up behind him through the stone ceiling and up and out into a night sky filled with brilliant silver-white stars. In one hand, he held a dagger with a blade of brilliant light. Across his back was a mighty bow, and in his other hand was something shimmering so brightly that Quaeryt could not determine what it might be . . . a key, a small book, a coiled chain of gold . . . ?

The silver-haired figure surveyed Quaeryt before he

spoke. "The road back only goes forward. What is done is done forever."

"I know that," protested Quaeryt.

"You know it, yet you do not, for you know, and do not believe what you know. The road forward always reveals what should have been seen in the past and was not. That is the lot of most men. You must not act or see as most men do."

"That's easy enough for you to say." Quaeryt regretted the words as soon as they left his lips.

"Words can always excuse. What is done is what matters." The silver-haired man smiled ruefully. "Do not argue over what is not and may never be."

The light faded, and Quaeryt found he could sit up.

"Quaeryt?" asked Vaelora, alarm in her voice.

"I'm here." Quaeryt quickly stood and moved to the side of her bed, reaching down and taking her hands.

"That light . . . that figure. He looked like Erion."

"Did you see him?"

"He was talking to you, about the road going back going forward. You were talking, too." She struggled into a sitting position. "I could see a reddish silver road behind him, going through the roof into the heavens. The stars were so bright."

Quaeryt shivered, and not from the chill in the air. "I thought I was dreaming it. I couldn't move, and I couldn't hear you breathing." He said quickly, "You're all right, aren't you?"

"I'm . . . fine. I don't hurt." In the dimness, Vaelora's free hand reached out and touched his face, her fingers running down the line of his jaw. "You're here. You're real."

"I hope so."

"Then . . . either we both dreamed it . . . or . . ."

Quaeryt feared he understood. Had he actually imaged his dream into a half reality? Had it happened because of his worries about Vaelora's farsight? Or was there truly an Erion? He almost wanted to burst into ironic laughter. *For a man who doesn't even know whether there's a Nameless . . . to see and talk to Erion in the dark . . . and have Vaelora see him as well . . . Are you going mad?*

He shook his head.

8

Roughly two quints before midday, Quaeryt glanced to the woods east of the river road, then across the brush that sloped down to the waters of the River Laar, then back to the comparatively narrow track that passed for a road in southern Bovaria. After a time he turned in the saddle and asked Vaelora, riding beside him, "How are you feeling?"

"Dearest . . . you've asked that almost every glass since we left Kephria this morning. I will tell you if matters are not right."

Quaeryt winced at the clipped words and exasperated tone. "I can't help it." He ran his left hand over the staff in the holder, a staff he had imaged into being the day before, since his previous staff had disappeared in the last battle in Variana. He'd tested the new staff, and from what he could tell it was solid, yet not a dead weight.

"I know you worry. Asking me every glass or less isn't going to change things."

"I will try not to inquire often." He had trouble not asking, partly because Vaelora would seldom admit that she was ailing, but he could sense an outright lie or evasion if he asked her directly. *But then, she knows that.*

He would have liked to have waited longer to leave

Kephria, but Vaelora had been insistent, even citing his imaged dream—*if it truly had been that*. In the end, he'd dispatched the *Zephyr,* with three wounded troopers as couriers, at dawn on Samedi, and by seventh glass, he and Vaelora were riding northward in the van of first company, followed by Calkoran and his company, with Eleventh Regiment following and providing the rear guard. But he still worried about her . . . and how she was dealing with the loss she wouldn't mention.

The weather had been pleasant enough, if slightly chill with a high haze muting some warmth from the sun, although Quaeryt was glad for the lack of an appreciable wind, again worried about Vaelora.

Finally, he spoke again. "I'd like your thoughts on something. All through the Antiagon campaign, we kept expecting to run into muskets. The Antiagons had cannon, and they used them fairly effectively. But we never saw a musketeer or a single musket. Kharst had both, and Bhayar has been trying to find a way to produce muskets on a large scale, but no one even seemed to have thought of muskets in Antiago."

"Hmmm." Vaelora tilted her head, but said nothing.

Quaeryt waited, glancing again ahead and then to the woods and back to the river.

Finally, she spoke. "I know that Aliaro kept his imagers locked away from himself, and from others, and never allowed them to gather in groups, except for battles."

"Even then, except at Liantiago, there were never more than a half score imagers in one place," Quaeryt added.

"Could the absence of muskets be because a musket can also be used equally in battle or against individuals? It's also a weapon that can kill from a distance and doesn't take years to master. You've said that the entire land was ruled by the Autarch and a few score Shahibs."

"That might be it." Quaeryt shook his head. "I don't know. Maybe Skarpa will find out in time. I still worry." *About more than you ever thought possible.*

"You didn't have any more bad dreams . . . after Liantiago?"

"Not yet . . . except for the one. But I've been fairly exhausted most nights." He paused. "I worry about doing massive imaging."

"Rebuilding a five-hundred-yard-long solid stone pier wasn't massive imaging?"

"I meant the kind where I've killed thousands. Yet . . ." He let the words dwindle away.

"You could do less than massive imaging," she replied lightly. "Or you could let one of the younger imagers do it."

"There's a price to that." *And not all imagers can bear it, as you've found out with Horan.*

"There is, dearest. There's a cost to everything, but your school or collegium or whatever you want to call it won't last unless everyone has to bear part of that cost."

"Collegium . . . I like that. Maybe we should call it the Collegium Imago."

"Dearest, I'd worry about the name after you have Bhayar's absolute approval and your undercaptains are raising buildings."

"It doesn't hurt to have a name. That creates the impression of approval."

"If you start to give that approval now . . ." she warned.

"I know . . . Bhayar will be furious. So I won't. But I'll bring up the name when I talk to him."

"Knowing you, after that you'll keep using it with him."

"Of course, and he might start using it. I won't use it to others, except you, until he does."

"Nor will I, dearest." Vaelora smiled sweetly.

"Thank you for the name."

"You're welcome."

Looking north along the road, Quaeryt saw dust and stiffened in the saddle, then relaxed slightly as he saw that the rider was a Telaryn scout. Still . . . that meant some difficulty or another.

"Sir?" offered Zhelan from where he rode ahead of Vaelora and Quaeryt.

"I see. That means we have a problem."

Half a quint later, the scout reined in beside Quaeryt.

"Commander, sir, the bridge over that rise has been washed out. Must have been a recent storm. The water in the stream is still running high, and it's muddy."

Quaeryt looked to the east, but the sky was clear, and the shoulder of the road was slightly damp in places, but not muddy. "How wide is the stream? How long was the bridge?"

"The stream's not that wide, less than ten yards. The bridge was maybe fifteen yards from bank to bank."

Quaeryt nodded, then turned in the saddle. "Under-captain Horan! Forward!"

The narrow-faced older imager moved forward from where he rode beside Baelthm and then eased his horse alongside Quaeryt's mount. "Yes, sir?"

Quaeryt couldn't help but note that Horan's short beard, once sandy blond and mixed with gray, was now almost totally gray, as was his hair. *Imaging, battles, and strain do change us all.* "There's a bridge ahead over a small stream. Do you think you could image a replacement for us?"

"Yes, sir."

"I'm going to send Khalis and Elsior with you, Khalis to provide shields, if necessary, while you're working, and Elsior to observe."

"That'd be fine, sir."

Quaeryt turned in the saddle. "Undercaptain Khalis and Trainee Elsior! Forward."

"Yes, sir." Khalis led the slender Elsior, who looked less than perfectly comfortable on his mount, forward so that they were immediately behind Quaeryt.

"Horan is going to ride ahead to replace a bridge. I'd like you to accompany him and to provide shields . . . just in case. Elsior, you're to observe."

"Yes, sir."

"Undercaptains, head out."

Quaeryt watched as the three followed the scout northward.

"A large proportion of your imagers are Pharsi," Vaelora said.

"About half of us are," Quaeryt said.

"You know, dearest, I think that's the first time you've ever said that you're Pharsi."

"It probably is," he said with a wry smile. "It took long enough, didn't it?"

Vaelora offered a warm smile in return.

Almost two quints later, first company approached the point where the three undercaptains waited, with Horan on the west side of the road, and Khalis and Elsior on the east.

A solid but graceful single stone span stretched across

the stream, wide enough for two wagons abreast, and with a narrow stone guard wall on each side. Quaeryt couldn't help but think that the bridge was far better than the road it served. *But then, that's another problem we'll likely have to help Bhayar with.* How few really good roads existed in Bovaria had been one of the biggest surprises that had faced the Northern and Southern Armies as they'd advanced on Variana.

"We've ridden across and back several times, Commander!" Horan called out. "She's solid."

"Excellent!" returned Quaeryt, gesturing for the three to rejoin the column. "It's also a beautiful structure."

"Thank you, sir," returned Horan as he swung his mount back behind Quaeryt and beside Baelthm's horse.

"How are you feeling?" asked Quaeryt.

"It wasn't any trouble at all."

"Good."

Quaeryt was also pleased that Horan seemed so cheerful, given the imager undercaptain's despondency after the carnage that Quaeryt's imaging had created in Liantiago.

9

Outside of a light rainstorm early on Samedi afternoon, Quaeryt's force encountered little difficulty with weather . . . or with the locals, and as before, saw no sign of any high holdings or holders on the way to Ghaern, where they had spent the night. They were on the road early on Solayi, and again early on Lundi, after bivouacking in a nameless hamlet that Quaeryt did not even remember from the ride to Ephra.

By late midafternoon on Mardi, he was getting even more tired of the bad roads of Bovaria. He and the imagers had already replaced another two bridges—poor timber constructions washed out by spring floods. On the ride south, he'd wondered how long some of the bridges would last, and he'd definitely found out. Yet he had to wonder why the local factors or holders hadn't invested in stronger construction.

"Because they use the river, and they built the bridges just strong enough so that the locals can reach the market towns and their factorages," said Vaelora. "That's what you told me before. I can't believe that's changed."

"Except that we've had spring rains since then," replied Quaeryt dourly.

"Each bridge the imagers rebuild strengthens Bhayar's

rule, and it's another one someone won't have to replace anytime soon."

"You don't think people will actually be grateful, do you?"

"Some will. Some won't. At the very least, it will suggest that Bhayar can affect things anywhere. Isn't that what you're planning with the imagers?"

Quaeryt laughed. "Your point is taken, my lady."

The sun was almost touching the tops of the trees on the west side of the River Laar when Quaeryt noted that the cots along the east side of the river had gotten closer and closer together and that the tended fields took up far more of the land than did orchards and woodlots. He also noted that while the holders and others working the land gave the troopers wary glances and did not approach, none of them fled. He also didn't see shuttered windows and closed doors. "We must be getting close to Daaren."

"That's good."

"We need to take a break to rest the mounts and you."

"I don't know that I like the way you worded that, dearest."

"I obviously need a rest as well," replied Quaeryt. "How are you feeling?"

"Like I need a rest . . . a rest, dearest."

Quaeryt offered a doleful look, then grinned.

"Sometimes . . ." Vaelora shook her head.

"I know . . . but you wanted someone who appreciated all your qualities."

"*All* of them," replied Vaelora tartly. "You appreciate some excessively at times."

"They're worth excessive—"

"Quaeryt . . ."

Quaeryt sighed, excessively.

Vaelora put her hand on the hilt of her sabre.

Quaeryt grinned and pointed. "Look. You can see the bridge that Threkhyl imaged."

"It is impressive," Vaelora agreed cheerfully.

Quaeryt did not sigh in relief, much as he felt like it.

The bridge that the imagers had constructed over the Phraan River on their ride south months before looked dusty, and the road on the south side looked more heavily traveled than before, but there were no signs of wear otherwise as first company led the way over the span and then into the main part of Daaren. The locals did clear the streets as the Telaryn riders appeared, but only so far as the sidewalks.

The innkeeper at the Grande Laar Inn only looked moderately discouraged when he caught sight of Zhelan and Quaeryt. "How long . . . might I ask, sirs?"

"One or two days, most likely. No more than three," replied Quaeryt. After that, he left the arrangements for quartering first company and Calkoran's troopers in Zhelan's hands, while he went over instructions with Khaern for quartering his men in the inns farther north along Daaren's main boulevard. Once he was finished with that, he rejoined Vaelora in the main entry hall of the inn.

Before Quaeryt had more than a few words with Vaelora, a squad leader hurried into the inn. "Commander, there are some factors who would like a moment with you."

Vaelora raised her eyebrows.

"They can have a moment with me and Lady Vaelora, but give us a little time to set up one of the private chambers."

"Yes, sir."

Quaeryt quickly made arrangements to use the first private room, then hurried in to rearrange the furniture so that he and Vaelora would sit behind the circular table . . . and so that all the other chairs were against the side wall. The two of them had barely seated themselves when the two factors entered the room.

Quaeryt wasn't in the slightest surprised to see the comparatively young factor Jarell as the first of the two men to enter the private chamber, since Jarell had emerged as the most diplomatic of the factors when Southern Army had stopped in Daaren in the fall. As before, the clean-shaven Jarell had his straight brown hair slicked back from a high forehead, and he smiled winningly directly at Vaelora. With him was a much older man, white-haired, who Quaeryt thought might have been watching with Jarell at the time the imagers had rebuilt the bridge over the Phraan. He did not smile. Both men bowed.

"Might I present Factor Palumyn?" offered Jarell, his voice deep and pleasant. "He is the head of the factors' council of Daaren."

"You might," replied Quaeryt. "We are pleased to see you both in health."

"There have been many rumors," Jarell went on, "about your return, Lady and Commander . . ."

"And you would like to know what happened?" Quaeryt smiled. "Submarshal Skarpa now holds Liantiago and Antiago for Lord Bhayar. The Autarch Aliaro and his palace and most of his armies have been destroyed."

"Destroyed . . . not defeated?"

Quaeryt shrugged. "His forces were defeated at Suemyron and again at Barna, and twice more between Barna and Liantiago. From what we could determine he gathered all his remaining forces and imagers into the palace fortress at Liantiago in an effort to force us to concentrate our troopers so that he could destroy all of us. In the end, it worked out the other way. There is a rather large gully where the Autarch's palace used to be. There might be a thousand surviving Antiagon troopers."

"I see." Jarell paused. "Might I ask if this was a costly victory?"

"Not terribly. The submarshal's regiments remain close to full strength." Quaeryt smiled again. "They will likely remain in Antiago for a time, but the forces assigned to Lady Vaelora are more than adequate for any duties within Bovaria. We did rebuild several bridges on the river road between Daaren and Geusyn. You factors might be interested to know that before the last encounter, when we destroyed three Antiagon warships and their imagers, Aliaro's forces destroyed Ephra totally, and leveled Kephria and Geusyn. We rebuilt the harbor facilities at Kephria and left several companies there to maintain order while the city recovers. But with the destruction of Ephra and the far better harbor at Kephria under Lord Bhayar's control . . . and few Antiagon factors remaining . . ."

The older factor nodded. "Are you suggesting . . . or insisting?"

"Merely suggesting. I would think it would offer an opportunity, and certainly some factors will take advantage of it."

"Who would risk that?" asked Palumyn almost scornfully.

"I do know of one Antiagon factoring and shipping family that is very interested," replied Quaeryt.

"You would let Antiagons . . ."

"Lord Bhayar intends to treat all factors under his rule equally. As I said, I just wanted you to know, and I trust you will pass on the information to other factors."

"As you intimated might occur . . . when you were here in late fall, we have received notice from Lord Bhayar that all factors are being assessed an additional tariff of ten golds," said Jarell. "Such an amount . . . when we have already paid this year's tariffs . . ." He shook his head.

"If you had paid to have rebuilt the bridge across the Phraan . . . how much would that have cost you?" asked Quaeryt.

"We did not need a new bridge . . . and not one so . . . massive."

"I'd wager that every factor in Daaren has seen more trade and saved time because of the bridge." Quaeryt looked evenly at the pair, imaging projecting a slight compulsion to reply honestly.

"Ah . . . that may be . . . but . . ."

"You will not have to pay to replace it anytime soon, and there will be more benefits from Lord Bhayar's rule. He is not seizing your goods or your women. He is not taking your factorages and turning them over to Telaryn merchants. He is asking for reasonable compensation for putting Bovaria back together under a fairer ruler. Can you honestly tell me that Rex Kharst was fair?"

Neither factor would meet Quaeryt's gaze.

After several moments Vaelora said quietly, "Do you wish me to report to my brother that you refuse to pay this pittance?"

"Lady Vaelora . . . ten golds is not a pittance . . ." sputtered the white-haired Palumyn.

"To keep your factorages and your livelihood after

you supported a ruler as evil as Kharst . . . I would not call it exorbitant. Would you?" Vaelora raised her eyebrows.

Again, both men lowered their eyes.

"Are there any other matters you would like to bring before Lady Vaelora?"

"No . . . Commander," replied Jarell. "We appreciate your guidance and forbearance, and that of Lord Bhayar."

Quaeryt had strong doubts that either man felt much appreciation.

After the pair left, he shook his head. "I'm going to need to visit the factors' council tomorrow and obtain a listing of all factors . . . and make it clear that we really don't want to have to make an example of Daaren, but that we will . . . if we must."

Vaelora nodded sadly.

"Now . . . if you would like to repair to your chamber and wash up . . ."

"What about you? You aren't exactly the freshest of spring mint, dearest."

Quaeryt grinned. "I will follow your example . . . after I check with Zhelan."

Not surprisingly, Quaeryt found the major out in the side courtyard, watching as the squad leaders carried out their duties. When he finished with Zhelan, Quaeryt met with the imager undercaptains and gave them a simple duty for the next day—to ride up and down the streets of Daaren and to take note and write down the names of all factorages, first thing in the morning.

Finally, well after washing up—and sunset, if before complete darkness—Quaeryt and Vaelora joined Zhelan, Calkoran, and Khaern in the same private room at the Grande Laar Inn they had used months before, where they ate an adequate meal of mutton slices and gravy with slightly overfried lace potatoes.

"What are your plans, sir?" asked Khaern. "Will we be riding out for Laaryn on Jeudi or Vendrei?"

"I'm considering not going that way at all. There are roads up the Phraan. The distance would be shorter, and we'd rejoin the Great Canal at Eluthyn. After that we can use the road along the Great Canal."

"How good are those roads to Eluthyn? Do you know?" asked Zhelan.

"The maps I have show that there are roads. I doubt they're any better than the ones we've been traveling." Quaeryt decided against asking if they could be worse. He knew from experience just how bad the roads in Bovaria could be—except for those ancient stone roads laid down by the Naedarans, roads so durable that they still put to shame anything built more recently by Bovarians. "There's another reason I'd like to take the way along the Phraan. The people will see that Lord Bhayar does indeed hold Bovaria . . . and Bhayar won't have to send a regiment on a special trip along the Phraan. Since Meinyt has, or had, Fifth Regiment in Laaryn, we won't accomplish anything by going that way."

"The factors and merchants all over Bovaria need a little shaking up," said Khaern. "That's just my opinion, sir, Lady Vaelora. I think going up the Phraan would help."

"It will be harder," prophesied Calkoran. "They do not know what a true road is. For them a mud track is a road."

Quaeryt chuckled. "You're right, but we might as well travel in a way that will help settle Bovaria down and get them to understand Bhayar is here to stay."

"You do have that talent, dearest," murmured Vaelora in such a low tone Quaeryt doubted the others had heard.

"I'd like to hear about what each of you needs for your men and mounts," Quaeryt said quickly, "and what supplies you think we'll need, especially anything we might not find in smaller towns. There aren't likely to be many larger towns along the Phraan because it's shallower and narrower than the River Laar." *And most trade under Kharst and previous rulers relied on the rivers.* He looked to Khaern. "If you'd start, Subcommander."

Quaeryt had no doubt that he and Vaelora would be listening for a time, but he needed to know what was necessary as soon as possible.

10

❧

Much as he wanted to stay in bed on Meredi morning, Quaeryt was up early, worrying about everything from provisions to getting to the factors' council. While he still had over three hundred golds from what Skarpa had sent, that was not much, even if he spent it only on supplies, not for fifteen hundred troopers. And he was only paying half the going rate. He didn't want to commandeer the provisions, but he also wanted to get the point across that the merchants and factors would have to shoulder some costs beyond token tariffs.

Accompanied by a half squad from first company, he did manage to rein up in front of the small, two-story brick building off the lower main square in Daaren just before eighth glass. There was no sign or inscription on the structure, but Quaeryt recalled it from the last visit, if only because it was the sole unidentified building around the square. That, in itself, suggested the power of the factors.

Before he dismounted Quaeryt surveyed the square, an area paved with rough cobblestones, unlike the smoother paving blocks used in Telaryn or in the ancient Naedaran roads. In the center was a square pedestal, and on the pedestal was a statue of a man, cast in bronze old enough that it held a patina of brown and green. Presumably, the man depicted was a former rex, since Kharst had not ruled long enough for a statue that old, and Quaeryt doubted that any local personage would have spent the golds for what would have been regarded as Naming. Apparently, in Bovaria, the rex was above that particular sin.

All that reminded Quaeryt that it had been almost a month since he'd had to conduct a service or deliver a homily. So far . . . so far, he had to say he didn't miss it.

He eased off his mount and turned to the squad leader. "Just wait. This shouldn't take more than a quint or so."

"Yes, sir."

Holding full shields, he walked up to the door and opened it, stepping inside. Once in the entry hall, he tucked his uniform visor cap into the crook in his left arm and crossed the open space to the front table.

The clerk behind the table looked up . . . and seeing the uniform, and most likely Quaeryt's unnaturally white hair, nails, and dark eyes . . . froze.

"I'm here to see Factor Palumyn. I assume he's here."

The clerk swallowed, seemingly unable to respond.

"Where is he?" Quaeryt asked politely.

The clerk grasped a small bell and rang it.

After a moment the leftmost of the two doors in the wall behind the clerk opened, and Factor Jarell stepped out.

Quaeryt wasn't surprised.

Neither, apparently, was Jarell, who smiled and asked, "What brings you here, Commander?"

"I need to go over a few matters with Factor Palumyn. I assume he's there." Quaeryt pointed to the closed door.

"He should be," replied Jarell amiably, walking to the

door and opening it. "Commander Quaeryt is here to see you." He gestured.

Quaeryt smiled. "After you."

Jarell stepped into the study, and Quaeryt followed, closing the door behind him.

The study was small, some three yards by four, and held only a writing table and the chair behind it, in which Palumyn sat, almost as if sculpted of marble, and two other armless wooden chairs. Quaeryt did not bother to seat himself.

Palumyn's eyes fixed on Quaeryt's midsection, or rather on Quaeryt's visor cap and the hand and fingers that held it. After a moment he shook his head, then looked up at Quaeryt. "That explains much."

For the first time, a puzzled expression flitted across Jarell's face.

"I'll explain later, Jarell. The commander understands." Palumyn's voice took on a resigned tone as he asked, "What brings you here?"

"Lord Bhayar and I require a listing of all the factors and large merchants in Daaren. I'm certain you have such a listing."

"We have a listing of all those factors who belong to the council. Some merchants do, but not all do."

"I'd appreciate a copy by the end of the day," Quaeryt said politely. "Oh . . . and I've had my officers taking a count and notes on every large merchant and factorage in Daaren. Lord Bhayar's clerks, I'm sure, will be comparing your listing against the tariff rolls you submit and against our census."

Palumyn stiffened, if but for an instant. "We would expect thoroughness from a ruler as effective as Lord Bhayar."

"And I expect the same from the noted factors of Daaren. I assume you will have no difficulty in delivering the list by fourth glass this afternoon."

"I believe we can manage that, Commander."

"Excellent," replied Quaeryt.

"Is there anything else you need from us?"

"Not at the moment."

"Then Jarell will deliver the listing before fourth glass."

"Thank you." Quaeryt inclined his head politely, then stepped back to allow Jarell to leave the study first.

After Quaeryt had closed the door behind himself, he and Jarell walked several steps farther before Quaeryt stopped.

Jarell said, "Most senior officers wouldn't worry quite so much about matters such as tariffs."

"They would if they were married to Lord Bhayar's sister," replied Quaeryt. "If they had any sense, anyway. Lord Bhayar expects much from those who serve him, and more than that from those who are close."

The brown-haired factor smiled ruefully. "I've had a few inquiries made. It's said that you are a fighting commander, and that you are effective. Most effective. From those inquiries and from what you have said, it would appear that Lord Bhayar can be a hard man."

Quaeryt shook his head. "He makes a great effort to be effective and fair. He has been known to accept honest mistakes. Those who made them often have not remained in his service, or they have had to undertake duties that were demanding and onerous. He does not accept treachery, dishonesty, or duplicity."

"And you?"

"I've been one of those who has made mistakes. I'd prefer not to make others."

"I see."

"Perhaps you do, Factor Jarell. It might be wise if you conveyed that understanding to other factors. It might prevent any misunderstandings. Lord Bhayar will not be as tolerant of factor excesses as Rex Kharst was. He has already shown that he will not tolerate excesses by High Holders."

"Oh?"

"All five of the high holdings just north and east of Kephria have been leveled. Four of the High Holders have lost their lands. Three are dead. The fifth High Holder was removed and his heir installed as his successor. All the High Holders who were closest to Rex Kharst are dead. The factors of Laaryn attempted to deceive Submarshal Skarpa. Their reward was to supply the Southern Army and to support a full regiment quartered there until Lord Bhayar is convinced of their resolve not to attempt any further questionable actions. The leader of the deception fled and faces execution if he returns. His factorage and considerable wealth were seized."

Jarell tried not to swallow. He did not succeed.

"If you wish to send someone to Laaryn to inquire, by all means do so," Quaeryt added pleasantly. "As I've said, Lord Bhayar has no interest in arbitrarily punishing factors. He just doesn't like deception . . . or other actions that suggest a lack of loyalty." Quaeryt couldn't say anything about obeying the laws of the land, because Bhayar had essentially repudiated the old privileges of the factors, and Quaeryt wasn't aware that any new rules or laws had been issued. In fact, in his absence, he doubted that anyone had even considered the matter. *Another problem for you to resolve . . . if he'll listen and let you.*

"Loyalty . . . that can be an ambiguous term, Commander," offered Jarell.

Quaeryt faced the factor and projected a combination of power and withering scorn, so much so that Jarell stepped back several steps and paled. "Neither I nor Lord Bhayar care much for weasel-wording factors who seek to hide behind the meaning of words or who use them to shield themselves from punishment for doing what they know is wrong. You know what is right, and it is not always the same as what brings in the most golds." Quaeryt dropped the projection and said quietly, "Do you understand?"

"Yes, sir." Jarell inclined his head.

Just before Quaeryt turned to leave, he noticed that the clerk who had been at the front desk had fainted. *You weren't that violent.*

He didn't shake his head as he walked out of the building. *Why are so many of them always trying to avoid and evade? Is that truly what makes a successful factor?* Then he paused, considering. Palumyn hadn't tried to avoid. He'd been unhappy, and resigned, but he'd given every indication that he would do his best.

Quaeryt smiled ruefully. That suggested Jarell was another Myskyl, a lower-level schemer trying to get to the top by twisting everything to his advantage. *And Myskyl is another problem you'll have to face when you return to Variana.*

When he rode into the side courtyard at the Grande Laar Inn, Quaeryt reined up and saw Undercaptain Ghaelyn. "Undercaptain! Do you know if the imager undercaptains have returned?"

"No, sir. They haven't."

"Thank you." Quaeryt dismounted and led his mount to the waiting stable boy.

He needed to write out all the problems he faced—especially a set of rules to make things clear for the Bovarian factors and merchants, because it was all too obvious that the way they conducted business was not what was necessary for better trade between the different lands Bhayar now ruled.

Quaeryt took a deep breath as he walked toward the inn door.

11

In the end, Quaeryt, Vaelora, and their forces did not leave Daaren until Vendrei morning, partly because obtaining supplies took longer than Quaeryt had anticipated and partly because both Khaern and Calkoran felt that the mounts needed more rest. The additional day did give Quaeryt some time to start drafting what he thought of as a code for factors and trade. He had no illusions that what he wrote would be approved by Bhayar without change, but with three different sets of laws governing trade and commerce, Quaeryt felt that Bhayar would want some uniform code . . . and if Bhayar changed it, even for what Quaeryt might think was for the worse, one code was better than three—or four, if the High Councilors of Khel ever came to their senses and agreed to some sort of terms with Bhayar.

For the first eleven milles north on the east side of the Phraan River, all the way to the small town of Faantyl, the road was slightly better than it had been south of Daaren. In Faantyl, surprisingly, every building seemed to have been built of the pale yellow brick that Quaeryt had first observed in Daaren, except in Daaren, not every structure had been built of it. Once in the town proper of Faantyl, Quaeryt reined up and asked one of the local crofters, seated on his wagon seat, on the west side of the churned dirt open space that passed for a square, about the road to the north.

"Well . . . it's not as bad as it might be this time of year, after the swampy part a mille or so north."

"What about the roads on the west side of the river?"

The grizzled crofter shook his head. "Aren't none to speak of."

"How bad is the swampy part?"

"Right now, I wouldn't be going there. It's passable enough come summer."

"All the way to Eluthyn?"

"I wouldn't know about that. Never been farther north than Eelan, and not there recently."

"How far is Eelan?"

"Mayhap twenty milles, could be a shade more."

"Do people travel here from farther north?"

"In the summer, they do. Not now, most years."

Quaeryt asked more questions, but it was clear that the man had told him what he knew. And others around the square couldn't add much.

"We might as well push on," he decided. *And we'll likely need imaging in more than a few places.*

Less than two milles north of Faantyl, the outriders came hurrying back to Quaeryt and Zhelan.

"Sirs . . ."

"There's an impassable swampy stretch of road?" asked Quaeryt.

"Pretty much, sir."

"What does the road look like beyond the swampy place?" asked Quaeryt.

"Can't tell, sir."

"Is there a track that leads around it?"

"There's a narrow path, but Cloryt's mount's foreleg sunk so deep we had to use ropes to pull him clear."

"We'll have to see what the imagers can do, then."
Quaeryt turned in the saddle. "Imager undercaptains!
Forward!" Then he looked at Vaelora. "The road repairs begin. I hope we don't have to rebuild it all the
way to Eelan."

"If you do, that will make life better for the people."

"And take days . . ." he replied dryly, turning to
Zhelan and saying, "Have the men take a break, and
pass the word back to Calkoran and Khaern. Water the
mounts, and then move ahead to join us. But take your
time."

With the four imager undercaptains and Elsior, Quaeryt rode forward a good quarter mille along the section
of the road that rose very gradually, perhaps five yards
over the distance. He reined up where the outriders
waited on the gentle crest just south of an area that
looked like a gigantic mud puddle, stretching several
hundred yards to the north and east and some thirty to
the west. His first inclination was to have one of the imagers just remove the sloppy mess, but he saw that the
road was actually in a depression with higher ground
to each side, and that ground was a good two yards
higher. Still, that gave him an idea, and he guided his
mount toward the river, where he looked over the higher
ground between the muddy mess and the slope down
to the Phraan. Then he rode back.

"Horan . . . do you see where that bare bush is?"

"Yes, sir."

"Do you think you could image out a channel two
yards wide from the road through the higher ground?"

"So that the slop will flow toward the river?"

"That's the idea. Even if it doesn't, that will allow
drainage in the future so that this mess doesn't happen
again."

Horan concentrated, and in instants there was a channel from the west side of where the road might once have been through the higher ground to the slope leading down to the river, a distance of about fifty yards.

"There you are, sir." Horan blotted his forehead.

"Let's wait and see how much drains away."

While the water on top of the mud slowly flowed through the channel, after a quint had passed it was clear that the mud below the surface water wasn't moving. Not anytime soon, Quaeryt realized.

"Lhandor, image away a few yards of the mud, starting there." Quaeryt pointed several yards north of the slightly higher and drier ground where he had reined up.

"Yes, sir."

After just a few efforts by Lhandor and Khalis, and even a smaller amount being removed by Elsior, Quaeryt called a halt when he saw, at the bottom of the excavated area, the remnant of what appeared to be a stone wall.

"Take away a bit to the north," he ordered.

"Yes, sir." Khalis did so, revealing more mortared stone.

With the additional removal, Quaeryt could see that at some time in the past, someone had built a stone causeway through the swampy ground, and that the causeway had included two culverts to drain water away.

In the end, some two glasses later, a stone roadway, with three arched culverts beneath and smaller channels feeding into the larger one that Horan had created, stretched almost four hundred yards through what had been a swampy depression.

Once the last traces of frost from the imaging had faded, they resumed their journey.

"If the people here had just maintained what was built here in the first place, they wouldn't have had that problem," observed Vaelora.

"The local smallholders don't have the ability to do that, not without neglecting their own lands. There aren't any High Holders near, and the factors in Faantyl and Eelan don't want to spend the silvers or golds because they don't see any immediate coins from repairing the road. That's the problem with leaving everything in the hands of the factors. If it doesn't benefit them directly and immediately, most of them won't do things that help others, especially here in Bovaria, it appears."

Two milles north of the swampy area and the newly rebuilt causeway, Vaelora suddenly pointed to a low rise on which there were several scattered stone and brick walls. The brick was, once more, pale yellow. "Over there, on the hillside."

Just ahead, also on the left, was a double line of trees, although there were many gaps in the trees that had once flanked a drive leading to the buildings.

"Most likely, the former High Holder who once lived there built the causeway," suggested Quaeryt.

"This isn't that narrow a road. Or it wasn't. Look at how wide the shoulders are."

Quaeryt had noticed that earlier. "You're thinking that this was once the main way from Varian to Daaren before the Great Canal was built?"

"It was a more important road then."

"That makes sense. The route is shorter." It also proved to Quaeryt how much Kharst and his sire had neglected the roads of Bovaria.

For the rest of the morning and the first three glasses of the afternoon, the road remained passable, although in two cases, Quaeryt had the imagers replace small timber bridges with stone spans, but those were across small creeks.

Just after fourth glass, up ahead, he saw an oblong stone, upright, but half buried in turf that threatened to engulf it. When they rode closer, he could see that the millestone held letters carved into the stone that time and weather had softened until they were barely readable: EELAN—4 M.

"Have you ever heard or read of the place?" asked Vaelora.

"Except as a name on a map? No."

They rode another two milles. Then the road curved away from the river, running due east for a good half mille before turning back north again. Quaeryt also noticed that the Phraan River itself had bent more to the west, and he wondered why the road hadn't at least gone straight. After another half mille, he saw why. Off the road to the left was a high holding, not a huge one, but definitely a high holding with a large residence constructed out of pale yellow brick and gray stone situated on a low rise that presumably overlooked the river, although Quaeryt couldn't see the river from the road. Ahead was a set of gates, simple black iron anchored in two large yellow brick and gray stone pillars, with a low pale yellow brick wall running some fifty yards back from the gates on each side.

As they rode past, Quaeryt saw no indication of who the High Holder might be, although the well-kept grounds and thin trails of smoke from more than a few chimneys indicated that the holding was definitely in use.

"I would have thought," ventured Vaelora, "that the High Holder might have had some interest in better roads."

"His holding is on the river, and it's deep enough, barely, for travel and probably for small boats to bring goods down from Eluthyn. The last thing he'd have wanted is good roads for Kharst's forces to be able to reach him easily."

"So they all let the roads deteriorate to make it harder for Kharst to reach them?"

"Given what you know about him, wouldn't you?" Vaelora just shook her head.

"That brings up one other thing that has bothered me, on and off," Quaeryt ventured.

"Which is, dearest?"

"Imagers. There were always rumors that Kharst had imagers. We never encountered any. No one has mentioned them, either."

"That's not surprising," she replied. "When you turned the battlefield at Variana and the Chateau Regis to ice, you likely killed almost everyone who knew anything . . . and possibly the imagers themselves . . . if there were any. If they weren't there, don't you think they would have gone into hiding or fled?"

"Because of what they did for Kharst?"

"Well . . . anyone who had a company of assassins . . ."

Quaeryt nodded, but he wondered if they'd ever really find out.

Less than a glass later, they rode into Eelan, an old river town, with two river piers, old enough to look like they should sag out over the water, although they did not, and a single inn, across the river square from the piers. Clean and tidy as it was, the Silver Swan had seen better days, with slightly sagging and worn floorboards, and a public room. Every building in the town appeared to have been constructed of the same pale yellow brick that they had seen at the holding.

After the initial meeting with the innkeeper, Quaeryt left the details of settling the men in to Zhelan and Khaern. Barely allowing Vaelora a chance to wash up, he requested a squad of troopers from Eleventh Regiment to accompany him and Vaelora back to the high holding. Khalis also rode with them, before Quaeryt and Vaelora and alongside squad leader Kezyn.

They had scarcely ridden away from the inn when Vaelora turned in the saddle and said, "Do tell me we're doing this now so that we don't have to spend another day here."

"That's precisely why we're doing it." Quaeryt glanced at the small chandlery on the west side of the main street, its shutters already closed for the day, even though it was barely past fifth glass.

"What is the name of the High Holder?" asked Vaelora.

"I told you. It's Nephyl—"

"You may have told me, dearest, but you didn't bother to see if I happened to be where I could hear what you had to say."

Quaeryt held in a wince, and continued. "He has some contact with the town, but seldom has visitors from the north, except by the river . . . and not many of those. The innkeeper said that his family was here before the town, or so the story goes, and that his bricks built all of Eelan, all of Faantyl, and much of Daaren."

"I didn't see much sign of a brickworks."

"It's supposedly on the other side of the river, downstream and out of sight. The good High Holder doubtless did not wish his view spoiled."

When they reached the gates, Kezyn gestured, and a trooper dismounted and walked to the gates.

"The gates are locked, sir."

"Stand back, if you would," ordered Quaeryt, who gestured to Khalis.

The trooper backed away, and the undercaptain imaged away a link of the heavy iron chain.

"Try it now."

The trooper unwound the chain and then pulled back one gate, then the other. Both creaked loudly.

Quaeryt studied the short brick-paved apron leading to the gate, then nodded. "No recent tracks. Most visitors and supplies come by river." He looked to Khalis. "Shields up. Lead the way to the side entry."

Khalis led the way along the brick-paved lane to the entry on the north side of the hold house.

As they neared, Quaeryt could see that another brick lane angled up from a pier and boathouse on the river some ten yards lower than the side terrace that appeared to serve as a receiving portico. No one appeared on the unroofed terrace, which had four gray stone pillars on the east side and four on the west river side. Three wide steps ran from the paved lane up to the portico terrace.

A gray-haired man in pale yellow livery, trimmed in white, stepped out onto the side portico, a puzzled expression on his face.

"Lady Vaelora and Commander Quaeryt are here to see High Holder Nephyl," announced Khalis.

"He is not receiving," announced the functionary.

"I don't think you understand," said Khalis. "Lady Vaelora is an envoy and the sister of Lord Bhayar, who now rules Bovaria. Your master can receive them . . . or he can contemplate his failure to do so amid the ruin of his holding."

"I do not believe—"

Before the man could complete his sentence, Khalis

imaged away the first two pillars on the left side of the receiving terrace.

The functionary swallowed. "I will convey your message." He did not quite bolt inside.

In moments, a short and slender figure in an elegant blue jacket, a white ruffled shirt, and gray trousers above polished black boots appeared. His eyes darted to the missing section of the portico, and he smiled wryly as he turned to face Khalis, Quaeryt, and Vaelora. "I see that Vheran was not exaggerating. I'm Nephyl, current holder, if recently. Welcome to Lehyln. We did see your forces pass earlier. Will you be requiring the holding for quarters or the like?"

"No . . . not unless matters deteriorate," replied Quaeryt. "We were passing through on our return to Variana, and the Lady Vaelora thought we should pay our respects."

"You're welcome to enter, and we would be happy to receive you . . ."

Quaeryt smiled. "Thank you. Of necessity, our visit will be short. Undercaptain Khalis and the troopers will remain here. Khalis is, of course, quite capable of bringing down the entire holding by himself."

"I had heard that Lord Bhayar's forces were not unduly bothered by obstacles that had in the past thwarted other conquerors."

Quaeryt dismounted and extended a hand to Vaelora.

Her fingers barely touched his as she vaulted down from the saddle, a gesture expressing appreciation while making the point that she needed no aid. "Thank you."

As Quaeryt and Vaelora walked toward the slender holder, half a head shorter than Quaeryt, who was barely taller than average, Nephyl studied the two from behind a pleasant smile. Quaeryt maintained shields covering both himself and Vaelora.

The holder gestured toward the open door, then stepped through and led the way. Beyond the wide but single door was a modest entry hall with a slightly raised ceiling and a floor tiled in pale yellow and a dark gray. Waiting was a black-haired maid in the pale yellow livery of the hold. She stepped forward to take Vaelora's riding jacket, then looked at her closely. Her eyes widened and went to Quaeryt, running from his brilliant white hair and eyebrows, even to his fingers. She said nothing, but took Vaelora's jacket and Quaeryt's visor cap, bowed, and immediately retreated down a narrow hall immediately to the right.

"We had not expected visitors," said Nephyl, "and what refreshments we can offer are perforce limited."

"We understand," replied Quaeryt. "We had not intended to be visitors, but we could not pass up the opportunity to visit another High Holder."

"You have visited many?"

Quaeryt frowned, trying to make a quick mental calculation. "I would say a score or more, in one fashion or another, but that is just an estimate."

"You are the seventh hold in southern Bovaria," added Vaelora.

Quaeryt's eyes darted to the narrow side hall where he saw the maid whispering something to a taller young woman with curly brown hair, wearing a hip-length gray silk jacket over gray trousers and a bright yellow silk blouse. The taller woman slipped away from the maid and hurried into the entry hall.

"My wife, Mergiana."

"I apologize. I had just come in from riding. We had not expected such distinguished personages."

Mergiana's voice was warm, although her smile was tentative.

"We're pleased to meet you," said Vaelora warmly.

"If you would join us in the salon," suggested Nephyl. "It does have a lovely view of the river."

Quaeryt stayed close to Vaelora, his shields covering them both, as they followed the couple, both far closer to Vaelora's age than Quaeryt's, down the larger corridor that led straight back from the entry hall. Mergiana leaned toward her husband and murmured a few words. While Quaeryt could not hear them, he could sense the urgency behind them, and he strengthened his shields.

Some twenty yards down the corridor was an archway into a large chamber that stretched some fifteen yards toward the river. Wide windows overlooked a roofed terrace beyond, the roof clearly being necessary so that those on the terrace could enjoy the breezes and the river view in late afternoon.

Nephyl gestured toward a settee and the chairs flanking it, all facing the river.

Quaeryt guided Vaelora to the far end of the settee, then stood beside the chair, waiting for the holder and his wife to take their places, seating himself as they did, with Mergiana taking the place beside Vaelora.

"My wife informs me that you, Commander, are somewhat more than a commander, and that the lady is also more than that."

Quaeryt smiled. "I am a commander in the Telaryn forces, and I do have the honor to be married to Lady Vaelora, who is indeed the sister of Lord Bhayar, and who is returning from a mission as envoy to the High Council of Khel."

Nephyl frowned, as if uncertain as to what else he might say without being impolite.

"I believe my husband was referring to the fact that you both appear to have a Naedaran background, and such is rare these days."

"It is no secret that Lord Bhayar's family is half Pharsi," said Quaeryt, "and I was an orphan who did not discover I was of Pharsi blood until I was full grown." .

"My maid Semila is of that background," pursued Mergiana. "She says that you bear all the . . . attributes of those who are sometimes called sons of Erion."

Quaeryt shrugged, as if helpless to refute the statement.

"My husband can be modest about such," said Vaelora. "He has always believed that actions define someone better than words. He is the most effective commander in all my brother's armies. He just returned from the conquest of Antiago."

"Antiago . . . ? It is also in Lord Bhayar's hands?" asked Nephyl. "What of the Autarch . . . and his Antiagon Fire . . . and imagers?"

"The Autarch and most of his troopers are dead, as are most of the imagers," replied Quaeryt. "We also destroyed perhaps seven or eight warships as well. Submarshal Skarpa is acting governor of Antiago."

"The world has changed . . . greatly . . . in the last year," said Nephyl slowly.

"It will continue to change in the year to come," observed Quaeryt. "You may have received a summons to pay a token tariff for the past year. If you have not, you will."

"Token? How great a token . . . if I might ask?"

"A hundred golds, I believe."

"Some might not consider that a token."

"Perhaps not, but he is also requiring token tariffs

from the factors, and there is much that needs to be done in Bovaria, such matters as rebuilding neglected roads and applying the same laws to all. Lord Bhayar would prefer not to remove High Holders, but he will do so if they do not pledge allegiance to him and pay their tariffs."

"I had not heard . . ."

"There were four High Holders near Kephria," said Vaelora. "They did not believe the commander. Their holds no longer exist. There is not a stone remaining. There are other High Holders who did. Outside of the token payment, and occasionally the purchase of supplies at a cheaper rate, they remain untouched."

"Lord Bhayar is a man of his word," declared Quaeryt.

"And so are you, it is said," suggested Mergiana. "Can you assure us—" She stopped at a sharp gesture from Nephyl.

"We have no intention of doing you any harm," replied Quaeryt. "Lord Bhayar expects allegiance and loyalty. We're here to let you know that, not to strip your holding or destroy it." He smiled politely. "I understand that your holding is known for the fine pale yellow bricks that appear to have built every structure in Eelan, Faantyl, and many elsewhere, as in Daaren. Tell me about that, if you would."

"Ah . . . yes." Nephyl cleared his throat. "My great-great-grandsire was fortunate enough to discover that the lands on the far side of the Phraan contain great deposits of a fine clay . . ."

Quaeryt listened, but remained alert. So did Vaelora.

12

In the end, Quaeryt and Vaelora only stayed a little over a glass at Lehyln before they returned to Eelan. Although staying at Lehyln would have been far more comfortable than at the Silver Swan, Quaeryt wanted to save his impositions on High Holders for the times when they were truly necessary. He also hoped the combination of power and forbearance would make an impression on Nephyl and Mergiana, but there were times when he wondered if anything except absolute power made any impression on anyone. Still . . . he felt he had to try. *And hope it won't be your undoing.*

Both Vaelora and Quaeryt were happy to leave Eelan early on Samedi morning. Again they found the road to the north a packed dirt track in the middle of what once had been a road almost twice as wide. They also managed to travel almost fifteen milles before Quaeryt and the imager undercaptains had to replace and rebuild yet another bridge.

By the following Meredi afternoon, as they neared the town of Berryhyl, Quaeryt could take a certain satisfaction in the number of bridges and causeways that they had improved or replaced. At the same time, he was astounded and amazed at the number. *Was that a pas-*

sive defense against the depredations of Kharst and his predecessors? Or did Kharst create his elite corps of crossbow assassins because the roads precluded use of troopers with any haste? Or did they go together?

Quaeryt doubted that he'd ever discover an answer. He did know that one likely duty for imagers in the years ahead would be the gradual improvement of roads, if only to bring them up closer to the standards of Telaryn highways.

As he and Vaelora rode closer to the town, he saw low hill after low hill seemingly covered with bushes set in neat rows. A closer look showed that on more than half of the hills the bushes appeared not to have been that well tended recently, with undergrowth around them, and in places, goats, sheep, and cattle grazing in, on, or around the bushes.

Quaeryt did notice one young shepherd take a look at the troopers and immediately begin to use his dog and his staff to try to move the flock up over the hill and out of sight of the road.

"He didn't want us getting any ideas," observed Vaelora.

"Something like that," said Quaeryt.

Then, in the midst of the hills filled with berries, was a larger hill on the east side of the road. The top of the hill bore traces of a fire, and there were clumps of stone and brick scattered down from the crest across ground that held but a few scattered scraggly bushes and patches of weeds. The devastation continued on the slope west of the road, all the way down to the Phraan River, where Quaeryt could make out the charred remnants of several piers, some scarcely above the water, but most below it and barely visible.

"It looks like someone salted the ground," said Vaelora. "Is this what you were telling me you'd seen along the Aluse on your way to Variana?"

"This looks older, but the holding's been treated the same way."

"You think it was Kharst?"

"More likely his father or grandfather."

"And they didn't give the lands to another High Holder?"

"If they did, whoever received them doesn't seem to care much for them."

Vaelora shook her head.

Farther north of the devastated hold, for almost a mille, the berry-bush-covered hills continued. Then past a stone wall in advanced disrepair, there was a small holding with neatly trimmed and tended trees, apple trees, Quaeryt thought.

A few hundred yards later was another millestone: BERRYHYL—2 M.

Quaeryt gestured to Vaelora, then called to Zhelan, riding ahead of them with Baelthm. "Major?"

"Yes, sir?"

"According to the maps, there's nowhere else to stay for at least another ten milles, and it's already past fourth glass. If there's anything that looks feasible here . . ."

"Yes, sir."

Even from the southern edge of the town proper, with older, if small, stone and timber houses, all neatly kept, Quaeryt gained the impression of a place that had once been prosperous, but that still took pride in its appearance. They rode past several dwellings that looked to be empty, but which were still well kept.

There was a large inn on the square. That Quaeryt

could see from three blocks south. By the time they reached the square, it was clear that the three-story Berry Inn was the largest inn they'd seen since Daaren, and possibly even larger than the Grande Laar Inn there. Its timber and stone construction gave it a more rustic appearance. Quaeryt did see that all the windows on the south wing were shuttered, but even the shuttered wing seemed to be well maintained.

A glass later, Quaeryt and Brem, the innkeeper, a muscular but trim graybeard, had reached a satisfactory arrangement, and Vaelora, Quaeryt, and Brem sat at a circular table in the spacious public room.

"It's slow this time of year," admitted Brem. "When berrying season comes round, we get more visitors. Still can't fill the inn, not like in the old days."

"The town took its name from the berries on the hills, then?" asked Quaeryt.

"That'd be so, sir. Folks called the holder High Holder Berryhill. Don't rightly recall what the family's real name was. The place was burned out by Rex Kharst's sire when my da was a boy. He said you could see the flames from here in town."

"What did the holder do with all those berries?" asked Vaelora.

"They made jams and jellies and fancy sauces. They raised game fowl and fed 'em on the berries. My da said the holder shipped them downriver on his flatboats all the way to Kephria. That was when you could do that. River's never been the same since they built that Great Canal. Don't see why it was necessary. You could use the river all but three months out of the year."

Quaeryt nodded, not voicing the thought that one major difference was that the canal allowed goods from the north and west to travel to and from Variana, not just one way, all year around. "Why did Kharst's sire burn out the High Holder?"

"One day . . . one of the sons of the rex came to visit. That was Rex Kharst's sire, but it was before he was rex. No one knows what happened. Some say he fancied the young wife of the holder. Others say he fancied the brother of the wife . . . Anyway, he left in haste and in anger. Weeks later the troopers came."

"And no new holder came?" asked Quaeryt.

"The lands belong to the rex. Well, they did. I suppose they belong to Lord Bhayar now. Back then, the council sent a missive to Variana asking who to expect as the new High Holder. Never received an answer. So the folks graze their flocks there, careful like, and pick the berries. No one says much when travelers come during berrying season, but . . ." The innkeeper shrugged, then looked at Vaelora. "Might your brother be appointing a High Holder to bring back the berrying?"

"He will be appointing some new High Holders," Vaelora conceded, "and I will certainly bring Berryhyl to his attention."

"Be a shame for the lands to lie so poorly used," added Brem.

"But it would take the right kind of High Holder," Quaeryt said.

"Aye. Not ones like some around Semlem."

"What do you know about them?" asked Quaeryt, for whom Semlem was just a town on the map located some fifty milles upriver.

"There's two, maybe three, from what I hear. One was killed last fall when you folks defeated Kharst. He was the worst. Used to ride into town with his armsmen and pick up any lass he fancied. No one ever saw any of them again."

"No one did anything?" asked Vaelora.

"He had two hundred armsmen. He owned the silver mines in the hills to the east. They say his heir's not much better, but who would know?"

"And the others?" prompted Quaeryt.

"Can't say I know, except one of them would graze his cattle on the lands of freeholders whenever water or forage got short. He'd just laugh and tell them to ask Rex Kharst for relief."

After more stories, and another quint, Vaelora glanced meaningfully at Quaeryt.

Quaeryt smiled and rose, as did Vaelora. "We appreciated hearing what you had to say, but we've had a long ride today, and there are a few other matters we need to address."

"I'd not be meaning to take your time . . ."

"No . . . the pleasure was ours."

Quaeryt and Vaelora retreated to their room, one of the "grand chambers" overlooking the river, with not only a large and firm bed, but a separate bathing chamber, if one that required water be carried up by the inn's chambermaids, a task Quaeryt had arranged.

After bathing and eating with the officers in a large private dining room that Quaeryt suspected had not been used much, if at all, in recent years, the two returned to their chamber.

In the dim light cast by a single wall lamp, Quaeryt sat in a chair, while Vaelora, propped up with pillows, stretched out on the bed.

"This land is fertile enough," mused Vaelora. "It's as if Kharst and his sire went out of their way to ruin it."

Quaeryt shook his head. "I wouldn't say that."

"What would you say, dearest?"

"They didn't want to make the effort to rule it. So they laid down a few rules and let it go at that. The first rule was not to thwart or oppose the rex. The second rule was to pay your tariffs. So far as I can tell, there wasn't a third rule. That allowed the factors to act almost like local governments, but none of them dared to go further than that. The High Holders didn't dare to act together because the moment one of them said or did anything, he was killed and his hold leveled. I imagine Kharst kept an ear and an eye out for any High Holder who tried to build up his armsmen, and the other High Holders probably would tell the rex as well, because none of them wanted a truly strong ruler to replace Kharst."

"But why did Kharst attack Ferravyl?"

"You've seen the state of the Great Canal and of Ephra. He wanted an open route to Solis on the Aluse for his traders. They doubtless told him that would create more tariffs, and it would have. His marshals didn't see that many Telaryn forces around Ferravyl. Initially, your brother was heavily outnumbered. And most people tend to believe that other people behave the way they do. Kharst knew your brother was young for a ruler, and probably didn't understand that Telaryn was ruled far better than was Bovaria. He thought he had more troopers. His marshals thought so, too, and they knew Bhayar didn't have that much in the way of cannon or muskets. Given all that, they weren't about to tell Kharst they couldn't attack. By the time they realized Telaryn was far stronger than they thought, it was too late."

"That was because of you and your imagers, dearest."

"Partly, but not totally. Because Telaryn has better

roads, your brother could raise and bring more troops
to Ferravyl than Kharst's marshals realized. Even had
we not been there, in the end, I believe his attacks would
have failed."

"At a terrible cost."

"To both lands."

Vaelora frowned, then reached for the leatherbound
book on the side table. She paged through it quickly,
then nodded, and moved the bookmark, before handing the volume to Quaeryt. "You might find this interesting. Start with 'all men believe.'"

Quaeryt opened the book and began to read at the
phrase she had spoken.

All men believe in something. That was one of Rholan's
favorite sayings. Even those who claim to believe in
nothing are believing something, he would say. He
often confounded people by asking about what they
believed . . . and then told them things about themselves that he could not have possibly known. Conversely, he would listen to someone talk for a time,
and then say something like, "The Nameless in which
you believe weighs the acts of good and evil like lead
weights upon a scale balance."

The same was true of rulers, he believed, except
that since they often acted like they were gods, they
saw themselves reflected in the images of other rulers
that they built in their thoughts. Thus, Lord Ofryk
thought that Hengyst of Ryntar was more thoughtful, in the way that Ofryk himself was, while Hengyst
hesitated to attack Tela because he could not believe,
based on his own character, that Ofryk could have
failed to prepare for war. That being so, Rholan was
no fool, nor did he believe that shrewd men continued

to persist in seeing themselves in others, and that only fools did so. By those lights, he regarded Hengyst as shrewd and Ofryk as a self-deluded fool.

As he closed the book and handed it back to Vaelora, he nodded and said, "I hadn't remembered that passage. At least, I didn't remember reading it, but it must have stuck in my thoughts somewhere."

"Kharst was a fool, according to Rholan's definition."

"When I read that book, I get the feeling that Rholan thought most men were fools." *And, at one time or another, most of us are.*

"He didn't even bother to observe women," said Vaelora.

"I doubt he would have been any more or less charitable."

"In small ways, the book shows he was far less charitable."

Given Vaelora's firm tone and, he had to admit to himself, what he'd read, Quaeryt wasn't about to argue that. "You're right, and that's too bad."

"Are you placating me?"

"If trying to avoid an argument when you're right is placating . . . yes."

Vaelora laughed softly. "You're sweet when you try not to be so obvious in admitting something."

"I thought I was very obvious."

"You can be sweet about that, too."

Quaeryt was definitely not about to argue that.

13

By leaving Berryhyl early on Solayi and putting in a long day, although only one minor bridge repair was required, and by leaving the small hamlet of Souwal early on Lundi morning, first company came into sight of Semlem just before second glass that afternoon. Even the southern outskirts of Semlem were anything but inspiring, with houses that were little more than large boxes with single-slant roofs and overlapped plank walls with peeling gray-washed boards and small windows.

"The men will like the extra time in a town," said Khaern from where he rode beside Quaeryt.

"Even in this town?" asked Quaeryt.

"After all the hamlets, any town will do."

Out of the corner of his eye, Quaeryt could see the faintest headshake from Vaelora.

The not-quite-ramshackle dwellings on the south side of Semlem slowly gave way to roughly dressed stone-walled homes and shops as they neared the center of Semlem—a stone-paved square with yet another statue in the middle.

Is the worship of the Nameless only a pretense here? Quaeryt wondered, especially when he saw a large anomen a block north of the square. *Or did those who*

*had been Rex of Bovaria believe that Naming was not
a sin for rulers?*

On the north side of the square was the inn, a structure smaller, if not by much, than the inn in Berryhyl,
but one that was equally old, but more imposing by
virtue of its gray stone construction. Quaeryt turned
his mount toward the inn, and the necessary process of
obtaining food and lodging for sums that would not
exhaust his limited funds, but which would not also
amount to outright commandeering of what he needed
for men and mounts.

Once he had settled matters with the innkeeper, who
seemed, if not agreeable, grudgingly accepting of Quaeryt's offer for lodging and fare, Quaeryt relayed the billeting orders to Zhelan and the two subcommanders,
then returned with Vaelora to talk with the innkeeper
in the main entry hall.

"Who are the High Holders here?" Quaeryt asked.

"There's Lenglan of Norwal. The old holder died in
the battle at Variana. He's the heir. So he's the one owns
the mines in the hills east of here. Got a hold house just
north of town on the river. Then there's Patarak. He
doesn't leave his place much, not since he got thrown
in the hunt a few years back. Must be sixty if he's a day.
His estate is southeast, if you take the lane off the south
pier for two milles."

"Are there any others?"

"Depends on whether you count High Holder Far-
lan. Has a summer hold maybe ten milles north, right
on the river. Don't know where his main hold is, except
it's somewhere near Eluthyn."

When Quaeryt finished with the innkeeper, he walked
with Vaelora up the steps, following an inn chamber-
maid to their rooms.

"I think we'll send a message to High Holder Lenglan, saying that we'll be paying him a call between fourth and fifth glass."

"If you're going to give notice, I think you should bring a full company and the imagers."

"I'd thought that. While you're getting washed up and changed, I'll talk it over with Zhelan, Khaern, and Calkoran before I decide on the company."

"Changed? Into what?"

"Your best riding outfit."

"None of them . . ." She shook her head. "Never mind. I'll work something out."

After leaving Vaelora in their chamber, Quaeryt returned to the main level of the inn, sent a trooper with a message that he needed to meet briefly with his senior officers and the imager undercaptains, and repaired to the otherwise empty public room for Zhelan to gather the imager undercaptains and for Calkoran and Khaern to join them.

Calkoran was the first to arrive. Then came Khaern, followed by Zhelan and the undercaptains.

"Thank you all for coming quickly. This won't take long. It's only rumor, but I've been led to understand that High Holder Lenglan is a less than golden heir of a thoroughly disreputable sire who was a close acquaintance of Rex Kharst. The sire was at Variana and perished with Kharst. The father maintained an inordinate number of armsmen and specialized in the overt kidnapping and subsequent use of attractive young women who were never seen again. Lady Vaelora and I intend to pay a call on the High Holder between fourth and fifth glass. I need a company to deliver the invitation. The imager undercaptains will accompany the company and will provide the necessary persuasion. That persuasion is to be applied gradually, beginning with the removal of gates and walls and proceeding to the removal of guards and functionaries only as necessary. You under-captains will need to shield yourselves and the company because I want no injuries or wounds to our troopers. Is that clear?"

The four undercaptains and Elsior nodded.

"Subcommanders?"

"We would be pleased," offered Calkoran. "It would be a pleasure to deliver such a message to a Bovarian High Holder."

"Thank you. We'll await the results of your visit."

Quaeryt spent another quint inspecting the inn and checking the stables and the progress of billeting before returning to Vaelora.

From the window in their inn chamber, Quaeryt could see the center of the town, with the usual square. To the west, if he leaned forward, slightly out the open window, he could also see the two river piers, but the up-river pier was unlike any he'd ever recalled seeing. It was U-shaped, and there was a flatboat tied in place, its stem firmly against the middle shore section of the pier. From the inn window, Quaeryt watched while two dray horses pulled a narrow but strongly constructed wagon up a ramp from the flatboat and onto the pier, and then up a paved ramp to the main street. As the wagon passed below, he could see that it was empty.

"What are you watching?" asked Vaelora from where she stood before a mirror and worked on her hair.

"An empty wagon coming off a flatboat. They must cart ore or rough metal north somewhere, and then return the horses and wagons by flatboat."

"What would they do with the flatboats?"

"I don't know, but there must be some use for them."

A glass later, a ranker knocked on the door and informed Quaeryt that Calkoran's company had returned. Quaeryt hurried down to the public room, where the undercaptains and Calkoran waited.

"How did it go?" asked Quaeryt.

Lhandor and Khalis exchanged glances. Horan shook his head ruefully.

Finally, Calkoran spoke. "The hold has large iron gates. There is a wall all around the house and the other buildings. The guards at the gate refused to speak to me. So Landor removed the gates. Then some crossbowmen fired at us. Horan shielded us. Khalis imaged away their crossbows. I said that they should convey your invitation to the High Holder. Someone rang a bell. Before long two squads came charging at us. The undercaptains imaged pepper and smoke into their ranks. That stopped most of them. The head of the guards threatened us. He used vile language. So I called on Baelthm. He put out both his eyes with silver daggers. I told him we were doing our best to convey a polite invitation. He wasn't listening. His squad leader was. I told him that we really didn't want to kill them all, but that they weren't leaving us much choice." Calkoran shook his head.

"And?"

"He laughed," said Calkoran. "So I called on Khalis. He removed his neck and let his head fall on the ground. He stopped laughing. So did the others. The crossbowmen ran, and the riders rode away. The guards said they would convey your message."

Quaeryt nodded slowly. "It appears as though I'll need you all when we call again on the good High Holder."

"It would be our pleasure again," insisted Calkoran.

"We'll leave in a quint."

When Quaeryt returned to the chamber, Vaelora immediately asked, "Well? Was he receptive?"

"Not in the slightest." Quaeryt conveyed what had occurred.

"You're not going to level the place?"

"Not yet. I'll give the High Holder a last chance. Some of them do learn." *Besides . . . we don't want to get in the habit of leveling every hold for reactions based on what they did in the past. We'd have to level too many of them.*

Two quints later, Quaeryt, Vaelora, Calkoran, and the undercaptains rode up to the stone wall and the gate pillars that marked the entry to Norwal.

Four mounted guards with sheathed blades were stationed inside the walls.

While Quaeryt was ready to order the imagers to destroy a good section of the holding walls if there happened to be the slightest sign of resistance, the lead guard immediately called out, "High Holder Lenglan bids you welcome to Norwal."

Then the four guards turned and rode slowly up the gray-stone-paved lane that led to the long two-story dwelling situated on the top of a rise overlooking the Phraan River to the west. The entry portico was on the east side.

"Subcommander," said Quaeryt, "if you and the undercaptains will follow and remain in position near the hold house. Undercaptains, you're to provide shields if there is any indication of trouble. If we do not return, although I do not expect that, you are to reduce the entire holding to rubble."

"Yes, sir."

Two footmen stood at the top of the steps leading up to the portico. When Quaeryt and Vaelora reined up, one announced, "Holder Lenglan awaits you."

Quaeryt dismounted and held out the hand, his good one, that Vaelora did not need as she followed. They walked up onto the portico. Standing at the far side, just outside the open double doors to the hold, was Lenglan, a man of moderate height, with comparatively short brown hair, brownish hazel eyes. He wore a rich brown jacket over an ivory shirt, with trousers that matched his jacket, and well-polished brown boots. His welcoming smile included his eyes. The smile alone made Quaeryt exceedingly wary.

"The lady and the commander," offered Lenglan in a warm and welcoming tone, after a bow. "I presume, Lady, that you must be a relation to Lord Bhayar, his sister, perhaps, since it is known that his wife remains as regent of Telaryn."

That suggested to Quaeryt that Lenglan's sire, and perhaps Lenglan himself, had indeed possessed a close tie to the late Rex Kharst.

"His youngest sister," returned Vaelora.

"And returning from Khel as his envoy to the High Council," added Quaeryt.

"Ah hah . . . most interesting, and I would love to hear more. If you would join me in the salon. I would wish to provide my own lady, but I cannot, for I have not yet wed. I saw little purpose in that while my father was yet a strong and vigorous man." He gestured toward the doors, then turned to lead them inside.

Quaeryt made certain his shields covered Vaelora, then nodded to her. They followed, matching Lenglan's measured pace. Inside the doors was a large, but not overlarge, circular receiving hall with a lightly domed ceiling finished in smooth white plaster. The lower walls, up to the simple goldenwood crown molding that separated them from the ceiling, were covered in pale goldenwood paneling set off by goldenwood faux columns. The floor was composed of alternating squares of polished white and gray marble. There was a small closed door on each side of the hall and a large archway at the end of the hall. Beyond the arch was a long corridor that appeared to stretch the length of the house in each direction, and directly opposite the archway was another set of open double doors, leading into a long and narrow room with wide windows at the end, clearly overlooking a formal garden, with a less formal garden set out on the slope leading down to the river and an elaborate boathouse flanked by two piers.

In the space short of the windows, the young holder, certainly not any older than Vaelora, stopped and turned. "Whatever seating arrangements you prefer."

"Why don't you sit there," suggested Quaeryt, pointing to the chair at a right angle to the gray velvet couch.

Lenglan stood by the chair, but did not seat himself until Vaelora settled into the far end of the couch. Quaeryt took the other chair, the one facing the holder, then removed his visor cap and set it on the low corner table.

Neither Lenglan's eyes nor his expression changed as he looked at Quaeryt, although there was the faintest hint of a nod.

"I would offer refreshments, and will if you wish, but I doubt that such was the primary purpose of your call. Might I ask the purpose of your visit?"

"My brother has suggested that, in the course of our travels, we visit the more notable High Holders as we can," said Vaelora. "We were fortunate enough to arrive in Semlem early enough to see you."

"Notable? I fear not. What have I done, save inherit the holding?"

"The holding is considered to be quite notable, according to those up and down this part of the Phraan River," said Quaeryt mildly. "You have silver mines, and it would appear that you also quarry stone."

"The copper mines produce more, but there are costs that are not inconsiderable."

"You reduce the ore and ship it north, but refine the silver here?"

"That is so."

"What do you do with the flatboats once they return here?" asked Vaelora.

Lenglan smiled. "We sell them to High Holder Nephyl at a slight profit."

"And he uses them to ship his bricks farther downriver."

"I presume so."

"Most efficient," said Quaeryt, "in addition to being notable."

"Notable . . . a rather interesting word."

"Apparently, your sire had quite a reputation."

"Am I to be judged for what he did? Are the acts of the father the acts of the son?"

"Not unless the son does as his sire did," replied Quaeryt. "Your father paid for his close support of a reckless and poor ruler. You will not be held responsible for his support . . . so long as you pledge allegiance to Lord Bhayar, who has already proven both more successful and responsible . . . and so long as your conduct meets the standards that he has set for High Holders.

At present, there is no evidence that you have failed in either allegiance or in conduct. Lord Bhayar would prefer that you do not fail."

"Oh? How sure of that can one be?"

Vaelora smiled, then said sweetly, "It is so tiresome to remove High Holders and replace them. The commander has removed five since the beginning of the year, and destroyed their holds, but allowed one heir to retain the lands and rebuild. He has also found a number of other holders well suited to retaining their lands."

"How many, pray tell?"

"Something like a half score are hale and well . . . of those we have visited," replied Quaeryt. That was likely technically a slight exaggeration, because they had not visited some High Holders whose reputations had seemed adequate. "And only those High Holders in Antiago, Shahibs they call themselves, who fought and died in battle were removed, only to be replaced by their heirs." *So far, anyway.* But Quaeryt doubted that Skarpa would remove anyone without extreme cause.

Lenglan frowned. "Antiago? What might Antiago have to do . . ."

"Our pardon," said Vaelora quickly, before Quaeryt could reply. "You have not heard? Antiago is now under the rule of Lord Bhayar. The commander and Submarshal Skarpa destroyed the Autarch and his forces. The commander and I are returning to Variana to provide details to my brother."

Lenglan looked hard at Quaeryt. "Might you be the commander said to have destroyed the forces of Rex Kharst?"

"He is," replied Vaelora. "Twice. At Ferravyl and at Variana."

"And you are here talking to me . . . a small High

Holder along a modest river in the hinterlands of Bovaria?"

"It is the quickest way back to Variana. It has also allowed us to repair bridges and roads as part of an effort to restore the roads of Bovaria. My imagers do not just destroy. They also build."

For a long moment the young High Holder sat immobile. Finally, he said, "I must thank you for your forbearance." A rueful smile crossed his face, one that Quaeryt trusted not at all. "What else might you require of me, other than pledging allegiance . . . and respectable conduct."

"In time, if you have not done so already, Lord Bhayar will require a onetime token tariff of one hundred golds for this year. He knows you or your sire already paid the annual tariff, but he is incurring significant costs in his efforts to rebuild Bovaria and deal with many aspects of the land that have been neglected."

"I will pay you now . . ."

Quaeryt shook his head. "You will discover who to pay and when. We thought you should know." He glanced to Vaelora.

She gave the briefest and smallest of nods.

Quaeryt rose, extending a hand to Vaelora.

"It has been a pleasure to meet you, Lenglan of Norwal," she said. "I trust we will hear nothing but good of you in the months and years to come."

Lenglan rose quickly. "I will do my best to meet those expectations. Let me see you off properly." He turned and moved toward the grand entryway.

As they followed him, Quaeryt eased forward and said in a low voice to the young holder, "There is one other thing. I think Lord Bhayar would be very disappointed if any more young women disappeared from the streets of Semlem. I know Lady Vaelora and I would be, and I'd very much not wish to make a special trip here to deal with the situation. I'll also be letting it be known that such is our feeling to those in certain positions in town." Quaeryt smiled as warmly as he could. "I just thought you'd appreciate knowing that."

Lenglan flushed slightly and looked at Quaeryt as if to say something.

Quaeryt projected power and certainty.

The young High Holder paled, but said in a low voice, "I do appreciate your kindness in letting me know quietly. There will be no more instances of such, overexaggerated as such reports doubtless were."

"I'm glad to hear that such rumors were exaggerations, but I did wish you to know, as we have informed other High Holders that Lord Bhayar expects a far higher standard of conduct and behavior from all his High Holders, both here, in Antiago, and in Telaryn. He crushed those in Tilbor and those in southern Bovaria who failed to understand that."

"Why do you tell me this, then?"

"He also believes in giving High Holders an opportunity to show their allegiance and worthiness." After a moment Quaeryt added, "Once."

Lenglan nodded. "I believe I understand."

"I believe you do."

The young holder, clearly uneasy, stepped aside, but walked beside Quaeryt and Vaelora to the portico steps, then watched as they mounted and rode back down the wide stone-paved drive.

Once they were on the river road back to Semlem, the sun hanging just over the trees on the west side of the Phraan River, Quaeryt turned in the saddle. "What do you think?"

"He's a spoiled brat, but he's a very intelligent spoiled brat. You won't have changed the way he feels, but there won't be any trouble with his tariffs or with the local women."

"He'll seek out women elsewhere?"

"I think not. I suspect he'll have an inordinate amount of serving maids who are paid rather better than the local wages. Some may leave his service, but they will leave alive and in health. He likes being High Holder far more than he likes any other personal pleasure, and you frightened him to his core."

"But . . . ?"

"It might not hurt to send him a missive every so often, inquiring about his health."

Quaeryt nodded, knowing that his problems in dealing with High Holders and others of position were only beginning . . . especially if he continued to be successful. He reminded himself that he needed to write a short missive to High Holder Patarak, regretting that the nature of their travel to Variana made a visit impossible, but trusting that Patarak's allegiance to Lord Bhayar remained firm.

14

Interestingly enough, but not completely surprising to Quaeryt, was the condition of the road heading north out of Semlem. While still of clay, the surface was packed and smooth, as well as wide enough that the actual surface used by riders and wagons stretched from one original shoulder to the other, all signs that the metals mined east of the mining town continued to be valued and that they traveled north—most likely to the Great Canal and then eastward to Variana.

He was also pleased that he and Vaelora had received a nearly immediate, if brief, but pleasant reply to their missive to Patarak. The older High Holder had written that he appreciated their courtesy and their interest in High Holders, even in less frequented parts of Bovaria, and that he looked forward to the return of order across Bovaria and that the presence of Lord Bhayar's sister boded well for all those with that hope.

"I don't think he was too pleased with Kharst," Quaeryt had observed. "Or he wants us to think he wasn't."

"That could be, but the innkeeper did say that he'd been very quiet for the last few years. His riding accident might have provided an excuse not to travel to Variana or to see Kharst."

"That's possible." *But anything's possible the way Kharst ruled.*

Quaeryt had thought over the missive more than once as they had ridden northward over the next four days, especially after visiting, if briefly, two other High Holders who had been all too eager to profess their allegiance to Bhayar. But then, the nearer they came to the Great Canal and Variana, the more likely it was that information about Bhayar's victories had reached the various high holdings.

Although it was not yet midspring, by midday on Vendrei Quaeryt had long since shed his uniform riding jacket. He was also looking impatiently at the scattered cots and holdings, thinking that there should be signs that they were approaching Eluthyn. His impatience might have been partly because, in covering the last hundred milles, they had accomplished more road and bridge repairs, but mainly to strengthen existing bridges and causeways, since the road north of Semlem remained wide and in far better repair than the roads north of Daaren.

Roughly a glass before, they had seen a stone indicating that they had ten milles to go, yet Quaeryt saw no sign of the canal town or the canal.

"You're getting impatient, aren't you?" observed Vaelora.

"I suppose so."

"We still have nearly a week of travel left, eight or nine days, if the weather's bad. I worry that Bhayar's gotten rumors about what happened, and Myskyl and Deucalon are distorting them."

"With the state of roads in Bovaria, how is he going to find out? The only way he could get word is if someone sent a dispatch rider from Kephria . . . and there's no one who could. Even if he did get word, he wouldn't know how accurate it would be."

Once more, Quaeryt was reminded of just how long it took for messages to travel—and travel time had been bad enough just across Telaryn.

"You have that look," said Vaelora.

"I was thinking about how long it takes even for rulers to find things out."

"You could have sent a dispatch rider," she pointed out.

"That would have been worse. Imagine what problems we'd face if Myskyl and Deucalon had two weeks or more to plant ideas without us there." Quaeryt shook his head. "Either way, it's a problem. That's why Bhayar needs good roads and good regional governors. And dispatch stations." *And in Bovaria, at the moment, he has none of those.*

Quaeryt glanced to his left, down at the river, almost pondlike in its calm. It was definitely narrower, although that had occurred so gradually that Quaeryt hadn't really noticed before. What called his attention to it was that, in places, there were poles planted to show the channel for the flatboats, and there wasn't that much open water between the poles and the shore.

Ahead, above the trees, he saw the roofs of several buildings, although they looked to be to the west of the river. Then he nodded, recalling that most of Eluthyn actually lay to the west of where the canal and the river crossed, or rather where the river actually ran under the Great Canal through a culvert. The canal locks were just east of there.

"Well . . . finally," he said cheerfully. "There's Eluthyn."

"Where else would you expect it to be," replied Vaelora dryly.

Quaeryt thought he heard a smothered guffaw from one of the undercaptains who rode behind them. He grinned and replied, "For all I know, it could have vanished. But it does have a decent inn, I hear, although . . . there would have been advantages to having Rex Kharst's canal boat."

"Advantages for whom, dearest?" murmured Vaelora.

Quaeryt decided to refrain from commenting, at least until they were alone in the inn at Eluthyn.

15

Almost exactly a week later, on a sunny midafternoon, as Quaeryt and Vaelora rode along the last mille or so of the towpath of the Great Canal, Quaeryt gestured toward the northeast and the hold house of the late High Holder Paitrak. "It's hard to believe that it was almost two seasons ago since we were there."

"I don't find that hard to believe at all. I'm most certain that we'll find brother dear there." She pointed to the southeast where, glimmering white in the sun, was Chateau Regis, which had been Rex Kharst's and which Quaeryt's imagers had rebuilt and restructured almost two seasons ago.

"By now, Bhayar should have received word that we're almost in Variana." *Unless Deucalon delayed them.* Although Quaeryt had sent out dispatch riders when they had set out that morning, he was well aware that did not assure that their messages reached Bhayar in a timely fashion.

"So should Deucalon, and Myskyl, if he's around."

"Myskyl might not be."

Quaeryt wasn't certain whether it would be better if Myskyl was near Bhayar or distantly removed. In either case, the submarshal was likely to cause difficulties. *You can't do anything about that now.* "I still say that

Kharst's canal boat would have been welcome here," Quaeryt suggested, "not that it matters now, this close to Variana."

"You weren't thinking about sleep, dearest . . ."

"But I was," he half protested, with a grin.

"Just about sleep," Vaelora amended her words.

Less than a quint later, a squad of riders wearing the green uniforms of Telaryn approached under Bhayar's personal banner. The officer leading them was a major Quaeryt recognized by face, but not by name.

"Lady Vaelora! Commander! Lord Bhayar is most gratified that you have returned hale and successful. He awaits you at the Chateau Regis."

"I'll need billeting for Eleventh Regiment and two companies," Quaeryt replied.

"Ah . . . we have made arrangements for two regiments, sir."

"We didn't lose Nineteenth Regiment, if that's the concern. Subcommander Alazyn is supporting Submarshal Skarpa in the submarshal's capacity as acting governor of Antiago."

"Sir?"

"I'd appreciate your keeping that to yourself until we have a chance to brief Lord Bhayar personally." Quaeryt image-projected a sense of just how displeased he would be if the major let that slip.

The major stiffened for an instant, then nodded. "Yes, sir. I understand, sir."

Almost two quints passed before Vaelora and Quaeryt walked up the grand staircase of the rebuilt Chateau Regis to the upper-level foyer. The staircase, Quaeryt recalled, had needed few repairs, unlike the outer and inner walls and floors. The walls still held no ornamentation, and the main-level furnishings had been comparatively sparse, although part of that was doubt-less a reflection of Bhayar's wishes, since he'd never liked elaboration for the sake of elaboration.

"He is in the northeast study, not in the receiving chamber, Lady, Commander," said the captain who escorted them when they reached the second level of the chateau. He turned to the left and led them along a wide corridor toward the sole door with a pair of guards stationed outside.

The guards watched as the major rapped on the door. "Lady Vaelora and Commander Quaeryt to see you, sir."

"Have them come in."

The major eased open the door and nodded. Quaeryt followed Vaelora, and the major closed the door behind them.

Quaeryt did a quick survey. The northeast study was the kind of chamber Bhayar preferred, a corner chamber with windows on the north and east sides, which provided early light and a flow of air on all but the still-est of days.

Bhayar stood beside the wide writing desk. On one side was a stack of papers, and on the other a map. For a long moment he studied the two, then frowned. "I would not have thought you would leave your child."

"I lost her," said Vaelora simply. "Sometimes . . . it happens."

Bhayar's eyes went to Quaeryt, hardening from dark blue to stone.

"It was not Quaeryt's doing. There was nothing he could have done. He has done more than either you or I could ever have asked."

"Are you protecting him?"

"If I must. You should have seen him when he came to my sickbed to comfort me after I . . . lost her."

"Where was this?"

"In Kephria," replied Vaelora. "You should let us tell you how and why you now are the ruler of Antiago."

"What of Aliaro? Did you not bring him in chains . . . after all he has done?"

"That would be difficult, sir," said Quaeryt mildly. "We were forced to destroy his palace fortress with all his remaining armsmen and imagers in it. He was also there."

Bhayar sighed, the long and dramatic expression of exasperation, rather than the short and explosive sound of anger. Then he gestured to the conference table and the chairs around it. "You have had a long journey. I've ordered refreshments."

Once the three were seated, the Lord of Telaryn, Bovaria, and Antiago said, "If you would, tell me the sum of what you have accomplished, or not, before we dwell on the details."

Vaelora looked to Quaeryt.

Quaeryt cleared his throat quietly. "As you ordered, we accompanied Submarshal Skarpa along the Great Canal to Laaryn. We made major repairs to the canal this side of Eluthyn and put down a factor conspiracy in Laaryn. That required leaving Subcommander Meinyt, two imagers, and Fifth Regiment to assure compliance and receipt and payment of damages, and tariffs. You should have received a dispatch describing those events. We proceeded down the Laar to Geusyn and Ephra. Because Captain Nykaal had been unable to obtain enough ships to carry two regiments, we embarked with first company and Eleventh Regiment and sailed to Kherseilles. On the way we were attacked, and the imagers had to destroy two Antiagon warships. Since the High Council of Khel restricted the sale and use of mounts, only first company accompanied us to meet with the High Council at the ancient capital of Saendeol. The Council agreed to consider your terms, but only when you held all of Lydar." Quaeryt could see Bhayar open his mouth, but he continued to speak. "So we returned to Geusyn. Once there, we discovered that the southern Bovarian High Holders refused to pledge to you or to meet with either Skarpa or Vaelora. Then they fled into Antiago. We leveled all their hold houses and fortifications, breached the wall around Kephria and took it, and then rode to Suemyron and took it. After that, we took Barna and rode on Lianti-ago. Along the way, we fought four battles. We defeated and largely destroyed all who faced us. Aliaro holed up in his palace with his imagers. We destroyed the palace and almost all remaining Antiagon troopers and imag-ers. Skarpa remains as acting governor. In our absence from Kephria, Aliaro's troopers and imagers leveled Ephra, Kephria, and Geusyn. We commandeered a schooner and returned to Kephria. On the way we de-stroyed the four warships, and the troopers and imagers that had burned the three cities. The imagers rebuilt the main pier and constructed a trooper compound at Kephria, the best harbor of the three. We left two com-panies of the Khellan troopers to keep order during the rebuilding of Kephria and set out to return to Vari-ana. Here we are."

Bhayar was silent for a time. "I sent you out to obtain the allegiance of Khel. You seem to have accomplished everything except that." His voice was cool.

"I would respectfully disagree, sir. I believe you will be able to reach terms with Khel before long. Without taking Antiago, we had no chance of reaching such terms—except by fighting in Khel, and that would have meant fighting two lands to unite Lydar. Since Aliaro had already offered sanctuary to rebellious High Holders and attacked your warships three times without provocation, there were certainly grounds for the Antiagon campaign. Also, Antiago would have remained a threat and a temptation to the southern High Holders. Khel offers no such threat."

The lord of three lands nodded slowly. "It is always dangerous to send you to solve a problem, Quaeryt. You solve the problem, but in ways unforeseen. And those ways further your ends as well as mine."

"Would you rather have the problems unresolved, sir?"

Bhayar paused, as if to consider an appropriate response, when there was a knock on the small side door on the west side of the study.

"Bring in the refreshments," ordered Bhayar.

A Telaryn ranker appeared with a tray, followed by another ranker. In moments, each of the three at the table had a goblet, a small plate, and in the middle of the table were several platters, one of fruit, one of cheeses, one of sliced meats, and one of assorted pastries. There were also two carafes of wine, one of white, and one of red.

Once the rankers had departed and closed the door, Bhayar looked to his sister. "Red or white."

"The white, please."

Bhayar poured her white and himself red. Quaeryt poured himself the white.

"To your safe return." Bhayar lifted his goblet.

"To your forbearance, brother dear," replied Vaelora with a smile, "for our exceeding your expectations."

Bhayar's smile was half sour and half amused. "I knew there was great danger in having you two wed."

"It was your idea," Vaelora pointed out sweetly.

"Enough . . ."

Quaeryt noticed the tiredness in Bhayar's voice, but waited. So did Vaelora.

"Now tell me everything you left out, and the reasons why you did what you did."

Vaelora looked to Quaeryt.

"I'll start," he said, "but I trust Vaelora will add what I don't include."

Bhayar's lips quirked, almost as if to suggest that he would have been greatly surprised if his sister did not. Then he nodded.

"The first thing we noticed, after just a few days on the Great Canal," began Quaeryt, "was that it had not been that well maintained . . ." From there he described in great detail the harsh conditions of peasants on the lands of many landholders, the factors' deception and the problems in Laaryn, the conditions of the roads on the way to Geusyn, and what followed on their voyage to Kherseilles and the ride to Saendeol. Quaeryt deferred to Vaelora to let her describe the trial requested of them by the High Council and the subsequent meeting with the High Council of Khel.

When she finished, Quaeryt added, "Without the image that Vaelora made them see, there would have been no possibility of future terms."

Bhayar sighed again, a long expression of resignation, then said, "I begin to see the reasons for your actions. Go on."

Quaeryt took up the tale again.

When he got to the part where he and Skarpa, and the massed regiments, were about to leave Kephria on the ride to Suemyron, Vaelora interrupted. "I insisted that I remain with Eleventh Regiment and the troopers that would be returning from Khel. I *knew* that without all the remaining imagers, they could not prevail against the Autarch's forces. I also knew that I could not accompany them. I was too close to term. As you will hear, and he will not tell you, Quaeryt almost did not survive the final battle. Had there been even one less imager, he would not have." She looked to Quaeryt to continue.

Quaeryt went on to explain what happened in Antiago. He did not skip over his dread at discovering that Aliaro had sent warships to Kephria, and his efforts to reach there.

"He was close to being carried onto the schooner," interjected Vaelora. "That is what Major Zhelan told me. The captain was worried that he might not live."

"It wasn't that bad—" Quaeryt began to protest.

"It was a week later when I saw you, and half your body was yellow and purple," snapped Vaelora.

A faint smile crossed Bhayar's lips.

Quaeryt finished up with what happened on the way to Kephria, then turned to Vaelora. "You should finish this part. I wasn't there."

Vaelora did, speaking firmly about the Antiagon attack and what she had done, and her accident, adding quickly, "I was not trying to be a hero. I left Kephria as soon as I could. I was just unlucky."

"You were fortunate that it was not worse," replied Bhayar. "Still—"

"We have not finished," said Vaelora firmly.

From there the two recounted what had happened in repairing the harbor and building the trooper compound and on their journey to Variana.

When the two had finished, Bhayar looked to Vaelora. "At times, I wish you were not so headstrong as your grandmere. I cannot fault you, for the same blood runs in all our veins, but the price for these conquests you have laid before me has been high."

"Not so high as failing to succeed," replied Vaelora.

"I would talk to Quaeryt—"

"If it is about what has happened, I should be here," Vaelora said firmly.

Abruptly Bhayar laughed. "I will not insist. I would that my marshals showed even the slightest hint of the loyalty for each other that you two have for one another." After a moment he said, "I have questions. They are not about what you have done. What is done is done, and it was as well done as you could do with what you had. I would like your thoughts about what lies ahead. About what troubles you foresee." He looked expectantly at Vaelora.

"I have had no such foresights. Not yet."

"Then your feelings and thoughts."

"You need strong regional governors," said Quaeryt. "The factors cannot be trusted without someone over them. Nor can the High Holders."

"I thought your imagers would assure that," replied Bhayar sardonically.

"No, they can only do that if you have effective governors who can call upon us. That the governors report to you, and we support the governors, is necessary for the comfort of both factors and High Holders." Quaeryt took a swallow of the wine. All the talking had left him almost hoarse. "Have you heard from Subcommander Meinyt? I left him acting as a regional governor."

"He has sent dispatches every week, as well as the token tariffs from High Holders as he has collected them. He reports that all is going well."

"Good." *One less worry there.*

"You were saying?" prompted Bhayar. "About the imagers?"

"You need the imagers to repair the worst in the roads, as we can. We did improve the road from Eluthyn to Kephria, but the part from Semlem south to Daaren needs widening . . ."

Bhayar's questions continued for another glass before he said, "I will have other questions once I have thought over what you have said." He looked to his sister. "I need Quaeryt to brief the senior officers at fifth glass. Then, after that, we shall have dinner together, but I will not badger you with questions then. At least, not with too many. You have rooms on the south side, and I have ordered them to be as comfortable as possible."

Vaelora rose. "Thank you. Might Quaeryt escort and settle me, brother dear?"

"So long as he returns within the quint."

The three of them left the study and walked back south to the large foyer and across it to the corridor back along the east side. The doorway to which Bhayar led them was the first one outside an archway guarded by two Telaryn troopers.

"Your quarters?" asked Vaelora, gesturing in the direction of the guards.

Bhayar nodded. "Some precautions are necessary. That is another reason why I wanted you in these quarters, especially for those times when Quaeryt may be traveling."

"For now," replied Quaeryt. "Until we can build a suitable compound for imagers on the river isle."

Bhayar chuckled. "You never lose sight of goals."

"No," said Vaelora, "and one of those goals is to make you the absolute and secure ruler of all Lydar."

"For which I am grateful, if apprehensive about the means."

As if there were any others that were practical. Quaeryt opened the door to the quarters, discovering a sitting room with archways on both sides.

"You have a study, a sitting room, and a bedchamber with a small bath chamber," said Bhayar.

"Thank you." Vaelora smiled warmly at her brother.

"There should be several chambermaids up here shortly with warm water for a bath," said Bhayar. "I look forward to dinner." With a smile, he turned.

Once Bhayar had left, the two walked around the quarters, which Quaeryt could see were truly spacious and elegantly furnished. Quaeryt couldn't help but wonder from whom Bhayar had commandeered the furnishings, which included an overlarge bed with a pillared headboard and matching bed tables and a pair of armoires, a pale green velvet settee in the sitting room, with a pair of green velvet upholstered side chairs, and both a desk and a writing table in the study.

"These are quarters fit for the lord's sister, but far better than a commander deserves . . ."

"And far less than the man who has delivered most of Lydar to Bhayar deserves . . ."

"It's far better this way, that I remain a commander and not more."

"That remains to be seen, dearest. If . . . if matters turn out as you plan . . . that may be."

If not . . . Quaeryt knew what she meant, and the problem was that intrigue would determine as much as skill and imaging now that they had returned to Variana. "You didn't mention your farsight . . ."

"That was about you, not about Bhayar or Lydar."

Quaeryt didn't object. "I need to return to meet with Bhayar."

"Say as little as possible," cautioned Vaelora.

"Or as little as Bhayar will allow."

"He won't wish you to say more than necessary," observed Vaelora.

Quaeryt bent forward and gave her a brief hug. "I hope this won't take too long." Then he slipped out of the quarters and walked back to Bhayar's study.

The study door was open, and Bhayar motioned for Quaeryt to enter and close the door. Quaeryt did and walked over to the side of the desk where Bhayar stood.

"The two of us will talk tomorrow," said Bhayar, "about what tasks may be appropriate and necessary for you and the imagers. At this meeting, I just want you to give a solid briefing about what happened as far as Southern Army and your imagers accomplished. If asked about Khel, just say that the High Council is considering the terms you presented."

"If Deucalon or one of his commanders presses as to why we attacked Antiago and not Khel, can I say that it seemed unwise to attack a land that neither threatened us nor that presents a threat when Antiago sent troops and Antiagon Fire to support Kharst, offered sanctuary to rebellious High Holders, and attacked without provocation vessels under your flag on three occasions."

"If appropriate, you can mention that earlier."

Quaeryt nodded.

"We can walk down to the conference room. By now, Deucalon should have assembled all the senior officers who are available."

"Where might that be?"

"Oh . . . that's at the south end of the chateau on the main floor."

"Where is Submarshal Myskyl? I assume he's not here."

"He spent the winter, with half of Northern Army, in a place called Rivages. It's up the Aluse, supposedly as far to the north as Laaryn is to the west. He sent regular dispatches over the course of the fall, but I've heard nothing since the turn of winter. He observed that reaching the High Holders there is a time-consuming task because the roads are poor and the winter has been long."

And because he really doesn't want to do anything terribly difficult if he doesn't have to, thought Quaeryt.

"So far, he hasn't reported the trouble you had with High Holders."

"He wouldn't."

"Wouldn't report or wouldn't have?"

"It's hard to have trouble with High Holders you haven't met," said Quaeryt dryly.

"You've never cared much for him."

"I've never trusted him. There are officers I don't care for that I've still trusted."

"Why not?"

"In this case, I worry that he wouldn't demand allegiance of the High Holders. He'd just assume that they would be loyal, and he'd believe that he could later crush anyone who wasn't."

"Why is that so bad?" asked Bhayar, an amused tone in his voice, as if he knew what Quaeryt might say. "It does give them time to adjust."

"That approach has its advantages, and it's better suited to the north than the south. In some ways, it's similar to what Rescalyn did in Tilbor."

"Because there's no real escape in the north, except distance or outright rebellion?"

"Among other things," admitted Quaeryt. After a moment he realized something and asked, "You said that Myskyl hasn't sent any dispatches recently?"

"No. Not since the first days of Ianus, but I wouldn't have expected dispatches in the dead of winter."

But we're nearing the end of spring. Quaeryt frowned, but said nothing as the two walked down the grand staircase and to the southwest corner of the main floor.

Quaeryt had the feeling that Bhayar was having him brief all the senior officers present near the Chateau Regis just so that Deucalon or others would have a more difficult time misrepresenting what Quaeryt said.

As Quaeryt stepped into the conference room followed by Bhayar, as required by protocol and courtesy, Deucalon stood. "Lord Bhayar!"

The officers seated around the long oblong table rose.

Quaeryt could see that two places had been left vacant, the one at the head of the conference table, and the seat adjoining it at the left side. Deucalon stood at the first chair on the right side.

"As you were," said Bhayar. "Please be seated."

Quaeryt only knew a handful of the commanders and subcommanders by both face and name, including Subcommander Ernyld, who had been Deucalon's chief of staff from before the battles at Ferravyl. Quaeryt was intrigued to see Pulaskyr, because he'd thought Pulaskyr would have been with Myskyl at Rivages. The only other commander he recognized by both name and face was Dafaul. There were only two other subcommanders besides Ernyld present. That did not surprise Quaeryt because the majority of regiments headed by subcommanders had been assigned to Skarpa's Southern Army.

Quaeryt assumed the others were with Northern Army, and that suggested that the commanders present had not wished to brave winter in northern Bovaria, and that Deucalon had accommodated them.

Quaeryt took the vacant seat and waited.

Bhayar did not sit, but waited a moment before beginning. "I had you all summoned because Commander Quaeryt has returned with some news that I find . . . momentous, if unexpected. I've asked him to provide a short factual summary of events that led to the situation he will present." Bhayar nodded to Quaeryt and seated himself.

Quaeryt rose and stepped back from the table just slightly. "The news is simple enough. Lord Bhayar is now ruler of Antiago, and the High Council of Khel is considering terms presented to them from Lord Bhayar." He waited for several moments to let the import sink in before continuing.

"The mission assigned to Southern Army was to obtain the allegiance of the High Holders of southern Bovaria and to assure that the Autarch Aliaro did not continue hostilities against the lands held by Lord Bhayar. Lady Vaelora and I were dispatched to accompany Southern Army and then to depart from Ephra to present terms to the High Council of Khel, which has been reconstituted in a form similar to that which ruled Khel before the attacks and depredations of Rex Kharst . . ." From there Quaeryt gave a summary of the events that occurred, following Bhayar's instructions to limit himself to the military events and the results. He concluded by saying, "Once we rebuilt the piers at Kephria and created a working trooper compound, we set out on the return to Variana."

Quaeryt then turned to Bhayar.

Bhayar merely nodded.

"Might the commander answer a few questions?" asked Deucalon.

"I'm sure the commander can answer a few questions," replied Bhayar. "So long as they deal with the matters at hand."

"Did you not consider sending a dispatch rider to inform Lord Bhayar more quickly?" asked Deucalon.

"I did. Lady Vaelora and I considered it. We decided against it because we had determined to take the shorter route up the Phraan River. If we had sent a dispatch rider, because we have no dispatch stations established, the only place he would have been able to be assured of remounts would have been in Laaryn, and that route is much longer. If we had sent enough riders to assure his safety, he would not have arrived much sooner, if as soon as we did. Once we were close enough to assure that safety we did in fact send a dispatch rider."

"Surely . . . Bovaria is not that dangerous. There are no armies or marauding armsmen roaming the land."

"Marshal," Quaeryt said firmly but quietly, projecting absolute assurance, "once one leaves the towpath of the Great Canal, the roads range from passable to abysmal. On the way to Ephra we repaired roads as we could. One of our tasks on the return, and one which took little time, was to use imagers to repair bridges and the causeway on the stretch of road from Eluthyn to Daaren. That will speed travel considerably in the future."

"But surely . . ."

"I believe the commander has answered your question, Marshal," said Bhayar quietly. "Are there other questions?"

"Success is often best not questioned, Commander, especially in war," said Pulaskyr, "but could you say why you or Submarshal Skarpa felt you had a chance of defeating the Antiagons?"

"After seeing the pattern of Antiagon tactics, and noting how poorly defended Kephria was, and also seeing how much Aliaro relied on the Bovarian holders of the south to defend his northern borders, it appeared likely that Antiago was ruled by fear of the Autarch and that fear was reinforced by cruel and absolute punishment of those who disobeyed. In addition, Antiago is thinly populated in many areas. There are only three major cities, or four if one counts Westisle as separate from Liantiago, and the Autarch maintained a large fleet. It appeared unlikely that he had that many armsmen and troopers. And we had already destroyed a regiment or more of his troops on the advance up the Aluse to Variana. Because Aliaro had attacked us a number of times already and had given sanctuary to rebel High Holders, Lady Vaelora, Submarshal Skarpa, and I decided that it was best to take the risk and attack when Aliaro did not expect it."

Pulaskyr nodded.

Another commander cleared his throat. "Did you not think the prerogative of declaring war belonged to Lord Bhayar?"

"In the documents which named Lady Vaelora and me envoys, there is a section which empowered us to take action against any powers or forces either rebelling against the rule of Lord Bhayar or hostile to and threatening his lands. After all that the Autarch did, I don't believe we exceeded the authority he granted."

Deucalon glanced at Bhayar.

Bhayar smiled. "If I cannot trust my sister and the

commander who has been most devoted and most successful, who can I trust?"

Commander Dafaul asked, "Did you consider the use of force against Khel, rather than against Antiago? After all, by setting up this High Council, Khel is technically in rebellion against Lord Bhayar?"

Quaeryt knew from where that question had come—Deucalon, no doubt. He nodded. "Your question assumes that Rex Kharst actually held Khel. In fact, he held five port cities and not much more, except Khelgror, and that only briefly. More to the point, Bovarian traders largely held those cities. Once it became clear that Kharst had died and his armies had been destroyed, the Bovarian forces in Khel either fled or were killed piecemeal. That included the Bovarian traders. The toll on Khel was so high that only one in three of those who lived there before the Red Death and Kharst's invasion are still alive. Nonetheless, there were no Bovarian forces alive anywhere when we landed in Kherseilles. I did not have Southern Army at my beck and call, but one regiment, without mounts, and to make an attack on Khel would have taken at least a year, even with Southern Army. Khel represents no immediate threat. If Lord Bhayar orders an attack on Khel, then I will follow his orders, but the instructions he provided were to persuade the High Council of Khel to consider his terms. They are doing so. If they reject them, then Lord Bhayar will decide as to what shall be done."

The remaining questions were far more factual.

"What range of arms and weapons did the Antiagons use?"

"How did you escape the effects of Antiagon Fire?"

"Do you know how much of the Antiagon fleet remains?"

A half a glass passed before Bhayar rose. "I think we have tried the commander's patience enough for now. I'm going to have dinner with him and my sister."

As he left the conference room with Bhayar, Quaeryt still wondered about Pulaskyr's presence in Variana. The commander's question had been designed to allow Quaeryt to provide an answer before a more slanted question could be asked, and precluded a nastier attack in the guise of a question.

Still . . . that didn't address Quaeryt's concern. Was Myskyl planning something and didn't want a senior commander as competent and loyal as Pulaskyr around? Had Pulaskyr been left in Variana because he knew Myskyl too well from their years together in Tilbor? Both? Neither?

Quaeryt had no idea, except Pulaskyr's presence worried him.

16

Dinner with Bhayar on Vendrei evening was actually pleasant. Bhayar asked very few questions about their efforts, and the remainder of the evening was more than satisfactory, including the luxury of sleeping in a very good bed on clean and soft linens. Even so, Quaeryt woke up concerned, although he didn't say much about it to Vaelora until after they had finished breakfast, brought to them and served in the sitting room.

"I'm worried."

"Now? You certainly weren't worried last night, dearest."

Quaeryt flushed. "You take my mind off worries." He swallowed a last sip of tea. "There were too many pointed questions at the briefing yesterday. Deucalon's usually not that confrontational, unless he's been prompted by Myskyl, and Myskyl's hundreds of milles upriver right now."

"I imagine they're all angry," said Vaelora.

"Why? Because we were successful, and they didn't want us to be?"

"In a way. They wanted Bhayar to settle down and rule Bovaria, pacify it quickly, and then hand out high holdings to the senior officers . . . and lands to some of the others. Now they can see that occupying and pacifying three lands is likely going to keep them from what they view as their just rewards."

Quaeryt nodded slowly. "I should have thought of that. Only the officers who came from Tilbor have any real understanding of what it takes to establish a new ruler. Some of them are likely tired of fighting, much as they understand, while the ones from old Telaryn thought that they'd win battles, defeat Kharst, and immediately be rewarded."

"That can't happen yet."

Quaeryt could see that . . . and more. "If he hands out holdings now, they'll think they're being shuffled off . . . or that they won't get the best ones?"

"They don't know which ones are the best ones."

"We don't, either," Quaeryt pointed out. "That makes it chancy. And it's too early for that. But there are a number of high holdings without holders whose heirs won't be inheriting . . . except those are the ones that need work."

"They don't want that. They want to step into a spacious hold house . . ."

Quaeryt shook his head in disgust. "They want spoils."

Vaelora nodded.

"Not all of them, I'd think."

"Most of them. The difference is that the ones who've been with you and Skarpa are likely to be more patient."

Quaeryt was still thinking over what Vaelora had said when he arrived at Bhayar's study just before eighth glass.

The lord of three lands was pacing back and forth between the writing desk and the conference table. He looked up and gestured brusquely to the table, then walked over and seated himself even before Quaeryt had closed the study door and taken three steps. Quaeryt walked to the table and seated himself.

Bhayar looked at Quaeryt. "You've conquered almost all of Lydar for me. That's a Namer's gift. How in the Nameless's sake am I supposed to rule it without maintaining all these armies for years? They'll bankrupt me—if another senior officer like Rescalyn doesn't get ideas first."

"I didn't do it alone. Skarpa, Vaelora, and the imager undercaptains were all necessary."

"That may be, but the problem remains. And if I hand out high holdings right now, everything will fall apart. That's if I even knew what high holdings are available."

Quaeryt smiled. "That's your answer. For a bit, anyway. You need to discover which holdings lost their holders, which have heirs, which don't, and which merit being seized for the acts of their holders. If you don't have that information, how can you be fair?"

"They don't want fair . . ."

"Of course not. But you can point out to Deucalon that if you aren't reasonably fair, everyone is going to think all the other commanders got better holds. You also need to reward both accomplishment and seniority, and you can't do that without some evaluation. It will still be haphazard. There's no way we can find out everything quickly, not with the destruction of most of the tariff records."

"I've mentioned most of that. Deucalon understands, and he's not in any hurry to stop being marshal."

Quaeryt understood what Bhayar wasn't saying.

"Now . . ." Bhayar squared himself at the small conference table. "What are your plans for me to deal with the imagers?"

"First, you declare that, over time, the imagers will

be constituted into a permanent Collegium here in Variana in order to provide both a safe haven for imagers and to assure that their talents serve the rex and all the people of Lydar."

Bhayar nodded. "I did promise that."

"Second, you assign the Eleventh and Nineteenth Regiments to the maître of the Collegium permanently . . . and the Pharsi battalion under Calkoran—"

"What?"

". . . and then you send messages to all the High Holders, all your regional governors, including the Khellan High Council, and make it known to all factors that the code of laws you are issuing will be followed and that, in the future, dealing with any civil transgressions will transition from the armies of Telaryn to the regional governors you will appoint, who will be supported by the Collegium of imagers and its forces, and as a last resort by your armies. Then you offer some warm words about how you know that the High Holders would prefer to keep their lands and privileges and how you hope that they will act wisely and thus retain those privileges— unlike the High Holders of southern Bovaria who lost everything. . . ."

Bhayar's mouth remained open, as if he could not believe what he heard.

"You did ask, didn't you?"

"That's preposterous."

"Is it? Do you want a huge standing army that you have to pay? You just told me that you can't afford that. Without something like the Collegium, you won't have honest regional governors, and you'll have to have regional governors to hold all of Lydar together. You're going to have to build a navy before long to protect all the traders . . . or you won't have many traders who will trade with other lands, and the traders from other lands will reap the benefits. You can probably take over the remaining Antiagon warships . . . if you pay the crews and captains . . . but I wouldn't make Nykaal your sea marshal."

"Next you'll be telling me that whatever child you and Vaelora have will be my heir."

Quaeryt shook his head. "That can't be. It would destroy everything you've built. Imagers can only survive if they're seen to serve—honestly, reliably, and without any hint of personal greed. It would be best if you never talk about what the imagers have done . . . except to carry out your wishes."

"Why would I do this?" asked Bhayar, a definite edge in his voice.

"For one thing, except for two or three of them, every single imager remaining with me has the ability to bring down Chateau Regis, if not more. The only way that you can rule the kind of land you want to rule is with the help of the imagers. But if they're powerful enough to do that, the only way High Holders will feel safe from them is if they're clearly under control. Putting them in a few places across Lydar will emphasize that control. The imagers will only stay there if they feel they have a place safe from the fears and whims of those in power. You control me, as well you know. We will work to make sure that the Collegium is always a tool of the rex. Call the Collegium glue. The High Holders always want too much. The factors will always be too greedy. The crafters distrust anyone of wealth and power. A ruler cannot maintain a kingdom just by force, unless that force supports laws that are just. Sooner or later, those in power will realize that the imagers cannot be everywhere and do everything—they can only combat the worst offenses against the law and the rex. But if the laws are just—and great offenses are punished fairly—I have to believe that will allow the land to knit into one great unity."

"What else?" Bhayar asked dryly.

"You need to change the name of your land . . . I'd suggest Solidar, to express the idea of a unified Lydar— without directly saying so. Variana should also have a new name, one fitting for the capital of Solidar."

"Why don't you just rule instead of me?"

"I told you. Because it won't work. I saw how weak Antiago was because of the way imagers were used. They expressed Aliaro's will, not a rule of law. Besides . . . there will never be enough imagers. I wouldn't be surprised if, right now, I have a twentieth of all the living imagers in all of Solidar."

"I haven't agreed on that name, let alone anything else." Bhayar did not snap, but his voice betrayed exasperation.

"No . . . you haven't. And I agree that you shouldn't . . . not until you're convinced that either I'm right, or that I'm wrong and you have a better plan. You asked me for my views and plans. I've told you. You're the ruler."

"You're the most powerful force in all Lydar . . . and you say I'm the ruler? I'm not exactly dense, Quaeryt."

"No, you're not. Let me ask you this. Why are the imagers so powerful?"

"Because of what you all can do." Again, Bhayar's voice took on an exasperated tone.

"Vaelora told you what happened in Liantiago. You saw what happened here in Variana and what happened in Ferravyl. Just how long would any of us imagers survive—after those battles—without your support?

You can disband the imagers. Just let them return to their homes and families . . . or remove them quietly over time. Then Vaelora and I will be essentially your prisoners, living on your sufferance."

"You're exaggerating."

"Am I? Can I remain awake every glass of every day and night? Into what tower would I have to barricade myself to be able to sleep? Every imager living outside the Collegium would face that. Most of the imagers alive today are either schoolboys or younger or not much older, recluses or those hiding their abilities, or those with powerful protectors. What makes the imagers powerful is being able to protect each other. But even in the Collegium, they would be vulnerable. They have wives, and some have children. Some could not protect themselves for long."

"Just why and how would such a group defer to me? How, pray tell, will you assure that?"

"I've already begun. I've pointed out time and time again that they already have more freedom than imagers anywhere else in Terahnar. They've seen that you've paid them. They've also seen and heard how badly imagers were treated by Aliaro. They all know imagers who were killed or chased away. Most of them aren't stupid, either. They understand"—*and they will, one way or another*—"that only under your protection can they be truly safe."

"But how will I be safe from them?" asked Bhayar, his tone ironic.

"By making certain that all imagers to come understand their vulnerability and their debt to you and your successors. We'll need a council and a strict code of law and behavior for imagers—both for their protection and for protection of those who are not imagers. By making the Collegium a scholarium as well, you'll also be creating a place of learning, and that's never a bad thing. The Collegium could offer a gold or two for every young imager who comes to the Collegium . . . just as you did to build the undercaptains of first company. That way, imagers go to a place where they're welcome, and people know where the imagers are. If they wore uniforms as well, gray perhaps . . . that would also reinforce the sense of discipline, as well as let people know who the imagers are."

"This bears thinking upon."

"It does," Quaeryt agreed. "Would you be agreeable to the imagers beginning to build quarters on the isle of piers?"

"The isle is currently devastated, and only beggars and riffraff haunt the place," mused Bhayar. "I can't see that making it an orderly place would hurt. But not a word about this Collegium business or anything else we've discussed."

"Yes, sir. Would you mind if the imagers, as they can, improved some of the roads to the isle from here?"

"That wouldn't hurt. Neither would a better bridge across the Aluse."

"We'll see what we can do."

"Good." Bhayar smiled. "That brings up another matter. Now that you have returned . . . and there are no more battles to win . . . at the moment, there is another difficulty you are uniquely qualified to handle."

Quaeryt tried not to stiffen. "Yes?"

"You have been a princeps and a governor. None of my senior officers have that experience, especially not in dealing with factors and setting up ledgers and clerks and keeping records. There are almost no records remaining, and I fear far too many golds are being spent unwisely."

"How does Marshal Deucalon feel about that, if I might ask?"

"He agrees something needs to be done."

"Who is handling supplies right now?"

"Some majors under Subcommander Ernyld."

"And what's left of the treasury of Bovaria?"

"The same group."

"Do you want me to use Ernyld's clerks, find more, or gradually switch to clerks reporting to me and to you?"

"Come up with a plan and let me see. No later than Lundi morning. At seventh glass. We'll meet with Deucalon after that."

Quaeryt nodded. "Do you want me to control the Bovarian treasury, subject only to you, once you approve of a plan?"

Bhayar leaned back in his chair and cocked his head to one side. After several moments he leaned forward and looked at Quaeryt. "It won't work if you don't . . . but Deucalon will be furious. Don't mention that part of it when we meet with him."

Quaeryt had no intention of discussing anything he didn't have to with the marshal. "If this is going to work, I'll need an official position and title, or I'll spend more time arguing with commanders than dealing with problems."

"I'd thought about something like Minister for Bovarian Affairs."

"How about Minister of Administration and Supply for Bovaria? That is a less threatening title. Along with maître of the Collegium, of course." Quaeryt grinned.

Bhayar sighed . . . not quite explosively. "*IF* . . . if I approve of this Collegium plan, then you can call yourself 'Maître' . . . but not a word about that, either, until I do."

"Might I ask what progress Submarshal Myskyl has made with the High Holders of the north?"

"His last dispatch said he had met with three."

"That was in the fall, was it not?"

"There is snow in the north, unlike the south."

Rather than pursue the matter, Quaeryt merely nodded. "Has he encountered any High Holders reluctant to pledge allegiance to you?"

"He has mentioned none."

"How is Aelina coming in ruling in your absence in Solis?"

Bhayar smiled. "She has had no difficulty, and she would not hesitate to let me know . . . like someone else I know." The smile vanished. "I think I've tasked you enough." He gestured toward the study door. "Go." The last word was delivered humorously.

Quaeryt rose, then bowed. "We will begin with road repairs and bridge building while I consider how to accomplish the greater task."

"Limit yourself to what I requested. I know that's difficult for you, Quaeryt. But for now, it will be more than sufficient."

"Yes, sir." Quaeryt bowed again before turning and leaving the study.

He thought he heard a soft sigh behind him, but he wasn't about to turn and look.

17

Quaeryt had to ride quickly in order to make it by ninth glass to the headquarters building of the Telaryn armies in Bovaria—what had once been the Variana estate of the late Holder Paitrak, and then the temporary residence for Bhayar. Quaeryt's first meeting was with Khaern, Calkoran, and Zhelan. All three were waiting for him when he walked into the small study Skarpa had once used in the outbuilding. From the dust in places, and the grime on the sole window, it was apparent that the study had been seldom used since, unsurprisingly, since roughly half the Telaryn regiments that had comprised the force to take Variana were currently either in the north or in Antiago, with perhaps ten remaining in and around Variana.

"I'm sorry," said Quaeryt as he sat down behind one of the two desks, the one formerly used by Skarpa. "My meeting with Lord Bhayar lasted longer than I thought it would."

"We can't complain about that, sir," said Khaern with a smile.

"We have orders. Apparently, I'm going to have several duties. One of them is to organize supplies and finances here in Variana for all army operations in

Bovaria. The other is to work with the imager under-captains to aid in rebuilding certain areas. You all remain under my command, and your immediate duties will be light. You will need to provide protection for the imagers while they rebuild roads and bridges and then start to reconstruct the isle of piers, where they'll start to demolish the ruins and build quarters and support buildings there. This comparatively light duty will allow you to rotate companies and rest men and mounts."

"Quarters for whom, might I ask, sir?" inquired Zhelan.

"I'm hoping that the quarters will be for imagers and the troopers and officers assigned to protect the imagers, but that decision is up to Lord Bhayar. So far, he has only agreed that we may proceed."

Khaern raised his eyebrows, but did not speak.

"I'll be as direct as I can be at this point," Quaeryt said. "The imagers, as a group, or in groups, can be a powerful force. Without protection, though, they're more like unguarded cannon on an open field. Lord Bhayar and I are trying to work out a way to protect them and keep them safe and useful to him. If they are not kept safe and trained in peacetime, they will not be that useful in times of war."

"If Khel comes to its senses," said Calkoran slowly, "and can reach terms, who will there be for Lord Bhayar to fight?"

"I would hope Khel does come to its senses, Subcommander. If it does, and if most of the armies are disbanded over time, who will protect the ruler from factors and High Holders such as some we have seen? If Bhayar is forced to pay large armies to do that, where will the golds come from to make Lydar a better place, with roads and harbors? Not all the imagers in all Terahnar could build the roads we need. And he will need a navy to protect the harbors and ports and traders from pirates and brigands. So he must be protected in ways that do not cost thousands upon thousands of golds."

Calkoran smiled. "Spoken like a son of Erion."

Khaern frowned. "What do you mean?"

"A son of Erion is doomed if he seeks power for himself. He holds power only as long as he uses it wisely for others." When Khaern did not immediately reply, Calkoran went on. "When I first saw him, I was unsure of what kind of lost one he might be. Then I saw how often he used his powers to protect others. He protected the young imagers who knew nothing at first. He protected my men, and yours. In Khel, he underwent a trial he did not have to. So did Lady Vaelora. That was to avoid a war no one needed. I hope my countryfolk will come to understand that before it is too late. Do you remember when he defied the marshal to save our men from needless slaughter?"

Khaern nodded.

"There have been lost ones, and there have been sons of Erion before. Those who failed are remembered. Those who were true to their power are forgotten. That is the curse carried by all sons of Erion."

"That's already true," said Zhelan. "Lord Bhayar triumphed at Ferravyl and Variana. Submarshal Skarpa subdued Antiago."

"Enough!" Quaeryt laughed. "That's as it should be. Officers shouldn't be seeking glory. I'm an imager and an officer doing a job that has to be done. We all have a job that needs to be done." He wished he'd been able to think of a more eloquent way to downplay the entire idea of a son of Erion. "I'll need a company today. For now one company should be sufficient to accompany the imager undercaptains each day. We'll likely need help from the men later on, in setting up quarters and the like, but it won't hurt them to have light duty for a week, before they get back to drills and a regular schedule."

All three senior officers nodded.

"I'll leave it to you three to set up the rotation schedule. Let me know if there are any considerations I should be aware of. I need to meet with the undercaptains and their trainee, but I expect we'll ride out in two quints. Oh . . . and one other thing. I'll need a duty squad tomorrow afternoon to accompany Lady Vaelora and me."

"Yes, sir."

Once the three officers left, just a few moments later, Khalis, Horan, Lhandor, Baelthm, and Elsior entered the study.

"The good news is that we don't have to fight. The rest of the news is that we have a lot of work to do. Lord Bhayar needs some roads . . ." Quaeryt went on to describe their likely schedule for the remainder of the day, and then for the week ahead—after a day off on Solayi, before concluding, "You won't be working long days, but they will be hard days. That way, you won't lose your imaging strength . . . and neither will I." *And it will leave an impression of just how useful imagers can be.* "Do you still have those plans you drew up for the isle of piers, Lhandor?"

"Yes, sir."

"I'd like to see them. Lord Bhayar has agreed to a certain amount of building on the isle, after we repair and rebuild the road from the Chateau Regis and create a wide and solid bridge across the Aluse. If we're to be effective in rebuilding the isle of piers, we'll also need a bridge from the west bank of the isle to the river road."

"Sir?" asked Horan. "Are we done fighting? For sure?"

"I don't know. For the moment, if there is any fighting, it would be against brigands and the like. Whether we go back to war will depend on what the High Council of Khel does. It will also depend on what is happening in the north of Bovaria with the High Holders there. Lord Bhayar hasn't had a recent report from Submarshal Myskyl."

Khalis and Lhandor exchanged glances that Quaeryt ignored.

"I'd like you to assemble fully mounted in the courtyard in a quint. Lhandor . . . bring your drawings and maps. I'd like to look them over."

"Yes, sir."

Quaeryt watched as they left, then followed, closing the study door behind himself.

Three quints later, Quaeryt and the imagers were reined up on the slope south of the Chateau Regis, with a company from Eleventh Regiment two hundred yards farther south, although one squad was finishing up warning everyone away from the south side of the structure.

Quaeryt surveyed the Chateau Regis and the low hill on which it was situated. A single narrow road angled down the hill and then curved to the northeast, running relatively straight for well over a mille toward the River Aluse, reaching it at a point north of the isle of piers, where the river narrowed and a timber structure spanned the water. On the east side of the bridge lay most of Variana. He turned in the saddle, momentarily looking south across what remained of the earthworks and ditches that had been ripped out of the once lush grounds and hunting park to the south of Chateau Regis more than two seasons earlier. He nodded and turned back to the imagers.

"Undercaptains . . . what do you think of that road leading up to the chateau?"

Lhandor shook his head. "We built a wide archway and entry. The road's too narrow. It always was."

"What about a circular paved road around the entire hill, and then a gradually inclined paved drive straight from the southwest up to your entry, and then down to the circular road on the southeast?"

"We'd need a paved area for a lot of carriages opposite the entry," suggested Lhandor.

"I could flatten that hump opposite the entry," suggested Horan.

"It should all be in that hard white stone," added Khalis. "All the stone we image, I mean."

Quaeryt looked to Horan. "See what you can do with that hump. Just move the earth and stone to where the drive will be, starting at the top."

"Yes, sir." Horan concentrated.

The top of the hump directly south of the entry portico vanished, and cold white mist wreathed the ground, only to disperse slowly under the direct late morning spring sunshine. A long expanse of dirt and gravel, roughly a yard deep, evenly covered the uppermost section of the road leading down the slope on the east side of the entry.

"Lhandor," ordered Quaeryt.

More of the hump vanished, and the white mist was thicker as more of the overburden appeared on the eastern slope.

"Elsior, see what you can do."

"Yes, sir."

The trainee managed to move a fair amount for his age and experience, perhaps a fifth part of what Lhandor had done.

Even after just half a glass, Quaeryt could see that the more precise massive imaging, if that was the correct term for what they were doing, was going to take longer than he'd anticipated. *Doesn't everything?*

By the time Quaeryt and the other imagers were too tired to do any more imaging, without totally exhausting themselves and risking collapse, they had completed the drive up to and from the entry and almost down to where it would meet the circular road, as well as a paved circular carriage plaza south of the entry portico. They had bowed to the reality of the terrain by creating stone steps up to the entry to avoid the massive earth-moving that would have been necessary to keep the drive to and from the entry from being too steep for carriages and wagons.

They also had imaged away part of the higher ground to the west of the Chateau Regis so that the circular drive would be level—and that, in turn, would require stone drainage gutters.

Quaeryt also realized that they would need a paved service drive to the west side of the chateau to replace the rutted lane currently being used. *But then, there's always something you've forgotten.*

After riding back to the de facto Telaryn headquarters, and dismissing the imagers and the company from Eleventh Regiment, Quaeryt turned his mount over to an ostler, then crossed the courtyard and made his way into the library. From what he could tell most of the volumes remained.

After a quick study of the shelves, under the watchful eye of a junior squad leader, Quaeryt began with the thin volumes with the greatest height of spine. The first volume he took off the shelf was entitled *Plants of Varia* and contained drawings of various plants. The title, he realized, if belatedly, must have referred to the area around Variana. From the paper dust that rose when he opened the folio to the drawings, he wondered if "Varia" had been a separate land at one time. He didn't recall any histories that mentioned that, but then he hadn't read that much history about the western half of Lydar. *Was there ever that much written?*

Then he forced himself to move through the volumes quickly. The seventh or eighth bound folio that he opened contained maps of Bovaria, although he had the impression that they had been drawn at least several decades earlier. He set that volume aside on a reading table and continued to look. After close to half a glass, he found two other volumes of maps, one of which included maps showing hills and mountains and even roads, although it was clear it had been drawn before the Great Canal had been built.

He picked up the three volumes and walked to the squad leader. "I'm taking these maps for duties required by Lord Bhayar. They'll be at the Chateau Regis."

"Yes, sir."

Carrying the three volumes, Quaeryt walked from the library toward the stables where a half squad waited to escort him for the ride south to the Chateau Regis.

18

~

Quaeryt woke early on Solayi morning, out of uneasy dreams he could not remember. *At least, there was no ice . . . no dead troopers staring at you.* Rather than wake Vaelora by moving, he lay there, thinking, for what was likely a glass, trying to work out in his mind all he needed to do in the week ahead.

After dressing and a leisurely breakfast with Vaelora, in their chambers, he took out the three map folios he'd taken from Paitrak's library, and he and Vaelora pored over them together.

Less than a quint into studying the maps, Vaelora looked at Quaeryt. "There aren't any provincial or regional boundaries shown for Bovaria."

"But the maps have the old provincial boundaries for Telaryn," added Quaeryt. "If the mapmakers knew about those, then they would have drawn provincial boundaries for Bovaria . . . if Bovaria had provinces."

"No one said they didn't."

"People don't mention what doesn't exist," Quaeryt said dryly, "except for food and golds."

"You thought they didn't, though."

"I did, but Bhayar's going to need provincial governors, or the equivalent. That's why I got the maps together. I wanted to see if we could figure out reasonable boundaries for governors before he's forced into agreeing to governors' territories by Deucalon or Myskyl . . . or just by necessity."

"How many governors are you thinking about?"

"Telaryn had six, counting Tilbor. Bovaria isn't as spread out, and a lot of the north doesn't have many people, especially in the Montagnes D'Glace. I was thinking four, but I wanted to look at that map that shows the hills and mountains . . ."

"You know . . . this is just another thing . . ."

"I know. But you married me, and because of that, most of what we do will be forgotten or attributed to others. Calkoran mentioned that again the other day. The problem is that the alternative is worse."

"He said that in Khel, too." Vaelora smiled. "We'll just have to make sure that brother dear gets the credit and not Deucalon or Myskyl."

Somewhat more than a glass later, Quaeryt and Vaelora had sketched out rough boundaries for four regions of Bovaria, each with a larger town or city from which a regional governor could administer the surrounding area. Laaryn was one of those, and that would make an easy transition for whoever followed Meinyt, assuming Bhayar agreed to something at least similar to what Vaelora and Quaeryt had sketched out.

After that, he sent a messenger to have the duty squad ride to the Chateau Regis to meet them at the first glass of the afternoon. During the interim, he and Vaelora toured the Chateau Regis, taking notes on the still-vacant chambers of the large structure and determining where the best place for administration and logistics might be.

Both Quaeryt and Vaelora were on the front steps of the chateau a quint before the glass. The sky was slightly hazy, and a cool but not cold breeze blew out of the northeast.

"The entry and the drive look much better," observed Vaelora.

"They should." Quaeryt still didn't like the raw dirt around the carriage park and bordering the new drive, but imaging wasn't good for creating the growing plants for gardens and parks. That took gardeners and time.

"Where are we riding?"

"From the Chateau Regis along the road we'll have to rebuild all the way to the River Aluse, then down along the west shore to the isle of piers."

"You want to have a good look at what the imagers will need to do."

"And a better look at this part of Variana. You might recall that I didn't see all that much of it before we set out for Khel."

Before long a squad from Eleventh Regiment rode up the west drive and reined up.

"Good afternoon, Lady, sir," said the squad leader, inclining his head and motioning for a ranker to lead the black mare and gelding forward for Vaelora and Quaeryt to mount.

"Good afternoon," replied Vaelora cheerfully before mounting.

Quaeryt just nodded, smiled, and mounted. Then he and Vaelora led the way down the eastern drive toward the old road and the north bridge over the River Aluse. Although the calendar date was the first of Avryl, the midpoint of spring, most of the trees were still leafing out, and many of the spring flowers were still budding.

Was that because of what you did? Quaeryt half smiled at the thought, reminding himself that the trees and flowers had been leafing out just as slowly all the way along the last hundred milles of their ride along the Great Canal.

For the first half mille from the Chateau Regis, there were no dwellings, just the smoothed over remnants of earthworks that had been dug into what had been Rex Kharst's park surrounding the chateau. Closer to the river there were modest shops and dwellings, and while some still showed damages, most of them seemed to be occupied, although there were few people on the streets, unsurprisingly for a Solayi afternoon.

When they neared the River Aluse, Quaeryt and Vaelora reined up short of the north bridge itself, and Quaeryt studied the old stone structure barely wide enough for two wagons side by side. "We need a better bridge."

"The one south of the isle is worse," said Vaelora.

"I haven't seen it. You looked at it when I was recovering?"

"We came by the roads on the north side of the river. So we rode through Variana and over the south bridge. It's narrower and older."

"That figures. Neither Kharst nor any of his forbears wanted to spend much on roads or bridges—except for the road from Nordeau to Chateau Regis." Quaeryt shook his head, then turned to the squad leader. "We'll head south along the river road now." What he called the river road was more like a cobbled lane. *Another imager project.*

The river was still running high, well above its normal level. That, Quaeryt could tell because he could see that parts of a stone pathway on the east side of the river were almost a yard underwater.

Less than half a mille south of the north bridge, Quaeryt reined up to study the north end of the isle of piers, an expanse of mudflats, brush, and rubbish washed onto the flats, apparently by earlier spring runoff. The flats extended only twenty yards or so before ending in a rocky escarpment that rose at least a good five yards above the flats.

Quaeryt nodded. He'd thought that the majority of the isle was well above the river, and if the imagers built a stone retaining wall, almost like the prow of a ship, at the north end, that would help protect the rest of the isle as well.

After studying the northern part of the isle, he, Vaelora, and the duty squad continued southward until they reached a point opposite the middle of the isle, where he again called a halt.

"You'll need a bridge across to the isle," said Vaelora.

"I know. I'd thought about imaging one today, but . . ." He smiled wryly and shook his head.

"Why not?"

"Because as soon as there is a bridge, the poor and those with nowhere else to go will sneak across it in darkness, and that will make improving the isle just that much more difficult." He didn't mention that it was likely many of those who were homeless were likely so because of his own efforts in the battle of Variana.

As he looked across the river to the isle, amid the ruined buildings, toward the southern end of the isle, he thought he saw what might be—or have been—an anomen between two sagging warehouses . . . an old anomen. *Can you restore it?* He smiled at the thought, the idea that he wanted to restore the anomen to a deity he wasn't certain even existed. *You'd better find a good chorister first, or you'll end up being pressed into giving more homilies and conducting services.*

"Why are you smiling?" asked Vaelora.

"There's an old anomen over there in the ruins."

"I didn't say a word."

"I didn't say you did," he replied with a grin, "but you do have this penchant for fixing up anomens . . ."

"Only one." She smiled back at him.

He shook his head ruefully, then said, "We should head back. I hope the south road to the chateau is in better repair."

"It isn't," replied Vaelora.

"You would have to tell me, wouldn't you?"

"Of course."

They both smiled.

19

On Solayi evening, Quaeryt and Vaelora dined with Bhayar, who peppered them with questions about what they had observed on their journey back from Kephria. Their observations on the High Holders and factors led into Bhayar's tales of the endless petitions he had received from factors, not to mention the suggestions for improving trade, and removing the tariffs on trade sent down the River Aluse to Solis. That Bhayar had received almost no communications from High Holders tended to confirm Quaeryt's sense of how Kharst had ruled.

A quint before seventh glass on Lundi morning, Quaeryt was in Bhayar's study.

"Deucalon will be here shortly," announced Bhayar, standing beside his desk. "I thought you might have a few things you wanted to talk over first."

"I do." Quaeryt spread the rough map on the writing table, remaining on his feet. "This is the map we mentioned to you last night. It shows the boundaries for four regions of Bovaria, with regional governors located in Laaryn, Villerive, Rivages, and Asseroiles. In time, as roads improve, you might wish to change those cities, but all of them are located on rivers for access."

Bhayar studied the map, then nodded. "I need to think about this."

Quaeryt had expected no less, especially given the small number of regional governors he and Vaelora had suggested. "There's also the question of how soon you want me to begin as Minister of Administration and Supply. There are unoccupied studies on the main level"—*more than a few, in fact*—"but I'll need clerks and some small amount of golds for tables and cases. Not to mention ledgers. I'm assuming that you don't want me operating out of the headquarters holding."

"Take the studies you need, and I'll get you some golds."

"Do you want me to take custody of the Bovarian treasury, or just draw on it?"

"Draw on it until you think you can handle it, and then we'll talk again."

"Also, I'd like to involve Vaelora. She has a good head, and she's trustworthy." *And I can trust her if you send me off somewhere.*

Bhayar frowned, tilted his head, but finally nodded.

"I'm going to have to find clerks as well. I thought I'd ask for rankers or squad leaders who were wounded, leg injuries, and the like, who know their letters and numbers and who are well recommended. If there aren't any . . . then I'll have to look to local clerks from factors who've lost their master to failure or death." From there Quaeryt went on, until he'd reached the last matter dealing with administration. "How do you want me to proceed in notifying the factors about their 'token' tariffs? I'd suggest my having letters prepared for your signature."

"I'm agreeable to that. Anything that brings in more golds would be useful."

"Has Deucalon said anything about Meinyt acting as a regional governor? Or Skarpa as acting governor of Antiago?"

"Only that he hopes such can be temporary." Bhayar's smile was sardonic.

"Temporary? In Antiago? When you still have a marshal as governor in Tilbor after twelve years?"

"Oh . . . he certainly thinks there will be a need for a governor there for years."

"He'd prefer, perhaps, Commander Kharllon? Or would he like the position?"

"Kharllon, I would think," replied Bhayar. "In time, Deucalon would likely prefer a high holding and the position of whatever regional governor whose territory includes the River Aluse from Ferravyl to Variana."

"Deucalon might actually be adequate at that," conceded Quaeryt. *Maybe.*

Bhayar's eyebrows lifted. "You've never cared for him. Why would you approve him as a regional governor?"

"Because the behaviors I dislike in him as a marshal are those that might make him useful as a governor. He's cautious and deliberate." *And I don't want to give the impression of disliking all the old senior officers.* "Myskyl is the one I not only dislike, but distrust. When the time comes, if you have to, give him a high holding in the most distant locale possible, but one with a great deal of land, most of it rugged or inhospitable."

Bhayar chuckled. "And you . . . you don't want such?"

"You know what I want."

Bhayar nodded. "You've made that clear. You've also shown how useful the imagers can be under you, just since your return. What are your immediate plans for them?"

"To finish a circular avenue around Chateau Regis

with paved avenues to the north and south bridges. To rebuild both bridges, and then to rebuild the isle of piers . . . as you agreed."

"I did agree," said Bhayar. "I didn't say when." He held up a hand. "I'm not telling you to stop with your projects. I hope I don't have to, because they'll benefit everyone. I do reserve the right to call you and the imagers in case of need. There's no need at present, but I still have not had a recent dispatch from Submarshal Myskyl."

That sounds like trouble. But Quaeryt said nothing, and only nodded.

There was a knock on the study door, and the squad leader stationed there announced, "Marshal Deucalon, sir."

"Have him come in."

Deucalon stepped into the study.

Quaeryt thought that the slender, if wiry, gray-haired marshal looked more haggard, and definitely older, as if he had aged five years in the time Quaeryt had been away from Variana. *But why? He hasn't been doing any fighting . . . and what he's been doing can't be as hard as handling Northern Army was during the campaign.* Or was it just the fact that Deucalon was getting older, and his age had caught up with his looks?

"Good morning, Lord Bhayar . . . Commander." Deucalon smiled pleasantly.

Bhayar motioned to the conference table, but did not speak until the three were seated. "I've given Marshal Deucalon a brief description of your mission to Khel and the events that followed. Do you have any questions, Marshal?"

"I have many more questions than would be profitable, especially given that what has occurred has apparently turned out for the best." Deucalon looked at Quaeryt. "I am somewhat surprised that you did not insist that Submarshal Skarpa send advance notice of his decision to invade Antiago . . . or even to request the approval of Lord Bhayar." Deucalon smiled warmly.

"I can certainly understand your concerns, Marshal, but the submarshal was tasked with obtaining the allegiance of the southern High Holders. That would have been impossible and remained so as long as Aliaro continued as Autarch of Antiago. As you may recall, Antiagon forces and Antiagon Fire were deployed against Southern Army in the campaign to take Bovaria. In addition, Antiagon warships attacked the *Montagne* and the *Solis* on their voyage to Kherseilles. All element of surprise would have been lost, had the submarshal waited for approval."

Deucalon nodded sagely. "I can understand that, but do you not feel that the effort of subduing and governing Antiago might . . . overextend our forces?"

"If we were talking about such an effort in Khel," Quaeryt replied, "I would agree wholeheartedly. Even after years of battles and effort, Rex Kharst still only controlled Khelgror and the major port cities. Truly subduing Khel would be impossible at this time. Antiago is a very different land. There are only six cities, and one of them, Kephria, was little more than a shell of itself, while three will accede to whoever holds Liantiago. That leaves Liantiago and Westisle, and the submarshal's forces are well able to control both."

"You do seem to have considered those factors. Tell me," asked Deucalon, still smiling, "if you would, when we might expect the allegiance of Khel?"

Quaeryt smiled politely in return. "The High Council of Khel is considering the matter. Once they receive word that Lord Bhayar holds Antiago, it is likely that they will reach a decision, but it will not be in the next few weeks. It is also possible that they may send a delegation here . . . or request another delegation to meet them in Saendeol or Khelgror to work out the terms of that allegiance."

"Terms of allegiance?"

"Terms," replied Quaeryt. "Even after the Khellans lost a third of their people to the Red Death, they still destroyed over half of the forces Kharst sent to conquer them. The land is rugged, and as you pointed out, any campaign to force a total capitulation from the High Council will be unfeasible for years. On the other hand, Khel has much to gain from pledging allegiance to Lord Bhayar, and negotiated terms would be far less costly, and far more beneficial."

"What about your imagers? Surely they could force favorable terms."

Quaeryt shook his head. "We could indeed level every town and city in Khel . . . but the Pharsi would flee into the hills, leaving us with a barren wasteland of little value. There is also the fact that the Pharsi have dealt with imagers for generations. We lost two of ten imagers in dealing with Kharst's forces, who had never faced trained imagers. We would likely lose more in fighting Khel . . . and gain far less."

"That seems . . ." Deucalon paused.

"Strange as it may seem, it is likely true," interjected Bhayar smoothly. "Commander Quaeryt has been unusually effective . . . and accurate . . . in his understanding of the strengths and weaknesses of our enemies."

Deucalon nodded. "I have seen just how effective he is at that, and how he has used that knowledge to the benefit of his forces."

And you still can't forget that I stopped you from squandering my men unnecessarily. But Quaeryt refrained from commenting.

"There is one other matter," said Bhayar. "Commander Quaeryt has considerable experience in matters of supply and logistics. You may recall that he was princeps of Tilbor. Marshal Straesyr recommended his skills highly, and he put the Montagne governorship to rights more quickly than anyone could have imagined. Governor Markyl even wrote me to note how well organized he found matters in Extela."

Deucalon's forehead bore only the trace of a frown as he listened.

"I've decided to put his experience to use. For now, he will be acting as a minister for administration and supply for Bovaria."

"The armies will be sad to lose such a valuable commander," said Deucalon.

"Oh . . . he will remain a commander in charge of Eleventh Regiment, the Khellan battalion, and his first company," replied Bhayar. "I'm just using his talents as I did in Montagne, to get matters better organized while we work out a permanent arrangement for governing three lands."

Deucalon nodded.

"He will need one of your clerks who is familiar with the supply ledgers for the armies, but he will be finding others as well."

"Will he be taking on the army logistics?"

"No. Your staff will function largely as it has. At some point, of course, the commander's temporary ministry and the finance ministry of Telaryn will have to be combined, but that cannot happen for some time. The commander first has to build a staff that can be combined."

"Of course."

"I wanted you to know this so that there would not be any confusion."

"I understand, sir," replied Deucalon.

"Do you have any further inquiries of Commander Quaeryt?" asked Bhayar, in a tone that suggested further inquiries were unnecessary.

"No, sir."

"Then you may go, Commander. I look forward to seeing the results of your imagers' work."

"Yes, sir," replied Quaeryt as he rose, then inclined his head politely. He did not don his visor cap until he left the study.

Once he left the Chateau Regis, Quaeryt rode to meet with Khaern, Calkoran, and Zhelan in the headquarters study he'd taken over, after inquiries and negotiations with Subcommander Ernyld, since Skarpa wouldn't be needing it anytime soon, and since Commander Luchan was in the north with Myskyl.

"Any news, sir?" asked Khaern.

"No. Lord Bhayar hasn't heard from Submarshal Myskyl for a time, but we're to make reasonable haste on his roadworks projects and the bridges before we can work on the isle of piers."

"How long do you think the roads and bridges will take, sir?" asked Zhelan.

"Longer than I'd like, but we have fewer imagers."

"The young one is already getting better, I hear," said Zhelan.

"He is improving," Quaeryt acknowledged.

"Do you think there's trouble in the north, sir?" asked Khaern.

Wherever Myskyl is, there's likely to be trouble. "If

there is, we'll likely be sent there. So far, there's no word of trouble. There's just no word."

"Some have said that no word is a good word," said Calkoran slowly. "In matters of arms and war, having no word is seldom good."

"You could be right," replied Quaeryt, "but we report to Lord Bhayar, and we're to remain here until he says otherwise."

When he finished with his senior officers, Quaeryt left the study to join the imager undercaptains and the day's duty company from Eleventh Regiment. All were formed up and waiting when he stepped out into the rear courtyard of the headquarters building. In moments he had mounted and led the column out.

Lundi was similar to Solayi, except that the day was longer, and knowing that, Quaeryt spaced out the intervals between imaging. Part of that delay was required because the duty company had to clear people away from the area of imaging, and as the imagers proceeded, Quaeryt could see more than a few locals staring with eyes almost popping out of their heads.

He also heard a few remarks, some of them repeated more than once by different bystanders watching on different blocks.

". . . do things like that, no wonder they defeated Rex Kharst . . ."

". . . wish every street were like what they did here . . ."

". . . Pharsi officers . . . may be good . . . don't trust 'em . . ."

". . . you want to tell them they're blocking your shop?"

". . . all for show . . . what good are a few stone roads . . ."

Quaeryt could have told them, but he just kept a pleasant expression on his face as the imaging proceeded. Even so, by just before fourth glass, when he and the imagers rode back to headquarters, he was satisfied. He and the imagers had finished the ring avenue around the Chateau Regis, and the service road, and had widened slightly and paved the north road halfway to the bridge. He did decide to begin with replacing the bridge first on Mardi before paving and replacing the street heading west from the bridge until they joined up with the already replaced section of the north road from the Chateau Regis.

As he rode back from the headquarters building, after dismissing the imagers for the day, he couldn't help but worry about what was happening in northern Bovaria.

Vaelora had obviously been watching for him, because she was standing by the service entrance door when he rode into the rear courtyard of the chateau and reined up outside the modest stable, but she just waited for him while he turned the black gelding over to the ostler and then walked to join her.

"How was your day?" he asked.

"Tedious. I'll tell you after you wash up. The most exciting thing was planning dinner for us—and we're eating alone in the family dining room."

"I'm sorry," said Quaeryt as they walked into the chateau and then through the lower-level foyer and toward the east side staircase that circled up to their chambers.

"It's not your fault. It's almost as bad as when I was in Solis."

That worried Quaeryt—a lot. He remembered Vaelora telling him how much she'd felt like a prisoner in

Bhayar's palace in Solis. "I do have some news for you, and something for you to do . . ."

"What? Write out a meaningless description of our trip to Khel and back?"

"No. You know that Bhayar asked me to act as a temporary minister of supply and administration."

"Yes?" That single word contained a sea of wariness.

"I asked if you and I could work together on that. Bhayar agreed."

"Why did you do that?"

"Because it's going to be a bigger job than I can handle, and he and I need someone whom we can trust—especially if he sends me and the imagers off somewhere to fix something. You did an admirable job of finding the governor's house in Extela, staffing it, furnishing it, and getting it running. Then you worked with Aelina as a partial finance minister in Solis. All we have here will be one clerk from Deucalon and three studies on the main level . . . and some golds. I'm supposed to be rebuilding roads . . . and I'd like to get the imagers started on the isle of piers."

"That would be better than sitting around."

Quaeryt refrained from speaking as they climbed the circular staircase to the upper level. When they reached the top, he replied, "If you have to go someplace to get goods, supplies, or people, though, you'll need at least a squad of troopers."

"I can see that," Vaelora conceded.

While Quaeryt washed up, he and Vaelora discussed how they should set up their temporary ministry, although Quaeryt had his doubts that it would be all that temporary, given what they had observed of Bovaria.

Later, they sat down to dine in the chamber Vaelora had taken to calling the family dining room.

Quaeryt poured them each a goblet of white wine, then raised his. "To the lady who will likely end up doing much of the finance and logistics."

"At least *you* recognize that." Vaelora smiled before she sipped her wine.

Quaeryt looked at the platters between them on the table.

"It's a river trout poached in wine, then fileted over rice grass with a lemon cream sauce." Vaelora paused. "And don't look at the dinner rolls first."

Quaeryt laughed. He had been looking at the dinner rolls.

"Try the fish."

"It's not the fish, but the rice grass."

"It's tender, and nutlike in a way."

Quaeryt served her and then himself. He took a bite of the fish and the rice grass, chewing slowly before swallowing. "I've had much worse." He kept a straight face.

"Much worse?"

He grinned. "It's quite good. You were right."

"You need to say that more often."

"Most men probably do," he admitted.

"You should tell Bhayar that."

"Better that you tell him . . . or Aelina."

"She already has."

That didn't surprise Quaeryt, not at all.

"You know, in some ways, Bhayar is as close to a brother as you'll ever have."

"Why do you say that?"

"In my more than ample spare time," Vaelora paused before continuing, "I was reading *Rholan*. The author mentioned that Rholan didn't believe in brotherhood."

"That makes sense. His half brother was a wastrel, and he didn't have any other brothers or sisters."

Vaelora took a sip of wine, then said, "There's something about that passage. I'd like you to read it again."

"I will . . . after we enjoy this tasty dinner."

Vaelora shook her head.

Quaeryt smiled.

Later, while Vaelora was preparing for bed, Quaeryt paged through *Rholan and the Nameless*, finally locating the passage Vaelora had mentioned. He quickly read the entire section.

So often do men talk about brotherhood, as if it were some lofty ideal that transcends the boundaries of all lands, that some may find it interesting that Rholan never did. That is less than surprising. Rholan had no siblings except his half brother Nial, and they were never close. In fact, Rholan went out of his way to avoid Nial, not that such was difficult. Yet, Rholan's mother was most close to her sister Clyana. Although his mother died when Rholan was only ten, Rholan often visited his aunt throughout his life and made no secret of their relationship. What is more interesting was that Clyana was a cabinetmaker of some skill, and several of her pieces adorned Rholan's home. Yet he never mentioned that, even to his closest friends, perhaps because having an aunt who was a crafter of note did not fit his image. This was possible only because Rholan's friends and acquaintances were entirely drawn from the ranks of those of considerable golds and property, either merchants, factors, or the younger sons of High Holders. Yet, for all of his private concern about finances and golds, and his rather hidden appreciation of the finer life, he understood and could speak to those of a more common background, perhaps just because of his closeness to Clyana. At the same time, he never seemed to accept the fact that sisterhood existed; even as he had seen it before his very eyes.

"What do you think?" asked Vaelora.

"It does seem strange that he couldn't see either sisterhood or brotherhood."

"Do you see it?"

Quaeryt smiled sheepishly. "Not really. Living with all the scholars wasn't exactly brotherhood. Voltyr was the only one I felt even halfway close to."

"That wasn't what I had in mind. Do you see what's strange about the passage? How did the writer know that he hadn't told his closest acquaintances about his aunt? And if he hadn't . . ."

"How did the writer know," finished Quaeryt.

"Exactly."

"I'll have to think about that . . . later." He turned toward her.

20

Vaelora had barely joined Quaeryt for breakfast in their sitting room when she announced, "There are no tables or chairs or even cases in the studies we'll be using."

"We also don't have golds for them."

"Skarpa sent a paychest with you," she said.

"That's from Southern Army." Quaeryt paused. "I suppose we could lend from it to the Bovarian Ministry of Supply. There must be a hundred golds left, and Bhayar did say he'd pay for our expenses."

"Good. I'll come with you to headquarters and get the golds."

"And take a squad and one of our supply wagons with you?"

"Why not? Is anyone else using it?"

"No." Quaeryt laughed. "Just purchase or order solid and simple table desks, chairs, or cases, and chests? Where, might I ask?"

"You're almost being disrespectful, dearest. I have made inquiries of the staff and the serving maids."

"Aren't most of them from Paitrak's house holding?"

"Not all of them. Some came from other High Holders. Some are locals who heard that Bhayar was fair and paid as promised."

You should have known. "Why don't you come with me when I leave for headquarters, then?"

"Thank you for asking, dearest."

Quaeryt winced at the cool edge to her voice. "I'm sorry. I was thinking about how we need to get the roads and bridges finished before something else happens."

"Did you have a dream or a farsight?"

He was relieved to hear curiosity. "No . . . but it seems as though, whenever things are quiet, it doesn't last."

"So we should enjoy the quiet while it lasts."

"So we should." He smiled at her, then took a swallow of the lukewarm tea, before picking up a biscuit, splitting it, and slathering it with mixed berry preserves.

Before all that long, they rode north to the headquarters holding, accompanied by a half squad of duty troopers, where Quaeryt made arrangements, including disbursing golds, for Vaelora's logistics expedition. After seeing her off, he met quickly with the senior officers, and then headed out with the imagers and the duty company toward the north bridge over the River Aluse.

Under a sun that was much warmer than on either Solayi or Lundi, by two quints past third glass, Quaeryt could tell that the imagers were exhausted. He couldn't complain. They'd imaged a solid bridge across the Aluse and finished the rest of the north road so that it ran smoothly all the way from the chateau to the bridge and across it. The Bovarians or the factors of Variana could Namer-well make improvements on the east side. They'd even replaced the south bridge, and completed a few hundred yards of stone paving heading west from the bridge. Further roadwork would have to wait until Meredi, and Quaeryt hoped that the imagers could begin work on the isle of piers on Jeudi, beginning with a permanent bridge.

With those thoughts in mind, he gave the orders to stop imaging and to form up for the return to the headquarters holding.

"Have you heard anything from Submarshal Skarpa, sir?" asked Khalis as he rode up to rejoin the others.

"No. I wouldn't expect a message or a dispatch anytime soon. We've been here less than a week, and it would take almost that long for a rider to reach Kephria from Liantiago. Even with fresh mounts, without established posts along the way, dispatch riders couldn't make the rest of the ride to Variana much more quickly than a week less than it took us."

Khalis nodded. "I hadn't thought of that."

"We don't because dispatch stations exist all over Telaryn." *Just another thing that we need to establish here.* Quaeryt mentally noted to add that to his list of logistic improvements needed in Bovaria.

"Do you think we'll be called to build some of them?"

"I hope no one thinks of that immediately. We need to get started on the isle before anyone gets any ideas of what else we might build."

"So that imagers have a place that's theirs?"

Quaeryt nodded.

A heavyset man, a merchant of some sort from his jacket, hurried toward Quaeryt as he rode at the head of the column past a cluster of shops on the section of the south road that they had not rebuilt. "Officer! Sir? Will you be repairing this road the way you did the north road?"

Quaeryt slowed the gelding, but immediately checked his shields, hoping that the man wasn't a diversion for an attack. "Why do you ask?"

"Because folks have already stopped using the south road."

Quaeryt smiled. "We've already replaced the south bridge and some of the south road. If there's no trouble, we should finish this part of the road all the way to the circle around the Chateau Regis in the next few days."

"It wouldn't hurt if the west river drive got stone paving, sir," suggested the merchant.

"I'm sure it wouldn't, but we can only do so much."

"Thank you, sir." The corpulent merchant, breathing heavily, inclined his head and stepped back.

Quaeryt looked to Khalis.

The young Pharsi undercaptain shook his head. "Everyone always wants more, don't they?"

"When did you not notice that?" asked Quaeryt dryly.

Khalis laughed.

A good two quints passed before Quaeryt reined up in the rear courtyard of the headquarters holding. The Eleventh Regiment duty squad leader hurried toward Quaeryt.

"Sir . . . there's a chorister waiting for you in your study."

"A chorister?"

"He says he served under you in Tilbor."

"Gauswn? He's here?"

"Yes, sir . . . Some others as well. Youths."

Imager students? "I'll see him. If you'd see to my mount. I'll be needing him later to ride to the Chateau Regis."

"Yes, sir."

Quaeryt dismounted and hurried across the courtyard. *Why is Gauswn here? Has Tilbor turned against the young imagers . . . or just the scholarium?*

Quaeryt had barely stepped inside the study when he was greeted exuberantly.

"Commander!" Gauswn's eyes widened slightly as he took in Quaeryt, but that was the only indication of surprise. He remained slender, but he was clearly a chorister in gray and with the short black and white traveling scarf. "I see you've been promoted since your last letter."

"Such can happen in wartime. How are you? Why are you here?" Quaeryt's eyes went to the four youths standing behind the chorister, whom he had once thought of as a young officer, yet Gauswn was at least ten years older than Khalis and Lhandor were. The four youths looked to range in age from around ten to twelve or thirteen. Two wore the student browns of the scholarium in Tilbora.

Gauswn half turned to the students. "This is Commander Quaeryt. He is also a scholar, and as I've told you, if he wished, he could be the best chorister in all of Lydar."

"Your chorister is too free with his praise," demurred Quaeryt, "and he's a fine chorister in his own right."

Gauswn extended a sealed envelope to Quaeryt. "This is from Governor Straesyr. It might be best if you read it first, sir. I can answer any questions after that." He turned to the four youths. "Wait outside in the corridor. Don't stray. This is an army post, and you could get hurt . . . or worse."

"Yes, sir," came the chorused response.

Quaeryt opened the letter and began to read.

Dear Quaeryt—
I won't even attempt a title. You've had so many in such a short time. I've made the decision to suggest that Chorister Gauswn and his two students travel across Telaryn and Bovaria to meet you in Variana. I've supplied mounts and golds, and they will ride with our dispatch riders.

I have my doubts that the scholarium here is the best place for the students, and Gauswn is wasted there. With what I gather is your objective, you'll need someone like Gauswn, and you will certainly need the imagers, as will Lord Bhayar, and any others that Gauswn can find along the way.

Mistress Eluisa D'Taelmyn sends her regards and her appreciation for your redressing a situation that she could not. Her father, if he is still alive, is Taelmyn D'Alte, and her youngest sister is Rhella. She would be pleased if you would contact them, if it is possible.

Try not to destroy more than necessary in seeking your aims.

Quaeryt couldn't help but smile at the last line. He had to admit that he missed Straesyr, even though they had not always seen eye-to-eye, especially in the beginning, but he'd learned a great deal from the governor. *And you should have learned more.* The message from Mistress Eluisa was definitely unexpected, but welcome . . . and a good suggestion. He tucked the letter inside his uniform shirt.

"Do you have any questions, sir?"

"About the letter? No. I take it that matters at the scholarium did not turn out as you might have wished?"

Gauswn smiled, slightly ruefully. "The governor is overly concerned. The scholarium will survive. It will likely prosper modestly . . . so long as . . ."

"The scholars are not required to deal with imagers as students?"

"Yes, sir."

"Then why did you leave . . . or are you planning on returning?"

"No, sir. Not if you can find a position for me as a chorister."

Quaeryt burst into a grin. "I'd be glad to have you as a chorister. Not only that, but we might just have an anomen, in a few weeks, for you." He went on to explain about his plans and the ruined anomen on the isle of piers.

After he had finished, Gauswn said, "I still might request an occasional homily from you."

"Very occasional . . . if matters work out." Quaeryt made the qualification because matters hadn't yet worked out in the fashion he'd anticipated. "We'll have to find temporary quarters for you and the students, but we can call them trainees, and no one will complain. And since Eleventh Regiment has no chorister . . ."

At that moment there was a solid rap on the door.

"Yes?"

Begging your pardon, sir," came a voice from the corridor, "but there's a junior squad leader here with dispatches for you personally. They're from Liantiago. He's most insistent."

"If they're from Liantiago, it's urgent," replied Quaeryt. "Show him in."

The young squad leader who entered the study looked totally exhausted, with deep circles under his eyes. Even so, he looked askance at Gauswn as he handed the two sealed envelopes to Quaeryt.

"Captain Gauswn was one of my officers in Tilbor," Quaeryt explained. "He's acted as escort for some student imagers."

"Yes, sir. The top dispatch is from Undercaptain Voltyr, the other one, sealed in green, is from Subcommander Alazyn. I have another for Marshal Deucalon, but he is at the Chateau Regis with Lord Bhayar. He's not expected back soon."

"Is the other also from Undercaptain Voltyr?"

"I don't know, sir. It's sealed. Twice."

Quaeryt felt a cold chill. "It will take you close to two quints to reach the Chateau Regis. You'd best hurry." He offered a smile he didn't feel. "Thank you."

"Yes, sir."

As soon as the squad leader left, Quaeryt used his belt knife to slit the envelope, opening it quickly and unfolding the sheets within.

Commander—

Submarshal Skarpa is dead. He was killed by a man named Chaellonyt, who claims to be the heir of Chaelaet, the former High Holder of Laetor. Chaellonyt used a small crossbow from cover when the submarshal left a staff meeting, from which we were excluded. We could not move quickly enough to shield him because of where we had been placed as a result of Commander Kharllon's concerns about our reporting on the meeting. Threkhyl imaged a block before Chaellonyt's mount, and we captured him. The assassin stated that he killed Submarshal Skarpa because the submarshal had personally destroyed his holding and ruined his father, who died in the battle for Barna . . .

Quaeryt paused. *Personally destroyed?* Then he swallowed as he recalled that the assistant steward had called him "submarshal," and he had not corrected the man. The assistant steward must have passed on that the "submarshal" had personally destroyed the hold. *And Chaellonyt thought that Skarpa had done it.*

"Sir?" asked Gauswn.

Quaeryt looked up from the partially read dispatch. He swallowed again. "Skarpa. He was killed by the heir of a rebel High Holder because the imagers and I leveled his hold house and forfeited his lands to Bhayar."

"But you were under Commander Skarpa's orders, weren't you . . ."

Quaeryt shook his head. "My command was independent. Skarpa agreed reluctantly, but it was my decision and my act. And he paid for it." *All because you didn't correct a misunderstanding.* But that was something Quaeryt couldn't afford to admit publicly, because it would reflect badly on Bhayar. *Are you sure?* Was there any doubt? Deucalon, Myskyl, and Kharllon would all use any admission against Bhayar . . . and Quaeryt and the imagers. *And you can't afford that.* "Excuse me. I need to finish reading the dispatch."

. . . Commander Kharllon has assumed the position of acting governor of Antiago.

Under the command of Subcommander Alazyn, Nineteenth Regiment and first company have removed from Liantiago to Westisle, where we have begun to establish a Telaryn base to assure that Lord Bhayar retains control of the port at Westisle. I felt that accompanying Nineteenth Regiment was in accord with your orders, but do not hesitate to change those orders as you see fit. I did inform Commander Kharllon of your orders and that I would request your confirmation or change to them.

For your information, we have also obtained two trainees, and may receive a third in the next week.

Quaeryt's smile was bittersweet. Voltyr had more nerve than Quaeryt might have had in his position, and both Alazyn and the imagers were far better off separated from Kharllon. Even so, Voltyr would have his hands full. He slipped the sheets back into the envelope and then slit open the one from Alazyn.

Commander—

Submarshal Skarpa was killed by a Bovarian High Holder's son earlier today. With his death, Commander Kharllon assumed command of Southern Army. He insisted that Nineteenth Regiment was under his command. I noted that Nineteenth Regiment was assigned to the envoys directly, and that you and Lady Vaelora had requested that the regiment support Submarshal Skarpa. With his death, command reverted to you or those under you.

The compromise we reached, until we receive orders from you or Lord Bhayar, is that Nineteenth Regiment and first company would invest the port of Westisle to assure that Telaryn controls all major ports of Antiago, save Hassyl. The imagers have begun to convert old warehouses adjoining the port quarter into barracks and facilities. These can be used by any Telaryn forces as necessary.

I felt you should know these facts in order to present them, as you see fit, to Lord Bhayar and Marshal Deucalon.

Obediently yours.

The signature was that of Alazyn Zyntarsyn, Subcommander.

Quaeryt quickly folded the sheets and stuffed them back in the envelope. "I'm going to have to leave you. But let's get you and the boys settled for now." He stood and headed for the door.

Gauswn followed.

Quaeryt quickly explained the situation with Gauswn and the new trainees to the duty squad leader, since Zhelan was not immediately available, gave him instructions, then reclaimed his mount.

As he rode quickly toward the Chateau Regis, Quaeryt thought about the dispatches. Both had been dated the nineteenth of Maris. That meant the dispatch riders had covered the distance in a little less than three weeks. Quaeryt shook his head. They could have covered the same distance in Telaryn in less than a week. *A week and a half. The roads aren't that straight.* Then there was the fact that the dispatch rider hadn't said anything about a dispatch to Bhayar . . . and Skarpa—and thus Kharllon—reported directly to Bhayar.

Did Chaellonyt kill Skarpa because he thought Skarpa was me? Or because Skarpa was in command? Or for both reasons? Why did it have to happen that way? And then there was the problem of Voltyr and Threkhyl not being able to protect Skarpa because of Kharllon's concern about the imagers finding out something. Quaeryt didn't think that was an excuse by Voltyr. Voltyr had never made excuses. *Threkhyl, perhaps, but not Voltyr.*

Two rankers were waiting at the side entrance to Chateau Regis to take Quaeryt's mount.

"Lord Bhayar is in his study, sir."

"Thank you." Quaeryt dismounted. "Is the marshal there?"

"No, sir. He left half a quint ago."

Quaeryt held back a frown. He hadn't seen Deucalon or any riders on the road from headquarters. "Do you know where he went?"

"No, sir, but he was riding west."

"Thank you." Quaeryt hurried through the oak door and then down the lower-level hall to the circular staircase that rose two flights to the upper level of the chateau.

The ranker by the study door opened it for Quaeryt even before he reached it. He stepped inside.

Bhayar was indeed waiting, pacing back and forth in front of the windows. "I sent for you, but I see you already know. When did you find out?"

"Two quints ago. The dispatch rider said that he had a dispatch for Deucalon, and I'd heard he was meeting with you." Quaeryt wondered why he hadn't seen a rider heading for headquarters.

"He had dispatches for both Deucalon and me. They were both the same . . . from Kharllon. Acting governor Kharllon."

"I didn't see any rankers riding to headquarters," Quaeryt said blandly. "Or Deucalon."

"I'm not surprised. Deucalon asked permission to send a courier a back way."

"To see how soon I'd arrive?"

"I imagine." Bhayar smiled faintly. "Would you care to read my dispatch?"

"I would. I thought you might read the two I received."

"Two?"

"Voltyr and Alazyn."

"Ah . . . yes."

Quaeryt extended both dispatches and took the one Bhayar handed him.

Both men began to read.

Quaeryt had no doubts as to how the matter would be presented, except how delicately Kharllon would do so.

Lord Bhayar,
Lord of Telaryn, Bovaria, and Antiago

It is my sad duty to report to you that Submarshal Skarpa was murdered earlier today by one Chaellonyt, who claims to be the heir to a holding in southern Bovaria and who was disinherited for his father's failure to pledge allegiance to you. The assassin escaped the notice of both the imagers and Submarshal Skarpa's men and killed the submarshal with a single shot. The submarshal's men did capture the assassin, and he will be executed once we have extracted as much information as possible.

I must report, regretfully, that Subcommander Alazyn insisted that his orders from Commander Quaeryt did not place him under the direct command of Southern Army, but only as a supporting regiment under independent command. I did not choose to contest this after first company and the imagers also supported this convoluted interpretation of the chain of the command. As a temporary measure, subject to change upon receipt of your direct orders, Nineteenth Regiment and first company, supported by the imagers, are investing the port of Westisle to assure its loyalty to you. This action, of necessity, has left Southern Army's main forces without the capabilities of the imager undercaptains, a fact I must reluctantly emphasize . . .

Quaeryt shook his head but continued to read the remainder of the dispatch, which consisted of a report on the status of the six regiments now commanded by Kharllon and the progress Skarpa had made in returning Liantiago to some semblance of order in the nearly three weeks between the capture of the city and Skarpa's assassination.

Quaeryt lowered the dispatch and waited for Bhayar to speak.

"You'd best keep these for now," said Bhayar, extending the two envelopes and their enclosures to Quaeryt, "but if you or Vaelora would make me copies, I would appreciate it."

Quaeryt understood exactly what Bhayar's request meant. "You'll have copies tomorrow." He handed back Bhayar's dispatch.

"What would you recommend that I do in Antiago?" asked Bhayar.

"Confirm Kharllon as acting governor, but don't make him a submarshal for now, and inform him that he reports to you and that you will assure that any dispatches he sends to you will also reach Marshal Deucalon. Tell him that governors always report directly to the lord."

Bhayar nodded. "And Alazyn?"

"Let him hold Westisle. That's also a good place for the imagers."

"I thought you wanted them all here."

"What happened in Antiago changed my mind. I think there should be two Collegiums. Or rather one Collegium with two locations. That way, you'll have two bases of power. Also, you could tell Kharllon that he can certainly call upon the imagers for specific tasks, but not for continuing duty. That way . . ."

"I understand that much, Quaeryt," Bhayar said sardonically. "Unfortunately, so will Deucalon. What else did Alazyn do? Not that avoiding orders wasn't enough to enrage Kharllon . . . and Deucalon."

"During the campaign, Alazyn pointed out some discrepancies in Kharllon's views . . . or rather how he tended to position himself and his forces in ways most favorable to himself, and how his reports were not always in accord with how events had actually happened. Both Skarpa and Subcommander Paedn supported Alazyn. I also observed that Commander Kharllon's view of matters accorded more with what he wished to believe than the situation that often faced Southern Army. Subcommander Alazyn made the mistake of observing that publicly once." That was stretching matters slightly, but only a bit.

Bhayar smiled sardonically. "I thought as much. That was why I wished to see you without Deucalon present. He was most proper in hearing my decision to discuss matters with you alone."

"He didn't like it, but respects your decision."

"I'm not sure he even respects it." Bhayar paused. "I suppose I should promote Voltyr . . . to major, you think?"

Quaeryt thought for a moment. "For now, that would be good. Once the Collegium is established, I don't think imagers should have military rank at all."

"You'd give up being a commander?"

"For being the maître of the Collegium? Absolutely."

"What if I made you a submarshal?"

Quaeryt shook his head. "Begging your pardon, sir, but I believe that would be unwise."

Bhayar laughed, a short and harsh sound. "When a man refuses promotions and honors, and means it, I should heed his advice."

"Can I instruct Voltyr to build and plan for a branch of the Collegium in Westisle?"

"You can. I will also send him a dispatch telling him that in all matters involving imaging and imagers, you remain his superior." Bhayar fingered his chin, then looked back to the windows. "You are not to discuss the events in Liantiago with Deucalon. I have already told him he is not to question you about them. It would be better if you busied yourself with imager efforts for the next few days. I will confirm that, for the next few months, Subcommander Alazyn will govern the isle of Westisle, supported by the imagers. After that . . . we shall see."

"You have not heard recently from Submarshal Myskyl, have you?"

"No."

Bhayar's tone told Quaeryt to drop that subject. So he said, "If the weather holds, we will finish the road from the avenue around the Chateau Regis to the south bridge in the next few days. We've replaced both the north and south bridges."

"The imager roads are a great improvement. We will need more . . . in time. How are you coming in setting up your ministry?"

"Vaelora went looking for tables and furnishings for the studies . . . And ledgers and chests. I have had Zhelan and Khaern making discreet inquiries about clerks."

For the next quint, the two discussed Bhayar's requirements for the new Ministry of Administration and Supply for Bovaria.

After leaving Bhayar's study, Quaeryt walked to the east side of the chateau, but Vaelora was not in the quarters. He found her on the main level, working with three troopers in arranging writing tables and chairs, and stacking chests.

"You've been busy," he observed.

"We can't do much until we have the furnishings and supplies."

He glanced around. "Are you about finished for now?"

"Just about." Vaelora looked at him. "Something's happened, hasn't it?"

"There's nothing we can do at this moment. I'll tell you when you're finished."

Less than a quint passed before Vaelora dismissed the rankers, and the two of them walked up the main staircase to the upper level of the chateau and to their quarters. Quaeryt had barely closed the door to the sitting room when Vaelora turned to him.

"Something from Antiago?"

Quaeryt nodded. "Skarpa was assassinated. Read these." He handed her the two dispatches and let her read them before he went on to tell her what had happened at Chaelaet and then about his meeting with Bhayar. "I didn't tell him about my not correcting the steward."

"You were right not to. That would only make matters worse without benefiting anyone."

"I should have corrected the steward. I should have." Quaeryt shook his head.

"How were you to know?" asked Vaelora. "Besides,

it might not have changed anything at all. Skarpa was the submarshal in charge of Southern Army, and all the dispatches you sent to the High Holders said that Skarpa and I would receive the allegiance of the High Holders."

"But it *might* have," said Quaeryt.

"You can torture yourself about that forever, dearest, and it won't change anything."

"I know that. You know that. Skarpa would probably even have said that. But it doesn't make it right."

"Will telling anyone but me make things better? Here? Or in Antiago?"

He shook his head. "It's just that I owe so much to Skarpa."

"He owed much to you."

"I put him in danger."

"He would have been in danger without you, and he might well have died in battle without everything you did. It's not as though you gave an order that caused his death. And you weren't the only one, dearest. Kharllon made it impossible for the imagers to protect Skarpa. Don't forget that."

Quaeryt just stood there for a moment. "That's true . . . but he wouldn't have needed protection—"

"Are you sure of that? He was still the submarshal. In the minds of all the southern High Holders, he was the one responsible. Also in the minds of all the surviving Shahibs of Antiago."

Quaeryt said nothing.

Vaelora stepped forward and put her arms around Quaeryt. "You're upset. You made a mistake. It was such a small mistake. How could you have known? But he was your friend, and you feel like all the blame is on you. I understand."

For a time, neither spoke.

Finally, Quaeryt stepped back. "I don't want to talk about it anymore right now."

Vaelora nodded, then asked, "Do you think that it's wise to set up two separate locations for your Collegium?"

"I thought I'd prefer one location, but what happened with Skarpa made me think differently. The imagers will always be vulnerable if they and those who lead them are in one place."

"And Voltyr is the best one to lead the imagers in Antiago. That was what you had in mind, wasn't it?"

"I did, but I was thinking of months, perhaps a year, when I did. Now . . ." Quaeryt shrugged, then shook his head. "Oh . . . with what happened to Skarpa, I forgot to tell you. Gauswn showed up this afternoon. Straesyr sent him and four student imagers."

"That's just the beginning," said Vaelora.

Quaeryt hoped so, but he couldn't stop thinking about Skarpa.

21

Quaeryt did not sleep well on Mardi night, disturbed as he was by vague nightmares, and one in which he tried to tell the assistant steward that he was not a submarshal even as the winds kept blowing his words away. That was followed by another in which a tree was falling on Vaelora, and he couldn't reach her . . . or do anything at all as she immediately gave birth to another daughter who died as he tried to hold her. He much rather would have had any of the dreams in which Erion appeared and admonished him, he reflected, as he dressed on Meredi morning.

He and Vaelora hurried through breakfast. Then each copied one of the dispatches Quaeryt had received. Next, Quaeryt wrote dispatches to Alazyn, and then to Voltyr, both confirming their actions. After that, Quaeryt made his way to Bhayar's study, while Vaelora headed down to finish setting up the studies for the supply ministry.

The guard didn't finish announcing Quaeryt before Bhayar called, "Send him in!"

Quaeryt immediately crossed the room and handed the copies to Bhayar, who, as usual, was standing beside his writing desk. "Here are the copies you requested."

"Thank you."

"There's one thing I forgot to tell you yesterday. I'm sorry, but it skipped my mind with everything about Skarpa's murder. That upset me more than I realized."

Bhayar nodded, but remained standing behind the desk, waiting.

"Chorister Gauswn, I may have mentioned him before. He was a captain in Tilbor, and when his term was up, he left to become a chorister at the scholarium. He arrived at headquarters yesterday with four young imager students. Straesyr sent them here."

"Straesyr sent him and four imagers?" asked Bhayar. "Four?"

"He sent him with the two student imagers I knew about when I left Tilbor. I didn't finish learning where Gauswn picked up the other two because I got the dispatches about Skarpa just after he arrived at headquarters. I made quick arrangements for them and then rode to see you as quickly as I could."

"It appears that fate and every officer I trust wants you to lead the imagers and build that Collegium," said Bhayar dryly.

"I had no idea that Straesyr felt that way, sir."

"I assume he sent a dispatch or letter?"

"Oh . . . yes, sir." Quaeryt extracted the governor's letter from his uniform and extended it to Bhayar, who set the copied dispatches on his desk before accepting and beginning to read the short letter from Straesyr.

Bhayar stopped reading and looked at Quaeryt, then said, "Straesyr saw what you had in mind. Otherwise he wouldn't have written, 'you will certainly need the imagers, as will Lord Bhayar, and any that Gauswn can find along the way.' Would he?"

"That might have been because Gauswn wrote me

while we were advancing up the Aluse, and I wrote Gauswn back, and advised him to consult with the governor if he had continuing difficulties."

"And what about his concluding lines, where he requests that you 'try not to destroy more than necessary in seeking your aims'?"

"He is a perceptive man. I never told him what I hoped for the imagers."

"He's also a good governor." Bhayar handed back the letter. "I don't need a copy of that one." He smiled briefly. "Is there anything else?"

"No, sir."

"Good. We've had enough news for now. I would like you and Vaelora to join me for dinner this evening. I've invited some of the councilors from Variana and a few High Holders and factors, and their wives. When and if appropriate, I thought you might tell them about the Collegium and how it will improve that isle of piers."

"We can do that. I'd thought that we might be able to build a bridge to the isle from the west shore today. Once we have more work done, when it seems feasible, we'll build one to Variana itself."

"You'd mentioned a change in names for the city. I'd like you to think about that." Bhayar held up his hand. "Don't say a word. That must wait, but the name for the city must be carefully considered. City names last a long time."

For successful rulers. "And the name of the lands you hold?"

"I have to admit that your suggestion of 'Solidar' does sound good, but not until Khel agrees to terms . . . one way or another." Bhayar's face turned stern. "That's another reason why I've agreed to your Collegium. It won't hurt to have those pigheaded Khellan councilors realize that you're building a force that could make what you did to Liantiago and Variana look small."

"I'd hope that building it will make its use unnecessary."

Bhayar's expression softened. "So would I . . . but there are those who fail to understand."

"If the matter comes up in dealing with Khel," Quaeryt suggested deferentially, "it might not hurt to mention that part of the Collegium is being built up in Westisle. It's much closer, especially by sea."

"Good point . . . even if it does serve your aims." Bhayar shook his head. "Your aims somehow seem meshed with mine."

"Several of those with farsight have told me that neither of us will succeed if we both do not."

"I can guess who one of those was. The others?"

"An old Pharsi woman in Extela that Vaelora rescued from the mob when we first arrived, and one of the Eleni in Khel."

"Eleni?"

"One of the outland wise women and seers we encountered west of Saendeol. There are two kinds of farseers in Khel. The *Eherelani* are part of the councils and the towns; the Eleni live isolated lives away from the cities and towns. Most of them are women." *But not all, because they didn't hesitate to claim you were* Eherelani *after the Hall of the Heavens, and that means there have been other men who are or were.*

"What else did they tell you?"

"That Vaelora and I would fail if we attempted to take credit or any power other than that which you bestowed upon us, and that neither of us could or should ever be rulers." That was true enough, reflected Quaeryt, if not phrased in the way the Eleni had.

"And you believed them?"

Quaeryt laughed softly. "I knew that before anyone told me anything. So did Vaelora."

"She's known too much before she was told."

"She told me she knew I would be in her future . . . and it frightened her for years."

"She was wise young . . . wise but willful . . . as I suspect you have discovered." Bhayar shook his head. "You need to go before Deucalon arrives."

"He's still furious, I assume."

"He'll be coldly angry for the rest of his days about how you've maneuvered around him. He can live with it."

Or die if he can't. Friendly as Bhayar was, Quaeryt had no illusions about the man he had known for half his life.

"We'll see what we can do with the roads today." Quaeryt inclined his head, then turned and left the study, making his way down and out to the stables behind the chateau.

Zhelan, Calkoran, and Khaern were waiting when Quaeryt walked to the study at headquarters that had become his, if largely by default. Together, they went over the plans for the day. Then, while Zhelan mustered the imager undercaptains, Quaeryt met with Gauswn.

"How are your students?" asked Quaeryt.

"They're tired." Gauswn smiled. "We had to keep up with the dispatch riders, and they weren't used to it at first."

"We'll be heading out to work on roads and a bridge. I think they should see what imagers can do. It won't be hard riding, and I've arranged for other mounts for them and you."

"Roads . . . bridges?" Gauswn raised his eyebrows.

"Some of the imagers can image stone structures, paving . . ."

"You're one of them, aren't you?"

"Yes. That's why I didn't want you making me into something I'm not . . . or claiming that the Nameless protected me."

Gauswn smiled. "But the Nameless granted you the ability, and you worked to make it so you could. I've found that is the way the Nameless most often works."

Even though Quaeryt had his doubts about the Nameless, he couldn't dispute Gauswn's view of the world. He also could see that Gauswn had matured a great deal over the past two years. *Haven't the past two years changed all of us? Or most of us?* He had his doubts about how beneficial the changes had been among some of the most senior officers.

With one thing and another, two quints passed before Quaeryt and the imagers, along with Gauswn and his students, and the fourth company of Khaern's third battalion, rode south from headquarters toward the Chateau Regis and the remaining section of the south road that needed rebuilding.

By slightly after noon, the roadwork was complete to Quaeryt's satisfaction, and the imagers continued eastward until they reached the west river road. From there they rode north, past dilapidated shops and warehouses, many of them empty, until they came to a point slightly north of the midpoint of the isle, a location across from one of the higher parts of land on the isle. There Quaeryt called a halt and ordered a rest for the company and the imagers.

Two quints later, Quaeryt assembled the imager undercaptains on the riverbank facing the isle of piers. "We're going to need a solid bridge across here, wide enough for two wagons and high enough above the water for flatboats and small sailing craft to pass under."

"How much clearance between the water and the bottom of the bridge?" asked Horan.

"Five yards at the current water level," replied Quaeryt. "The river's running a good three-four yards above normal, I'd judge. You've got the plans Lhandor drew?"

"Yes, sir."

"Just the basic bridge structure, Horan. Khalis will add the side walls and the approach causeways."

Quaeryt watched as the square-bearded and slightly graying imager looked at the plans, then at the river and the riverbank. Finally, Horan squared himself in the saddle and concentrated.

White mist swirled everywhere, but in the middle of the fog and mist was a gray stone structure spanning the river with a single massive pier in the middle, the two spans arched down but slightly on each side, only enough so that rain or melting snow would drain. A slight film of frost coated the stone, but quickly vanished. The layer of ice on the water beneath the span broke up into chunks that the current soon carried downstream and out of sight.

Once the mist and ice vanished, Quaeryt turned to Khalis. "The causeway down to the river road, if you would. Then the side walls. We'll save the causeway on the isle side for when we start work there."

In moments Khalis had imaged the walls and causeway in place, with some icy fog and mist.

When that had cleared, Quaeryt said, "Lhandor . . . can you image iron grillwork across the bridge so that brigands can't take wagons over it and steal everything that's left on the isle? Even without a causeway on the isle side, they'd try."

"Yes, sir."

After the grillwork was in place, and the imagers had some time to rest, Quaeryt announced, "Now we're going to ride up the river road to a point opposite the north end of the isle."

Given the uneven and neglected paving stones of the west river road, which explained why the merchant had suggested the need for repairs, it took almost two quints to reach a slight spur of riverbank a hundred yards north of the tip of the isle. From there, Quaeryt surveyed the rocky escarpments that suggested why the isle had survived years of flowing water and riverine abuse.

Finally, he spoke. "We need a gray granite wall deep into the riverbed and rising a good three yards above the stone ledges there. In time, we'll raise the entire isle close to that height. That will keep it above the spring floods." Quaeryt glanced back at the imager undercaptains, Elsior, and the student imagers. All of the undercaptains looked exhausted, their uniforms showing sweat.

He turned back to the isle and concentrated, drawing all the heat and power he could from the River Aluse.

A blast of wintry air rocked Quaeryt and all the others back in their saddles, and tiny crystals of ice rained down on them. A thick white fog covered the entire river from the water to a good ten yards up, totally obscuring the isle . . . and the view of Variana to the east. Quaeryt's head throbbed, and flashes of light flared across his eyes. He swayed in the saddle for a moment, then reached for the water bottle filled with lager. After several swallows, the throbbing subsided somewhat, and the light flashes became less frequent.

The gentle breeze out of the northwest slowly began to disperse the fog into fragments that revealed that the entire river was covered in ice from at least two hundred yards north of where the imagers had reined up to somewhere south of the fog. In addition, the north end of the isle, a distance of well over half a mille, was sheathed in what appeared to be white stone. As the imagers watched and the breeze and warm spring sun further shredded and evaporated the mist, the thin white ice that covered the stone began to crack and shatter revealing a stone battlement similar to the prow of a vessel, a structure that covered the entire end of the isle and a good hundred yards south on each side.

Quaeryt took another long swallow of lager from his water bottle, then corked it and replaced it in its holder. "I think that's enough for today." He raised his voice, image-projecting it slightly. "Captain! We'll head back to headquarters!"

"Yes, sir."

Quaeryt flicked the reins of the black gelding and guided him around north toward the north bridge—and the north road.

Gauswn eased his mount up toward Quaeryt. "If I might ride with you, sir?"

"As you wish." Quaeryt managed a smile, despite the continuing headache. *You shouldn't have let your impatience get the better of you.* He took another swallow from the water bottle.

"You didn't exactly explain why you're changing that isle," ventured Gauswn.

"I'm sorry. We've talked it over so much . . . I didn't think. Lord Bhayar has agreed that we can build a Collegium—a scholarium for imagers—on the isle."

"You mentioned the school, but not where."

"The isle is one place. There may be another in

Antiago." Quaeryt went on to explain the general idea behind the Collegium.

When they finally reined up in the headquarters' rear courtyard, Gauswn looked to Quaeryt. "Lydar will never be the same."

"That may be, but would we have wanted it the way it was heading?"

Gauswn shook his head. "I talked to some of the captains last night, and a major or two. They all say you're as powerful as any submarshal or marshal. Far more powerful from what I saw this afternoon. The students haven't said a word. Usually, I have to remind them not to chatter."

"That's not because of what I did. They were quiet before that."

"You're right. They never dreamed of what they saw today."

Quaeryt sighed. "Having them accompany us may have been a mistake. If you'd gather them up after the mounts are taken care of and bring them to the study . . . I'd better talk to them. Immediately."

"Yes, sir."

"I'm not trying to be commanding, Gauswn. If any of them try a fraction of what they saw, it could kill them. I need to get that across before they do."

Gauswn smiled sadly. "It's hard to believe you're only a commander."

"That's the highest rank I should ever hold, and I'll be happy when I can relinquish it."

The chorister nodded slowly. "I can see that. There are many commanders, and a few submarshals, and an imager who became a submarshal would create much fear in the hearts of the powerful."

"In the hearts of most people," corrected Quaeryt. "The idea behind the Collegium is that the imagers are protected and in turn protect the ruler who protects them. It will give parents hope for those few children who are imagers, and will provide a check on the power of the High Holders and the wealthy factors." He dismounted, then handed the gelding's reins to the waiting ranker. "I'll be waiting for the students."

Half a quint later, Gauswn and the four student imagers filed into the small study. Gauswn gestured to the two dark-haired and dark-eyed students at one end. "You might remember Chartyn and Doalak."

Quaeryt stood and nodded. He'd met Chartyn, but not Doalak, although he had arranged for the latter to study at the scholarium in Tilbor.

"Poincaryt, here, came from Santara, and Moraen from outside Cloisonyt."

"All four of you are welcome here. Matters are unsettled and will be for a few weeks." Quaeryt surveyed the four for a long moment before speaking. "Today, all four of you have seen what trained and skilled imagers can do. What you have not seen is what trying to image what you cannot do . . . or what is beyond your ability . . . will do. Have you ever thought of imaging golds?" His eyes swept across the four.

Finally, the small dark-haired boy on the left gave a small nod.

"Do you know what could happen if you tried that here . . . in this chamber . . . really tried it?"

"No, sir." But there was a question in the boy's eyes.

"It could kill you. That was how the Antiagon imagers who were captured killed themselves. They imaged a disk of gold large enough to kill themselves. That's because, when you image, you're drawing what you image from around you. If you image stone, that's easier than metal, because there's much stone beneath the soil—or beneath a river. Gold is rare and hard to find. It takes much strength. If you are strong enough to image gold, but there is no gold in the ground near you . . . it could kill you. Please don't try it. You can image coppers . . . one at a time . . . if you can do it. But don't pass them off on others. Not yet. Not until they're perfect."

"Isn't that counterfeiting, sir?"

Quaeryt gave a ragged grin. "If they're perfect and made totally out of copper . . . no. The value is in the metal. You won't cheat anyone if the copper is perfect. And you'll likely work as hard to image it as you would to earn it." *And every imager I know has tried it; so there's no point in forbidding it.* After a moment, he went on. "Before long, you'll be having classes, like in the scholarium, and some of those will be about imaging. Until then, until you learn more, please limit your imaging to small things and familiar things. Too many rankers and even imagers have died to give you this chance. Don't waste it by trying to image too much and killing yourself."

"Sir . . . did you know you were an imager when you were young?" The questioner was the small dark-haired boy.

"I was younger than you. I couldn't do even a small portion of what you saw today until two years ago. It takes time. Most imagers aren't patient. That's one reason why so many died young." Quaeryt looked to Gauswn. "Is there anything you'd like to add?"

Gauswn nodded, then turned to the students. "The

commander was a strong imager two years ago. He still took a crossbow bolt in the chest. Months later he almost died in the last great battle in Tilbor. I know. I was there. None of you are anywhere close to his ability. Heed his words."

Quaeryt offered a smile. "I'm not trying to frighten you. I want every one of you to become the best imager you can. There aren't enough good imagers. But trying to do more than you can will only put you in danger. You need to improve your imaging bit by bit." He grinned. "Now . . . that's enough homilies. They're all yours, chorister."

Gauswn ushered the four out, then paused in the study door and said, quietly, "Thank you."

"Thank you," replied Quaeryt.

For a time, he just stood there, half standing, half propped against the desk, before he roused himself for the ride back to the Chateau Regis.

By the time he reached the stables there, his headache was no worse, but not any better, and at times his vision blurred. He dismounted and handed the gelding over to the ranker ostler. "Thank you. I won't be needing him tonight."

"Yes, sir."

Then Quaeryt made his way to the three studies that would initially comprise the spaces for the Ministry of Supply and Administration for Bovaria. He found Vaelora in the middle study, going over a ledger with a ranker clerk.

She straightened and walked over to him, studying him. Then she said in a low voice, in court Bovarian, "You're exhausted, and your eyes are bloodshot. What did you do?"

"A little more imaging than I intended," Quaeryt admitted.

"What have you eaten?"

"I had some lager and a biscuit or two."

Vaelora gave a sigh even more expressive than the theatrical ones offered by her brother, then shook her head. She turned to the young ranker clerk standing beside one of the writing tables. "Stennyl . . . run down to the kitchen and get some bread and cheese. Tell them it's for Commander Quaeryt. If they protest, tell them that Lord Bhayar's sister insists."

"Yes, Lady." The ranker hurried out the study door, not quite at a run.

Once they were momentarily alone in the middle study of the three, Vaelora looked at Quaeryt and asked quietly, but far from gently, "Just what did you image? An entire anomen? A massive bridge across the Aluse?"

"Just the stoneworks on the north end of the isle."

"Just? The isle is more than a half mille wide."

"A bit wider," Quaeryt admitted.

"All at once?"

"It seemed better that way."

"Quaeryt Rytersyn . . . you may be the most powerful imager ever and a hand of Erion, but you are an idiot! It's one thing to have to do something like that in battle . . . but . . ." She shook her head again, almost violently.

"I feel like we're running out of time. This way . . . as the other imagers build on what I've done, they can't slack off. They'll have to match the height and strength of the stone walls, and that will keep the isle safe from flood damage. It will also create an image of power. That won't hurt." He lifted a hand to her lips to stop her protests. "People forget what they don't see. In a few years, all but the oldest person in Variana will have forgotten the devastation and the death. You wouldn't think so . . . but they will. A mighty stone isle—like a ship in the river—that's harder to forget."

"Dearest . . ." Her voice softened. "No one could ever accuse you of dreaming small dreams." She paused. "Please don't do quite so much again."

He could hear the plaintive concern behind her soft words. "I won't." *Unless there's no choice.*

After eating some bread and cheese, retiring to their quarters . . . and a glass and a half later, Quaeryt felt better, and ready to escort Vaelora from their quarters to the formal dining chamber at the south end of the lower level of the Chateau Regis. He found the formal dress uniform slightly looser than he recalled, and that surprised him, because the last time he had worn it, he'd been recovering from his injuries from the battle of Variana.

Vaelora wore the same black and silver dress and jacket she had worn then . . . and looked even more stunning, Quaeryt thought.

When they reached the main level, a ranker escorted them to the receiving room adjoining the dining chamber.

"Deucalon is here," Quaeryt murmured after they stepped through the open double doors and he scanned the forty or so people in the room, in groups of three or four.

"How could he not be?" replied Vaelora. "We should pay our respects to brother dear."

"Oh?"

"He gave me a look."

There can be definite disadvantages to brother-sister

communications, reflected Quaeryt as they made their way across the green and gold carpet toward where Bhayar stood, with his back to the closed doors leading to the dining chamber. Rankers circulated through the room, carrying trays with goblets of either white or red wine.

When Vaelora and Quaeryt neared Bhayar, he nodded to the trumpeter standing to his left and a pace back, and a short fanfare silenced the muted conversations around the reception room.

"Just so that all of you know a few of those attending . . . the distinguished gray-haired officer in the uniform of a marshal standing near the windows is Marshal Deucalon, in command of the armies of Telaryn . . . when I'm not interfering." Bhayar gestured toward the marshal, then waited several moments before continuing. "You might also wish to know this charming couple," announced Bhayar. "The beautiful one is my sister Vaelora, who was recently envoy to Khel, and the rugged-looking one is her husband, Commander Quaeryt, whose accomplishments are too numerous to discuss here."

Another fanfare followed those words as conversations threatened to rise once more. "I haven't even tried to seat anyone by position or protocol," said Bhayar, adding with a smile, "except myself. So when we enter the dining chamber, please do not be surprised or offended by where you are seated or by whom your nearest companions may be."

After a moment when Quaeryt felt that most eyes in the room remained on the three of them, the various conversations resumed.

"I assume we're to be charming and not terribly informative," said Quaeryt dryly.

"That would be helpful," said Bhayar. "I'm told that I only have—properly—until the end of Avryl before I should cease entertaining for the summer and the first month of harvest."

"I know how you love entertaining," said Vaelora. "You can hardly wait for Mayas."

"It's necessary," replied Bhayar.

"To let everyone know that the fighting is over and the intriguing can resume?" asked Quaeryt.

"Of course."

A ranker stopped and proffered a tray. Both Quaeryt and Vaelora took goblets of the white wine. Quaeryt just held his.

"The wine's not bad," said Bhayar. "It's just not good enough to keep some of the High Holders and their wives from complaining."

"People always like to complain," replied Vaelora, "in Solis or in Variana."

Bhayar glanced to the Telaryn captain stationed just inside the doors from the main foyer, who offered a raised hand and a nod, then said, "Everyone's here." He turned to the trumpeter, who played another fanfare, then turned and opened the doors to the dining chamber.

After setting their goblets on a ranker's tray, Quaeryt and Vaelora accompanied Bhayar as far as the head of the table, where he smiled and said, "Vaelora, you grace the far end of the table so that those lower will not feel excessively slighted. You're roughly in the middle on the right, Quaeryt."

Quaeryt inclined his head, then escorted Vaelora to the far end and seated her at the foot, directly opposite her brother. Quaeryt recognized the long dining table and chairs as those that had formerly graced the dining chamber of the late High Holder Paitrak's hold, as had several of the sideboards. With a smile, he left his wife and made his way toward his own chair.

He noted the placards before each place setting, with the carefully spelled out names. To his right was Malyssa D'Chamion. *Chamion . . . that's familiar, but why?* He couldn't remember and quickly took in the name to his left. Alynae D'Fyanyl-Alte. That meant she was the wife of High Holder Fyanyl, not that Quaeryt had any idea who Fyanyl might be.

The first of those seated beside him to arrive was Malyssa D'Chamion, who looked to be a few years older than Quaeryt himself, and that likely meant, given women's attention to appearance, she was probably older than that. Quaeryt seated her and then turned to seat the very much younger-looking Alynae, a chestnut-haired beauty in a deep green gown enhanced by a filigreed gold neck choker. Across the table from Quaeryt were two men and a woman he did not know.

Once everyone was seated, and the ranker servers had filled all the goblets at the long table, Bhayar stood and raised his goblet. "To peace, prosperity, and order across all Lydar."

While many repeated the toast, some merely sipped their wine.

"I did want to meet you, Commander," offered the older Malyssa. "My husband was most impressed when he dined with you last fall. I understand you and your wife have been traveling."

"You might say that," replied Quaeryt, now knowing that she had to be the wife of the chief councilor of Variana. "We both traveled to Khel to meet with their High Council. My wife was made envoy."

A quick look of confusion appeared and vanished from Malyssa's face.

"Vaelora is part Pharsi. The High Council of Khel is entirely Pharsi, and most are women. All but one, in fact."

"Ah . . . and since she is Lord Bhayar's sister . . ."

"Exactly."

"Commander," came the almost silky smooth voice from his other dinner companion, "Lord Bhayar praised your achievements . . . but never mentioned what they were."

"No, I don't believe he did," replied Quaeryt politely.

"If I might offer a few words, distinguished lady," interjected Malyssa, "that the commander would be unable to offer without seeming excessively self-important, he was the one who destroyed two Bovarian armies, first at Ferravyl and then at Variana. I understand he accomplished a similar feat in Liantiago as well." She looked at Quaeryt with the hint of a smile. "Did you not?"

"For better or worse, I did," he admitted. "Now . . . you know of me, and I know nothing of either of you, except that you, Madame Malyssa, are the wife of the chief councilor of Variana, and you are either the daughter or the wife of High Holder Fyanyl, whom I have not had the honor of meeting."

"Daughter?" Alynae laughed softly. "You're most kind, Commander. I'm his wife, and the mother of four children."

"I honestly would not have guessed." And that was true enough, Quaeryt knew.

"Nor I," added Malyssa.

"Are your lands near Variana?"

"Not terribly near—some fifty milles northeast of here. My husband was fortunate enough not to be an intimate of Rex Kharst."

"I suspect you were the one fortunate that he was not," said Quaeryt dryly.

"He was most careful, Commander. He presented me to Rex Kharst when I was almost full-term with our second child. I was not at my best."

Quaeryt managed not to smile or grin, but he did note that Fyanyl sounded like a High Holder to watch. "He was most careful."

Alynae nodded.

"My husband said that you are an imager, and the officer in command of all of Lord Bhayar's imagers."

"No more so than any officer is in command of those over whom he is placed," demurred Quaeryt, before adding, "Your observation raises a question that has puzzled me for some time. What happened to the imagers who served Rex Kharst? We heard that there were such, and yet we never encountered them."

There was a moment of silence, then the man across the table from Quaeryt spoke. "Commander, Laevoryn D'Alte. I might be able to shed some light on that."

"Please . . . if you would."

"Rex Kharst relied on less than ten imagers, and he kept most of them close . . . but not too close. I have heard that most of them were in the field when you and your imagers froze the Bovarian forces. Several whom I trust have suggested that perhaps three of them were either not there or somehow escaped the violence of the winter that destroyed Rex Kharst and his forces."

"Do those whom you trust have any idea what happened to those who escaped?"

High Holder Laevoryn shook his head. "They have left Variana. Of that, I am certain. Where they might be . . . that is another question, and one to which I have no answer. It is not a question, I hope you understand, that I would wish to pursue."

"I do understand." Quaeryt did, especially given that any imagers powerful enough to survive what he had wrought were certainly powerful enough to wreak disaster on anyone who got in their way. "That does give some answer to the question of what happened to his imagers." He paused. "He must have had some way of controlling them."

"His usual methods," replied Laevoryn. "He kept close watch on their families . . ."

Effectively holding them hostage.

". . . and that is all I know," concluded Laevoryn.

Or all you're willing to say. "That is most useful, and I thank you."

"My pleasure, Commander."

After another moment of silence, Malyssa cleared her throat delicately. "It is said that you were also a scholar," said Malyssa. "A scholar who learned much about Bovaria, perhaps?"

"Some . . . but I made a practice of talking to many in the course of the campaigns. I ran across a High Holder, a less than agreeable man, who had been banished to his estates . . . and I learned a great deal from him."

"Fauxyn?" asked Alynae.

"I believe that was his name."

"He died this past winter . . . from injuries he suffered . . ." Alynae's mouth opened. "Were you the one?"

"The one what?" asked Malyssa.

"Fauxyn was . . . despicable, among other things. He was also a duelist who murdered anyone who displeased Kharst. Even for a duelist, he cheated. He challenged a Telaryn officer, it was said. The officer used a staff and crippled him. He never recovered. Some said he poisoned himself to punish his wife."

At that moment Quaeryt realized that Alynae was not nearly so surprised as she should have been, but he said nothing, only waited.

Malyssa looked to Quaeryt. "Were you?"

Quaeryt shrugged. "He tried to kill me so that his wife would lose her family lands. When that failed, he tried to taunt me into killing him to reach the same goal. I wouldn't. Now it appears he tried a third way to the same end." Abruptly . . . Quaeryt turned and studied Alynae. Then he smiled. "How did you manage it?"

"I was bold enough to ask Lord Bhayar if I might be seated near you. He thought it might be interesting . . . I think."

"You're her sister? Cousin?"

"Cousin."

"I'll do what I can." Quaeryt didn't know whether to laugh or shake his head . . . and this was only the first dinner of what he feared might be many.

Yet, thankfully, that was the only surprise of the dinner.

It was close to ninth glass before Quaeryt and Vaelora were able to return to their quarters, and both were thankful that they only had to climb the main staircase to reach their quarters and bedchamber. While they undressed, Quaeryt told Vaelora about his conversation with Alynae D'Fyanyl-Alte. When he finished, he looked to her and asked, "Should I bring this up with Bhayar . . . or should you?"

"It might be best if we both did tomorrow."

"I also want to talk to him about those missing imagers. If there were three imagers strong enough to shield themselves, they could be a problem."

"Do you think you should . . ." She shook her head. "Of course, because if they show up and make trouble he'll want to know why you didn't tell him."

"If they do, it will still be my fault somehow. I'd still like to know where they went."

"It could be anywhere," Vaelora pointed out. "They wouldn't want anyone to know they're imagers . . . or that they supported Kharst."

"Except to others who did."

"Or to someone who wanted to use their abilities and could protect them."

"I can't see that there's anyone who could assure them of that."

"Dearest . . . there's always someone."

Quaeryt laughed. She was so right about that . . . but he still wondered about the imagers. He nodded. "Now that I've told you what I've learned, who were those around you, and what did you discover?"

"I was seated between High Holder Fhernon and a factor named Welsarius. The factor was far more interesting. He was likely almost as wealthy as many High Holders, and he wanted to know if Bhayar would be improving the roads outside of Variana, the way some of the roads to Chateau Regis had been repaved. He was very enthusiastic about that."

"He wants to bring goods into Variana, and that's hard. The only easy travel to the city is by the Great Canal. What about Fhernon?"

"His holding is somewhere near Tuuryl. He has a place north of town on the Aluse, but he shuttered it when Kharst became rex. He claimed that it needed repairs. That's what he said, anyway. He let it slip, deliberately, of course, that he was one of the less endowed

High Holders, and that had allowed him to avoid Rex Kharst on most occasions."

"What do you think?"

"Cat and rodent. He has more than he admits. It was still not enough for Kharst to pursue him, and his wife is less than attractive. He pointed her out to me."

Quaeryt shook his head and continued to listen.

22

Vaelora and Quaeryt were in Bhayar's study by a quint past seventh glass on Jeudi morning. First, Quaeryt brought up the issue of the late High Holder Fauxyn. When he finished, he looked to Bhayar.

The Lord of Telaryn and Bovaria smiled. "I think that all these complaints about succession for High Holders should be a matter handled by the Minister of Administration and Supply for Bovaria, jointly with Vaelora. You know more about the implications and laws, Quaeryt, and you have the blood, sister dear, so that these prickly High Holders can't complain that they're being dismissed by a mere commander."

Quaeryt couldn't argue with Bhayar's logic, and neither, he saw, could Vaelora.

"Whatever solutions you two adopt should not deviate too far from existing practices. I don't want you disciplining High Holder after High Holder."

"What about allowing widows to hold and administer the lands for their children?" asked Quaeryt. "If a child is a boy, until he reaches maturity. If there are only girl children, until the eldest is old enough to marry the son of another High Holder. That preserves the bloodlines, and doesn't force quick and unsuitable alliances."

"You might add something about the widow also being allowed to marry someone of equivalent suitable rank," suggested Vaelora.

"What do you have in mind there, sister dear?"

"Any single or widowed officers of the rank of commander or higher in the Telaryn forces," said Vaelora. "There won't be many, but there might be a few younger widows or those whose heirs died in the war. It would also offer another possibility."

"That exception will have to receive my approval on a situation by situation basis," replied Bhayar. "What else did you want to talk over?"

"The missing Bovarian imagers," replied Quaeryt. "Ever since the battle of Variana, and even before, I've wondered why we never encountered any Bovarian imagers. We'd heard that Kharst had them . . ." He went on to recount the conversation of the night before.

When he finished, Bhayar nodded slowly. "That makes sense, unhappily. You don't have any idea where they might be?"

"None, but I wanted you to know that there was the chance that they might appear or cause trouble in the future." Quaeryt paused, then asked, "You haven't heard any rumors, have you?"

"No. Not a one, but it's unlikely I would. What are your thoughts?"

"The Khellans won't want them, and Bovarian imagers wouldn't feel safe there for long, even now. Sooner or later, if they stay in Lydar, there's a chance we'll likely hear something." Quaeryt shrugged. "Then again, we might not, but I don't want you to be surprised." *Rulers don't like surprises, especially unpleasant ones.*

"What are you two doing today?"

"I'm going to survey the isle of piers with the imagers and get them started on making the place suitable for a Collegium."

"I don't want you there personally all the time," said Bhayar.

"After I survey the place and have Lhandor and Baelthm draw up plans and approve them, I won't have to be. That will likely take the next few days." Quaeryt grinned. "It will remove an eyesore and will be another part of your efforts to improve Variana into a most excellent city."

"Don't push it, Quaeryt," said Bhayar genially.

"Sir . . . have I ever not acted in your interests?"

"Just leave it at that." Bhayar looked to Vaelora. "Try to keep him from acting in interests I don't even know I have."

"Yes, brother dearest."

Bhayar offered a long and dramatic sigh. "Go . . . both of you."

Neither Vaelora nor Quaeryt spoke until they were alone in the smallest of the studies they had taken for their ministry, the one with a desk and a conference table. Quaeryt had insisted that the desk was Vaelora's.

Vaelora looked at her husband. "What are you going to do first today?"

"As I told your brother, start working to turn the isle of piers into the grounds for the Collegium Imago."

"Bhayar hasn't approved the name . . ."

"I'm not using it except with you and him until he does." Quaeryt smiled. "He will."

"So long as you keep yourself safe and don't try something like the other day."

"I won't."

Vaelora looked at him firmly.

"I promise."

"Can you finish surveying and hand things over to the imagers?"

"I haven't even started because we were working on the roads and the entrances to the Chateau Regis."

"I think he's right."

"I'll see what I can do today and early tomorrow."

She nodded, then slipped her arms around him for a moment.

Even so, in less than a third of a quint, Quaeryt was mounted and riding toward the headquarters holding with half a squad, and by a quint past eight glass, Quaeryt, the imagers, and Elsior, and the duty company were at the bridge to the isle of piers.

Imagisle . . . in time, thought Quaeryt, *you hope.*

"Lhandor . . . a gate in your grillwork, please."

"Yes, sir." The Pharsi undercaptain concentrated but briefly, and a set of double gates replaced a section of the iron grillwork.

One of the duty company rankers rode forward and swung the gates wide.

"Company! Forward."

At the end of the bridge Quaeryt called another halt and turned in the saddle. "Elsior! Forward."

The Pharsi trainee from Liantiago rode forward. "Yes, sir?"

"See what you can do to create a causeway from the end of the bridge down to that ruin of a road."

"Yes, sir!" Elsior straightened in the saddle and concentrated.

White mist appeared at the end of the bridge, extending perhaps five yards. When it cleared, there was a stretch of paved causeway. The young imager frowned, then wiped his brow.

"It's harder than it looks," observed Quaeryt mildly. "Have some lager from your bottle and a biscuit. I'll do a little stretch and then you can try again."

"Yes, sir."

All in all, it took two quints to finish the fifty yards of the causeway, with Quaeryt alternating with the young trainee. When it was done, Elsior was pale and shaking, and that was fine with Quaeryt, because that kind of stressful imaging was what it took to strengthen any imager. After that, as he rode down the last section of the newly imaged causeway toward the warren of rubbish behind the ruined buildings fronting the river and the sagging piers, Quaeryt could immediately see that the destruction was far worse than he had thought. Nearly all the warehouses either were roofless or their roofs had collapsed onto empty and sagging interiors, as if most had been abandoned years before. In a few places he could see charred timbers and signs of a fire, but even the charred sections of wood had faded into a dark gray.

He turned to Baelthm, riding beside him. "It doesn't look like the isle's been used in years."

"No, sir. I'd wager that it flooded too much." The older imager pointed to the northeast. "That section over there . . . looks like it's only a few yards above the water."

"Then we'll just have to deepen the river on each side and image the spoil onto the isle."

Quaeryt turned in the saddle and grinned at Lhandor and Khalis. "That will keep you both in practice . . . and strengthen Elsior and the student imagers."

For a moment Lhandor looked stricken, until he glanced at Khalis, who had grinned back at Quaeryt and said, "Yes, sir, but what do you want us to do with the cataract that will create at the north end of the isle?"

"Maybe we'll have to widen the channel, too," replied Quaeryt with a smile. "We need to ride north and see how bad it is. Keep sketching any ideas you have, Lhandor."

"Yes, sir."

Quaeryt gestured and then urged the gelding forward.

Riding to the northern end of the isle, a good mille from the bridge, took a good half glass, just because of the need to image rubbish and rubble out of what had once been a road or a lane behind the abandoned buildings on the west side. As Quaeryt had surmised, though, the last quarter mille or so sloped upward to the rocky outcrops that had partly protected the southern section of the isle from being eroded completely by the River Aluse.

He reined up short of the rough ground that held no structures and surveyed the back side of the granite ramparts he had earlier imaged. From what he could tell, they were solid enough. "We'll head back along what passes for a lane on the east side." He turned the black gelding.

The east side of the isle was even more dilapidated than the west side had been. At the lowest point, roughly a third of the way south, the floodwaters had apparently earlier flowed over the isle embankment, and then receded to leave a small pool.

"We'll definitely have to build up this part of the isle," said Quaeryt.

"You want me to do some of that now, sir?" asked Horan from where he rode behind Khalis and Lhandor.

"Not right now. You'll have enough to do shortly."

Near the southern tip of the isle on slightly higher

ground to the west, they came to the ruin of the anomen, standing between two tumbledown buildings that might once have been warehouses of some sort.

"Sorry-looking anomen," observed Baelthm.

Quaeryt studied the building. Despite the years, or possibly century or more of neglect, the tan stone walls appeared solid, and behind the heavy sagging beams that blocked the entrance, the ironbound, age-darkened, double oak doors looked sturdy. The roof tiles were chipped and cracked, but most appeared still in place, if most precariously. "It's held up well against time and neglect. As you can, Baelthm, I'd like you to take charge of restoring it. You'll need to call on the others to help, but we do have a chorister now, and he should have a proper anomen."

"I can see that, sir."

The only other buildings Quaeryt judged worth saving were a pair of newer and very solid long warehouses near the south end of the isle, but north and east of the anomen, and south of the new bridge. As with the anomen, they were located on somewhat higher ground and looked to be able to be converted into good barracks.

Once he completed his informal survey, Quaeryt gathered the imagers, as well as the company captain and the squad leaders, then began to outline the plan for the remainder of the day. "Most of the buildings aren't worth saving, except for the two stone warehouses and the anomen, and most of the ground is lower than it should be. We'll begin by clearing the south end of the isle, except for the anomen and the two warehouses. You're to flatten the buildings into small pieces but not to remove the pieces because we'll need all the fill we can find. After that, we'll see where we need to build up the isle the most . . ." He went on to explain before turning to Lhandor. "You'll likely have to modify the plans you drew earlier because I want you to work with me—as we can—on a plan for the entire isle." At the looks that crossed the imagers' faces, Quaeryt smiled. "No . . . we won't be doing all that this week or the next, but we need a plan so that we don't have to do things over . . ."

By the time fourth glass had approached, every structure on the isle, except the three buildings, had been reduced to fill, not that it had taken as much effort as Quaeryt had thought it might because most of the buildings would have collapsed before long anyway.

"That's more than enough for today!"

As the tired imagers and troopers rode off the west end of the bridge, Quaeryt could see people watching from the east side of the old river road. Those nearest the bridge eased away quickly.

For all their trepidation, Quaeryt couldn't help but wonder how long that deference would last. *A few years after the last building is in place—unless we do something else massive and mighty.*

He didn't shake his head as he led the column toward the north road.

23

Quaeryt didn't sleep all that well Jeudi evening, what with visions of Imagisle flitting through his dreams, and with unseen imagers imaging away buildings as soon as they were constructed . . . not to mention a raging flood that inundated everything. He woke up with a start and covered in sweat. Beside him, Vaelora was asleep, apparently peacefully. He eased the sheet away and just lay there cooling off, trying to compose himself, mentally going over the code of laws that he and Vaelora had begun putting together. He wished he had the treatise on law and justicing that he'd briefly borrowed from Aextyl, the old high justicer of Montagne, who had helped him so much before his death . . . a death, Quaeryt recalled with bittersweet clarity, for which he had been blamed, even while the dead justicer's family had been appreciative of all that Quaeryt had done for their father.

Still, with the centuries-old law code Vaelora had unearthed from somewhere, and from what they both recalled, they'd made a decent start on a basic code of laws for the land that Bhayar hoped would be Solidar before too long.

"What are you thinking?" asked Vaelora, breaking into Quaeryt's reverie.

"About the law code. I thought you were sleeping."

"I was . . . until you started sighing so loudly."

"I'm sorry."

"We both ought to be up—" Vaelora raised an arm. "That's not what I meant."

"After last night . . ." Quaeryt began suggestively.

"Last night was last night. We both have too much to do today." Vaelora sat up in the wide bed.

Quaeryt tried hard not to look too closely.

"I said enough . . . dearest."

The "dearest" was offered warmly enough that Quaeryt didn't feel quite so rejected as he got up to wash and dress.

When they sat down to the cool breakfast delivered to their quarters, he looked to Vaelora. "Has your brother mentioned anything about Myskyl?"

She shook her head.

"I think I'll tell him how we're coming on Imagisle—"

"Don't call it that yet."

"I won't, except to him. I can report and then ask about Myskyl."

"He'll know what you're doing."

"Of course. But he did ask to be kept informed." Quaeryt ate a bite of the cool egg toast. The sweet syrup helped in getting it down, and the tea was at least warm.

Immediately after breakfast he made his way to Bhayar's study, where Bhayar was looking out the west window.

"What is it now?" asked Bhayar.

"I just thought you'd like to know that we cleared all the ruined buildings from the isle of piers. There are two sturdy warehouses we can convert to barracks, and an old anomen that shows possibilities. The rest wasn't worth saving. I've got Lhandor working on plans for the isle. We'll have to build up parts of it so it doesn't suffer in the spring floods."

"You won't have to be there all the time now, then?"

"I wouldn't think so, but I'll likely have to be there a bit of most days for a time to make sure things go as planned."

"You didn't when the chateau was rebuilt."

"That was because Voltyr was there. He's in Antiago. Once we get started here, though, I think Baelthm and Horan can keep matters in order."

"Good."

"Have you heard anything from Submarshal Myskyl?" Quaeryt asked.

"No . . . and neither has Deucalon."

Or Deucalon says he hasn't. Quaeryt wasn't about to verbalize that thought.

"Why are you so concerned? I didn't hear anything from you and Vaelora all winter."

"We were in Khel and in Antiago, much farther away, and it's approaching summer, and you haven't heard from Myskyl in more than two months."

"What do you suggest I do? Send you to see what's happened?"

It might not hurt. "That's your decision, sir."

"I've thought about it . . . If there's no word in another week, we'll have to consider it." Bhayar shook his head. "It's not like Myskyl."

To the contrary, it's very like him. He only communicates when it suits him . . . or when he has to. "That is a bit worrisome."

"Quaeryt . . . I know you distrust Myskyl, but he has yet to prove that he is not to be trusted."

He can be trusted to serve his own ends. "For your sake, sir, I hope that such proof never occurs."

"Enough. Just go on and get your isle in order so that you can spend time administering all the troubling details that are cropping up."

"I will . . . but you could send some of them to Vaelora right now."

"I already have, but I'd feel better with both of you working on them." Bhayar paused. "When will you have the draft of that codex done?"

"In a few days, we hope."

"What about tariff schedules?"

"We're working those out as part of the code."

"And the tariff notices?"

"There's no way we can send those yet, but they're not due until the end of Erntyn." *Almost four months away.* "We don't have enough dispatch riders yet, and no dispatch stations, and we're still working on a census of High Holders. The ones we've met with know what's expected, and what happened to those who didn't pledge allegiance should encourage all of them to pay. The factors already know they have to send them in." *Because we made that clear in every town through which we passed.*

"We need dispatch rider stations to the west first. We have them along the River Aluse, all the way to Solis."

"We could set the ones in the west up if we could use a battalion from the marshal's forces," observed Quaeryt.

"You plan where they should be. You're the only one who's ridden the entire way to Liantiago."

"We can do that. I'll have a recommendation for the locations for you by Lundi."

"Good. That's the sort of thing I expect from you."

"Yes, sir."

It was still barely before eighth glass when Quaeryt

reached the headquarters holding and met with Khaern, Calkoran, and Zhelan. He asked all three for their thoughts on where the dispatch rider stations should be located. All of them agreed on the main locations in Eluthyn, Laaryn, Daaren, Croilles, and Kephria, but after that, there were other considerations.

"Talk it over with your experienced majors and captains, and the most senior squad leaders. I'd appreciate your complete recommendations by fourth glass this afternoon . . . if you can. Lord Bhayar is interested now . . ."

All three officers nodded.

Then they discussed the plans for the following week and other matters.

Next came a meeting with the imagers. Quaeryt began by saying, "After today and tomorrow, you're all going to be working more on your own to build and rebuild the isle of piers. Lord Bhayar has made it most clear that he needs my efforts at rebuilding the administration of Bovaria. Given the work you did in rebuilding the Chateau Regis, I expect you will do well in rebuilding the isle. It will take longer."

He smiled, then looked to Lhandor. "How are you doing?"

"I have several rough plans, sir," offered Lhandor.

"Let's see them."

"They're only rough, sir."

"I understand. There's little point in doing more than rough plans until we've cleared away the isle . . . but let me see them, if you would?"

Lhandor extended the sheaves of paper.

Quaeryt looked through them once, noting the careful drafting. He'd seen supposedly finished plans that didn't compare. Then he went back to one plan and studied it again, placing it on the top of the stack he handed back to the young Pharsi undercaptain. "The one on top is the sort I have in mind. Bring that with you today, so that you can compare it to the lay of the isle."

"Yes, sir."

After a brief outline of what he planned for the day, Quaeryt dismissed the undercaptains. While the imagers readied their mounts and the duty company, Quaeryt sought out Gauswn, who had already started the student imagers on their lesson in an empty tack room.

The chorister walked to the door. "You won't be needing them today?"

"No. Keep them at their lessons. We're headed to the isle. With some fortune, it shouldn't be long before we have a functioning anomen for you. We could use it as a place for lessons in the beginning . . . if that wouldn't be a problem."

"I doubt the Nameless would object, Commander." Gauswn smiled. "Undercaptain Baelthm was asking my thoughts about what might be necessary for refurbishing it."

"Good." Quaeryt paused, then asked, "How are you finding things here? I apologize for leaving you to your own devices so much. You only got here a few days after we returned from Antiago, and there's been quite a bit to do."

"You intend to rebuild that entire isle?"

Quaeryt nodded. "It's not going to be just a military post, but a community, and that will require not only regimental quarters, but stables and housing for imagers and their families as well as housing for the senior rankers and officers who have families. And the anomen, of course."

"Lord Bhayar agreed to that?" Gauswn smiled. "Did you give him much of a choice?"

"The situation gives him little choice," said Quaeryt, going on to explain the difficulties of maintaining order in Lydar over time primarily by the use of or threat of force.

When Quaeryt finished, Gauswn looked evenly at Quaeryt. "And what of you and the imagers? After all the power you have shown . . . will you be content to allow another to rule less wisely than you might?"

"Content? Possibly not, but that is the only fashion in which Lydar can be ruled. The Naedarans used the power of imagers, and it failed them. Using imagers as a direct arm of the ruler made Antiago weak and a poor place to live."

"And three heads are wiser than one," concluded Gauswn.

Quaeryt suspected what the chorister meant, but asked softly, "Three?"

"Lord Bhayar's, yours, and Lady Vaelora's."

"As well as the heads of those we consult," added Quaeryt. "I already miss Skarpa. He was practical. So was Meinyt."

"Did something happen to the major?" Gauswn looked concerned.

"Oh . . . no. Not that I know. He's a regimental sub-commander, and the acting regional governor for the area around Laaryn. But you can't talk to someone when they're hundreds of milles away."

"That was your doing, wasn't it?"

"Skarpa's and mine," Quaeryt admitted. "Meinyt's practical and fair. He knows what he knows and what he doesn't, and he's got two imagers who are also practical to help him."

"*That* was your doing."

"It made sense." Quaeryt laughed softly and ruefully. "But sometimes what seems to make sense doesn't always." He couldn't help but think about his failure to correct the steward at Laetor, when he'd thought it hadn't made sense to make what he'd thought was a minor correction in rank. *A minor correction . . . and Skarpa is dead.*

Gauswn looked at Quaeryt for several moments before speaking. "Only the Nameless is infallible. The rest of us must do the best we can."

And sometimes I wonder about just how infallible the Nameless is, thought Quaeryt, *if there even is a Nameless.*

"Sir . . . ?"

"Yes?"

"Subcommander Ernyld—I understand he is the chief of staff for the marshal—he approached me about conducting services . . ."

"Go ahead . . . but you really don't need my approval. You might let Khaern and our other officers know also."

"I'd thought to. You aren't doing services . . . ?"

Quaeryt shook his head. *After all that I've done . . . ?* He forced a smile. "I need to be going."

Gauswn smiled back.

Quaeryt just shook his head and hurried out to join the imagers and the duty company for the ride south to the north road and then east to Imagisle.

A half glass later, once the imagers were on Imagisle, Quaeryt decided that the first task was to build up the isle, especially the low spots on the east side, rather than have them work on buildings. First, he laid out what needed to be done. Then he undertook some moderately heavy imaging himself in lifting a layer of small boulders and large rocks into the flood pond, leaving a drainage channel and letting the displaced water flow back into the river, until the ground was level with the surrounding area and all the stagnant water was gone. After the other imagers had done another rotation of imaging in fill, he imaged in another large layer of rocky fill.

Before leaving them, he put Baelthm in nominal charge of the work.

As Quaeryt rode back toward the Chateau Regis, he hoped he could keep up that pattern for at least a week. By then, with luck, they might be done with the heavier earthworks, and the imagers could begin to put together the roads and initial buildings the Collegium would need. *That will also give you the time to determine what buildings, besides barracks and stables, should be built first . . . and where.* He also wanted to see what settling there might be, although his initial plan was to locate heavier buildings on the rockier and solid sections of the isle.

He reined up in the side courtyard of the Chateau Regis by slightly after first glass, turned the gelding over to the duty ostler, and hurried to the main floor chambers set aside for the Ministry of Administration.

Drawing a concealment around himself, he eased into the first chamber, where Vaelora was going over the ledgers with a pair of new clerks.

"If you have a question about where to make an entry, first look in the instruction book . . ." Vaelora held up a slim volume bound in red leather.

Quaeryt smiled. The folder had been a sheaf of papers until he bound them by imaging and turned the leather crimson.

He let her finish her instructions before dropping the concealment and clearing his throat.

"You're back for the day . . . or just for a while?" she asked.

"For the day, unless Lord Bhayar decides otherwise. I thought we could try to finish the codes . . . or make an effort on them."

Vaelora nodded, then turned to the clerks. "Tylasor . . . you're to go through those papers and sort out all those dealing with stables, mounts, and fodder and anything else dealing with horses. Remember . . . the entries have to be in separate categories. Grain and fodder, gear, and that includes shoes and the costs of farriers; and the acquisition of mounts. Don't forget to debit mounts that die or are sold to the knackers or renderers . . ."

Almost half a quint passed before Vaelora and Quaeryt were alone in their own ministerial study.

"How are they coming?" he asked.

"Slowly. The army clerks did the best they could, but . . ." She shook her head. "It will be a year before we have ledgers that are even close to accurate."

"That's what happens in a war . . . and when the land you conquer didn't have good accounts to begin with . . . and none of them have survived."

"Not in readable fashion." Vaelora frowned just slightly. "I was looking over the part of the code we talked about last night."

"Limiting the justicing rights of High Holders? What about it?"

"We need to make it clear that Bhayar isn't really taking away their existing rights, but clarifying what has always been the practice."

"That's why we decided to differentiate between high and low justice."

"There needs to be a better explanation about why

the code is just setting forth what the practice has always been," Vaelora said.

"Even if the most powerful High Holders had a tendency to ignore it?" asked Quaeryt almost humorously.

"That's why . . ." Vaelora broke off, shaking her head. "You write it, then."

"I did. You're right. It could be better, but you try this time."

Second glass came and went, as did two revisions of the introduction to the section on high and low justice before they were both satisfied with the wording.

They had turned to the revisions to the definitions of high crimes and treason when there was a knock on the door.

"Yes?" Quaeryt managed to keep the irritation from his voice.

"Commander, sir . . . Lord Bhayar would like to see you at your earliest convenience."

"Me? Or Lady Vaelora? Or both of us?"

"You, sir. He didn't say why."

"I'll be right there." Quaeryt sat up, laid his pen on the rest, and looked at Vaelora. "You know more about this than I do anyway."

"You write better."

Quaeryt shook his head, then stood. "You write better. I write more plainly."

"You don't write that plainly. Neither of us does. That's part of the problem."

She's right about that. "I'll be back as soon as I can be."

"I'll not be holding my breath, dearest."

They both smiled, and then Quaeryt walked to the study door, opening it behind him, closing it, and nodding to the waiting squad leader.

When Quaeryt entered the study, Bhayar looked up from the conference table, stacked with papers . . . and an old map. "When will you be able to take over the Bovarian treasury?"

"At least a month, and that's if we can use Deucalon's guards."

"Why can't you just use your troopers?"

"Because that's a very bad idea, and it will be worse once things on Imagisle become obvious. I don't think you want the head of the imagers having physical control of the treasury. It's one thing to keep records and set forth the laws, but you need control of those golds here. Everyone should know that they're your golds, under your control, and that they're not being passed out by a Pharsi imager."

"For an officer Deucalon worries about being too ambitious, you certainly aren't grabbing at golds or power." Bhayar's voice was dryly sardonic.

"I want enough power to protect the imagers and to set up the Collegium so that future imagers will always be protected by their service to the ruler."

"That's another question. I can't really go on being Lord Bhayar of Telaryn, Tilbor, Bovaria, and Antiago . . . and Khel . . . if that idiotic High Council ever agrees to terms."

"You've already said that the combined lands would be called Solidar. Why not call yourself 'Lord Bhayar, Rex Regis'? That way, you're still Lord Bhayar, but you're asserting that you are the rex of all lands."

"Hmmm . . ." Bhayar fingered his smooth-shaven chin. "That might work. I'll have to think about it, though."

Quaeryt waited.

"This imager business," mused Bhayar. "I must say

that I have my doubts about why this Collegium is necessary."

"It's most necessary, sir. Where do your doubts lie?"

"You and most of your imagers can do great things, yet you continue to insist that they need the protection of your Collegium. I'm hesitant to dispute you. I've learned that you are usually right when you feel strongly. Could you explain why you feel this strongly? In a way that I could explain to others?"

"I will, but I would prefer that you keep the complete explanation between you and Aelina . . . and Clayar, when he is older. I trust you will see why when I finish."

"So do I," replied Bhayar dryly.

"The imagers who serve you now—except for the student imagers—are the survivors. They've survived being distrusted and attempts on their lives before they became undercaptains. A number survived by living away from others, and some of the undercaptains didn't survive the battles. Akoryt died because he couldn't learn new skills quickly enough. Shaelyt died because he was required to do more than his body could take. I suspect two or three times the number of imagers we have gathered likely died all across Lydar just during the time these wars have gone on. Baelthm is an accomplished and precise imager of smaller things, and he might be able to protect himself against single assailants, but not against many or for long. As I told you weeks ago, even I would have trouble protecting myself day in and day out against the threat of attacks. None of the student imagers could come close, and if young imagers are killed year after year before they can protect themselves, where will the imagers come from to support and protect Clayar? The Collegium can protect its own, especially with guards from the regiments for the first years, until the Collegium is established, but there will never be enough imagers born, even across all of Lydar, to pose a threat to the land. The land is what poses the threat to the imagers."

Bhayar nodded slowly. "I must confess, after seeing the destruction you created, I had not considered that side of matters."

"It's like Clayar. You protect him while he is young so that he can grow to be strong. The same is true of the imagers. Why do you think so many parents have given up their children when they learned there might be a place for them? Even in Antiago, parents felt that having a child serve the Autarch as an imager was a better life for them—and he kept them under lock and key much of the time." Quaeryt cleared his throat before going on. "Part of the problem is exactly what you observed. People see what the strongest of imagers can do, but they don't think about how unprotected the weaker imagers are. By necessity, those remaining undercaptains are the strongest—and there are just nine of us left." *Ten, if we count Elsior.* "Nine in all of Lydar. Without keeping them together and training the young ones, in less than a decade there would be few left, and you would again have to be especially concerned about ambitious commanders or marshals like Rescalyn . . . even more so, given the size of Lydar."

"You give me few choices, Quaeryt."

"A fool has many choices, a wise man far fewer."

"Sometimes . . . talking to you can depress and discourage a man. There are times when I wish you were in places like Antiago or Khel."

Quaeryt nodded. "That's another reason why you

need me as maître of the Collegium, busy on Imagisle and not too close to you, but close enough that you can call upon me and the Collegium as necessary."

"Enough of that. What am I to do with Telaryn . . . and Aelina?"

"You could send Commander Pulaskyr to Solis as a submarshal and as regional governor . . . That will free Aelina to join you here."

"Why Pulaskyr?"

"Who else could you trust?"

"Do you trust him?"

"Far more than any other commander you have, except my two, and Meinyt, and my two aren't experienced enough for anything like that. Meinyt's better as a regional governor where he is."

"There are others I trust besides Pulaskyr."

"Such as?"

"Am I ruling . . . or are you?"

"You are, but I'd like to know. I don't know all the commanders."

"Justanan and Moravan are both trustworthy."

"Is either here?"

"They're both with Myskyl."

Quaeryt noted that Bhayar hadn't mentioned Luchan. "Then my recommendation of Pulaskyr stands, sir. But you asked. I suggested. The choice is yours, sir."

Bhayar shook his head. "At times, you remind me of my father, and you're younger than I am."

Not by that much. But Quaeryt wasn't about to say that.

"You might have something there. I'll think about it. Now . . . you said you'd have recommendations for setting up dispatch stations . . . ?"

"On Lundi, sir. Some of the locations are obvious. Others . . ."

Bhayar nodded, but his question reminded Quaeryt that he would have to ride back to headquarters to see what his officers had come up with in recommending dispatch rider posts.

After a moment Bhayar grinned. "That's enough for now. I'm looking forward to reading that code of laws. No one will be pleased, you know, if you and Vaelora do a good job on it."

"We've considered that."

"We'll have a family dinner tonight."

"No High Holders?"

"There aren't any left near here that I haven't seen enough of, not that matter. I'll see you two later." Bhayar turned toward the window.

Quaeryt slipped out of the study, heading back to Vaelora . . . and the issues of high crimes and treason.

24

On Lundi, Quaeryt had ended up working longer than he had anticipated with the imagers to repave the west river road from the Nord Bridge to the Sud Bridge after Gauswn had pointed out that getting goods, furnishings, and supplies would be difficult, given the sad state of the road serving the bridge to the isle. That had delayed some of the earthworks on the isle, but by fourth glass on Meredi afternoon, Quaeryt was satisfied with the basic earthwork on Imagisle, although it would likely be weeks, if not months, before he and the imagers would be able to complete the granite bulwark entirely around the isle.

In the meantime he and Vaelora delivered the first draft of the proposed Solidaran code of laws to Bhayar on Mardi. Bhayar read and reviewed it, and then went over it with Vaelora and Quaeryt in great detail after dinner on Meredi. Neither Quaeryt nor Vaelora could dispute his observations and corrections, but making the revisions clear and consistent was likely to take several days, Quaeryt suspected, especially given that more "administrative" problems were finding their way to their small ministerial study.

On Jeudi morning, Quaeryt showed the imagers where he wanted the first roads on Imagisle—the ones connecting the bridge with the two warehouses being converted and the anomen—but he had insisted on a less direct route to leave a central green along the middle of the isle. Then he hurried back to the Chateau Regis.

He'd barely stepped inside the ministry study he shared with Vaelora when he stopped dead in his boots after seeing the expression on her face. "What is it?"

"Chamion D'Council will be here shortly." Vaelora looked up from the desk where she had been perusing a ledger. Short as it was, her wavy brown hair still looked disarrayed.

"What does the Council want now?"

"I have no idea, but one of the squad leaders said Chamion would be here shortly."

"Something Bhayar doesn't want to deal with, no doubt." *But what?* Quaeryt shook his head. There were all too many things about which the Council might be upset . . . or wanting favors or something done.

"No doubt," said Vaelora sardonically. "There will be more of that."

Much more.

At the knock on the study door, Quaeryt said, "Yes?"

"Councilor Chamion is here to see you."

"Have him come in."

Vaelora closed the ledger and stood. The two said nothing as the councilor stepped into the study.

"Commander . . . Lady," offered Chamion in the deep and raspy voice that Quaeryt found particularly annoying.

"Councilor," returned Quaeryt.

"I understand that you . . . and Lady Vaelora, of course," added Chamion quickly, "are acting for Lord Bhayar in . . . administrative matters." Chamion's voice was polite, although Quaeryt thought he detected a hint of exasperation.

"He appointed us as joint Ministers of Administration and Supply for Bovaria," replied Quaeryt. That wasn't technically correct, since Bhayar had appointed Quaeryt and then told him to work things out with Vaelora, but Quaeryt wanted to assure anyone coming for a decision that either of them could decide. The last thing he wanted was for decisions to stack up if Bhayar sent him elsewhere . . . or for those decisions to be deferred to Deucalon. He and Vaelora might not always agree, but he was far more likely to be comfortable with any decision she made than one made by Deucalon . . . or possibly even Bhayar himself, at least in certain matters.

"I see." Chamion nodded politely. Not a single dark gray hair on his head moved.

"How might we help you?" asked Vaelora.

"It has come to the attention of the council that Lord Bhayar has commissioned . . . his forces to repair and rebuild certain roads." Chamion looked to Vaelora and then to Quaeryt.

"That is true," said Quaeryt.

"All of the roads that have been repaired are on the west side of the river," Chamion said blandly.

"The west side of the river is where the greatest part of the damage from the battle occurred," replied Quaeryt. "I would note, however, that the repairs included replacement of both the Nord and Sud Bridges. Those bridges serve both sides of the river."

"A number of factors and tradespeople are concerned that the better roads on the west side will affect them adversely."

How could they possibly tell this soon? Quaeryt

smiled and said, "The other reason for rebuilding those roads was to provide adequate access to the isle of piers. Lord Bhayar has decided that the isle should be turned to practical purposes, rather than remaining a useless eyesore."

"Might I ask those purposes?"

"For the time being, two of the old warehouses are being converted to barracks so that fewer of Lord Bhayar's forces will be required to impose on the people of Bovaria for quarters."

"Ah . . . I see. But only two barracks?"

"No city was built in a day, honored Councilor," interjected Vaelora smoothly. "Nor can all the repairs created by war be made as quickly as one might like." She paused. "What was it, exactly, that you wished to bring to our attention?"

"Some . . . have suggested that an improvement of the east river road might demonstrate Lord Bhayar's concerns for the people of Variana."

Quaeryt managed a puzzled expression. "I thought those who live on the west bank of the River Aluse were within the city of Variana. Have we misunderstood something?"

"Oh, no. That is true. But . . ." Chamion frowned. "It is difficult to explain . . ."

"Do try," suggested Vaelora warmly. "We would not wish to do something or fail to do something through lack of understanding."

Quaeryt managed not to smile as he waited for the councilor to reply.

"Most of the city, and most of its people, lies east of the river. They do not see or encounter improvements across the river."

"I can see that," acknowledged Quaeryt, "but almost

all the damage to the city occurred west of the river. That is why Lord Bhayar's forces have been busy repairing things there."

"I understand that, Lady . . . Commander. Still . . ."

"You feel that at least some gesture, some improvement, on the east side of the river would be beneficial? Is that it?" asked Quaeryt.

"Precisely. Precisely."

"Such as a portion of the east river road?" asked Vaelora.

"That would be helpful . . . although . . ."

"At present, it will be difficult even to rebuild a section of the east river road opposite the isle of piers," Quaeryt said mildly.

"The Council had hoped . . ."

"We all hope, Councilor," said Vaelora, her voice warm, "but there is much to do. Improving a serviceable road, alas, must often wait until those areas that need roads and have none are satisfied. Or for repairs on those roads required for Lord Bhayar and his forces to be completed."

"Still . . ." pressed Chamion, his deep raspy voice taking on almost a whining tone.

"We will look into it," promised Quaeryt, "and see what is possible."

"I suppose that is all that can be done."

"For now," replied Quaeryt, "unless, of course, the Council wishes to undertake such a project."

"With the state of the Council's finances . . . that is not possible. That is why we came to Lord Bhayar."

"We appreciate the Council's faith in Lord Bhayar," replied Vaelora, her voice still warm. "We will do what is possible when it is possible."

Quaeryt image-projected warmth, as well as the sense

that it was time for Chamion to depart, then stepped forward. "We do hope it will not be too long before we see you and your wife again."

Once he had escorted Chamion out of the study and closed the door, Quaeryt dropped his smile and turned back toward Vaelora. "They're like leeches . . . all of them."

"That reminds me," said Vaelora. "There's also a dispatch from Subcommander Ernyld to you. I didn't open it."

Quaeryt walked to the desk and picked up the envelope, addressed to "Ministry of Supply and Administration, Commander Quaeryt," then reached for his belt knife. "You could have opened it."

"Me? A mere woman? When it was addressed to you?"

"It was addressed to the ministry, with my name penned almost as an afterthought."

"Even less would I wish to open it."

"You don't care for the subcommander?"

"I've never met him."

"Then why—"

"Deucalon chose him."

Quaeryt decided not to pursue that line of inquiry, slit open the envelope, and began to read. After skimming the brief courtesies, he centered his attention on the second paragraph.

As you doubtless know, Lord Bhayar has made it most clear that the armies of Telaryn should purchase supplies and not seize them. We are to seek the most favorable prices. It has become clear, however, that, unlike elsewhere, near Variana there is only one price from all merchants and factors for most basic goods. This seems

*most unreasonable, and far too dear for the forces of
the Lord of Telaryn and Bovaria . . . hoping that the
Ministry of Supply might be of assistance in this
matter . . .*

*With the implication that we aren't of much use if we
can't.* Quaeryt finished reading the letter, then turned
to Vaelora. "Ernyld's complaining about the prices he
has to pay to provision the armies, but he never says
what the prices are. Do you have any idea what they're
paying for goods like flour, potatoes, mutton, and the
like?"

"No. We've just been getting simple reports on the
total amount spent on a weekly basis for flour, mutton,
root vegetables. With everything else . . ."

"I'll have to go inquire of his clerks, then. We can't
complain about prices until we know what they are."

"You don't want to send a message?"

"The clerks will tell me the real costs."

"You don't trust Ernyld any more than I do."

"Did I ever say otherwise?' After a moment he added,
"I'd best deal with this now."

"Better you than me, dearest."

"Thank you."

"You're most welcome."

They exchanged smiles before Quaeryt donned his visor cap and left the study.

As he walked back to the chateau stables, Quaeryt had
to search his memory for the prices Skarpa's forces had
paid for similar goods in Extela. After a moment he recalled that the High Holders had wanted at least a gold a
barrel for flour, but the price had been eight silvers before
the eruption, and that had been in spring in the north.

Two quints later, at the headquarters holding,

Quaeryt found Zhelan outside the dilapidated stables that held first company's mounts.

"Zhelan . . . I need your help, again . . ."

"Sir?"

"Have you been able to purchase grain and flour for first company and Eleventh Regiment?"

"I did, sir, until Subcommander Ernyld requested that we requisition that through his clerks. Saved us silvers, because the Northern Army pays for it, and not you."

"What were you paying?"

"Grain . . . less than a copper a barrel . . . flour . . . was running around six silvers, likely be higher now . . ."

Quaeryt listened, then asked, "Where are Ernyld's supply clerks?"

"They're in the rooms at the far end of the second stable."

"Do you know the name of the head clerk?"

"No, sir." A puzzled expression crossed the major's face, but he did not offer a question.

"Apparently, the marshal is having difficulty with local factors. I'm supposed to look into it, but Subcommander Ernyld failed to supply details. I thought it might be useful to gather that information myself."

"I see, sir."

Although Zhelan's voice was even, Quaeryt could see the amusement in the major's eyes. "Not a word, Major."

"No, sir."

"Good." Quaeryt grinned, then turned and headed for the far stables.

The stables were indeed distant—close to a third of a mille from the main courtyard of the holding—and Quaeryt was sweating considerably in the late spring sunlight by the time he opened the battered ironbound door to the domain of the supply clerks.

A young ranker looked up from the narrow table just inside the door. "Commander, sir?"

"Commander Quaeryt. I'm here to see the head clerk. Who might that be?"

"Senior Squad Leader Alylor, sir."

"If you'd escort me." Quaeryt projected absolute authority and certainty.

"Ah . . . yes, sir."

At the table in the far corner of the room sat a graying senior squad leader, with several ledgers before him. His eyes followed Quaeryt as he approached, and he finally stood.

"Commander . . . ?"

"Commander Quaeryt."

"Oh, yes, sir. What can I do for you?"

"I need some information from you in order to follow up on a request by Subcommander Ernyld." The sound of a door closing behind Quaeryt suggested that the young ranker who had escorted him—or someone else—had hurried out the front door as soon as he could. *Doubtless to let someone know that a strange commander is querying the clerks.*

"Sir?"

"Lord Bhayar has asked me to assist in dealing with factors and suppliers who appear to be unwilling to supply provisions except at, shall we say, questionably high prices. To do this, I need the names of those factors, and the recent prices." Quaeryt smiled politely at the head clerk.

"Sir . . . this is . . . unusual."

"Anything involved with Lord Bhayar usually is. It is also generally urgent." Quaeryt smiled once more.

"We could certainly supply that, sir."

"Excellent. I'll wait while you or one of your clerks write down what I need."

"Now, sir?"

"What better time? I can't solve the problem without the information. You have the information. You write it down, and I get on with resolving matters."

"This is unusual."

"I believe you said that before."

"Yes, sir."

A quint later, Senior Squad Leader Alylor handed Quaeryt a short listing. "These are the prices we've been paying for the last month. In a moment Forawal will finish the listing of the factors with whom we've been dealing." Alylor's eyes flicked toward the door. "Oh . . . Subcommander Ernyld is here."

Quaeryt neither turned nor rose until Ernyld was almost upon him. Then he stood and smiled politely.

"Commander Quaeryt . . . I hadn't expected to find you here among the clerks." Ernyld offered a wide smile in return, and one as false as warm sunlight in Ianus.

"I've been following up on your request for assistance in obtaining a fair price for provisions."

"We should talk about it in my study."

"We should indeed," agreed Quaeryt. "After I finish here. It shouldn't take long." He image-projected friendly warmth.

For a long moment Ernyld said nothing. Then he nodded. "My study is above the main stable. Take the end outside staircase."

"I'll be there after I get the second list from your clerks."

"Splendid!" Ernyld's smile was clearly forced.

Alylor's eyes followed the subcommander's departure.

"The second list?" prompted Quaeryt.

"Oh . . . yes. Let me see if Forawal has finished it." Alylor rose and scuttled to the other side of the study filled with clerks, tables, and ledgers.

Shortly he returned. "The first sheet is that of the factors with whom we have placed large orders. The second are those used but occasionally, usually for items of smaller quantities."

Items for the marshal's personal mess, most likely. "Thank you." Taking the small sheaf of papers, Quaeryt stepped away from the desk. "I do appreciate your courtesy and haste."

"We do try to please, Commander."

"Lord Bhayar will appreciate that." With a last polite smile, Quaeryt turned, left the clerks' study, and began the walk back to the main courtyard.

Quaeryt could sense Ernyld's agitation from the doorway to the study of the chief of staff, but he said nothing as he entered and took a chair across the table from the subcommander. Then he smiled and said, "Your clerks were most helpful."

"I had not expected such . . . an immediate response. I would have been pleased to have supplied the figures you needed without your having to take your valuable time to come and obtain it."

"I am most certain you would have been," said Quaeryt. "But, having been a princeps and a governor, I knew exactly what information I needed, and I would not wish the marshal to pay a silver more than required any longer than necessary. Lord Bhayar's coffers are not endless, and maintaining thirty regiments far from Solis is costly."

"That is true, but at times . . . perhaps not in this instance . . . failing to follow the chain of command can lead to misunderstandings."

"You are most correct about that," replied Quaeryt. "But this is one of those instances. The marshal, I know from experience, believes that certain accomplishments need be done in a most timely fashion, and your dispatch suggested that this was one of those times."

"Ah . . . yes. He was most concerned."

Most concerned to make the Ministry of Administration and Supply look slow and unresponsive. "You can convey to him that we will be taking matters to the factors once we have made a quick investigation."

"Might I ask . . ." At the look on Quaeryt's face, Ernyld said quickly, "I suppose not."

Quaeryt rose. "Once we have looked into the matter, I will let you know." He could feel the subcommander's eyes on his back as he left and walked down the outside stairs and made his way to where the gelding was tied.

Two quints later, he was back at the Chateau Regis talking to Vaelora.

"I've only glanced over the prices Ernyld is paying, but they look to be too high by one or two parts in ten. I didn't tell him that because—"

"He'll want you to do better than that . . . and he'll take the credit."

"He will anyway. I'll have to meet with the factors' council."

"They're restricting supplies like the factors in Laaryn did, aren't they?"

"Most likely," replied Quaeryt. "People don't change the way they do business unless they can make more golds or unless their lives or their businesses are in danger. That seems to be especially true here in Bovaria."

"There's one other matter," said Vaelora. "I was about to tell you, before the councilor arrived, that several factors who are located south of the Sud Bridge on the west river road sent a petition—"

"And they want the paved section extended to their factorages and warehouses? Preferably yesterday?"

"Of course."

"And before long, those north of the Nord Bridge will be asking for the same. And if we manage to rebuild some of the east river road, then whoever isn't served by the new good road will be complaining that they're left out." Quaeryt shook his head. "I thought the High Holders in Montagne were bad, but the more I encounter the factors of Bovaria . . ."

"They really haven't been ruled in generations. Not effectively."

"No. All Kharst wanted was his palaces and privileges." *And his way with women, whether they were willing or not.* "We'll have to change that, I think."

Vaelora nodded, but there was a sadness to her small smile.

25

After they had dined on Jeudi evening, alone in the "small" family dining chamber of the Chateau Regis, a chamber a good ten yards by six, at one end of a table that could have easily seated half a score, Quaeryt and Vaelora repaired to their quarters on the upper level.

In the dim illumination of twilight, Quaeryt found himself pacing back and forth in front of the windows in the sitting room.

"What is it now, dearest?"

"I can't help it," Quaeryt said. "Every time I think about the Bovarian factors, or the High Holders of Montagne, I get angry."

"Because all they think about is how many golds they can amass without counting the cost to others?"

"That's part of it. But only part. Once they saw that the imagers could repair and improve roads, everyone wanted their road improved . . . as if the imagers had little else to do."

"They see what they see. To them, it takes little time, and they think it is easy."

"They only think it is easy. They don't see that a moment of imaging can leave an imager so exhausted he can do nothing for a glass . . . or a day."

"Or for weeks," added Vaelora softly.

"They don't see the thousands of deaths it cost to strengthen and perfect those skills. They don't see all the imagers who died all across Lydar for generations because they were different. They don't see the imagers who died because they couldn't do enough or tried to do too much." *Like Akoryt and Shaelyt.*

"They don't see how many nights you do not sleep or sleep badly," added Vaelora. "They ignore the white hair, and the fingers you cannot move. Or that your bad leg troubles you more."

"Are they all so greedy?" Quaeryt paused. "Are we greedy as well? And do not see it because we only see what we wish to see?"

"There are those who are greedy and those who are less so."

"Rholan said something about that," mused Quaeryt. "I don't remember exactly how he put it."

"Do you want me to find it?"

"You might as well." *I'm too agitated to settle down.* Vaelora rose and walked into the bedchamber.

Quaeryt stopped pacing and looked out the window to the south. With the spring had come greenery, and most of the scars of the previous fall's battle had either been removed by the imagers, by Bhayar's forces, or been muted by the growth of grasses and bushes. Yet, for a moment, Quaeryt saw a land covered in ice, with everything in sight white, even though he had not ever actually seen that. *Only felt it . . . and endless ice within you.*

Vaelora returned, holding the small leatherbound volume. "Would you like me to read it?"

"If you would." He turned from the window and looked upon her, taking in once more the warmth that infused her, despite all she had been through . . . because of him.

She cleared her throat and began.

"Rholan claimed to be ambitious, but not greedy. He insisted that the distinction between ambition and greed was simple enough. Ambition was the setting of desired and fixed achievements and striving to accomplish them, while greed was the unending quest for more of whatever was desired, with no end in sight. Yet . . . what is the difference between a greedy man and one who, after establishing his one set of goals and achieving them, immediately determines upon another and greater set of achievements? Is there any difference? When asked this question once, Rholan simply said, 'Knowledge,' and refused to discuss the subject more. That was a practice he often used when he did not wish to defend a position that might have revealed any weakness on his part . . ."

Vaelora looked up. "There's more, but it's about his stubbornness."

"Thank you, dear one. That's the part I was thinking about," Quaeryt said. "At least by Rholan's definition, you and I aren't greedy. Excessively ambitious, perhaps." He paused. "I don't do that, do I?"

"Do what?"

"Retreat behind a fortress of one-word cryptic statements."

Vaelora laughed softly and warmly, closing the book as she did. "Never with me."

"Are you saying I deluge you with words and ideas?"

"Sometimes. Sometimes I have done so with you."

"Especially in your letters. I still read them."

"I know. It pleases me."

"You please me."

"Then let us talk of other matters than of greed and golds, of power and pride."

"Such as?"

"Will you have gardens upon Imagisle? Fountains to cool the air on long summer days?"

"You've seen the plans. There will be gardens and greens, and there will be fountains, and places for children to run and play . . ."

Vaelora eased onto the settee. "Sit beside me. Tell me more."

Quaeryt walked from the window and seated himself beside her. "I can only tell you of what I dream, for little beyond the roads and three buildings is there now."

"Then tell me dreams, dearest . . ."

26

On Vendrei, Quaeryt was up early, and waiting in Bhayar's study when the Lord of Telaryn entered.

"What disaster is about to befall us?" asked Bhayar sardonically.

"Why do you ask?"

"For you to be here well before seventh glass . . . it must be urgent."

"Not urgent. Merely troublesome." Quaeryt pointed to the conference table. "I need your seal and signature on these."

"For what?"

"To deal with Bovarian factors, and possibly High Holders, in order to keep them from demanding prices that are excessively high, particularly in selling provisions to your armies, and so that I don't have to do something to them that all of us might regret."

"You will . . . and I will anyway, no doubt."

"There are two documents. One for me, and the other for Vaelora. Each requires your seal, and each states that we are empowered to act in your name, as full ministers, in matters of administration and supply within the boundaries of Bovaria for the purpose of dealing with matters of import in administration and in obtaining any and all supplies necessary for the needs of Lord

Bhayar, including but not limited to those required for the maintaining of forces or officials in the pursuit of law and order."

"You think they'll suffice?" Bhayar walked to the table and picked up one of the documents. "Without the threat of force?"

"They'll make a veiled threat more veiled and thus more palatable. If nothing else, they'll provide a rationale for punishing someone for not obeying."

"Always useful," said Bhayar dryly. "Why does Vaelora need one?"

"To do the same when you've sent me somewhere— like to Rivages to see why you haven't heard from Submarshal Myskyl."

"We'll wait a few days."

"As you command, sir."

"Don't press it, my friend."

"No, sir."

"I suppose another signature or two won't raise significantly more problems than you've already created." Bhayar sat down and signed one document, then the other. "Is there anything else?"

"Besides the fact that every factor in Variana wants a new road to his front door?"

Bhayar laughed. "I'll leave the determination on which roads are built where to the Ministry of Administration and Supply for Bovaria."

"That might be for the best."

After exchanging pleasantries with Bhayar, Quaeryt left the study and walked down to the ministry studies, where he bestowed Vaelora's certificate to her. "Your personal authorization to browbeat High Holders and factors."

"I'm overwhelmed."

"That makes two of us. I'm going to meet with the head of the factors' council this afternoon . . . if he's in."

"You aren't sending word?"

"No. I don't want to leave the impression with Ernyld, and Deucalon, that we're not acting immediately on his problem. If the chief factor's not in, I'll just leave an invitation for him to visit us on Lundi. The kind he'd be foolish to ignore."

"You're acting like a governor again."

"I don't think I did in Montagne . . . as I recall everyone telling me. This time . . . I'll try to do it with polite meetings and a veiled approach." *Not that your approach in Extela was in the slightest veiled.*

"You can't veil the power you hold, dearest."

"No . . . but I can give them the chance to be reasonable."

"Some will force the issue."

"I hope not. I really don't want to make too many examples."

"You may not be able to avoid it."

At that moment, there was a knock on the study door. "Amalyt D'Anomen to see you, Lady and sir."

"The chorister at the Anomen Regis?" murmured Vaelora.

Quaeryt nodded to her, then said, "Have him come in."

Amalyt, white-haired and as tanned as when Quaeryt had seen him nearly half a year before, stepped into the study. His lined face bore an expression that Quaeryt might have called stern but kindly . . . had he not already met the chorister. Amalyt's gray vestments, unsurprisingly, were of a far higher quality than those worn by Gauswn.

"Greetings, honored chorister," offered Quaeryt.

"Greetings to you, Lady Vaelora, and you, Commander."

"What brings you?" asked Quaeryt.

"You may recall that Lord Bhayar was kind enough to employ his imagers to repair and rebuild the Anomen Regis . . ."

Quaeryt managed to smile politely, although that was difficult, since he had been the one to arrange for and oversee the repair. "I do indeed."

"It has been brought to my attention that the Anomen D'Variana, located near the River Aluse, also suffered damage, if not so grievous, as a result of the battle of Variana . . ."

"And?" Quaeryt kept his voice pleasant.

"The imagers did such a good job in restoring the Anomen Regis that I naturally thought that they should be considered to repair the Anomen D'Variana."

"I see." Quaeryt kept his voice pleasantly neutral.

"It would appear that they are not unduly occupied."

"Actually, they've been quite occupied, chorister, and there are only half the number of imagers here in Variana that there were when they repaired your anomen."

"Still . . . it should not take that long."

"All I can promise is that we will look into the possibilities."

Amalyt looked from Quaeryt to Vaelora. "Lady . . . if you might intercede. The faithful would appreciate any assistance."

"I fear, Chorister Amalyt, that what Commander Quaeryt has told you is quite true. The number of imagers is limited, and the tasks assigned to them already will take some considerable time."

And one of the precepts of the Nameless is for those who can to make the best efforts they can, for the Name-

less helps best those who help themselves. Quaeryt kept that thought to himself, recalling all too well how intransigent the chorister could be.

Amalyt offered a heavy sigh. "Chorister Bryal will be most discouraged. We had so hoped." He paused. "I would not wish to have to be the one to tell Bryal that Lord Bhayar could offer no encouragement."

"You do not have to tell Chorister Bryal anything," replied Quaeryt, "save that you have brought the matter to Lord Bhayar's attention. There are many demands upon him and upon his men and resources."

"That is so, but I would have hoped, especially with your scholarship and knowledge of the Nameless . . ."

"As Rholan once said," replied Quaeryt, "to imply or to seek the favor or lack of favor on the part of the Nameless to obtain a human goal or end is in itself a form of Naming."

Amalyt's eyes hardened.

"We will look into the matter," Vaelora promised, gently.

"I do hope it will be soon, Lady."

Vaelora smiled warmly. "We will do what we can."

Neither Quaeryt nor Vaelora spoke until the study door was firmly closed behind the departing chorister.

"If we don't do something," Quaeryt said, "he'll spread the word that the imagers are creatures of the Namer, or something like it."

"And that Lord Bhayar cares little about the anomens of Variana." Vaelora gave the smallest of headshakes. "I've only seen him twice, but there's something about him . . . like he's a creature of the Namer."

"You haven't had another farsight?"

"No. Only the one about you being surrounded by something."

"You can't tell me more?"

"No. You were in light and then suddenly trapped in total darkness."

Quaeryt almost shivered. He'd never liked confined quarters . . . ever. "Why do you feel that way about Amalyt?"

"It's a feeling."

"He's definitely a hypocrite. The richness of his vestments alone proclaims that."

"He's worse than that. I couldn't tell you why."

"He's likely to be the first of many. The way matters are going, everyone with any degree of power is going to come through that door asking for the imagers to do this or that. If we say no, because they're involved with something else . . ."

"They'll claim Bhayar doesn't care . . . or the imagers are too proud to help anyone."

"I think we're just going to have to tell them all that the imagers have nowhere permanent to live, and that until they have time to build their own quarters, they'll only be available for the most urgent of tasks—such as replacing failing bridges across the River Aluse. Or something equally vital."

"What will you do about the Anomen D'Variana?"

"I'll send Baelthm to look at it. Then we'll figure out what we can do. It might only need moderate repairs."

"It needs more than that," said Vaelora. "Chamion wouldn't be here begging, otherwise."

Quaeryt had no doubts that she was likely correct.

For the next several glasses, he and Vaelora worked, with more than a few interruptions, to finish the changes to the proposed code of laws, which now included a section on factors. Then Quaeryt went over the simple supply reports from Ernyld's clerks in an effort to get a better feel and understanding of the supply problems. Then he wrote out a shorter version of one of Alylor's lists.

A little before noon, he rode out from Chateau Regis, heading along the road toward the Nord Bridge, accompanied by four rankers, the smallest number that seemed appropriate for a commander and a minister. He also carried full imaging shields, both to maintain his abilities and with the awareness that after what had happened to Skarpa there was always the possibility, however small, that he could be a target.

The sky was overcast, unlike the previous days, and a cool, almost chill, wind blew out of the northwest, where in the distance Quaeryt could see darker clouds, but the gray clouds overhead were high enough that he didn't expect rain immediately. Whether the rain would hold off until he was back at the Chateau Regis was another question.

While people on the street glanced at him, taking in the uniform of a Telaryn officer, the looks were almost cursory—as they had been in most places in Bovaria after the initial shock of seeing Telaryn forces had passed. *Almost,* mused Quaeryt, *as if who ruled mattered far less than how they rule.* Or perhaps the apparent attitudes of people reflected a fatalistic feeling that Bhayar and his troopers couldn't possibly be any worse than what they had endured under Rex Kharst and his sire. There did seem to be more vendors and people along the north road, but whether that was because of the improvements to the road or simply because life was getting back to a normal fashion was something Quaeryt had no way of telling.

Had he not made inquiries he might well have dismissed the modest structure situated on the corner of the east river road and an unnamed lane just past the Hotel D'Variana, which looked less imposing than many inns he had encountered over the past two years. He reined up outside the small two-story building, dismounted, and handed the gelding's reins to the nearest ranker.

"I hope not to be too long, but one never knows . . ."

"We'll be here, sir."

Quaeryt strode toward the door, almost stumbling as his left boot heel caught the top riser of the three stone steps leading to the entry. He caught himself, opened the door, and stepped into a small and low-ceilinged entry hall.

The clerk seated behind a narrow table in the middle of the hall looked up as Quaeryt walked toward him. His eyes widened as he took in the uniform and Quaeryt. "Sir?"

"Commander Quaeryt. I'm also Minister of Administration and Supply for Lord Bhayar. I'm here to see Factor Chaekyr."

"Is he . . . expecting you?"

"I hope not, but he will wish to see me." Quaeryt projected a sense of authority.

"I will tell him you're here, sir." The clerk rose and headed for the door at the right side of the hall, through which he disappeared after opening and closing it barely enough to squeeze through.

Quaeryt waited, not terribly long, but enough to observe a fly making several circuits around the table that the clerk had hastily vacated, before the clerk returned.

"Factor Chaekyr will be happy to see you, sir."

Happy? I think not. "Thank you." Quaeryt nodded and made his way to the door that had been left just slightly ajar, stepping through it, and closing it behind himself.

Chaekyr D'Factorius had dark brown wavy hair, pale and watery green eyes, and a full square-cut beard of a shade redder than his hair. He looked to be roughly ten years older than Quaeryt as he rose from behind a broad and empty polished wooden desk that was likely older than Quaeryt.

"What can I do for you, Commander? Or is it 'Minister'?"

"It's both, but 'Commander' will do for now. I'm here to discuss the price of flour and other supplies." Quaeryt gestured for Chaekyr to sit, then sat down in the left chair of the two facing the head of the factors' council of Variana.

Chaekyr frowned. "I don't see what that has to do with me. Prices are set by each individual factor, not by the council."

"Once . . . I would have thought that as well." Quaeryt smiled politely. "I doubt you know this, but I served as the princeps to Governor Straesyr of Tilbor. The princeps deals with matters of commerce. Then I was appointed governor of Montagne. The war came along, and Lord Bhayar needed my talents in that fashion. Recently, Lady Vaelora and I concluded a mission to Khel. Along the way, we encountered, shall we say, a misunderstanding about grain and flour shipments from Laaryn, and I had to investigate how prices were set . . ." Quaeryt looked directly at Chaekyr. "Now, I find, as was the case in Laaryn, that every factor who supplies grain and flour, as well as other items, sets his price at exactly the same level as any other factor, and that price is far higher than it was before or during the war. Some of that, obviously, occurs because we are farther from last year's harvest. That, I understand. A gold and two silvers for a barrel of flour, I don't. Especially when it appears that others pay lower prices." That was a calculated guess on Quaeryt's part, but it fit the patterns he'd seen.

"I cannot tell others at what price . . ."

"Head factor . . ." Quaeryt said mildly, but projecting authority. "I am merely suggesting that those factors who attempt to obtain excessive prices for goods traded at lower prices to those besides Lord Bhayar's forces are acting most unwisely, particularly since it appears most likely Lord Bhayar and his successors will be ruling Variana for many, many years."

"What do you expect of me, Commander?"

"Expect? From what I have thus far seen of factors here . . . very little. But . . . if a chief factor were wise, truly wise, he might explain to other factors that pursuing excessive gains in the short run might lead to changes that they would find most . . . unsatisfactory in the long run. And if prices remain high, it is possible that the long run will arrive rather soon."

"I still do not see . . ."

Quaeryt smiled again, tired as he was of the game. "As Minister of Administration and Supply for Bovaria, with Lord Bhayar's approval, I can issue laws affecting commerce and trade. I would prefer not to. Lord Bhayar would also prefer that, but that preference will change if he finds that his forces are paying higher prices than others. The laws will change, and those who break the laws will find themselves broken. There is at least one factor in Laaryn sentenced to death for his failures. Now . . . it would seem that such unpleasantness is unnecessary . . . unless greed cannot be restrained by your factors."

Chaekyr took out a large white kerchief and blotted his forehead. "Rather warm in here, I find."

"It could be much warmer."

"I take your point, Commander. You understand that I can only pass on your words."

"I do indeed. I also understand that the chief factor can be most persuasive . . . or he would not be chief factor."

"Not always so persuasive, I fear, as some think."

"That is also true." Quaeryt shrugged. "But replacing a chief factor who offers good counsel with one who would refuse to see what well might occur would suggest that greater . . . oversight of the factors might well be necessary." He extended a sheet of paper. "This is a listing of those factors who provided identical prices to Lord Bhayar's forces. We would not be so concerned about the fact that the prices were similar, because prices in trade do tend to gather around the same level . . . but when they are identical and excessive for but one buyer . . ."

"I see your point, Commander, and I will endeavor to convey that to the factors in question . . . as well as others."

"For now . . . I can ask no more. I look forward to your success." Quaeryt smiled a last time, then rose, nodding to Chaekyr before turning and leaving.

On the ride back to the Chateau Regis, Quaeryt shook his head more than once in thinking over his meeting with Chaekyr. While he'd been more diplomatic in dealing with the chief factor than he had been in Montagne, he had no doubts that he'd come across as less than tactful to the politely slimy factors of Variana. *How can you be tactful to men whose only god is not the Nameless but the pursuit of golds at any cost to anyone but themselves? Without a resort to force on your part, or the threat of it, nothing will change their conduct and practices.*

Quaeryt had barely dismounted in the courtyard of the Chateau Regis when an older ranker limped forward toward him.

"Commander, sir . . . Lord Bhayar would see you immediately in his study."

"Thank you. I'm on my way." *Now what?*

For the first time in weeks, Quaeryt actually found Bhayar seated behind his desk. The lord motioned for Quaeryt to sit down.

"You requested me?"

"Where were you? With the imagers?"

"No. I was meeting with the chief factor of the factors' council of Variana about excessive prices charged to Deucalon by local factors."

"And?"

"I was more diplomatic. I suggested that he might persuade the factors to be reasonable, but that you have little patience for greed at the expense of your forces."

"If he doesn't?"

"I'll have to be more direct."

Bhayar nodded. "There's a High Holder's widow who wants to see me. It's something about inheritances and the like. See if you can resolve it. She's in the small audience room."

"Along the lines we discussed?"

"Just don't go farther."

"I won't."

"Good." Bhayar waved Quaeryt away.

Quaeryt made his way across the hall and down two doors, where another ranker opened the door for him.

"Good afternoon, Commander." The ranker inclined his head.

"The same to you."

The blond woman seated in one of the chairs at the side of the chamber rose immediately as Quaeryt entered. A momentary frown passed across her brow and then vanished.

"Good afternoon, Lady." Quaeryt stopped a yard or so from the woman and studied her.

She was tall, if not quite so tall as Vaelora, and fair-skinned, with penetrating gray eyes, although those eyes had dark circles under them. Quaeryt judged her to be roughly his age. She wore a tailored black skirt, a dark silver-gray blouse, and a black jacket that matched the ankle-length skirt that showed polished riding boots. Her hair was drawn back from her face.

"You're not Lord Bhayar. Who are you?"

"I'm Commander Quaeryt. He asked me to meet with you. You are?"

"What can you do about High Holder inheritances?" Her tone was somewhere between angry and resigned.

Quaeryt also detected a strong accent in her Bovarian that he could not immediately place. He replied in Tellan. "I can see that whatever your difficulty may be is either addressed or not."

"Or not?"

Quaeryt smiled and waited.

"Oh . . . I'm sorry. I'm Tyrena D'Ryel. At least for the moment." Her Tellan—and her name—suggested several things.

"You are the widow of High Holder Ryel, the late

minister of waterways and the reputed spymaster of Rex Kharst?"

"Not reputed. All Bovaria appeared to know that." Her voice was firm.

"You are concerned about the holding . . . and what will become of it . . . and you?" Quaeryt reverted to Bovarian.

"In my place, would you not be?" she replied in her lightly accented Bovarian.

"In your position, especially, Lady, I would be most concerned." Quaeryt paused. "Almost as concerned as if you had . . . written critiques of military commanders in books."

"I'm certain I have no idea what you're talking about, Commander."

"Did the jewels and golds provide a sufficient dowry for Ryel?" Quaeryt asked gently. "Or was it the enticement of a holding sufficiently distant from Variana . . . and from Rhecyrd, Khanara?"

"Will you drag me before Bhayar in chains, more than twelve years later?"

Quaeryt admired the cool calm in her voice, not to mention the fact that she refused to dissemble or plead.

"I have no intention of doing such. Nor, at this point, does anyone in the Chateau Regis, including Bhayar, know who you are."

"What do you want, then? Favors?"

Quaeryt smiled. "No. Answers from you to see what is possible. Do you have children?"

"What does that matter?"

"Please answer the question."

"I have a daughter."

"From Ryel, so far as anyone knows?"

"She is his."

"Is she the only blood heir?"

"So far as I know. Ryel doubtless had other offspring, but that was a matter he kept to himself."

"How old is she?"

"Iryena is nine."

"You are telling me the truth?" Quaeryt image-projected both authority and the sense that lying would be fatal.

While Tyrena paled, she did not move. "I am. Would that I were not."

"Good. You are to write a petition to Lord Bhayar stating that you are the lawful widow of High Holder Ryel D'Alte and that you wish to act as guardian and administrator of the holding for his daughter Iryena D'Alte until she is of age to marry a man suitable to become High Holder and approved by Lord Bhayar." After a pause, Quaeryt said, "This is not a ploy to put you off. If you wish to write that petition here and now, in the study of the Ministry of Administration below, I will wait until you have finished, and then I will write a writ for Lord Bhayar's signature which will affirm your guardianship and the finding that the holding and lands of Ryel will remain with your daughter and her offspring."

"Why are you doing this?"

"It is best for Lydar that you did not inherit Tilbor, and it is also best for Lydar and Bovaria that you retain Ryel."

"What, really, do you want?"

"If you can provide it, any information on Submarshal Myskyl and what has happened to his regiments. I will approve your petition, regardless, but that would be helpful."

"You are not a mere commander."

"Nor are you a mere widow, Lady Tyrena."

"I did not expect this."

"Nor I. About the Telaryn forces in the north?"

"The submarshal has visited many of the high holdings near Rivages, including Ryel. He went over it like
a tariff collector, and he demanded a hundred golds as
a token tariff. My . . . husband was most careful in not
displaying his wealth . . ."

"Especially since he had less of it than was sufficient
for his aims?"

"Yes. That worked in our favor. The submarshal has
settled his forces at other holdings. He has made Fiancryt his headquarters. Some of that might be because
Lady Fiancryt was widowed, without heirs, and is said
to be modestly attractive."

"What else can you tell me?"

"It is said that the submarshal has met with many
High Holders over the course of the fall and winter, and
has neither attacked nor dispossessed any of them.
He has imposed the same tariff of one hundred golds
on all."

"Has he sent regiments any distance from Rivages?"

"No. He has sent small parties to towns. His officers
have met with the wealthier factors, but the factors have
said little. His regiments drill and conduct maneuvers
almost every day. He is keeping his forces ready. That
is clear."

"Does he have visitors that seem . . . unusual?"

"That . . . I would not know. It seemed better not to
be unduly interested."

"Why do you say that?"

"I have no facts, only feelings."

Feelings from a woman who had effectively

ruled Tilbor for a time suggested more than mere emotion. Quaeryt frowned. "Did not Rex Kharst have imagers?"

"Ryel said he did. I never saw or met them."

"Do you know what happened to them?"

"I thought they were killed with the others in the battle here."

"Is there anything else you can tell me about Submarshal Myskyl?"

"Only that I would not trust those whom he seems to trust among the High Holders. Although . . ." she paused, "he is said to be most careful of those who enter his presence, and he is said to receive them always in the same small study at Fiancryt."

Quaeryt asked a number of other questions, but it was clear Tyrena had told him all that she knew about Myskyl's operations and maneuvers. Then he asked, "When the submarshal visited Ryel, was he unpleasant?"

"No. He introduced himself, then merely ignored me as much as he could."

"As Rhecyrd did in years past?"

"How did you know that?"

"I spent a little time as princeps of Tilbor," Quaeryt admitted. "One of the sisters mentioned it."

"They talked to you?"

"They believe I did them a service, righted a wrong."

"Did you?"

"What I did in that instance righted several wrongs, I believe, theirs among them. It had to do with an unfaithful commander of the Khanar's Guard, or rather his son." Quaeryt smiled. "Shall we go down to the ministry studies so that you can write your petition?"

Tyrena stiffened. "How will you treat the widows of other High Holders?"

"In a similar fashion to you—with the possible exception of one or two whose husband's acts may merit the loss of the holding."

"Such charity." Her words were dubious.

"Practical. Lord Bhayar would prefer not to dwell on the past. He will be most severe to those who do not pledge allegiance, pay their tariffs, and support his rule. Shall we go?" Quaeryt gestured toward the door.

When they reached the ministry study, Quaeryt opened the door and escorted Tyrena inside. Vaelora rose from her desk, an expression that held puzzlement and amusement.

"Lady Tyrena D'Ryel, might I present you to Lady Vaelora Chayardyr, the other Minister of Administration . . . and also my wife."

Tyrena glanced from Vaelora and then back to Quaeryt.

"She needs to use the conference table to write a petition to Bhayar so that he can approve her guardianship of her daughter until she is of age to marry."

"She may use my desk if she wishes," said Vaelora, easing away from her desk.

"Chayardyr? You're . . . a sister of Lord Bhayar?"

"I am."

"He let you marry . . ."

"No," replied Vaelora. "He ordered us to wed." Vaelora looked to Quaeryt.

"I will leave you ladies." He looked to Tyrena. "Did you leave retainers somewhere?"

"They are waiting in the main entry."

"I will let them know that it will be a time before you

return." He nodded and left the study, not without wondering what might transpire.

Once away from the two, he walked swiftly to the main entry, where he found two guards and an older woman. "Lady Tyrena is meeting with Lord Bhayar's sister at the moment. It may be a glass or so before she returns."

All three nodded.

Quaeryt left them and returned to the clerks' study, where he spent a quint going over the summary reports from Deucalon. There was no mention of expenditures by Myskyl. Quaeryt hadn't expected any entries, but there was always the possibility.

Then he returned to the study that held the two ladies.

Vaelora immediately said, "I had Lady Tyrena add a few items to her petition. I thought that, should she remarry, the lands would still go to her daughter."

"That shouldn't be a problem . . ."

"You need to sign next to me," added Vaelora.

At the end of the petition, beneath Tyrena's signature, was a single sentence that bore Vaelora's perfect penning: "Approval of the petition of Lady Tyrena D'Ryel-Alte is recommended."

Quaeryt signed beside his wife, then imaged his seal beside hers.

Beneath their signatures was another short line. "It is so ordered, in spring after the fall of Variana to Lord Bhayar of Telaryn, this day of thirteen Avryl."

"We should present the petition, and Lady Tyrena, to Lord Bhayar while he is present in the chateau," announced Vaelora, stepping back from the desk.

Although Quaeryt had not intended to do that, he could see Vaelora's point. "Shall we go, Ladies?"

None of the three spoke until they reached the ranker by Bhayar's door. The ranker looked to Quaeryt.

"Commander Quaeryt, Lady Vaelora, and Lady Tyrena D'Ryel-Alte."

The ranker repeated the names, then opened the study door at Bhayar's gruff, "Have them enter."

The three advanced to where Bhayar stood beside the conference table.

"Lord Bhayar, might I present Tyrena D'Ryel-Alte, the widow of the late Ryel D'Alte, High Holder of lands near Rivages."

Tyrena curtsied gracefully. "Lord Bhayar."

Vaelora presented the petition. "There is but one heir, a daughter, and according to your instructions, the petition requests the lady be appointed as guardian until her daughter is married, and that the lands follow the bloodline of Ryel and Lady Tyrena."

Bhayar took the petition, read through it carefully, then walked to his desk and signed it, then applied his seal. "Hold the lands in allegiance, Lady, and all will be well."

"That I can do, Lord Bhayar, in full faith and thanks." Tyrena curtsied deeply. "As I can, I will speak of your sense of fairness and justice."

Bhayar looked to Vaelora, who stepped forward and took the sealed petition, and murmured almost voicelessly, "Thank you."

"We will not take more of your time, sir," said Quaeryt, inclining his head.

Bhayar smiled, then added, "I trust your return to Ryel will be peaceful, Lady, and give my greetings to your daughter."

"I will indeed, Lord, with gratitude."

The three left the study and walked down to the main

entry. The two guards in black and silver livery looked relieved to see Tyrena, as did the older woman, also in black and silver.

Tyrena looked to Quaeryt, then to Vaelora. "I cannot thank you enough. One hopes for justice, but one cannot always expect it."

"Lord Bhayar has always attempted to be just," replied Quaeryt.

"It helps greatly when those who serve a ruler also believe in justice. That has seldom been the case in Bovaria, but I can hope that it will be so now." Tyrena curtsied once more, then stepped back.

While Tyrena's voice was firm, Quaeryt thought he saw a slight brightness in the eyes of the former Khanara.

As Quaeryt and Vaelora walked back toward the ministry studies, he asked, "How was your conversation with Tyrena?"

"You are a very naughty man, dearest."

"Why?"

"Because you neglected to mention who she was . . . or to inform her who you are."

"I told you her name—" Quaeryt couldn't help but grin, even as Vaelora interrupted him.

"Dearest . . . that was most disrespectful. I didn't tell her that." She paused. "What did Bhayar say before you met with her?"

"I didn't tell him who she was, except that she was Ryel's widow. I wasn't sure, not until I met her."

"He'll find out, sooner or later."

"Possibly, but I doubt she'll ever set foot in Variana again. She'll raise her daughter and pay her tariffs and rebuild her holding."

Vaelora nodded. "You may be right . . . this time."

"What did she ask you?"

"That is between us. You did impress her, though."

"And that's not disrespectful—"

"Impressing other women might fall in that category . . ."

"Not unintentionally," Quaeryt mock-protested.

Vaelora smiled sweetly, then grinned.

27

After a quiet dinner in their quarters, Vaelora set down the glass of red wine that she had barely touched and asked, "What did Tyrena say about Myskyl?"

"That he inspected the hold at Ryel like a tariff inspector . . ." Quaeryt went on to relate that short conversation word for word, at least as he recalled it.

"So Myskyl has just been sitting a few hundred milles away for two seasons, doing nothing?"

"Nothing except drilling his troops, meeting with lots of High Holders, and living off the land, collecting tariffs . . . and not telling your brother anything. That doesn't make sense unless he's planning something."

"Because he knows that you could destroy him if he were to try something like Rescalyn did, you mean?"

Quaeryt nodded. "But he hasn't done anything overt. He could claim that he is carrying out Bhayar's wishes, meeting with High Holders, obtaining the token tariffs, and keeping his regiments in fighting shape."

"But he hasn't sent any dispatches."

"No. We don't know that. We know Bhayar hasn't received any."

"You don't think Deucalon is keeping them from Bhayar? That he's the one planning something?"

"I don't know what to think. I've never trusted either one, but I trust Myskyl less."

"What if it's all a ploy to get you and the imagers away from Bhayar?"

"To set up something like what happened to Skarpa?"

"That's possible."

Quaeryt frowned. "I could be wrong, but . . . Aelina and Clayar are in Solis. If anything happens to Bhayar, Deucalon and Myskyl would know that we and the imagers would support Clayar."

"Unless you're not around to support him," Vaelora pointed out. "Most of the senior officers are beholden to Deucalon, except for Pulaskyr and Paedn . . ."

And one is in Antiago, and you've recommended Bhayar send the other to Solis.

". . . Half your imagers are elsewhere. You've only got the youngest and those that aren't that strong. Without you, with the imagers scattered . . ."

"That would mean that there's a plot against Bhayar and me."

"Possibly just against you, dearest. What options would Bhayar have without you and the imagers? Would he not have to treat with Myskyl and Deucalon?"

"So . . . what do I do if Bhayar asks me to go see what is happening with Myskyl? I can't exactly charge Myskyl and Deucalon with plotting. There's no evidence of that, and I don't think we'll find any here in Variana, even if they're up to their necks in something. And I'm the one who suggested I might have to go look into Myskyl's lack of action."

"Take all your imagers, first company, and Eleventh Regiment."

"There's no point in taking Horan or Baelthm.

Baelthm isn't that good a combat imager, and he can be helpful here. And you know I promised Horan . . ."

Vaelora frowned.

"What about you? Who will protect you?"

"If they're plotting against you, dearest, they'll have to leave Bhayar's family alone . . . for now."

Except in time, "accidents" and illnesses would befall you all. "You'd think they'd wait. Khel hasn't agreed to terms."

"Do you think they care?" retorted Vaelora disgustedly. "Myskyl and Deucalon would prefer a campaign that crushes Khel. They feel that you and Bhayar are making things too easy for the Khellans. An all-out war would make them feel better . . . and they could pit the remaining imagers against the Khellan *Eherelani* and Elani in a way so as to remove the threat of the imagers."

"What should we tell Bhayar, then?" asked Quaeryt.

"Just what Tyrena said."

"There's not that much, but I'd like to see his reaction. He has a good feel for things, and he knows Deucalon far better than I do."

"But not Myskyl."

"I'm not sure anyone truly knows Myskyl, maybe not even Myskyl himself." *But then, do any of us truly know ourselves?* Quaeryt paused. "Now . . . what did you two really talk about? You and Tyrena?"

"Her petition, of course."

"Just her petition?"

"That was what she was there for." Vaelora smiled mischievously.

Quaeryt sighed. Loudly.

"We talked over the petition. As I told you, I suggested she add the words about remarrying."

"And then what?"

"A little bit, just a bit, about you. She wanted to know if you were the commander who defeated Kharst."

"And you told her?"

"I said that you were the one who defeated Kharst twice and Aliaro once and forever. She said that she thought it had to be you because no one else would dare speak for Bhayar."

"Except you. What else did she say?"

"She was surprised that you knew who she was almost as soon as she spoke."

"I was fortunate that I remembered . . ." Quaeryt broke off his words as he recalled what Skarpa had said about his using phrases containing the word "fortunate." *He was right about that . . . and many other things.*

"What is it, dearest? You had the strangest look."

"I just remembered how Skarpa told me how he distrusted my statements that I was just fortunate. Sometimes, I just was, but he was doubtful."

"His death still bothers you, doesn't it?"

"Yes." *It likely always will.* "Was there anything else?"

"She said that being at Ryel was like being in a large prison, but better than being executed. That was about it."

"Did she say any more about Myskyl?"

"Not directly. She's tried to avoid getting involved with anyone in anything more than a cursory fashion since she came to Bovaria. I got the feeling that she and Ryel weren't getting along that well. She did say that all the tales about Kharst were true, and that there were worse. Ryel sometimes told her horrible stories about the man. He seemed to find them amusing, she said. She said there was one about an imager . . . and a chastity belt, but she just shook her head. She didn't tell whatever it was."

"So there was at least one imager."

"I asked if she knew what happened to the imagers. She doesn't know. She never met any of them."

"I still wonder who else might know anything."

"Knowing isn't enough. We have to know who they are, and it would be helpful if they were inclined to talk to us."

"Who else . . ." Quaeryt froze. "Taelmyn D'Alte, Mistress Eluisa's father . . . and her younger sister Rhella."

"I didn't know you knew her family."

"I don't. Rather, I didn't. That was in the dispatch from Straesyr that Gauswn brought. I read it moments before I got the dispatches from Alazyn and Voltyr about Skarpa's death. I'd forgotten about that." Quaeryt offered a rueful smile. "I was somewhat distracted, you might recall. Anyway, Straesyr wrote that Eluisa had sent her best and asked us to contact her father and sister . . . if they survived Kharst and the battles."

"Where would we start? We don't even have a complete listing of High Holders."

"There have to be some High Holders who would know. Even some factors. Taelmyn had to have had a house or holding around Variana, because Eluisa's sister had to have been close enough for Kharst to notice her."

"Not necessarily."

"You're right . . . but he had to have a holding close to Variana . . . or on a river. Those were the only ones Kharst visited, and Taelmyn wouldn't have presented them unless he had to, meaning that Kharst already knew of them. That wouldn't be the case if the holding were hard to get to. That should limit the possibilities."

"I can have the clerks go over the records and have them make a few inquiries."

"I'd like to meet Taelmyn and Rhella before Bhayar sends me off."

"He might not do that immediately."

"And he might."

Vaelora didn't have an answer for that.

28

What with one thing and another, Vaelora and Quaeryt did not get to sleep early on Vendrei evening and slept somewhat later on Samedi morning, not more than a glass, but that was enough that by the time Quaeryt had dressed and eaten, Bhayar had left on a morning ride through the hunting park to the south and west of the Chateau Regis.

Rather than wait for Bhayar's return, Quaeryt gathered up the dispatch to Subcommander Ernyld he had written the afternoon before and then saddled the black gelding and rode to the headquarters holding. There he had one of the duty rankers deliver the dispatch to the subcommander, directing the ranker to inform Calkoran and Khaern that he wished to meet with them. Zhelan had already left for Imagisle with the imagers and first company.

The ranker had barely left when there was a perfunctory knock on the door of the small study, and the door opened immediately to reveal Marshal Deucalon. The wiry, gray-haired officer stepped inside the study and closed the door.

"Marshal." Quaeryt immediately stood.

"Greetings, Quaeryt. Somehow, we've largely missed seeing each other in quite some time, and I thought I'd stop by to see how matters are coming." Deucalon's smile was warm, both on his lips and in his eyes.

"Lord Bhayar has kept me busy, sir." Quaeryt smiled. "As I'm sure you're aware."

"Subcommander Ernyld showed me the dispatch you sent him this morning. I must say that I'm impressed with your speed and diligence in meeting with the chief factor." Deucalon hesitated just an instant before continuing. "Do you think your suggestions will have an effect?"

"I would think so, but if they don't, then we'll take stronger measures, and we'll point out to the factors that they were warned."

The marshal nodded. "It's always best to allow someone the opportunity to do the right thing first . . . before taking stronger action."

"You've made that point before, sir, by your considered acts."

"You're most generous in your words, Quaeryt."

Quaeryt thought about asking about Myskyl, then immediately decided against it. That would only alert Deucalon, if he were part of what Quaeryt believed Myskyl was doing, and would accomplish nothing if Deucalon were not—although Quaeryt had his doubts about that. "I try to be both honest and accurate in my words."

"I have noticed that. So has Submarshal Myskyl."

"Thank you, sir." Quaeryt ignored the opening to ask about Myskyl.

"I understand that we have your imagers to thank for the better roads around the Chateau Regis and the improved pavement on the roads to the Nord and Sud Bridges over the river. Will Lord Bhayar be having you do more road improvements or will they be working on building that compound on the isle of piers?"

"He has given them several tasks, sir. We've also improved the entrance and access to the Chateau Regis and rebuilt the west river road all the way from the Nord Bridge to the Sud Bridge."

"Your undercaptains have been busy, it seems."

"Yes, sir."

"You're not with them as much these days."

"No, sir. Lord Bhayar has asked me to devote time to rebuilding and replacing the administrative structure of the rex . . . except we've discovered that there wasn't that much even before the Chateau Regis was damaged. Telaryn is far better organized than was Bovaria—at least Bovaria under Rex Kharst."

"Yet he had many troopers," said Deucalon skeptically.

"That was where all his golds went, sir. The Great Canal was in poor repair, and no work to speak of has been done in years on any of the roads we have traveled. He trusted the factors to collect tariffs, and spent them all on either his own pleasures or on his troopers."

Deucalon nodded. "That would explain much." He shook his head. "I will not keep you longer. I just wished to see how you were doing." Another pause followed. "How soon do you think it will be before Lord Bhayar hears from the Khellan High Council? It's been, what, well over a season since you met with them."

"Several weeks at the earliest, I would suspect. They needed to inform their local councils, and that would take a good month for the exchange of dispatches, and it would take a month to send an envoy here. That would be if everything went smoothly. As we both know, that seldom happens."

"Midsummer, at the earliest, you think?"

"Sir, I'm not about to guess. I do believe that the Khellans will agree to terms. I also believe that hammering out those terms will take some time." *And certain short-term concessions if you want to avoid a bloody war.*

Deucalon nodded. "That was true in Tilbor as well. Myskyl has pointed that out."

"He would know. He was there and saw it all happen."

"He did indeed." After a moment Deucalon smiled. "I'll leave you to your various duties, Quaeryt. It's good to see you."

"Thank you, sir."

After Deucalon left, Quaeryt wanted to shake his head. The marshal's immediate response to the dispatch, within less than a quint from when Ernyld had to have received it, certainly indicated how closely, if indirectly, Deucalon was observing Quaeryt and the imagers.

Several moments later there was a rap on the door.

"Come in." Quaeryt remained standing.

"Begging your pardon, sir," offered Calkoran as he entered the study, "but was that the marshal we saw?"

"It was. He came to see how we're doing. He was very pleasant and complimentary."

Khaern, following the Khellan subcommander, raised his eyebrows, but did not comment.

"What do you have for me?" asked Quaeryt, gesturing toward the chairs and seating himself behind the desk.

"We're almost caught up on reshoeing the regiment's mounts. . . ."

Once he finished hearing the reports from the three,

Quaeryt made his way to the courtyard, where he mounted the gelding, and he and four rankers rode to Imagisle, where he observed the progress the imagers were making. Over the past week, the three stronger imagers had already added another half mille of granite river wall as well as laid down the basic stone roads for the isle. After Horan had strengthened the walls and foundations earlier in the week, and Lhandor had reimaged the roof tiles into solidity, Baelthm had begun to repair the anomen bit by bit.

After talking to Zhelan about detaching a squad to accompany Baelthm, since first company had the duty of guarding the imagers and patrolling the isle, Quaeryt reined up outside the anomen roughly two quints before eighth glass.

At the sound of mounts, Baelthm had hurried from inside and come to meet Quaeryt.

"You've already improved the anomen considerably," Quaeryt offered, gesturing to the flat stone front of the building, which appeared as it might have a century earlier, or whenever the structure had been built. The oak doors were golden again, and level, with the ironwork shimmering dark gray, the dark stone steps smooth and crisp. The two windows flanking the door . . . Quaeryt frowned. "The windows . . ."

"Yes, sir. Lhandor and I thought they were too low and too small. We made them a bit wider and taller. Not enough to weaken the wall, but enough to let more light in. Did the same with some of the others on the sides."

"What are you working on inside?"

"Refinishing the walls. I can image a lot these days . . . if I just do it in smaller bits. Still be a while before I finish here . . ."

"I'm afraid I'm going to have to ask you to undertake

another quick duty that will take a good portion of the day."

"Sir?"

"The head chorister of the Anomen Regis has requested that the imagers repair damages to the Anomen D'Variana. Before we can commit to that, I'd like to know just how severe those damages are. You seem to know about the basics of construction. Major Zhelan will be detaching a squad to escort you there. It's across the river and south of Imagisle, but not so far as the Sud Bridge. Make a careful inspection and take your time. Then, later today, after you return to the headquarters holding you can brief me on what you'll need to do."

"Yes, sir." The older imager frowned, if slightly.

"Neither I nor, I presume, Lord Bhayar wishes to commit to anything such as the chorister's request without knowing what fulfilling that request will require."

"I can see that, sir. I'll do my best."

"Thank you."

After seeing Baelthm and third squad off, Quaeryt rode back to the Chateau Regis by taking the river road north to the north road west—a route that was a good mille shorter than by the south road from the Sud Bridge.

When Quaeryt reached the Chateau Regis and walked the gelding into the stable, he asked the stable boy who came to take his mount, "Do you know if Lord Bhayar has returned from his ride?"

"Yes, sir. Two quints ago . . . about that, I'd say."

"Thank you."

From the stable, Quaeryt crossed the side courtyard and then made his way to the ministry study.

Vaelora looked up from a stack of papers as he entered.

"How did everything go?"

"I had the dispatch delivered to Ernyld. Within a fraction of a quint, Deucalon was at my study, saying it was good to see me and giving me a backhanded compliment for being so prompt and attentive to Ernyld's concerns."

"That wasn't all, I take it?"

"No. He inquired about what the imagers were doing, insinuating that they might be better used for road projects than on building a compound on Imagisle. He brought up Myskyl twice, and I didn't ask a thing . . . and then he asked about when the Khellan High Council might reply to Bhayar. He didn't seem all that worried that their envoy might not arrive until after midsummer."

"I don't like any of that, especially his reaction to the Khellan response."

"Neither do I, but I don't think it's something we can bring up to Bhayar."

Vaelora shook her head. "Not unless there's something more. It's one thing to voice concerns about Myskyl, but Deucalon's done nothing to merit distrust."

"Except support Myskyl . . ." At Vaelora's expression, Quaeryt said, "I know. I know. And you're right."

"Yes, dearest. Brother dear does give the benefit of the doubt, even when sometimes he shouldn't. If he didn't, we wouldn't be together."

Again, that was a point Quaeryt wasn't about to argue. "After Deucalon left, I went over things with Khaern and Calkoran, then inspected the work at Imagisle. Baelthm's on his way to the Anomen D'Variana."

"For all that Deucalon said to you, he and Ernyld won't be happy with your just talking to the head factor. He'll want an assurance of lower prices."

"I pointed out that we have to request first, and

Deucalon agreed, and then said something along the lines of it being better to allow someone to choose what was the wisest course—"

"He said that?"

"He did, but I think he knows Bhayar would be unhappy if we demanded lower prices immediately."

"It's also another message," Vaelora said.

"I know, but it's so seemingly innocuous. I can't say that I would expect anything different."

Vaelora shook her head, then said, "While you were gone, I went through what records we have. There is a Taelmyn D'Alte in the listing of High Holders who have paid their token tariffs to Bhayar. The listing only states that his holding is east of Variana. I sent Hullyt out to make further inquiries."

"Thank you. Shall we go see your brother and inform him of what Lady Ryel said?"

"We should. I'm not looking forward to it."

"That makes two of us."

They left the study and walked up the grand staircase to the second level, and then along the west corridor to the study, where the duty guard announced them and opened the study door.

Bhayar turned from where he stood by the northernmost window, which was open, but did not speak.

"How was your ride?" asked Quaeryt.

"Pleasant enough, if warm." Bhayar looked from Quaeryt to Vaelora. "You're here as well. What unpleasant news do you two have to convey?"

Vaelora nodded to Quaeryt.

"You might recall that you approved the guardianship of Lady Ryel yesterday?"

"Yes?" Bhayar's voice was wary.

"Her holding is near Rivages, and in addition to hearing about her position as a widow, we asked her a number of questions about what she has observed since last fall. We thought you should know what she has seen. Vaelora and I talked to her separately, of necessity. What she told me was that Submarshal Myskyl has visited many of the high holdings near Rivages. . . ." Quaeryt related all that Tyrena had told him, then stopped and waited.

Bhayar was frowning, but he nodded to his sister. "What did she tell you?"

"Some of what she told Quaeryt. What she also said was that Myskyl had spent most of his time with the widow of High Holder Fiancryt. He keeps all his regiments close to Fiancryt, although he has sent small parties with commanders in charge to visit many high holdings. He gathered extensive supplies over the late fall and the winter, and his officers met with a number of the wealthier factors. There were also some repairs or changes to the hold house at Fiancryt, although Lady Ryel had no idea what was involved, except that she wondered if a powder magazine were being constructed, since a certain amount of iron plate was carted to the hold house."

"How did she know that?"

"The Ryel holdings include an interest in the local ironmongery."

"What else?"

"Dispatch riders left or returned to the Fiancryt lands several times a week. She had no idea where the riders were headed or from where they came, except that they always wore Telaryn colors."

"Nothing more than that?"

"Oh . . . she did say that Kharst was far, far worse than the stories about him, and that she was less than pleased in the way that the High Holders bowed to him, but that they felt they had no choice. In the ten years she was married to Ryel, she knew of at least five high holdings that were destroyed, with the entire families executed. As we surmised as a result of our mission, the factors were indeed agents of the rex, and often provided information to him."

"Dispatch riders several times a week? Do you think she's telling the truth?"

"Why would she not?" replied Vaelora. "I asked what she knew and had seen. That was what she told me."

Bhayar shook his head. "This is troubling. Myskyl has done largely what he was sent to do. He has met with the High Holders. He's collected the token tariffs, and he has kept his forces in readiness."

"He has not sent those golds to you," Vaelora said, "and you have not received any dispatches in more than a season."

"Has Deucalon?" asked Quaeryt.

"He says not." Bhayar looked to Quaeryt. "What do you think? I know you don't trust Myskyl, but he's done nothing disloyal, and certainly, for all his caution, Deucalon has not."

So far . . . and that we know. "Myskyl has never trusted me, sir, but, as you say, the only evidence that something untoward is occurring is that he has not reported in months, and that he has enough dispatch riders to send them off often . . . and that he has not sent the High Holder tariffs—and any tariffs he may have collected from factors—to you. I might add that Subcommander Meinyt has managed regular dispatches. On the other hand, Submarshal Myskyl may have felt that the winter was too severe, or he may have sent them, and they have not arrived." Quaeryt paused. "You also know how I feel about the ties between Commander Kharllon and the submarshal . . . and what happened in Liantiago."

"I'm well aware of those feelings." Bhayar paused, then asked, "What would you do in my place?"

"I would send a small force to discover what has happened. One large enough that if some uprising has occurred at least a full squad of riders could return and report. If nothing has occurred, the officer in command could point out that the lack of communications necessitated a modest force so that you could be apprised of the situation, one way or the other."

"That means you, I suspect. And a few imagers."

"A few. Not all of them. Some need to remain here to undertake work."

"On your Imagisle?"

"Not just on it, I fear. More and more requests are arriving at the Ministry of Administration, as you know. Some of them may require at least token imaging."

"You seem to have created a bit of a problem for yourself and the imagers, haven't you, Quaeryt?"

"For the next few weeks or months, sir."

"You won't get out of it that easily." Bhayar shook his head. "I need to think things over. I'll let you know by Lundi. You don't have anything else in the way of facts to add to what you've said, do you? Facts . . . or other solid indications."

Quaeryt caught the quick look from Vaelora. "No, sir."

"Until later, then." Bhayar turned back toward the window.

Neither Quaeryt nor Vaelora said much until they returned to their private ministry study.

"He was rather short with us," observed Quaeryt after he shut the door.

"He was upset. Deucalon and Myskyl served Father, and they've served him. He can't see why they're acting the way they have. Oh . . . I know power or the temptation of it changes people, but Bhayar always thought fair and firm treatment would keep people loyal, and now he's worried that it won't. He won't dither, but he needs some time to think it through alone. If we'd said more, he would have felt we were pushing, and his reaction would be to delay deciding. It would help if Aelina were here."

"I told him to send for her, and to send Pulaskyr to Solis as the regent of Telaryn or some such."

"He can't do that yet, dearest."

"Why not?"

"He doesn't think Variana is safe enough for her. If we're right, it isn't."

Quaeryt couldn't disagree with that, although he couldn't help observing that Bhayar had less compunction about risking his sister.

"That brings up another question," said Vaelora softly. "If he does send you, who will you take?"

"Khalis, Lhandor, and Elsior. I promised Horan he wouldn't have to do battle imagining. Given how he feels about it, he'd be limited. Between them, he and Baelthm can handle most imaging. If necessary, Horan has strong shields, and he could protect the Chateau Regis."

"You don't think it will come to that, do you?"

"Not so long as Bhayar remains healthy and alive. Even the senior officers beholden to Deucalon and Myskyl would balk at an attack on Bhayar. But if Bhayar dies in an accident or of illness, Deucalon will certainly step forward to hold together what the great Lord Bhayar has unified. If you can, persuade Bhayar never to eat with Deucalon except at his own table here at the chateau."

"You want *me* . . ."

"He's far more likely to listen to you than me about poisons and intrigue."

Vaelora nodded dubiously. "I said this earlier, but what if all this is designed just to get you away from Variana?"

"That's possible, even likely, but Myskyl's being insubordinate. You heard your brother. He's ignoring dispatches. If Bhayar can't bring him into line, then Decaulon will have reason to supplant Bhayar."

"That means they're both in this together."

"I don't see how it could be otherwise." Quaeryt paused, then added, "Although they could be playing each other off."

"Even if they are, Deucalon can't take over from Bhayar without killing him if you're alive."

"He can if we do nothing. What happens when tariff time comes, and no tariffs come in? Kharllon may well be in on this plot as well."

"We don't even know if there is a plot, dearest."

"No . . . we don't. But if it waddles like a goose, hisses like a goose, and has a nasty disposition like a goose . . . then it's probably a goose."

A knock on the study door punctuated Quaeryt's words.

"Yes?"

"Lady, sir, it's Hullyt."

"Come in."

The dark-haired clerk entered with a broad smile on his square face. "Lady, I found where High Holder Taelmyn is. Or where his mansion in Variana is . . ."

Vaelora nodded.

"His holding proper is fifty to sixty milles east north-east of Variana off what they call the old pike road where it crosses the Lusee River. His city place is two milles outside Variana on the east pike beyond the Saenhelyn Road."

Vaelora and Quaeryt exchanged glances, Quaeryt's expression reflecting that he had no idea what those directions meant.

"We're not terribly familiar with the east side of Variana, Hullyt," said Vaelora. "Could you draw a rough map of where the city mansion is?"

"Yes, Lady. It sounds hard, but it's not. You just follow the Boulevard D'Este from the Nord Bridge until you reach Saenhelyn Road—that's where all sorts of roads and streets come together, and some folks say that there ought to be a plaza there, but there's not . . ." The clerk paused, then said, "Best I draw it out."

"Did the people you talked to have any idea about the High Holder?"

"No, Lady . . . well, excepting that he must be alive, because they're delivering goods and one of 'em saw him last week."

"How long would it take to ride there?" asked Quaeryt.

"Two glasses, maybe a bit more, sir."

"Tomorrow, then," Quaeryt said to Vaelora. "I'd rather not show up just before they might be entertaining. Do you wish to come?"

"I'll think about it."

Quaeryt couldn't quite conceal his surprise at her diffident tone.

"It's not that. I just don't know that I want to ride four glasses when the reason deals with something I had nothing to do with."

Her smile reassured Quaeryt.

"And now," Vaelora added, "we need to go over more than a few things in case you have to travel next week." She turned to the young clerk. "If you'd draw that out, please, Hullyt, and then you can get back to the work we disrupted."

"It was a pleasure, Lady. I don't mind getting out now and again. I'll go back to my table and draw it out proper."

"Thank you."

When the door closed, Quaeryt said, "He seems quite well mannered and pleased to be here."

"His father was a clerk for a High Holder who fell from Kharst's favor. He was working for a miller as a wagon boy."

"How did you find him?"

"I have my ways." Vaelora flashed a smile, then said, "I watched Aelina."

Quaeryt wasn't sure that was an answer, but decided against pressing.

29

Quaeryt woke, then stiffened, glancing around the chateau chamber. The shutters were secure and the door barred. In the dimness, he turned toward Vaelora, but she was facing away from him in the wide bed. He could hear a faint pattering sound, almost like rain, except that it wasn't. Then the shutters over the center window flew open and a swirl of rain sprayed across the chamber—except the raindrops were large and each glittered with silver light.

He started to rise, to close the shutters, but some of the swirls of silver rain cascaded over him and formed into chains of light that pinned him against the headboard of the bed. The silver rain intensified, even as the pattering dissipated into silence, and formed a silver archway, with the reddish silver road beyond it leading upward into a brilliant star-filled sky.

Silently, as if unable to speak, Quaeryt watched as a figure strode down that reddish silver road until he walked through the archway and halted. Erion, for it had to be he, stood there for a moment, then gestured.

Vaelora started, then turned over and half sat up against the headboard.

In the light that poured from and around and behind the silver-haired man, Quaeryt could see Vaelora's eyes open, and an expression of shock cross her face. As before, Erion held a dagger with a blade of brilliant light, yet part of the blade held a dark reddish substance. Across his back was the mighty bow, and in his other hand was something shimmering so brightly that Quaeryt could not rightly determine what it might be . . . Yet he felt that it must be a book.

The silver-haired figure surveyed Quaeryt and then Vaelora, before turning back to Quaeryt and speaking. "You have seen treachery, and yet you have not seen it. There is always treachery, especially by those who are powerful, but for whom no amount of wealth and position will suffice, for they know their failings and will not see them, and seek forgetfulness in the elixir of power. You, my son, will never know forgetfulness of your failings. Never."

Quaeryt could believe that, and he could feel the cold certainty of those words.

"In all treachery there is greater treachery, for the greater the scheme, the greater the deception, and often those who seem to be great traitors are only the lesser traitors."

Great traitors only turn out to be lesser traitors? Quaeryt could believe that in a way, but whom was Erion talking about . . . and how did the all-too-real dream figure know?

"Take comfort in doing what is right, and not in what brings power, for power is fleeting, and seeking power for its own sake brings only grief . . ." The silver-haired figure offered an enigmatic smile, then turned and walked back up the red-silver road through the archway that had been a window . . . and was once more, leaving the bedchamber lit in a silver radiance that slowly faded.

"Did you see . . ." Quaeryt asked.

"I saw . . . and heard." Vaelora's voice seemed unsteady. "He talked about treachery, and seemingly great traitors only being small ones . . . and that you have to do right."

"Seemingly great traitors . . ." mused Quaeryt.

"Rescalyn?" asked Vaelora.

"It could be . . . but then, it could be Myskyl or Deucalon?" Quaeryt paused. The greater question in his mind was the apparently real appearance of Erion. Yet how could that be? Was Erion real? An actual god? Or were his dreams taking over his imaging? *So much so that they seem real . . . even to Vaelora.*

Neither possibility was exactly comforting.

He looked to Vaelora, and she looked at him.

"You're making your dreams so real that they're . . . disturbing."

"How about frightening?" he said, attempting to make his words dryly humorous. "They're a bit more than disturbing. I just wish I knew what my dreams seem to know."

"I can see that." Vaelora shivered, even though the bedchamber was not that cool.

Quaeryt eased closer to her and put his arms around her. "I'm glad you're here."

"So am I."

Quaeryt lay there, half awake, long after Vaelora drifted back into sleep.

30

Unsurprisingly, Quaeryt woke early on Solayi morning, thankful that he'd had no other dreams, of even the conventional type, at least not that he could remember. Although he tried to be quiet, before long Vaelora woke, and they summoned breakfast, a luxury that Quaeryt, and Vaelora, did appreciate greatly.

As they lingered at the small table after eating, Vaelora asked, "Do you have any more thoughts about last night?"

Quaeryt set down the mug of lager—the morning was too warm for tea—and thought for a moment. "Nothing that we didn't already talk about."

"Who else might be a traitor besides Myskyl or Deucalon?"

"Any number of people neither of us might know or think about," replied Quaeryt. "In Tilbor, there were some who turned traitor because they thought it might benefit them, and in the end, they lost everything. They would have benefited more from being loyal."

"Is that always so, though?" asked Vaelora. "We remember those for whom treason did not pay. What about those for whom it did?"

"You're right," replied Quaeryt with a laugh. "They

don't call it treason then . . . like when your great-grandsire revolted against the Lord of Telaryn. Or when Kharst's forbears quietly removed the direct heirs to the throne of Bovaria."

"Sometimes, it works. That's why people try."

"Because they'd rather fail in attempting to achieve great power than accept modest power in service of another?" Quaeryt took another swallow of the lager. "That raises another question. What did they want power for? For the sake of having it?"

"That's the difference between them and you, dearest. You have a very direct and specific goal, and you want just enough power to accomplish it."

Much as he wanted to believe Vaelora, Quaeryt couldn't help thinking, *Just enough power? How much is that? Will you ever know? Or will you be like so many others? Others who wanted power to do good and ended up just doing well for themselves.*

After a moment of silence, Vaelora added, "You need to finish dressing and ride out to see if you can talk to Taelmyn."

Quaeryt nodded, if reluctantly.

In less than two quints, he and four rankers from the duty squad were riding south. Before long they were on the north road headed toward the Nord Bridge. The road was less traveled than on other days, but far from deserted, even though most of the shops fronting the road were closed, most of which were located in the last half mille before the west end of the bridge, and again for another half mille east of the bridge. The paving on the east side of the river consisted of uneven and mismatched cobblestones, and modest dwellings lined the road for perhaps a mille beyond where the shops ended. Then the paving ended totally, and several hundred yards farther east, amid ramshackle dwellings, he came to a point where four roads and several lanes all met in an area of packed clay that was likely a muddy morass when there was any significant rain.

"This must be what Hullyt meant by a place that ought to be a square someday," Quaeryt observed quietly to himself.

He turned the gelding southeast along the heavily packed clay road that he thought might be Saenhelyn. After he rode about half a mille, following Hullyt's directions, he turned onto what looked to be the East Pike, since he could see the mill on the creek on the left side of the road. After a few hundred yards, the pike began a curve around a hill, surrounded at its base by a stone wall two yards high, with a substantial dwelling perched near the top. The next hill was lower, but only the burned-out remnants of a dwelling crowned its crest.

Quaeryt looked for a gate or an entry road to the dwelling on the next rise, since that supposedly held the "city" dwelling of High Holder Taelmyn, although calling a hilltop dwelling a good mille from any real congregation of houses or shops a "city dwelling" seemed to stretch that description. The wall around the long rise was clearly older and of reddish brick, as was the modest dwelling situated on the north side just below the crest. A brick-paved drive led from the brick gateposts and angled up through a lawn interspersed with three gardens of varying sizes.

A single guard waited beside the small gatehouse. His too-ample midsection flowed over a wide brown leather belt that seemed challenged in its efforts to restrain his girth, but his gray livery was pressed and clean. As Quaeryt reined up, the guard smiled cheerfully. "Sir?"

"Commander Quaeryt, to see the family."

"Didn't know as anyone was expected, sir."

"I wasn't. I'm bringing word about one of the daughters, Mistress Eluisa."

"Mistress Eluisa? She's been gone for years."

"I know. She's been living in Tilbor. I was princeps of Tilbor, and I have word from her."

"The High Holder isn't here, sir."

"What about Mistress Rhella?"

"I suppose I could announce you."

"That might be a good idea. Lord Bhayar might just be somewhat annoyed if you didn't."

"Lord Bhayar? He's not coming, is he?"

"No. He sent me."

"Oh . . . then I had best let you announce yourself, sir."

"Thank you."

The guard unfastened the heavy catch to the iron gates and swung the right gate back, then held it while Quaeryt and the others rode through and started up the brick drive just barely wide enough for a single carriage. The drive sloped gently upward for a hundred yards or so and then made a wide turn in a flat area cut out of the slope before continuing upward to an uncovered brick-paved area large enough for several carriages. The entry to the two-story mansion was flanked by a small terrace. The terrace roof extended out only about three yards, and was supported by two square brick columns on each side.

Two servitors in livery appeared on the brick steps at the end of the covered terrace just before Quaeryt and the four rankers reined up. One was a dark-haired and sharp-featured man most likely ten years Quaeryt's senior. The other was probably a junior footman, closer to Lhandor's age.

"Sir . . . the family is not receiving," announced the footman imperiously.

Quaeryt smiled. "I'm not making a courtesy call. I'm Commander Quaeryt. I'm the Minister of Administration for Bovaria, and I'm here on Lord Bhayar's business to see Mistress Rhella."

"She won't be receiving, sir."

"I'll ask you to announce me once more. Politely."

"Sir . . . those are my instructions."

Quaeryt image-projected absolute certainty and authority, along with the sense that any servant who blocked the lawful request of a ruler might as well be dead.

The footman paled, then fainted. The steward also paled, then took a step backward.

"Now, if you'd announce me to the lady." Quaeryt dismounted and handed the gelding's reins to one of the rankers. He also made sure he was carrying full shields.

The steward took another look at Quaeryt and swallowed. "Sir . . ."

"I know you're only doing your duty, but I'm only doing mine, and I really don't think it would be in your interests, or the family's, to try and stop me. Especially since I mean no one any harm, and since Mistress Rhella will likely wish to hear what I have to say."

"Lady Rhella will have to determine that herself, sir." The steward looked to the young footman, who was slowly getting to his feet.

"She will hear me. Now . . ."

"Yes, sir." The steward turned.

Quaeryt followed him into the entry hall, then tucked his visor cap under his arm and waited with the footman while the steward hurried through the archway and down a short hallway, before stepping through a doorway on the left side.

The conversation that occurred in the room Quaeryt could not see was too muffled for him to make out the words, but the tone was anything but pleasant. The steward reappeared and walked back to the entry hall.

"Lady Rhella will be here shortly, sir."

"Thank you." Quaeryt suspected he would be made to wait, not for a long time, but enough so that Rhella would not be seen to hurry to his summons.

Half a quint later, a woman emerged and walked in a measuredly fashion along the corridor. She took exactly one step into the entry hall and halted. Rhella was tall, almost as tall as Quaeryt, slender, and imperious, even in what looked to be riding clothes. Her black hair was comparatively short, cut at jaw length, and her eyes were like blue gems. She appeared to be close to Quaeryt's age. For just a moment, her eyes widened as she studied Quaeryt. "Why indeed should I talk to you, officer?"

"Commander, Lady Rhella. And you should talk to me because, first, as one of the ministers who will determine which High Holders will keep their lands and holds, it would be foolish not to, and, second, because I'm not your enemy, no matter what anyone may have told you, and, third, because your sister Eluisa requested that I contact you and your father."

"Eluisa's dead." The words were flat.

"On the contrary, she is alive and well at the Telaryn Palace in Tilbora, where she is a musician for Governor Straesyr and his wife. She also, several years ago, taught several clavecin pieces to my wife, who is, by the way, the youngest sister of Lord Bhayar."

Rhella's eyes softened from gem-hard to merely ice-hard. "Why did we not hear this earlier?"

"Because Lord Bhayar did not know of the connection of Mistress Eluisa to Taelmyn, and because I only received the correspondence from Governor Straesyr a few days ago, and it took some time to locate your dwelling. All of Rex Kharst's records about High Holders were destroyed when he was."

Rhella sighed, resignedly. "We might as well go into the parlor." Her gesture to the archway from the entry hall was barely perfunctory.

Quaeryt followed her back along the corridor and into the same chamber from which she had emerged. The salon was modest in size for a High Holder, perhaps seven yards by five, with a small writing desk at one end and a fireplace and hearth at the other. Twin settees faced each other, with a low narrow table between them, and there was an armchair at each end of the table.

Rhella took one armchair. Quaeryt took the other.

"What else do you have to convey, Commander? Or is that it, in which case you may report that you have conveyed your message?"

"The dispatch asked that I inform you and your father that Eluisa was well and in health. Before I left Tilbor, almost two years ago, I had the pleasure of hearing her play. She played a piece by the former court composer here, but I cannot remember his name."

"Covaelyt. She liked his compositions."

"She also mentioned your other sister . . . but asked I not press. I did not."

"And now you wish to know?"

Quaeryt shook his head. "I have already discovered

more than I ever wanted to know about the acts of Kharst . . . and that was without asking."

"So now you will inform me that we will lose our holding?"

"No. So long as your father pays his tariffs and pledges allegiance to Lord Bhayar, he will keep the holding. Lord Bhayar has already agreed to consider letting widows hold the lands until the majority of a son or the marriage of a daughter."

"Agreed to consider?"

"One widow has requested that. He granted the request. He has said he will consider others."

"How generous of him after he caused so many deaths."

"The only High Holders we killed were those in the battle or in the Chateau Regis with Kharst, and I doubt you had much love for any of them." Quaeryt looked directly at Rhella.

Abruptly she looked away. After a moment she said, "You said your wife had learned compositions from Eluisa. Might I ask where your wife is?"

"At the Chateau Regis. We recently returned from a mission and a campaign."

"Then you're the one."

"The one?"

"The one who destroyed Kharst and conquered Antiago."

"I had something to do with that." Quaeryt laughed softly. "There was one other line in the dispatch. It mentioned Eluisa's thanks for my acts."

"Do you expect mine?"

"No." *Although it would be gracious.* "I would like you to answer a few questions if you can."

"Oh?"

"What do you know about Kharst's imagers? They are often mentioned, but we have found no traces of them, and several people have said that while some were killed at the battle of Variana, not all were, and there is no trace of those who may have survived."

"There wouldn't have been. They were lodged in a holding belonging to High Holder Paitrak. Kharst did not wish them any closer. There were supposedly three of them who did not support the armies. Everyone called them the three evils."

"Do you know who they were?"

"No one knew their names. Few ever saw them, and most of those who did were unlikely to survive long. Kharst used them to fire and destroy the holdings of those High Holders who were not obedient . . ."

"Or those whose daughters were not obedient."

"He regarded that as disobedience."

"Eluisa confided in my wife, but only on the condition she not tell me. Vaelora did not, except to say that his acts were far worse than the stories about him."

"Your wife's summary is accurate, Commander. If anything, it is a terrible understatement."

Quaeryt nodded. "Have you heard anything about those imagers since the battle? No one seems to know where they might have gone."

"We don't know, either. Kharst was secretive about them." Rhella shook her head. "They were never used in battle, Father said. They were sometimes used to keep the marshals and commanders in line because they could kill at a distance."

"How great a distance? Did he say?"

"He thought it was over a hundred yards." Rhella paused. "He did say that one of the marshals had his study lined with iron and lead."

"I've heard that the Autarch of Antiago had his imagers housed in iron-lined chambers. I hadn't heard about lead, though."

"Father said that was because lead was heavier and thicker than iron."

Quaeryt nodded. "Put that way, it definitely makes sense."

"Why do you paint your nails?"

For a moment that question gave Quaeryt a start, because it hadn't come up recently. "I don't. They turned white after the battle for Variana, and they keep growing in that way. That was when my hair turned white as well."

Rhella frowned, but did not speak.

"Did you have another question?"

"Did you really kill fifty thousand troopers?"

"What I did killed most of Kharst's troopers, as well as anyone who was in the Chateau Regis. I have no idea how many people that was."

"And you can live with yourself?"

I almost didn't. Quaeryt looked directly at Rhella. "Is that a rhetorical question, or do you want an honest answer, or at least the best answer I can give."

"It's not rhetorical. I can't see how you could. That's why I want to know."

"I spent almost a month after the battle locked in a room that my ravings and imaging turned solid white. I had a solid month of nightmares about the battle. I still have them . . . just not all day and all night. But . . . as my wife pointed out, as a commander I did not have a choice as to whether men would die. My only choice was which men would die. Given the stakes of the battle, and Kharst's avowed intent of destroying all of Lord Bhayar's forces and then marching down the Aluse, taking Ferravyl and then Solis, and then conquering Telaryn, had I not done what I did, at least as many men would have died. It just would have taken longer."

"That's sophistry."

"Is it, Lady? Knowing what you know about Kharst? Seeing what you have seen? Is it?" Quaeryt waited, not pressing.

"But all at once?"

"Would you have had both lands bled dry? When we first marched up the Aluse, Kharst ordered the fields and crops of all holders burned to deny us food. This was long before the crops could ever have been harvested. We only took the supplies we needed, and we paid for them. Not full price, I admit, but we destroyed nothing we did not use."

"You're almost convincing, Commander."

"Lady . . . I am not trying to convince. I am telling you what we did . . . and did not do. You can ask anyone, and if they are honest, they will tell you what I have told you. Whether you believe me or not depends not upon the truth of what I have said, but upon whether you wish to consider what I have said based upon facts or whether you wish to believe what you will based upon what you wish."

"You sound more like a scholar than the commander with the bloodiest hands in the history of Lydar."

"In fact, I'm both. I was a scholar until Bhayar's commanders made me an officer."

"Father always said that scholars were the most ruthless of men."

"He was likely correct."

Rhella shook her head. "How can you be so matter-of-fact? Tens of thousands of men died."

"As I said earlier . . . tens of thousands of men were

doomed to die once Rex Kharst ordered the attacks on Ferravyl. That was not the question. The question was only which men and under what circumstances."

"But you . . . you executed them."

"I've seen men maimed. I've seen a young imager with his body so bruised and crushed that he died in agony. I've been wounded as well. The men I killed died quickly, and they did not suffer, and I have to believe that far fewer died than if I had not acted."

"I imagine you do have to believe that. How else could you live with yourself?"

"That doesn't make it less true, Lady." Quaeryt image-projected a gentle sense of truth and assurance, as well as a hint of the agony he had felt when trapped in his own mind after the battle.

Rhella paled, then swallowed. "You . . . can project that . . . and you feel it?"

"More than that," he replied. "I am not without feelings, no matter what you may think." He offered a rueful smile, then rose. "I will not take more of your time. You know your sister is well. You can certainly write her in care of the governor at the Telaryn Palace in Tilbora."

Rhella stood, slowly. "This has been a . . . a most interesting visit."

"If you would convey what I told you to your father."

"Where could he find you?"

"The Ministry of Administration at the Chateau Regis . . . unless I've been dispatched elsewhere by Lord Bhayar, but if I am gone, Lady Vaelora will be there as minister. I do serve at his pleasure." He inclined his head. "Good day, Lady."

"Good day, Commander."

Quaeryt *thought* her voice was less imperious and icy. *But is that just what you want to think?* As he walked from the study toward the entry hall, and his mount outside, he couldn't help but wonder.

31

By the time Quaeryt returned to the Chateau Regis and stabled the gelding, then walked up to his and Vaelora's chambers, it was slightly past second glass. He found Vaelora in the sitting room reading.

"What are you reading?"

"The most recent history of Bovaria that I could find." She closed the book and set it on the side table. "Was Taelmyn there? How did matters go?"

"He wasn't there, but Lady Rhella was. She was less than enthusiastic about my presence or my past actions. . . ." Quaeryt went on to recount the conversation, word for word, as well as he could recall it. "She seemed slightly less imperious, just slightly, when I left."

"Few who have not been in your boots, dearest, will ever understand. They will only look at the numbers slain in a single battle and ask why it could not have been different. Most will fail to understand that a long war has a far greater toll, both on those who fight and on those on whose lands battle after battle are fought. Little you or I can say will change that. Those who advocate restraint or mercy against a ruler who has attacked without provocation and who has terrorized his own people understand neither rulers nor war."

"That may be. It was almost as though my telling her

that her sister was alive happened to be some sort of imposition."

"It may be. Perhaps the 'honorable' thing for Eluisa to do was to slash her wrists in her bath or throw herself in the Aluse and drown. Or perhaps Eluisa's flight in some way disgraced Rhella . . . or she feels that it did."

"I hadn't thought of that, but I did give her the address where she could write Eluisa, if she chooses."

"You did what you could. She didn't know any more about Kharst's imagers?"

"She said she didn't, and I don't think she does."

"The three evil ones . . . That almost sounds like Kharst never had any more than three dedicated to his personal . . . uses. Not recently, anyway."

"That may be, but I don't like the idea of three imagers that powerful remaining hidden in Bovaria . . . or anywhere in Lydar, for that matter."

"They wouldn't have fled to Khel," Vaelora pointed out.

"No. I'd guess that they're somewhere in Bovaria, likely in the north or northeast, and most likely as guests of a High Holder, who may not even want them as guests. I'd wager that the three are together for mutual protection."

"The same idea you have for the Collegium, but with a less worthy end."

"That bothers me. We might have to visit hundreds of High Holders. . . ." Quaeryt paused, then asked, "Have you and the clerks been able to come up with any listing of High Holders? Do you have any idea how many there are in Bovaria?"

"We have a partial list and there are almost four hundred, but some of those may have run afoul of Kharst for all we know."

"Do you know how many there are in Telaryn?"

"Father once said that there were more than six hundred in Telaryn, but some were barely that. Why?"

"I was just wondering how many the imagers might have to deal with . . . assuming we can make the Collegium work."

"Too many," said Vaelora with a laugh.

Quaeryt nodded. "The other thing she mentioned was the use of lead to protect senior officers against imaging. They must have worried that Kharst would use imagers against them."

"I'm surprised that Kharst's imagers survived, if he used them as assassins and destroyers."

"I wonder if all of them did. Rhella said no one knew their names. He could have had more than three so that if one of them were killed—"

"Or failed."

"With no one knowing their names . . . they could be anywhere, even somewhere here in Variana."

"That's why you need to hold your shields at all times, dearest."

"At almost all times," Quaeryt quipped back.

"All times when you're out of the chateau and even those times when you're in groups here in the chateau."

"Almost like a prisoner."

"That's why you need Imagisle. Why I need Imagisle. I want you around for a long time."

"I'm glad to hear that." Quaeryt glanced toward the window. "I wonder if we should line the bedchambers of the imagers with lead . . . at Imagisle, I mean."

"Because other imagers might image in their sleep?"

"That was my thought."

"Wouldn't lead be hard to image in place?"

"It might be possible, so long as they were imaging

from outside, but we'd have to be very careful. We might even have to have lead ore carted to Imagisle." He shook his head. "That part of things will have to wait for a time. Bhayar still doesn't have full control over Bovaria. Rather, we don't know if he does, and we won't until we know more about what's happening with Myskyl."

"Do you honestly think that Myskyl and Deucalon are planning to overthrow Bhayar?"

"I worry that they're trying to set up matters so that they could, if everything goes well for them, but that there will be no traces of what they plan if matters don't. That way, they can always be the perfect obedient marshal and submarshal, just carrying out orders."

"What about the dispatches—the ones Bhayar hasn't received?"

"I'd wager that Bhayar never directly ordered them to report. There is also a faint possibility that the couriers are being waylaid and killed by Bovarians."

"Very faint, but you're right about the orders. Brother dear would never think that necessary."

Quaeryt couldn't help but wonder what else Bhayar would not have thought necessary. *Or what you've overlooked and not specifically required or inquired about.* He hoped that whatever it might be, it wasn't serious.

"What are our plans for dinner?"

"A quiet dinner with brother dear."

"I could ask him if he actually ordered Myskyl to report. . . ." Quaeryt shook his head. "He can't have done that. Myskyl reports to Deucalon. Even if Bhayar asked Deucalon for reports . . ."

"Myskyl could claim he never received such orders."

"Which he likely didn't because it wasn't in Deucalon's interest to make that specific. It's an assumed order in the chain of command."

"What do you think Bhayar will do?"

"Sooner or later, he'll send me to see what's going on."

"And Myskyl and Deucalon know that, and Myskyl will be waiting for you."

"Not if he doesn't know I'm coming."

"He knows. He just doesn't know when," Vaelora said. "If you and Bhayar keep your departure and destination quiet and don't tell Deucalon, you just might arrive before he expects you."

"That's likely the best we can do."

"What are you going to do before dinner?" asked Vaelora, standing.

"At some point, I want to study the maps of the land and towns north of Variana."

She eased closer to him. "At some point?"

"Later . . . I think," he said as her hands took his, and their eyes met.

Much later, as Quaeryt lay beside Vaelora in the wide and comfortable bed, he couldn't help but smile. Never would he have dreamed that he would marry, let alone be wed to a woman as beautiful and intelligent as Vaelora.

"Do I make you happy?" she whispered in his ear.

"You do . . . deliciously. Do I make you happy?"

"You do. Tell me again what you were thinking that afternoon in Finitas when Bhayar summoned you into the governor's study."

"I was worried. He told me that I was a problem, that I solved problems he didn't know he had in ways he wouldn't even have considered, and that he'd thought long and hard about what he needed to do to keep me in line. I was wondering if he was going to assign me to a post in Midcote or somewhere even more remote, and then he said he'd come up with a solution, and that we'd come to like it. I wasn't even sure what he meant . . . until he opened the door and you were standing there. And then you said, so sweetly, that you'd find a way to have my jacket tailored around my splinted arm for the wedding. I was stunned."

"You looked stunned."

"Happily stunned," Quaeryt said. "Now . . . you tell me what you were thinking. Again. I like hearing it."

"Brother dear kept telling me the whole long ride to Tilbora that I was proving a terrible challenge to him. He said I was so much of a challenge that he dared not leave me alone with Aelina in Solis. He kept asking why I persisted in writing a penniless scholar. I told him that there was no one else to write who dared return my letters, especially with wit . . . and that you were proving that he was right to send you to Tilbor. He grumbled that you'd left him no choice, either in sending you or in forcing him to ride to Tilbora. I didn't quite believe him, but he can be incredibly headstrong . . . and by the way, you have curbed that, dearest."

"Why do you say that?"

"Because he knows that you can stand up to him, and that he can't bully you."

"He also knows that I'll back you."

"That, too." Vaelora smiled and kissed Quaeryt's cheek.

"What were you thinking when he dragged you into the governor's study?"

"He didn't do that. He put me in a side study and told me to stay there until he dealt with pressing matters. He even posted one of his personal guards there to make sure. I wasn't sure whether he was going to force me to tell you never to write me again, or tell you the same. I really didn't expect what happened."

"Go on," said Quaeryt with a grin.

"When he started talking about us . . . and he never actually said we were to be wed until he'd talked around it for half a quint—"

"It wasn't that long."

"It *seemed* that long. I wanted to stomp on his boots with mine. He couldn't even admit that we might actually like each other."

"He does have a strange sense of humor." Quaeryt grinned again.

"Dearest . . ."

Quaeryt didn't let her finish the complaint. Instead, he kissed her.

Later . . . they had to wash up and dress in a hurry in order to make it down to the family dining chamber in time for dinner with Bhayar.

Even so, Bhayar was waiting outside the archway. "I trust you had a pleasant afternoon." He smiled. "I am envious."

"I did suggest you send for Aelina," said Quaeryt.

"As did I," added Vaelora.

"I will . . . after certain matters are resolved." Bhayar gestured toward the table beyond the archway. "We're having a Bovarian beef dish, similar to paprikash, but somewhat less fiery, I'm told."

Once the three were seated, with Bhayar at the head of the table and Quaeryt and Vaelora on each side of him, Bhayar looked to Vaelora. "Red wine?"

"Please."

"And pale lager?"

"Of course," replied Quaeryt, "although I'm certain the wine would be excellent as well."

"It is, but at family dinners, personal taste outweighs protocol."

The serving girl poured the red wine into Bhayar's and Vaelora's goblets, and then filled Quaeryt's beaker from a separate pitcher. Then she and another server brought in two platters and a covered casserole dish. After that, the servers departed.

Bhayar served Vaelora, and then himself, both the rice grass and the mushroom beef paprika over it, and the early almond beans. Quaeryt served himself.

Bhayar lifted his glass. "A toast to family."

"To family," replied Quaeryt and Vaelora.

Then Bhayar lifted his knife. For a time, no one spoke. The beef was mildly seasoned, and far more to Quaeryt's taste than the fiery Yaran paprikash so often served in Solis and Extela, and the rice grass had been cooked well enough that it was only slightly crunchy. The almond beans were perfect.

After a time, Bhayar set down his utensils, took a swallow of wine, and then said, "There is another reason for this dinner besides enjoying it with family."

Quaeryt nodded and waited.

"I wouldn't expect otherwise," said Vaelora demurely.

"I know you wouldn't, sister dear."

"I've been considering what you both told me yesterday. I also have to confess that the lack of dispatches bothers me greatly. I'm inclined to think that some Bovarians are waylaying dispatch riders in order to disrupt matters . . . and possibly create mistrust and confusion between Myskyl's forces and Variana."

"That is possible," said Quaeryt evenly. "It would take considerable resources to intercept every single rider over two months. If that is what is happening, that would indicate a group of High Holders or wealthy factors."

"Precisely," rejoined Bhayar. "But . . . there is also the

possibility that Myskyl has somehow been made a captive of sorts, either by plotting High Holders or by Kharst's imagers. I honestly do not see him as a traitor . . . but I also cannot dismiss that possibility." Bhayar looked to his sister. "But that is only one possibility."

"So Quaeryt must look into at least three possibilities, none pleasant."

"Who else better?" Bhayar raised his eyebrows.

"What exactly do you have in mind?" asked Quaeryt.

"I'd like you to take first company and Subcommander Calkoran's remaining company and ride north to investigate the situation. I leave to you the matter of imagers. I see no point in dispatching Eleventh Regiment."

"Because one regiment will make no difference, one way or another?" asked Quaeryt.

"Do you think it will?" countered Bhayar.

"No, but I'll agree to that only if you issue orders that Eleventh Regiment reports only to you or me, and not to Deucalon." Quaeryt paused. "Or to the Minister of Administration and Supply for Bovaria."

Bhayar shook his head ruefully. "I think that's unnecessary, but if it will make you feel better, I'll issue that order."

"In writing, so that I can give a copy to Subcommander Khaern before we leave."

Bhayar nodded.

"We'll leave on Meredi morning, if that's agreeable."

"Good." Bhayar paused and took a sip from his goblet. "I don't like this . . . I have to tell you. I've sent messengers with instructions twice in the last six weeks . . . and I've heard nothing."

Quaeryt refrained from commenting, only acknowledging that he had heard Bhayar's words with a nod and an attentive expression.

"I've also considered what you heard from the widow of High Holder Ryel . . . do you think her report is accurate?"

"I fear that it is very accurate," replied Quaeryt.

"As do I," added Vaelora. "I talked to her privately for a time as well."

"Well," Bhayar said almost ruefully, if with a touch of humor in his voice, "you did say that holding Bovaria would be difficult."

"I did," admitted Quaeryt, "but I would that I'd been wrong." *And I didn't expect Myskyl and Deucalon to play matters out in quite this fashion.*

"I won't give you instructions, because you'll do what you will in any case. Just do what you think is best."

Haven't I always? "I do have one request, though."

"Oh?"

"It would be most helpful if you avoid talking to Deucalon about anything before Meredi, but especially about what the imagers and I will be doing."

"You think that's necessary?"

"I don't know. If there's some collusion between the two, the delay could make a difference. If there's no collusion, the delay won't matter."

Bhayar nodded. "I can see that. But won't he see what you're doing?"

"Someone will see two companies going in two different directions, but not Eleventh Regiment, and neither will head north immediately."

"I'll take care not to say anything." Bhayar's tone was resigned.

"Thank you. I'll do my best on this, and I'm certain Vaelora can handle the ministry in my absence."

"She can, but some might not be too pleased."

Such as Deucalon. "They won't say anything," replied Quaeryt, "not to you."

"Now that we covered that," Bhayar said, "I'd like Vaelora's thoughts on how the grounds you and the imagers re-shaped might be planted, and what sort of gardens might be appropriate."

"I would think that you might wish a stone promenade down from the carriage waiting area to the circular road, with narrow gardens on each side. . . ."

Quaeryt was happy to listen as the two discussed the grounds. He had his own ideas for Imagisle, and he doubted Bhayar even cared, so long as the Chateau Regis was to his and Aelina's tastes.

Later, after a dessert consisting of cherry tarts, the three rose, and Bhayar made his way to the rear staircase that led directly to his study.

"I don't like the idea of your not having Eleventh Regiment," said Vaelora as she and Quaeryt walked up the grand staircase toward their quarters.

"If this is a Bovarian plot, I certainly don't need a full regiment."

"Do you really think that?"

"I think it's the least likely possibility, but sometimes it is the least likely possibilities that are what has happened . . . as we discussed earlier this afternoon." Quaeryt grinned at his wife.

"You don't believe that Bovarians are behind this, do you?"

"I don't know who or what is, but if Myskyl's in full revolt against Bhayar, one regiment won't make a difference, not when he has six, and I can trust Khaern to protect you and the remaining imagers. Besides, if there is a revolt or plot, I'll have to figure out how to deal with it without destroying Bhayar's own regiments. Otherwise, everything will fall apart in any case."

"Why can't people be loyal?" Vaelora shook her head. "I know. They all think they can do a better job."

"Sometimes they might be able to," said Quaeryt, thinking of Rescalyn, "but usually they never think of the costs to others caused by their efforts to gain the power to do what they think is best. That's why trying to overthrow a decent ruler because you think you can do a better job often leads to a far worse situation . . . even if you succeed in toppling the ruler. And nothing works very well for months or years. Look at the mess we had in Extela and how much remains to be done here."

"You think Bhayar is only decent?"

"He's better than that, but he's not outstanding yet, and he won't be until he learns more and consolidates his power. Deucalon might be a bit better as an administrator, but he doesn't really know when to take risks. Myskyl would be worse, and he doesn't know it, but he's a very able schemer, the type of man able to undermine anyone, but not all that good as a leader. He's been fortunate because he's always had a capable superior officer and good subordinates."

"And what about you, dearest?"

"I'm decent, maybe a bit better with small groups, and I've had very good subordinates. I'm very good at getting distasteful but necessary tasks done for a ruler. I'd make a good maître of the Collegium."

"I think you're better than you think."

"Even if I happen to be, no one—not High Holders, not factors, and not most of the people—would ever want a known imager to be the head of anything except other imagers. But no one except a strong imager can hold a group of imagers together. My experiences with the ones I command have made that very clear."

"Let us hope that events unfold in a way that allows your expectations, dearest."

"They won't." Quaeryt laughed softly. "Whatever may be occurring with Myskyl won't unfold the way we wish without a great deal more effort. I know that, and so, I suspect, do you."

"One can hope."

"One can always hope, but hope without great effort is usually fruitless."

Vaelora reached out and took his hand as they reached the top of the grand staircase, squeezing it gently.

32

Quaeryt was at the headquarters holding before seventh glass on Lundi morning, meeting with Khaern, Calkoran, and Zhelan in the small study that had become his.

"Matters aren't looking good, sir?" asked Calkoran in his accented Bovarian, if with a knowing smile.

Quaeryt smiled back. "Why do you say that?"

"You're here earlier than in weeks."

"As a matter of fact, there may be some problems." Quaeryt paused. "I'm going to ask the three of you not to mention a word of what I'm about to say to anyone else, and I do mean anyone. Nor are you to discuss it with each other unless you are absolutely certain that no one can overhear anything you may say. Is that clear?"

"Yes, sir." All three spoke as one.

"As you know, Submarshal Myskyl was dispatched to the north of Bovaria last fall. He sent dispatches reporting on his progress in meeting with High Holders until the beginning of winter. Lord Bhayar has received no dispatches since then. He has sent dispatches and couriers north, but they have not returned. Nor has he received any couriers sent from the north. Yet we have good information that Submarshal Myskyl is headquartered at a high holding near Rivages, and that his regiments are there as well, and that they conduct maneuvers on a regular basis. Lord Bhayar has ordered first company and your company, Subcommander Calkoran, to accompany me and whatever imagers I choose on a mission to investigate these circumstances. We are to leave tomorrow morning. I will provide the order and direction of riding tomorrow morning."

"Not Eleventh Regiment, sir?" asked Khaern.

"Eleventh Regiment is required for duties here in the area of Variana. Lord Bhayar will be providing written orders for the regiment, which you will receive tomorrow. I do approve of those orders, however." *Unlike some.*

"Begging your pardon, sir," offered Zhelan quietly, "but this stinks like month-old fish in midsummer."

"It does, one way or another," replied Quaeryt. "It could be as simple—and nefarious—as a small group of Bovarians waylaying dispatch riders going in both directions in order to create confusion and distrust among our forces. Or it could be something else entirely. Our task is to discover what the problem is and resolve it, if we can, and to send word back to Lord Bhayar if we cannot. We can guess or speculate on the reason for the lack of dispatches, but since we do not know, please keep all that among the four of us until we do. You're to tell the men that the two companies are being dispatched on scouting missions and that you will be receiving complete orders tomorrow. I cannot see this taking less than a month, and possibly two. You may convey that as well."

"You don't want to say much, sir," observed Khaern.

"No, I don't. And I'd prefer that you say nothing at all. Tell your men the same, and tell them that since we will be likely traveling in areas where we're less than welcome, and where others might be very happy to attack, letting anyone outside the companies and the regiment know that we'll be setting out can do no good and could cause casualties."

All three nodded.

"It still stinks, sir," added Khaern.

"True, but since when didn't we get orders that had a certain stench about them?" asked Quaeryt sardonically.

That brought reluctant nods from the three.

"Any questions?"

"What about extra mounts?" asked Zhelan.

Calkoran nodded in agreement.

"Work out what you think is a reasonable number, and we'll find a way to get them." *Even if it means borrowing them from Eleventh Regiment.*

"Supplies?"

For the next quint the three officers offered questions, and Quaeryt did his best to address them.

When they left, Quaeryt summoned the imagers into the study. He looked over the small group, consisting of Baelthm, Horan, Lhandor, Khalis, and Elsior. Then he spoke. "Lord Bhayar has a problem, and that means we have one. In fact, there are several. So . . . I'd like to go over the smaller problems first. Elsior, you're acting as a provisional undercaptain. You should be uniformed as one. Ask Major Zhelan what you need to get two sets of uniforms today, even if they don't fit well."

"He can have one of mine," said Khalis.

"Thank you. Work it out as you can. Second—Baelthm, you looked over the Anomen D'Variana. What did you discover?"

"I wouldn't call what needs to be done there a small problem, sir. We're not talking about repairs. The walls have huge cracks. It's been neglected for years, maybe a whole lot longer, and, begging your pardon, sir, the robes and vestments the chorister wears are of the finest quality. So are the furnishings in his private quarters. They consist of a good five rooms for him and his wife and children."

"You're saying that the building has been greatly neglected while the chorister has not neglected his own comforts."

"Yes, sir,"

"How long would it take, say, for you and Horan to put it back in shape?"

"A good week, maybe two . . . if we could do it at all. Have to replace each section of each wall. Nameless knows if we could even do that without bringing down the roof. Timbers there don't seem as solid as they should be. If we try to replace the timbers without strengthening the walls, the walls could give way." The oldest imager shook his head.

Quaeryt nodded. "For now, I'm going to recommend to Lord Bhayar that the reconstruction of the Anomen D'Variana would require too much work and might even result in the destruction of the anomen. I might say that we will consider it once the imagers have greater experience in constructing buildings from scratch."

"Yes, sir."

"There's one other matter. I'd like you to check with Chorister Gauswn on a daily basis while you finish repairing the Imagisle anomen. I'd appreciate it if you'd accommodate him as much as you can."

"We can do that, sir."

"I'd appreciate that."

"Now . . . there's the major problem, and that is the fact that first company and Subcommander Calkoran's company, and those imagers that I feel necessary have been ordered to investigate the lack of recent communications from Northern Army. . . ." Quaeryt went on to explain the situation, then said, "I've decided that Lhandor, Khalis, and Elsior will accompany me and this force, while Baelthm and Horan will remain to continue the work in repairing and building the Collegium structures on Imagisle. In one sense, I'm reluctant to split up the imagers but I feel that Baelthm and Horan can do more good for both Lord Bhayar and the rest of the imagers by remaining here in Variana.

"That's all I have for all of you for now. Horan, Baelthm . . . if you'd remain a moment. Undercaptain Lhandor, please stay nearby. I'll need to talk to you about some plans, possibly the ones you already have or some variation on those . . . or new ones."

"Yes, sir."

Once the imagers who would be accompanying Quaeryt had left the study, he looked at the narrow-faced and graying Horan. "Outside of the fighting, how do you like being an imager?"

"Have to say I like the building and making good roads a lot better than the fighting. Pay's good, too."

"This mission to Rivages is likely to take longer than a month, and if you and Baelthm accompanied us, there'd be no work done on Imagisle. There's also another aspect to this. You know I've mentioned building a place for imagers, with quarters for wives and families as well. That's part of what you'll be doing. When we return, I'm hopeful that it won't be too long before we can have those of you with wives and children send for them. We'll be able to send some coin so that they can make the journey."

"Sir?" asked Baelthm. "Would we still be paid?"

"Lord Bhayar has agreed to building and supporting the Collegium. You will be paid, but I can't speak as to future pay scales, only that you'll get what you're getting now, but you'll also get quarters as well."

Both imagers grinned.

"Because I don't know how long we'll be gone, I will have Lhandor provide plans for what you can image beyond the two barracks and stables. As you can, Horan, I'd like you to add to the granite river walls. . . ." After finishing his instructions of what buildings he wanted imaged and in what general order, Quaeryt added, "I'd also like you two to start instructing the new student imagers as you can. If you have any disagreements about imaging, Horan, you're to defer to Baelthm. Is that understood?"

"I can do that."

"You're also not to leave the holding here without ranker escorts. Part of that is not because I don't think you can protect yourselves, but because I don't want you to have to use imaging to do so."

"That makes sense," offered Horan.

"Do you have any questions?"

"I'd be hating to ask this, sir . . ." ventured Horan.

"But what are you to do if something happens to me?"

"Yes, sir."

"Keep building the Collegium and gather and teach young imagers. The Lady Vaelora will be able to help you with that. If that does happen, and I hope it doesn't, have her have Lord Bhayar summon Major Voltyr from Westisle."

"Yes, sir." Horan nodded. "That'd be all I wished to know."

"Once I finish with Lhandor, you can all head out to

Imagisle for the day. Pass the word to the others and the duty company . . . and would you send word that I'll need to talk to Chorister Gauswn after I'm through with Lhandor?"

"Yes, sir."

When the two left, Lhandor slipped into the study.

"I'd asked you to draw up some plans for Imagisle a while ago. How far did you get in that?"

"You saw the drawings for the fountain and for the central green . . . I also did one for a sort of headquarters building . . . and the ones to adapt the two barracks buildings."

"What about family quarters? For each of the imagers who has a family?"

"I did a rough sketch and floor plan. . . ."

"Do you have it close?"

Lhandor smiled and lifted the leather folder. "When you mentioned that Horan and Baelthm would be staying here, I went and got all my drawings."

"Let's see the rough sketch and floor plan."

Lhandor opened the folder and leafed through the sheaf of drawings, handing one sheet to Quaeryt and then a second.

Quaeryt studied them, then laid on the desk the drawing that showed the front view of a cottage, with a pair of windows flanking an entry door. "I like this, but I think the door needs to be higher, with two stone steps up to it and with a wider stoop, almost a small porch, with at least an overhang to protect the entry."

"You're worried about flooding, sir?"

"More about heavy rains. We've largely flattened the isle, although there is a slight slope from the center to the edges. Still . . ."

In the end, he spent only a quint with the young

imager undercaptain before dismissing him with orders to make changes once he returned from the day's imaging so that if Horan and Baelthm had time, they could start work on a few cottages in the area laid out in the master plan Quaeryt and Lhandor had earlier developed.

Gauswn entered the study when Lhandor left. "You requested my presence."

"I did. We need to talk over some matters. What do you think about the imaging repairs to the old anomen?" Quaeryt shifted his weight on his boots, suddenly aware that he'd been standing for well over a glass, and that his bad leg was reminding him of that.

"It's hard to believe how well your imagers are doing. They've been most careful, but they've also told me that what they've done was only possible because the basic structure was sound. There's only minor rain damage, and the ground there is high enough that whatever floods there might have been in the past didn't leave any lasting damage."

"Will it serve you?"

"It's large enough to serve almost an entire regiment, if all the rankers attended."

"That won't ever happen," replied Quaeryt with a laugh. "Can you teach your students there, once we have quarters ready on the isle?"

"There are several rooms on the main level that would be suitable for instruction. The chorister's quarters are in the rear and more than suitable. Well . . . there are no furnishings, of course."

"Creating them might be a good learning project for the student imagers—under the eye of an older imager— but I wanted to talk to you about another matter. I'm going to have to leave on a mission for Lord Bhayar shortly. Please don't mention it to anyone. While I'm gone, I'd like you to keep an eye on what happens on Imagisle. If anything seems amiss or strange, I'd appreciate it if you would inform Lady Vaelora. I've already told Baelthm to check with you about matters with the anomen."

Gauswn smiled. "He's been doing that."

"Good. That will also give you a reason to watch what's happening." Quaeryt paused. "In time, we'll have more students, and we may need a separate building for schooling, but that shouldn't happen for a while."

"It may happen more quickly than you think," suggested Gauswn.

"If it does, that will show Lord Bhayar the need and value of the Collegium."

"Collegium?"

"I'm calling it the Collegium Imago. Bhayar hasn't protested the name." Quaeryt grinned.

"I still say that the Nameless has a purpose for you, Commander."

"And I still have to point out that I have no idea whether the Nameless exists or not."

"Your belief or disbelief doesn't matter to the Nameless."

Quaeryt laughed. "If there is a Nameless, you're right."

"You have a purpose, and that purpose is too great for the dreams of one man, even one so great as you are."

"I'm talented, but not great, Gauswn, and I'm doing what needs to be done."

"Many men have said that in pursuit of self-interest, and they have all failed."

"I know that. That's been clear to me from the

beginning." Quaeryt paused. "That's not quite true. There's nothing wrong with some self-interest. It's when self-interest consumes a man or a woman that the trouble begins, and those with great abilities have the most difficulty in distinguishing between necessity and self-interest. I'd submit that failure often comes from that loss of ability to distinguish."

"Or from the will of the Nameless when self-interest becomes too great."

"Either way, you and the Eleni and the *Eherelani*—and events—have made it clear that I must try never to seek power for myself and to dream beyond what I would wish personally."

"Would that more men thought so."

But . . . would that be good if all men and women thought to pursue great dreams? Quaeryt had his doubts. *But then . . . who should determine who dreams great dreams and who should not?* "Perhaps." Quaeryt offered a rueful smile. "In any case, I've said what I have to say for now, and I need to send off the imagers for the day. *Or, really, the afternoon, since the morning's largely gone.*

"I'll be here," replied the chorister, before turning and leaving the study.

In a fashion, you always have been.

After giving final instructions to all the imagers, Quaeryt saw them off with a duty company to Imagisle, then mounted the gelding and rode back to the Chateau Regis, where he found Vaelora in the ministry study they shared, with ledgers piled up around her.

She looked up, an expression between anger and exasperation on her face.

"What is it?" asked Quaeryt.

"There's no real frigging information on almost any

of the High Holders, except their names and the general location of their holdings and, occasionally, the location of a mansion near Variana."

"We lost a lot as a result of what I did," Quaeryt said.

She shook her head. "I've been sending out the clerks and talking to people. Kharst didn't have much more than that—except for tariff payment records."

"How did he—"

"He didn't! That's the problem. And the records for factors are all held by the local factors' councils."

"We need copies of those records," said Quaeryt. "We could start by sending dispatches to Meinyt and Kharllon."

"You'd have to have Bhayar send the dispatch to Kharllon and request the information be sent back to him. Brother dear wouldn't have a problem with that if I drafted it."

"No, he wouldn't. We also have a problem with the Anomen D'Variana. According to Baelthm, the place is practically collapsing, but the chorister has fine raiments and finer furnishings. I'll have to draft a letter to Amalyt about the state of the Anomen D'Variana and tell him that my builders have inspected the structure and that it has been so badly neglected for so long that any major imaging to attempt to repair such massive neglect could jeopardize the entire structure, and that it would be best if the congregation and the chorister devoted their efforts to raising golds for trained artisans and masons to rebuild it. I may add something about the contrast between the quality of the furnishings and vestments and that of the structure was rather remarkable."

"You probably should, if delicately, and send a copy to Bhayar."

"I will . . . and there are a few other items I need to take care of before we leave tomorrow."

"More than a few." Vaelora frowned. "You're sure about not taking Baelthm and Horan?"

"There's no point in it. Baelthm can't add that much, and Horan still isn't in any shape to do imaging that will kill people. I'm not sure he ever will be. Just as important, they can continue to build Imagisle." Quaeryt shook his head. "I don't want that to stop because there's another problem. There are going to be problems for months, if not years, and if the building stops anytime there's a problem, we'll never get anything built."

"You also need to get enough of it built soon so that people can see it and understand that the Collegium is an accomplished fact."

"That's part of creating the impression that the Collegium is more than an imager fighting force." Quaeryt shook his head. "And I need to stop talking and start writing dispatches, just to get them out of the way so I can complete planning the departure roads tomorrow . . . in a way that will leave Deucalon somewhat confused."

"Until he talks to Bhayar."

"That will still give us enough time . . . if your brother keeps his word about not saying anything for a day or two after we leave."

"You have plans, I take it?"

"I do. Let's hope they work." Quaeryt pulled out the chair and seated himself at the conference table.

33

Mardi morning began far too early for Quaeryt, even
though he'd gotten Khaern's orders from Bhayar late
on Lundi afternoon. After that, he and Vaelora had
briefed Bhayar on where they stood on all the matters
they had been handling, including the business of the
Anomen D'Variana, which Bhayar dismissed with a
laugh. Then Quaeryt had written out the order of riding
and departure directions for each company and put
each with maps in a folder, one for first company and
one for Calkoran. Finally, he and Vaelora discussed possible ministry problems and what options she might
have for dealing with each, should they arise.

A little before sixth glass on Mardi, after checking on
the gelding and strapping his kit bag behind the saddle, Quaeryt met with Khaern at the headquarters holding, handing him the document that held his orders.
"Please read this right now."

The red-and-gray-haired subcommander frowned
momentarily as he took the single sheet, then said, "Yes,
sir."

Quaeryt watched as Khaern's eyes widened, but said
nothing until Khaern looked up from the orders. "Do
you understand that order?"

"Yes, sir. It says that I am to support Lord Bhayar,

and to accept and undertake orders only from you or him, or in the absence or unavailability of either of you, of the Minister of Administration and Supply for Bovaria."

"Do you have any questions?"

"Aren't you the Minister of Administration, sir?"

"I am, but so is Lady Vaelora."

"Begging your pardon, sir, but this order suggests Lord Bhayar doesn't trust the marshal."

"That's not quite true. I don't fully trust the marshal, and if you recall what happened on the advance up the Aluse last year, I have a few reasons to be wary of his decisions."

"Yes, sir. So do all of us who were in Southern Army."

"I requested the orders you hold so that you can refuse any order from Marshal Deucalon. Obviously, you should use that ability with discretion, and if you don't have to use it, it's probably for the best. But you have it, in order to use your own discretion in protecting the Chateau Regis, Lord Bhayar, and Lady Vaelora—or the two imagers who will be remaining to work on the Collegium buildings on Imagisle."

"Yes, sir." Khaern looked at the order sheet again.

"I hope it doesn't come to that, but I trust your judgment."

"I'll do my best to keep that trust, sir." Khaern paused. "If Marshal Deucalon or one of his officers asks where you've gone, what should I say?"

"Tell him that I took first company out to investigate some problems Lord Bhayar had with High Holders and that you know I headed east of Variana to begin with. That is true. If he presses you, tell him that you would feel uncomfortable saying more, since you report to me, and I report to Lord Bhayar, and that saying more would be contrary to the chain of command."

"That might reveal where you're headed, sir."

"It might, but I'd rather you didn't lie outright." *And if it does, that's another indication that Deucalon's involved with Myskyl.* Quaeryt paused. "It might be helpful if you dispatched two companies for maneuvers heading west fairly early this morning."

"Yes, sir." Khaern grinned. "You wouldn't be minding if we took a supply wagon, just to give the men some practice?"

"I think that would be an excellent idea. You're to join Zhelan and Calkoran while I give them their riding orders."

In moments, all three of Quaeryt's senior officers were in his study.

"Are there any problems?" asked Quaeryt.

"No, sir," replied Zhelan. "First company is ready to mount up."

"We are as well," added Calkoran.

"Here are the maps, and directions." Quaeryt handled Zhelan the folder he and the major would be using and then the other to Calkoran. He waited while the two looked over the materials, then went on. "Subcommander Calkoran, in leaving Variana, you're to take the south road from the Chateau Regis to the Sud Bridge, cross the River Aluse there, then ride to the Sudroad and turn north. In the middle of Variana, it turns into the Nordroad, and it eventually becomes the river road to Rivages. First company will take the north road over the Nord Bridge and past Nordroad all the way out to Saenhelyn before turning north. We'll join up just south of Talyon. That's the first true town north of Variana.

It's about fifteen milles. Whoever reaches Talyon first waits. Is that clear?"

"Yes, sir."

"There's one other matter. You're to stop any dispatch riders, seize their dispatches, and detain them, by force if necessary. That also includes any rider who might be a courier for someone else as well."

Zhelan frowned. "Sir?"

Calkoran only nodded, sadly and knowingly.

"There's something wrong happening with Submarshal Myskyl's forces. There have been no dispatches back to Variana in more than two months, and we don't want to alert anyone who may be intercepting dispatches. We also don't want dispatches to anyone else heading north."

"You do not wish to let the submarshal know we are coming, either," said Calkoran.

"No, I don't. I'd like to be able to scout around, if we can, without his knowing we're near. Then again, that may not be possible because he may have scouts in many areas around Rivages, but if no dispatches reach whoever is at the root of the problem, they'll have less time to prepare to deal with us." Quaeryt turned to Khaern. "Any other diversions you can arrange here would be useful. I leave the details to you."

"Yes, sir. We can do that."

Quaeryt turned his eyes on Calkoran. "Any questions?"

"No, sir."

"Then have your men mount up. You'll leave first. We'll follow."

"Yes, sir."

Calkoran and Khaern hurried off.

Zhelan looked at Quaeryt. "Begging your pardon, sir, but how are we going to take on six regiments?"

"We can't, and we aren't. Lord Bhayar needs every regiment he has. We have to find a way to get to the bottom of this without losing those regiments." *One way or another, and only the Nameless knows how we can manage it.* Quaeryt almost smiled at the thought of his calling on an unnamed deity whose existence he wasn't even sure of.

"That's . . ." Zhelan shook his head as if unable to even come up with an appropriate assessment of the situation.

"Yes, it is." Quaeryt offered a smile. "We might as well get moving." He gestured to the study door.

Two quints later, first company was riding south toward the north road under a hazy sky. Quaeryt hadn't seen any sign of any senior officers watching, and he hoped that the fact that one company or another had been riding out every day would have numbed any observer to anything particularly special, although the fact that each company had a supply wagon was different. He also worried about rain later in the day, because there was a hint of dark clouds to the southeast, and he'd learned that the heaviest rains always blew into Variana from that direction.

Early as it was, by the time first company reached the Nord Bridge, they were slowed by wagons on the road and bridge, and even more so on the narrower avenue east of the River Aluse. A good glass passed before Quaeryt, flanked by Zhelan, with Khalis, Lhandor, and Elsior riding directly behind them, reached Saenhelyn Road and turned north on the dusty track that would eventually rejoin the river road to Rivages.

"Do you think this will do any good, sir?" asked Zhelan.

"Given how far and how long we have to ride, it can't hurt. And if the Bovarians are involved, it's definitely a good idea."

"Yes, sir."

From Zhelan's tone, Quaeryt could tell that the major had strong doubts that the Bovarians were in the slightest involved.

"And," Quaeryt added loudly, so that the imagers could hear, "we can do some roadwork along the way so that travel and dispatch riders will have an easier time of it in the future. That way, we won't have to wonder if bad roads slowed dispatches."

Clearly understanding what Quaeryt was doing, Zhelan grinned and replied loudly, "Yes, sir."

"We might even build a few good bridges along the way."

"Maybe they could build some really big bridges and causeways and pave a good portion of the river road all the way to Rivages."

"That might be a good idea," replied Quaeryt, grinning back at the major.

꩜

34

The river road as far as Talyon proved not only to be paved all the way from Variana, but the paving continued for the next two towns beyond, the second of which, Caanara, was where Quaeryt and the two companies spent Mardi night, using both inns. Quaeryt and the imagers and first company stayed at the Black Bear, whose innkeeper had observed occasional riders in Telaryn livery riding both north and south, but none for the past week or so.

"Couldn't say for certain, sir, but as I recall, there were four Telaryn riders moving quicklike through town a week ago last Samedi. Sometimes, they stop here, but those fellows barely slowed to a walk in the town. They just might have wished they did, seeing as it had rained the day before."

"The road's not paved north of here?"

"For another five milles, mayhap. All that was done in my grandsire's time. All the roadwork hereabouts stopped when Rex Kharst's father took the throne."

Another mystery of sorts. But Quaeryt just nodded, then asked, "I heard that Kharst's imagers might have fled north from Variana."

The innkeeper shrugged. "Could be, but who'd know

an imager from any other party of travelers 'less they were fool enough to let anyone know?"

"I take it imagers aren't exactly welcome in the north?"

"Not sure they're welcome anywhere, especially for High Holders out of favor. There's word that a few High Holders welcome them, but which ones, I couldn't say. Likely 'cause they're relatives. Anyone else'd turn out an imager whelp."

"They say that Lord Bhayar is starting a school for them in Variana," said Quaeryt, "offering a gold to parents who send young imagers there."

"Might not be a bad idea. Keep them under control and give their parents a reward for raising 'em and putting up with 'em." The innkeeper frowned. "How'd you be knowing that?"

"He told me to arrange for building the school. I was a scholar before the war."

"Scholar-commander . . . don't know what the world's coming to . . ." The man shook his head, then brushed back a lock of lank black hair. "Used to have scholars, too. They started disappearing some twenty years ago, something about the rex not letting them earn coins. Small scholarium here when I was a boy. Been gone for years, though."

"That's true all across Bovaria, I've heard."

"Terrible times . . . terrible . . . You said you'd pay?"

"I did. Two golds for food for the men, and a gold for lodging."

"Not all that much . . . but any boat in a flood."

Quaeryt didn't learn any more of interest from the innkeeper, and on Meredi morning he and his forces were on the road north well before seventh glass.

North of Caanara, the river road ran along a low

bluff beside the Aluse, the edge of the pavement some fifty yards from the edge. The undergrowth on the top of the bluff between the road and the dropoff to the river was mainly weeds and a few scraggy bushes, and only a handful of trees. At first Quaeryt wondered why, but then he began to notice all the stumps. *Everyone logs the lands of the rex . . . where they can. At least, it keeps it easier to see the river.* On the side of the road away from the river were scattered cots, with woodlots and fields, some more well tended than others, and occasional patches of grass.

The top of the bluff paralleling the river was flat enough, but to the east of the road the ground rose unevenly, gently in some places, and those areas held fields, sometimes terraced. The steeper slopes were often rocky and rugged covered with grass and sparse trees, while the steep stretches that were not excessively rocky were thickly wooded, and in a few instances, the branch tips were within yards of the road's shoulder.

Quaeryt had just ridden past a millestone that, on the north side, read: CAANARA—5 M when one of the scouts rode back toward first company.

The ranker called out, even before he swung his mount around and up beside Quaeryt and Zhelan. "Sir! There's a gorge ahead with a bridge."

"And there's a problem with the bridge or the gorge . . . or both? Or the paving ends?"

"Best you see for yourself, sir."

Quaeryt led first company forward for almost half a mille along the bluff road before he could see a bridge, but the ground was so level it was difficult to make out what the problem might be. Only when he was within a few hundred yards did he begin to see. The timber bridge was narrow and crossed a space of no more than ten yards. It also appeared rickety.

Then . . . some fifteen yards short of the bridge, the stone paving ended. Although Quaeryt had expected that from his talk with the innkeeper at the Black Bear, what he hadn't expected was the nature of what the bridge spanned.

Quaeryt reined up a few yards short of the bridge, then eased the gelding forward until he could see fully. The narrow timber bridge crossed a gorge some ten yards wide, but one that had been eroded more than that in depth so that the stream that had cut it flowed almost lazily westward into the Aluse. Quaeryt doubted that anything larger than a single light cart drawn by a small horse or donkey could safely cross the gorge. For a time, he studied the earthen walls of the narrow canyon, but it was clear that with each year, more of the walls would crumble away. He glanced to the east, but the narrow gorge was at least seven or eight yards deep even a half mille to the east, and there the trees ran to the edge. In fact, in one place a young fir angled out over the stream, as if the ground under a portion of its roots had been washed away. His eyes went back to the bridge. The second time he noticed that the planks and timbers were relatively new, certainly less than a year or two old.

"I'd not want to risk more than a rider at a time on that," said Zhelan.

"If that." Quaeryt turned in the saddle. "Imagers, forward!"

The three young imagers rode forward and reined up just behind Quaeryt.

"Undercaptains . . . and Elsior . . . take a good look."

Quaeryt waited until the three had studied the bridge

and the gorge. "How would you suggest you image a bridge across this little canyon?"

After a time, Lhandor said, "It depends on what's at the bottom of the gorge. If there's rock not too far below the stream level, we could image away the dirt and stones above the rock, and then image a bridge pier on each side. We'd need an arch across the middle to support the roadbed, and a half arch from each pillar to support the approach causeway on each side. That ought to work for at least five or ten years. It could be longer."

"Khalis? What do you think?"

"I won't disagree with Lhandor on this."

"Elsior?"

"I would not disagree . . ."

"But you have a suggestion?"

"Yes, sir. If we can image retaining walls away from the piers on each side, no more than three yards up from the base of the pier, that would channel the stream away from the back of the piers. The stream is not much higher than the river now. It can't dig down that much farther."

Quaeryt held back a smile. "Go to it. If you want me to image part of it, I will, but you have to describe what you want done. Since it's your idea, Lhandor, you're in charge."

"Yes, sir."

Quaeryt watched as the three dismounted and then walked just a few steps onto the bridge to study the gorge. They conversed quietly before Lhandor stepped close to the edge of the gorge and focused on the far side. At the base of the gorge on the far side, a trench appeared, at the bottom of which Quaeryt could see stone—before it was covered with stream water.

All in all, the imaging of a new stone bridge, wide enough for two wagons, if barely, took almost two glasses—and Quaeryt ended up imaging the retaining walls proposed by Elsior, as well as the last sections of the approach causeway.

The three undercaptains crossed the new span first, followed by Quaeryt and Zhelan, and then first company.

Halfway across, Zhelan turned to Quaeryt. "You could have done that yourself, could you not?"

"I could have created something, but what they did is a better bridge, and they need the experience of thinking it out and then doing it. I've done more in battle because too much was at stake. Now is the time for them to do all they can." Quaeryt laughed softly. "I won't always be around them, and I certainly won't be here forever."

"You're young as commanders go, sir."

"That may be, but things can happen to young commanders as well. The greater the experience they have, the more likely the Collegium is to be successful." *And a permanent part of Bhayar's Solidar to come.* After a moment Quaeryt added, *You hope.*

The bluff road stretched ahead for what looked to be another mille before it looked to slope downward toward a level closer to that of the River Aluse.

More mud and problems, thought Quaeryt. But he did not voice those words.

35

By midday on the following Solayi, Quaeryt and his two companies had just passed through a small hamlet some 150 milles north of Variana . . . or so he judged from the maps and his own calculations. He had used the imagers, as well as his own talents, to repair and strengthen a handful of bridges, although none had required the amount of imaging necessary just north of Caanara, and in one place, to fill and pave a section of the river road where it had descended into what would be a morass with the slightest amount of rain. Along the way, they had passed two older ruins of what might have once been high holdings, one of which appeared to have been abandoned and dismantled in an orderly fashion, with only the foundations remaining. The other had been burned, but not recently

When Quaeryt had inquired about local High Holders, he'd discovered that there were several in the areas where he asked, but all at least ten milles from the River Aluse. That didn't exactly surprise him, and he continued to be appalled at the state of what was the major road north from the capital. And, according to the maps he had and what he'd asked of the locals, no one knew of any better roads.

The weather continued hot and damp, and Quaeryt

was continually drenched with sweat. He had decided to alternate the lead companies, but keep the imagers with him, as well as ride for a time with each imager. On Solayi, Elsior was riding beside Quaeryt for the first time, with Calkoran and the two imager undercaptains immediately behind.

"Where were you from?"

"Navarou . . . it's a fishing village on the coast south of Westisle, sir." The slender dark-haired youth sounded almost apologetic.

"Your family is Pharsi?"

"My mother is."

"Are there many other Pharsi in Navarou?"

"No, sir. She washed up on the beach after a storm. She was clinging to some timbers."

"Where was she from?"

"She would never speak of what happened or where she was from, sir. All she said was that the past was a closed book, and that only the hand of Erion would ever open it." Elsior smiled. "She never expected I'd run into one."

"Beware of names placed on you by other people." Quaeryt shook his head. "Tell me about you and her, if you would."

"She was a seamstress, and a fine one. Folks come from towns along the coast for her to sew their fine garments, for weddings and the like. We had a little cot at the base of the hills. There was enough to eat, for the two of us, anyway."

"Did your mother ever speak of your father . . . or was that part of the closed book?" Quaeryt tried to keep his voice light.

"No, sir . . . excepting she did once say that his station was naught to be ashamed of. I was born soon after she washed up."

"I'm assuming that when your mother said something was closed, it was closed. Did she have the farsight?"

Elsior tilted his head, as if considering, although Quaeryt couldn't tell whether he was considering whether his mother did or whether he should say anything. Finally, he said, "She never said she'd seen something that would happen, but there were times when she should have been surprised and she wasn't."

"What about you?"

Elsior shook his head. "If anyone needed farsight . . ."

"How did you end up as an imager for the Autarch?"

"What else would I do after she died?"

"Oh . . . I didn't realize . . ."

"Folks didn't say much so long as she was there, because there wasn't anyone who could sew like she could, but they always looked away from me."

"Did you image a few extra coppers for her?"

Elsior grinned. "Of course. Not too many, and I gave them all to her. She knew, but she said that so long as I never had coppers no one would think about my being an imager. If she had a few more coppers, who would know?"

"Did you have trouble being accepted as an imager by the Autarch?"

"It wasn't easy. Before you're apprenticed to a master, you do anything wrong, and you could be blinded."

"How long . . ."

"I was lucky. Only a year after they took me in."

Elsior's tone conveyed anything but luck, but Quaeryt didn't pursue that. Instead, he asked, "What do you think about Imagisle and the Collegium?"

"You are right, sir. Imagers do need a place where they're not special and not feared. I think that living in Navarou would have been hard as I grew older. Even the imagers' quarters in Liantiago were better than what most of the others went through before they became imagers for the Autarch."

"Do you have any suggestions as to what might make Imagisle better?"

"Good beds and a library! Khalis has been working with me to improve my reading and writing so that I can write Bovarian as well as I can write Pharsi."

"Why do you think a library is important?"

"Because my mother said it was. She taught me Pharsi, but she didn't speak Bovarian that well."

"She must have been from Khel, then."

"She never said."

"You said that, but it makes sense. Navarou is south across the Gulf from Khel. If she were shipwrecked coming out of Kherseilles or Pointe Neiman . . . or even coming from the ports on the west of Lydar . . ."

Elsior nodded.

Quaeryt couldn't help but wonder just what lay behind the covers of the closed book that had been the past of Elsior's mother, just as he'd wondered the same about his own parents when he'd been as young as Elsior. But there was little point in pursuing that. Instead, he asked, "How are you coming with your shields?"

The young imager smiled happily. "Khalis says that mine are almost as good as his. Well . . . if I keep them close to me. I can't extend mine as far as he can. Mine aren't nearly as strong as yours."

"How do you know that?" Quaeryt asked, almost in jest, because he didn't think Elsior had ever been that close to him when his shields had been under attack.

"Oh . . . I can sense shields." Elsior looked almost embarrassed.

"By pressing yours against others?"

"No, sir. I've always been able to sense shields. Yours are stronger than any imager's, even the best of the Autarch's imagers. You always carry strong shields all the time, don't you?"

"I do that to keep in practice. You ought to try the same."

"I've been doing that, sir. So have Khalis and Lhandor. They told me that."

Quaeryt smiled wryly. *Those two would.* "Do you know if other imagers can sense shields the way you do?"

"I don't know, sir. I never told Magister Trewyno."

"Because revealing something was dangerous?"

Elsior nodded.

"From how far away can you sense shields?"

"Not all that far. It depends on the shields. For you . . . maybe a hundred yards."

Quaeryt pondered that for a moment and was about to ask another question when he saw one of the scouts riding back toward them. He waited until the trooper had turned his mount and was riding beside him before grinning and asking, "What is it? Another bad bridge or a swamp?"

"No, sir. The road's about the same as always. Just thought you'd like to know. There's another burned-out hold up ahead, sir, maybe a half mille around the bend in the river. Doesn't look like anyone's nearby, but there are sheep in the pasture to the north and in the fields across from it to the east."

"Thank you."

As the scout rode forward to rejoin the other scouts,

Elsior asked, "Sir? Is it true that Rex Kharst burned the places of High Holders he didn't like?"

"He burned the holdings of those who displeased or angered him."

"Why? He could have killed them and kept their goods and valuables." Elsior immediately added, "I don't mean . . . I mean that's not good, but . . . if you're going to take people's things, why destroy them? That's stupid."

"He may have taken their valuables and any livestock. He probably did, but we don't know for sure."

"But these hold houses . . . they're worth a lot."

"And in some cases, he salted the land immediately around the house so that little of value would grow there."

Elsior shook his head. "The Autarch wasn't even that bad."

"Did you ever meet him?"

"No, sir. Most imagers never did. That's what Magister Trewyno said. Will we ever meet Lord Bhayar?"

With a slight jolt, Quaeryt realized that none of the imagers had properly actually met Bhayar—and that wasn't good. After a moment he said, "Some of the imagers who were with me from the beginning have seen him, fairly close up. I will make sure, once we get back to Variana, that you all get a chance to meet him."

"What is he like, sir? They say you were students together."

"We studied with the same scholar. It might be stretching matters to say that we were students together, although that is how we came to know each other." Quaeryt paused. Exactly what could he say that was both accurate and not misleading in some way or another? "He wants to be a strong ruler, but not a cruel one. He does his best to be a just ruler. I cannot recall a time when he has executed a High Holder or someone who served him, although he has discharged those who have failed him, or sent those who made mistakes to lesser posts, sometimes in most remote regions. He is deeply in love with his wife and, to my knowledge, has never taken a mistress. He does have a temper, but when he is truly angry he turns stern and cold. He has, I believe, deferred too much upon occasion to the High Holders of Telaryn, but that is because he relies more heavily on their tariffs than he should." Quaeryt thought about saying that Bhayar wanted to unite Lydar into one land, because Bhayar believed that there would always be war if someone did not, but decided against saying that because he suspected that was as much his own goal as Bhayar's. Bhayar had only talked about the need to conquer Bovaria because whoever had been rex there had always caused trouble for Telaryn.

"How well do you know him, sir?"

That's a very good question. "I suspect I know him as well as anyone besides his wife and mine. It helps that Lady Vaelora can offer insights."

Elsior nodded.

Before that long, Quaeryt and Elsior were approaching the burned-out hold house. As was often the case in Bovaria, along the rivers, the road swung away from the water, so that the hold house sat at the top of a slope overlooking the river. Only the stone foundations of the gateposts remained, and a stone-paved drive ran due west toward the ruins.

The hold house had been extensive. That didn't surprise Quaeryt. What did was the fact that the damage looked to be comparatively recent . . . sometime within the last year, possibly less than six or seven months ago.

The remaining brick walls held soot that was largely still black, but there was no odor of smoke or recent fire. The grounds were still black, and nothing grew up through the charred soil, a fairly good indication that the ground had been salted as well—and, given the lack of tilling, possibly through imaging.

Why did Kharst have imagers torching and destroying high holdings in the middle of a war? The more Quaeryt saw of Bovaria, the less he felt he understood.

"It was a large hold." Elsior shook his head.

"Most of those burned were," replied Quaeryt.

Once they were well past the ruins, Quaeryt sent Elsior back to rejoin the other imagers and motioned for Calkoran to rejoin him.

"The young one, he looks like he came from Khel," observed the older subcommander.

"It's likely his mother and father did, but he doesn't know."

Calkoran nodded. "There have been many like that over the past years."

Quaeryt removed his visor cap and blotted his forehead, then replaced the cap. He turned toward Calkoran. "It may be two weeks before summer's here by the calendar, but I'd say that it's already arrived. This is almost as bad as Solis at this time of year."

"Then I would not wish living in Solis on anyone," replied Calkoran in his accented Bovarian.

"At least, we haven't had much rain—except for that shower on Vendrei, and not having rain has been good for travel," said Quaeryt.

"Don't speak that too loudly," replied Calkoran. "The rain listens and will come when you least desire it."

"You're probably right about that," admitted Quaeryt ruefully.

"Commander, sir!" came a call from the shoulder of the road behind Quaeryt. He glanced back to see a ranker riding forward. "Sir! Major Zhelan requests your presence. Fifth squad captured some dispatch riders."

Quaeryt's reaction was immediate. "Company! Halt! Pass it back!"

Once everyone had reined up, Quaeryt turned to Calkoran. "Subcommander, I'd appreciate it if you'd accompany me. I'm certain Major Eslym can guard the road."

"He can indeed."

"Undercaptains! You're to remain here to protect the company. Major Eslym is in command."

"Yes, sir!" rejoined Khalis and Lhandor.

"That includes you, Elsior," Quaeryt added.

Quaeryt followed the ranker back along the worn shoulder of the rutted dirt road, finally coming to a halt at the end of the column, where Zhelan rode up to meet them.

"What happened?" asked Quaeryt, reining up.

"The rear scouts saw three riders in uniform in the distance. I thought they might be dispatch couriers. So I stationed a squad in the woods beyond the ruined hold, and they let them pass and then captured them."

"Didn't they see first company?" asked Quaeryt.

Zhelan smiled. "I asked them that. They did. They were given orders that if they came upon Telaryn troopers, they were to hold back. When they could, without being seen, they were to go around the troopers and continue on. They were told that was to avoid unnecessary delays, since the dispatches didn't concern us. They didn't hold back far enough."

"Do you have the dispatches?"

"There was only one in the pouch." Zhelan leaned forward and handed the sealed missive to Quaeryt.

Quaeryt imaged the seal onto another section of the oversized envelope, careful not to break it, and then extracted the single sheet of paper. He scanned the contents, hurrying over the heading and getting to the key paragraph.

It might be of interest to you that Commander Quaeryt and at least two companies of his forces set out from Variana on Mardi, the seventeenth of Avryl. Since the commander reports directly to the rex and lord, I received no information on his destination, nor did I ask, for obvious reasons. One can but imagine what that destination may be, and I thought that information might prove useful to you.

That was the only mention of Quaeryt or his forces. After that, there were two sections suggesting how to deal with High Holders and factors, with most of which Quaeryt had little difficulty. But one part did catch his eye, and he read it twice.

. . . As you suggested in your earlier dispatch, I heartily agree with the proposition that when speaking to them, one should always refer to the power of Telaryn and its forces, and never mention any individual by name or position. That way, their allegiance is to Telaryn and not to any individual.

Quaeryt stopped reading. There was something about that idea. Then he stiffened. That was exactly what Rescalyn had done in addressing the Tilboran forces on the campaign against the rebel hill holders. *Had that even been Rescalyn's idea at all?* Quaeryt had no way of knowing, but those sentences were definitely suggestive . . . and then some.

He kept the envelope and handed the dispatch to Calkoran, who read it without speaking, then snorted, and handed it back to Quaeryt, who in turn passed it to Zhelan.

The major read it and returned it to Quaeryt, offering in a low voice, "I did say that matters had an odor, sir."

Quaeryt replaced the single sheet in the envelope and then re-imaged the seal back into its original position. "If you'll give me the dispatch pouch, I'll keep both."

Wordlessly, Zhelan handed across the battered leather pouch.

Quaeryt fastened it to one of the saddle rings, opposite the one holding his water bottle. "Where are the couriers?"

The major gestured south along the road to a group some ten yards south. "They're over there."

Quaeryt eased the gelding toward the three. All had their hands bound, and rope tethers around their waists, stretching to the saddles of three solid fifth squad rankers. There were also three spare mounts, a necessity when there weren't dispatch stations set up. He reined up and surveyed them.

"Sir, begging your pardon, but why are we being treated like captives?" asked the dispatch rider, a small and lean man with the dispatch insignia on his sleeve, along with the insignia of a junior squad leader.

"For your protection and ours," replied Quaeryt.

The rider squad leader looked puzzled.

"Have you talked to any dispatch rider that has come from Northern Army in the last two months?"

"Yes, sir. Caromyt returned three weeks ago. Well . . . three weeks before we set out. And Gosting, a week before that."

"By the way, when did you leave Variana?"

"First thing last Jeudi. Why?"

Quaeryt caught the quick look of surprise that crossed Zhelan's face.

"All that's rather interesting," said Quaeryt. "Not a single dispatch rider sent north by Lord Bhayar has returned. He sent us to investigate why."

"I don't understand, sir."

"Neither does Lord Bhayar. Neither do I. But until I do know why, you'll be remaining with us. And if any of you attempt to ride off, you're liable to end up dead."

"Begging your pardon, sir, but I'd not be knowing you."

"Quaeryt. Commander Quaeryt."

The two ranker escorts exchanged worried and knowing glances. The courier moistened his lips before speaking. "I still don't understand, sir. Marshal Deucalon sent us . . . said the dispatch was urgent."

I'm certain he did. Quaeryt smiled. "I'm afraid I'll have to decide that." He turned to Zhelan. "Keep them close."

"Yes, sir."

"We need to talk." Quaeryt rode north until he was well away from the captive couriers, then reined up and waited for Zhelan and Calkoran to join him.

"Yes, sir?" asked Zhelan.

"Lord Bhayar indicated that he would not be mentioning our departure or destination to the marshal, and it appears he did not. It is clear that he was watching us closely, and a day after our departure, he chose to send a special dispatch informing the submarshal. That concerns me slightly." Quaeryt's understatement came out in an ironic tone.

"The riders don't know anything," Zhelan pointed out.

"Of course not. I'm certain that everything going on is along the lines of the dispatch—suggestive and little more."

"Do we still ride on to Rivages as if nothing has happened?" asked the major.

"Nothing has happened," Quaeryt pointed out. *Even if you're convinced that something will happen.* "We've been ordered to go there, and until we have some sort of solid proof that there's a problem, that's just what we'll do. We'll just try to keep the submarshal from getting any advance warning of our arrival."

Both officers nodded, if reluctantly.

Quaeryt didn't feel much better, but he only said, "We'll just have to be more alert than ever, both in the vanguard and the rear guard."

"Yes, sir."

As he rode north along the narrow shoulder of the road, Quaeryt couldn't help but think about the second part of the dispatch that had concerned him. Emphasizing Telaryn power without mentioning Bhayar? That put a whole different light on what had happened in Tilbor . . . as his "dream" had suggested.

After he rode a bit farther, he began to think about Elsior's sensing of shields. *Is that something you can do?* He just tried to feel the shields of the imagers behind him, but he could sense nothing. He kept trying, but after a quint, he still felt nothing. Yet, if he extended a tiny projection of his own shields, he could feel when that projection touched another shield.

What else might Elsior be able to do? Was his ability to sense shields something unique to him? Quaeryt wondered. *You'll have to talk this over with the three of them.*

36

~~~

Lundi afternoon, Quaeryt, Calkoran, and Zhelan rode side by side at the front of the column.

"The roads haven't gotten any better," said Zhelan.

"Most of the ones we ride are worse than the worst lanes in Khel," added Calkoran.

"There don't look to be any large towns or even high holdings for the next twenty milles or so," said Zhelan. "Just small hamlets."

That they might have to occupy some hamlet or bivouac on some smallholder's lands was Quaeryt's fault, but they'd ridden through the last town of any size— Roleon—at ninth glass in the morning, and stopping there would have made no sense. Besides, they still would have faced the same problem on Mardi, and lost almost an entire day. Quaeryt couldn't help but worry that delays might be all too costly in one way or another.

"Calkoran, if you'd send out some scouts to look for any sort of holding that would provide some sort of shelter for the men." Quaeryt glanced back over his shoulder at the darkening skies to the south.

The subcommander issued an order in Pharsi, and in moments another set of scouts rode out ahead of the column. Shortly, they passed the column outriders.

"You think we'll actually get rain?" asked Zhelan.

"Since we have no towns of any size nearby and few prospects for shelter . . . and since we've been highly fortunate with the weather so far, I think it's more than likely," replied Quaeryt dryly. They'd been fortunate, he reflected, with only light rains or showers or cloudbursts that had lasted but a quint or two, not enough to turn the road into a quagmire.

"I'll be returning to first company, sir," said Zhelan.

Quaeryt nodded, then asked, "Any signs of dispatch riders?"

"No, sir. The ones with us are behaving."

"Good."

While he continued riding, and worrying about the possible rain, Quaeryt tried again to sense the shields of the imagers, but he had no success, although he could now "feel" their shields with the lightest extension of his own, but from what Elsior had said, feeling wasn't the same thing as sensing, and since he could feel any probe of his own shields, and hadn't, it seemed that what Elsior was doing was different from what Quaeryt did.

A glass passed before the scouts returned and reported.

"Sir . . . there is a holding ahead. Near on two milles. It might be a high holding, but there are no gates, just gateposts."

"No gates? What about walls?"

"No, sir."

Quaeryt reflected for a moment. While it wasn't a requirement, most Bovarian high holdings did have gates or walls, at least around the hold house, although there had been a handful, one or two, mostly in hilly or rocky regions, that didn't have gates, but none that hadn't had either. "Are there enough outbuildings that might provide shelter?"

"There look to be plenty, sir."

Quaeryt looked to Calkoran. "If you'd have a squad accompany me, we'll ride ahead and see what we can do."

Calkoran turned in the saddle. "Major Eslym, second squad, escort the commander." Then he repeated the order in Pharsi.

For a moment Quaeryt wondered why Eslym was being detached. Then he almost shook his head. None of the Khellan rankers likely understood either Bovarian or Telaryn. He inclined his head to Calkoran. "Thank you."

"No thanks are necessary. You treat us as your own." Calkoran smiled.

Quaeryt smiled back and gave his own order. "Undercaptains, you report to the subcommander."

"Yes, sir."

Then Quaeryt urged the black gelding forward. For some reason, he couldn't help thinking about the mare that had carried him all the way across Lydar, only to die under him in the last moments of the battle for Liantiago. *She deserved better.* But then, so did so many who perished in war, like Shaelyt, who had shown such promise, and Akoryt . . . and the tens of thousands who had died, so many because of his acts.

The worst part of that was that he was no longer so sure about what Vaelora had said after the battle for Ferravyl—that he had no choice on whether thousands would die, but only which thousands. That had been true at Ferravyl, he supposed, and at Variana, and the battles between, but at Liantiago? In essence, he'd made the decision to invade Liantiago. *You made it believing that war with Aliaro was inevitable . . . and that sooner would cost everyone less. But you made that decision.*

He glanced over the bushes and high grass to his left and down at the River Aluse, its waters still a good fifteen to twenty yards wide, but the occasional mud bars near the shores suggested that it was shallower, at least in spots, than it appeared. To his right was a forest, or rather a well-managed if extensive woods where the undergrowth appeared carefully trimmed. In places he could see sharply defined lanes, reinforcing the impression that great care had been taken by the holder whose dwelling they approached.

As they passed where the woods ended, and a hedgerow three yards high began, the scout turned in the saddle and called back, "It's not that far ahead, sir!"

Quaeryt hoped not, because he could smell rain on the cool breeze blowing at his back. After he rode another hundred yards ahead, Quaeryt could see the gateposts on the right side of the river road, set just a yard or so out from the hedgerow. He glanced to the river side of the road . . . and frowned. While the area to the left of the road had been cleared and was pasture, in the middle of that green area was a long rise, as if a substantial dwelling had once been situated there, overlooking the river.

Why would someone remove a hold house from there and move away from the river? Quaeryt shook his head.

A fraction of a quint later, when he reined up before the gateposts, he saw they were brick and square, but looked almost squat, as if they had once been much higher. Still . . . each was topped with a stone square on the top of which was an ornate iron letter L, something Quaeryt had never seen before, but most likely representing the name of the hold or its holder. The lane beyond the gates ran straight back, almost due east to a dwelling on a slight rise that was anything but small—unless compared to most hold houses. The small mansion looked to be a simple two-story brick structure no more than forty yards from end to end with an extended and columned entry porch. The roof was fired tile, rather than slate.

After a moment he turned the gelding up the brick-paved lane, flanked by two of Calkoran's rankers. The bricks looked old, and in spots newer ones had replaced the originals, and intermittently the mortar between the bricks had been repointed, apparently as necessary, rather than all at once as Quaeryt would have expected at a high holding. The lane was flanked by simple pastures, and sheep were grazing on each side. None of the animals were close to the lane, and none looked up as the squad rode past at a walk.

The lane went straight up the low rise, ending in a brick-paved square some twenty yards on a side with the center of the eastern edge meeting the two wide stone steps leading down from the open space between the two brick columns that supported the roof over the entry porch.

Standing on the edge of the porch were a man and a woman.

Quaeryt gestured the squad to a halt and rode forward, reining up short of the two and bowing slightly in the saddle. "Greetings."

"You speak Bovarian as though you were from Kharst's court, officer."

The man who had addressed Quaeryt was tanned, unlike most High Holders, and wore brown trousers, a cream-colored open-necked shirt, and a sleeveless brown leather vest. His boots were brown and scuffed. Quaeryt doubted he was five years older than Vaelora. The woman wore a loose-fitting white linen dress, as simple as a shift, with a pale violet sleeveless vest, unfastened, since she was quite visibly expecting.

"Thank you . . . I think. I'm Commander Quaeryt, and I'm looking for shelter for the night for my troopers."

"Do we have any choice . . . Commander?"

"Not really, but I can offer some small recompense, and the assurance that no one will be harmed and nothing damaged."

"For the night only?" asked the woman in a deep voice, even deeper and huskier than Vaelora's.

Quaeryt glanced to the south and the dark menacing clouds that now covered half the sky. "Well . . . until the rain stops."

The young man laughed. "That's a souther storm. You might be here two days."

"We won't stay longer than necessary."

"How many troopers do you have? If you're a commander . . ."

"The squad was just to escort me. My officers are protective. Eight officers and a little over two hundred men."

"The officers we can accommodate in the house," replied the woman. "There's no way we can fit two hundred men there, even sleeping in the halls."

"I wouldn't have expected that. We were thinking about outbuildings, sheds, barns, and stables."

The man nodded. "There's a fenced pasture that will hold your horses for a few days. The stables have space for perhaps ten mounts. Since it's almost summer, the hay barns are mostly empty . . ."

"That will be fine. Thank you." Quaeryt turned. "Major, if you would send word back to the subcommander that the holder has agreed to let us stay the night."

"Yes, sir." Eslym in turn spoke in Pharsi, and three rankers eased away from the squad and headed back down the paved lane.

The man looked at Quaeryt curiously. "That didn't sound like Telaryn."

"It wasn't. It was Pharsi. I have a Khellan battalion under my command, but just one company is with us."

"If you don't mind my asking, Commander, just how big is your command?"

"Officially, it's two regiments and the Khellan battalion, but at the moment, one regiment is in Westisle, two companies are in Kephria, another regiment is in Variana, and the rest are here." Quaeryt shrugged. "Most commanders don't have such scattered commands, and mine usually isn't."

"So . . . it's true that Lord Bhayar has conquered Antiago as well as Bovaria," said the woman. "What next? Khel?"

"He's requested that Khel consider favorable terms."

"That's the sort of request they'd be foolish to reject . . . assuming the terms are favorable."

Quaeryt cleared his throat. "Ah . . . the rain is coming. Would you mind if the major and his men made a quick survey to see what might be the best way of billeting the men?"

The man smiled and shook his head. "We appreciate the politeness. Of course. I don't believe we've introduced ourselves. I'm Daalyn, and this is Laedica."

"I'm pleased to meet you." Quaeryt inclined his head, then turned to Eslym. "Major, if you would look over the buildings and then let me know your recommendations. I'll remain here with our hosts."

"Yes, sir." Eslym issued several commands, and ten of the rankers followed him as he rode along the lane that circled the dwelling on the north side. Five remained and formed a line behind Quaeryt.

"For Pharsi, they seem rather protective of you."

"We've been through a lot together." Quaeryt dismounted, then handed the gelding's reins to the end ranker, and walked up the steps to the porch.

Laedica looked closely at Quaeryt. Her eyes widened. "You're much younger . . ."

"Than the white hair? Yes. Every hair on my body turned white at the battle of Variana." Even as the words left his mouth, Quaeryt wanted to take them back, wishing he'd just said, "Yes, I am." *That just shows you're tired and off-guard.*

"Were you . . . I mean . . ." Daalyn fumbled for words.

"If you're asking if I was in the midst of the battle . . . yes, I was."

Laedica's eyes dropped toward Quaeryt's hands. This time her mouth opened. "You . . ." She turned to Daalyn. "He's the one."

Quaeryt instinctively checked his shields. "The one what?" he asked mildly.

"Everyone is talking about the unknown officer who called the storms that killed all of Kharst's troopers," explained Daalyn. "They said he was a young man with the hair of an ancient, and that he was some sort of son of a Pharsi god . . ."

Quaeryt shook his head. "I'm the guilty one, but I'm no more the son of a god than either of you. I am an imager. You'd find that out sooner or later."

"Why did you kill them all?" demanded Daalyn.

"As my wife once told me, once Rex Kharst started this war, tens of thousands of men would be killed. I could not stop that. My only choice was which thousands. Lord Bhayar had almost thirty thousand troopers. Kharst had close to fifty thousand. If I had not done what I did, half of those would likely have perished. Perhaps a third of Kharst's troopers and two-thirds or more of Bhayar's. My acts changed which troopers died, not that troopers died."

"That's justifying—"

"Daalyn," said Laedica firmly. "Officers don't get to choose which orders to obey. Not unless they want to get executed."

The way she looked at her husband, at least Quaeryt thought he was her husband, reminded him of Vaelora. That firmness hadn't changed when she'd been pregnant, either. For a moment the thought . . . and the feelings . . . of the daughter they had lost rushed over him, as they sometimes did in unguarded moments.

"What is it?" asked Laedica. "You looked so strange, Commander."

"Thank you," replied Quaeryt. "Let's just say it's been a long day, and a long journey." He could tell from the expression on her face that she didn't believe him, but she didn't pursue it.

Before long, the rest of the companies arrived, and Quaeryt was busy watching, but the officers and squad leaders were quick and effective in settling the men in and making arrangements for some hot food, although by the time the men were largely settled the rain began to fall, first as a drizzle, but within a quint, it pelted down with a steady rhythm that suggested Daalyn had been correct in his assessment. Amid it all, Quaeryt did manage to get his gear up to the bedchamber that Laedica had indicated was his.

The dinner prepared for the officers and their host

and hostess, well after dark, given the need to feed the troopers, was quiet, very polite, and short.

Afterward, Quaeryt borrowed the small study to talk with the three imagers. Although he was tired, after a day of riding he didn't feel like sitting and remained standing.

"How are you three coming with your shields?"

The three exchanged glances.

Quaeryt sighed. "Khalis. Hold the strongest shields that you can."

"Yes, sir."

Quaeryt probed and pressed with his own shields. While he could have broken through, it would have taken a fair effort and would likely have injured Khalis. He released the pressure and nodded. "That's good. Lhandor, you're next."

Lhandor's shields were strong, if not quite so strong as those of Khalis.

"Now you, Elsior."

"Sir . . . I'm not as strong as they are."

"I know. I'm not interested in hurting you. Now . . . shields, please."

For all of Elsior's protestations, Quaeryt was pleased to find that the youngest imager's shields were nearly as strong as Lhandor's. As he released the pressure on Elsior's defenses, he said, "You're doing well. I think we can count you as a full undercaptain, not just provisional."

"Sir . . . thank you."

"You've earned it . . . or you will," replied Quaeryt.

Khalis and Lhandor both nodded.

By the time he was finished with the imagers, Quaeryt was more than tired enough for bed, although he was anything but sleepy. So he made his way out through the front door of the dwelling that was not exactly a hold house, but more than a mere landowner's mansion, and stood under the roof of the extended front porch in the darkness, looking out into the darkness and the rain.

He could see light from one of the oil lamps in the hall as someone opened the door behind him, and he turned to see Laedica walking toward him, the door left ajar behind her.

She stopped a yard away. "Do you like to listen to the rain?"

"Sometimes," he admitted.

"You mentioned your wife . . . and you looked sad. I don't mean to pry. . . ."

"She's fine." Quaeryt debated whether he should say more, then found himself speaking. "I saw you were expecting. She . . . lost . . . our daughter . . . in Kephria . . ." For a time, Quaeryt could say no more. He shook his head, then finally said, "I'm sorry. I hadn't . . ." He shook his head again.

"You haven't talked about it, have you?"

"No."

"Do you want to?"

"You're kind . . . but I think not."

"You're a strange man, Commander. That is obvious. You can kill thousands, but you worry about your men treating a pair of holders you don't know with care. You obviously love your wife, and mourn the loss of your daughter. You're not much older than I am, but your hair is white. You limp, and I saw at dinner that several of your fingers don't work. Yet you paint your nails."

"You're very observant." *As many women are.* Quaeryt smiled. "I don't paint my nails, though. They turned white when my hair did."

Laedica looked intently at Quaeryt and was about to

speak when the front door opened wider, and Daalyn emerged.

"Oh . . . there you are. I wondered where you'd gone." Daalyn walked toward Laedica, then took her arm, gently.

"I heard the door open and went to see," replied Laedica. "I found the commander looking at the rain."

"We haven't seen much rain on our journey," said Quaeryt. "I imagine it will be helpful for your fields and pastures."

"It definitely will be," said Daalyn. "It's been a dry spring."

"Your lands are rather expansive, it would seem," offered Quaeryt.

"You're wondering why this isn't a high holding?" asked Laedica.

"The thought had crossed my mind."

Daalyn smiled. "It was once. But Laedica's great-grandsire renounced his standing as a High Holder. He made a point of bestowing the lands on his eldest daughter when he had no sons, and when she refused to marry any of High Holder blood who were interested in her . . . or the holding. The other nearest High Holders petitioned to have the lands seized. Before the rex was even informed or could act, the old man had her married to the man she loved, claiming he was a distant cousin, and officially bestowed the lands on him. Ever since then, the eldest child has received the lands . . . if at times through a similar stratagem. The lands are officially mine, but they will go to our eldest. She's five."

"But you're not a High Holder?"

"No one ever petitioned to be reinstated as a High Holder, and given the way Kharst and his sire treated them, it's likely worked out better."

"No one talks about it," added Laedica, "but there are quite a few landholders who are neither crofters nor peasants, nor High Holders."

"But . . . what about standing . . . tariffs?" asked Quaeryt.

"We're officially produce factors," explained Laedica, "and we pay factor's tariffs to the nearest factors' council. That's in Yapres, north of here."

"Not Roleon?"

"That didn't work out," said Laedica. "Yapres is better suited to our needs. Most landholders who are not High Holders have similar arrangements, and the factors are happy to collect the tariffs because that enhances their stature. The rex was always happy because we pay and are far less trouble than the High Holders."

"So only the High Holders are unhappy?"

"They were miffed that one of their younger sons didn't get a holding, but they didn't make a fuss for long because it might have drawn the attention of the rex."

Once again, Quaeryt was both amused and amazed at the complexity and unwieldiness he was finding in Bovaria. "That has seemed to work out for you."

"It has indeed." Daalyn looked at his wife. "You really do need some rest, dear. Tomorrow will come early, rain or no rain." Then he looked to Quaeryt. "Good evening. Commander. If you would excuse us?"

"Please go," replied Quaeryt warmly, looking at Laedica. "You do need to take care of yourself."

"You two would smother me," she replied, not quite tartly, "even if you are right. Good night, Commander."

Quaeryt inclined his head, then watched as they reentered the house. The door closed. He turned to look into the darkness and the rain.

37

In time, Quaeryt left the front porch, carefully closed the front door, and made his way up the steps to the end bedchamber on the second level, not without smiling as he passed the closed door where he heard the muffled voices of three young imager officers, with only a few clear phrases. For several moments, he paused and listened.

". . . be a muddy ride tomorrow . . ."

". . . not going anywhere . . . rain for days this way . . ."

". . . be clear by tomorrow . . ."

". . . no farsight in him . . ."

With a last smile, he turned and walked toward the end of the hall, and the bedchamber where he'd left his gear. That room was clearly the favored guest chamber with an overlarge bed, a writing desk and chair, as well as an armoire and even an adjoining washroom and jakes, for which Quaeryt was grateful. He undressed methodically, still half wondering why he'd been impelled to mention what had happened to Vaelora, even the little that he'd mentioned.

Tiredness . . . worry, he told himself as he climbed under the single sheet, certainly enough in the warm damp air. Outside, beyond the inner shutters of the room, the rain continued to fall, and he finally fell asleep.

Sometime later, he turned over, half aware, and realized that the rain was falling more heavily and that the air was cooler, then much colder, and that, outside, the wind was building into a low moaning. That became a howling, and the inner window shutters blew open with explosive force and icy rain sprayed into the room, coating everything.

Quaeryt struggled against the icy gale to get to his feet, and suddenly he was back on the mare, with ice pelting down on him, yet each sleeting pellet burned as if it had been a white-hot coal. Trying to escape the rain of ice and fire, he urged the mare forward, but she only reared as a curtain of rubble poured down toward them from somewhere unseen, even while the fire- and ice-fall intensified.

The mare reared again . . . and the ground opened up beneath her and Quaeryt . . . and Quaeryt could feel himself falling into the depths, the mare beneath him, as a tidal wave of ice and fire and rubble poured down on them . . . burying him in endless burning rock and rubble.

Abruptly there was stillness . . .

. . . and Quaeryt shook himself, struggling awake.

As had happened too often, he was surrounded with chill and whiteness. Everything in the room was coated with a thin film of brilliant white ice, even the sheets that half covered him. He sat up all the way and flicked the sheets, spraying icy fragments away from the bed. Then he stood and brushed the remaining thin fragments off the bed.

After a moment he walked to the window, ignoring

the icy fragments beneath his bare feet. He eased open one of the inside shutters, then pushed the window open slightly, and stood in the warm moist air that flowed past him into the chill room.

Outside it was pitch-dark, but he could hear the unceasing heavy patter of rain, rain that fell as if it would never cease.

Like some nightmares.

For a time, he stood there letting the warmer air remove the chill from the room and from his skin, hoping, futilely, that it would remove the chill from within. He did his best to image away the ice fragments, glad that the rain he had felt had been part of his dream, and that the room had not been drenched. Finally, he closed the window and shutters and walked back toward the wide bed.

He just hoped he could get back to sleep.

~~~

38

By early on Jeudi afternoon, even after losing an entire day to the rain on Mardi, Quaeryt and the two companies had passed the point where the Roiles River joined the Aluse, flowing out of the northwest, its waters a greenish blue, but lost within a few hundred yards in the grayer waters of the larger river. Another two milles past the junction, they reached the large town of Yapres, somewhat smaller than Daaren, Quaeryt thought, and very dissimilar, although both were river towns, but the dwellings and shops in Yapres were especially well kept, and the streets, and even the lanes and alleys, were largely clean. There were a number of inns, and several buildings that looked to be gaming houses, the first Quaeryt had seen, or at least noticed, in Bovaria. Quaeryt had noticed that for the last five milles into the town, the river road improved markedly. He also understood why Laedica and Daalyn had associated themselves with the factors of Yapres, rather than those of Roleon.

The Aluse was far narrower at Yapres than the Laar was at Daaren. Given that there were no towns of any size for another fifteen milles, or so the maps showed, Quaeryt decided to stop early . . . as well as to deal with some unforeseen reshoeing of a number of mounts.

The largest inn was the Copper Tankard, and Quaeryt

had few qualms about settling both companies there. The boats Quaeryt saw tied at the modest piers across the river square from the inn were narrower than the flatboats used farther south on the Aluse or those used on the Laar, but still had a comparatively shallow draft, suggesting that they were not that stable in rough water and that the Aluse had become fairly shallow. Then again, those boats might have come from farther upriver.

Once the initial arrangements with the innkeeper had been worked out and Quaeryt had seen to men and mounts being settled, he returned to talk to the inn-keeper and see what he could learn from the black-bearded Jhoseal, scarcely older than Quaeryt was himself.

"What would you be wanting to know, Commander?"

"Have you seen any other Telaryn forces recently?"

"A few couriers every week or so. No large forces since early last fall. Heard tell they're all settled some-where near Rivages."

"Who are the most important factors here in Yapres?"

"Might be Zoalon . . . mayhap Locand . . . or Sue-lyr . . . depends on what you mean?"

"The wealthiest, or the head of the factors' council."

"Wealthiest is likely Suelyr, but Zoalon is the head of the factors' council."

"What does he factor?"

"This and that . . . late apples and fruit downriver, when the southern orchards are done, hardwoods from his mill, because the southerners have mostly soft tim-bers, except oak . . . even sends some north to Rivages. Mostly pines north of there . . ."

"Where could I find him?"

"That'd be easy enough. He's usually at his factorage. Six blocks north, right on the river. Has his own piers. Only him and Suelyr do."

"What about High Holders?"

Jhoseal frowned. "Caemren'd be the only High Holder here. On the river four milles north. High stone walls. You can't miss the place. Doesn't like visitors. They say some who tried to visit ran afoul of his guards, and no one ever saw 'em again."

"Any others nearby?"

"Well . . . you want to travel nine-ten milles east or so on the road to Choelan, there's Magiian. Choelan's but fifteen milles east beyond his holding."

"Is there a town patrol?"

"Good one. Don't find the beggars here. No street sluts here. Not in Yapres."

Quaeryt raised his eyebrows.

"Don't get me wrong," said the innkeeper. "We got good women. Madame Besseri's got a fine house on Arbor Lane, and Laynela's is good, too. None of the low street types."

"Who's in charge of the patrol?"

"The chief patroller. That's Sabotyr."

"And how do the patrollers get paid?"

"None of the shaking down folks. Not here. The merchants and factors and tradesfolk all pay a tariff. Factors' council collects it last day of each season. Glad to pay it. Folks come here to have a good time, especially in the spring and late harvest and early fall. Well . . . most years. Been slow last fall and this spring. Still get folks from a lot farther than Choelan."

"From Rivages?"

"Only if they don't want folks in Rivages to know," replied the innkeeper with a laugh.

"What else can you tell me about Yapres?"

There wasn't that much else Jhoseal wanted to volunteer beyond saying how this and that happened to be good, and Quaeryt didn't know enough to ask more than general questions. In another quint, he was back on the gelding, headed north with four rankers as escorts.

The six blocks mentioned by Jhoseal turned into almost ten, and calling Zoalon's establishment a factorage was a bit of an understatement, Quaeryt decided as he approached the complex of buildings that included a large lumber barn, or so it appeared, and three sizable warehouses as well as three wide but short piers. In the middle was a handsome red brick building with stone windowsills and lintels, as well as stone corners and cornices and a slate roof. Since there was a bronze hitching ring by the stone steps to the entrance, Quaeryt reined up there and dismounted, then said to his escorts, "It shouldn't be that long." He checked his shields, reflexively, before he turned toward the entry.

"Yes, sir."

Immediately inside the center building was an entry hall, in which sat a gray-haired clerk. He looked up from the ledger in which he was either making entries or checking them. His eyes widened slightly as Quaeryt removed his visor cap and stepped forward.

"Commander Quaeryt to see Factor Zoalon."

The older man smiled, if ruefully. "I'd say that he probably wouldn't want to see you, but there'd be little enough point in that these days. Commander Quaeryt, you said?"

"That's correct."

"Let me tell him you're here." He paused. "You didn't come alone, I presume, Commander?"

"I have a few rankers with me here, and two companies in town."

"At the Copper Tankard?" The clerk stood.

Quaeryt nodded.

"The boys said something about that. Hadn't seen so many soldiers since last fall when all your regiments came through."

"They haven't been patrolling this far south, though."

"No. Haven't seen anyone in a Telaryn uniform since then except you . . . and the occasional dispatch riders."

Quaeryt nodded and then waited while the clerk walked down the corridor leaving the entry hall, pausing at what looked to be the last door on the right.

"Sir . . . a Telaryn commander here to see you. Commander Quaeryt."

Quaeryt didn't hear the response, but the clerk gestured and said, "This way, sir."

Quaeryt was well aware of the unevenness of his gait as his boots seemed to echo on the polished gray marble tiles as he walked to the open door and then stepped inside, finding himself in a square chamber of modest size, roughly four yards by five. Polished wooden cases lined the wall to his right, and two small bookcases flanked the door. Zoalon was younger than Quaeryt expected, only about forty, balding with short blond hair above his ears. He stood behind a table desk. Two armless straight-backed chairs faced the desk, although the desk chair had arms, with its back and seat upholstered in a tan leather. All the furnishings appeared to be made of the same wood, either natural or stained a dark brown.

"Might I ask, Commander, how much of your visit is courtesy call and how much will result in my losing goods or being paid less for them than they cost me?"

"That depends on what goods you have and what we need." Quaeryt offered what he hoped was a genial smile. "Although that wasn't the reason why I came to see you."

"Oh?" Zoalon's deep voice and expression expressed skepticism.

"I'm after other goods. Information, in fact."

The factor gestured to the chairs and seated himself. "What sort of information?"

"A variety. One thing that has always puzzled me is how exactly did Rex Kharst raise and pay some forty regiments of troopers."

"At great cost to the factors of Bovaria," replied Zoalon dryly.

"He required an additional tariff?"

"Four parts in ten above the normal for the past two years. Some factors failed. Not here in Yapres, but times have been lean for several."

"Where did he get the men?"

"Most towns managed to find blade fodder, one way or another."

"And the factors had a great deal to do with it?"

"I wouldn't say that. We did encourage the young fellows with few prospects and others. . . ." Zoalon shrugged. "You know how it is."

Quaeryt was afraid that he did. "There don't seem to be many High Holders between Talyon and Yapres."

"There were more, years ago."

"We ran across a holding that used to be a High Holder's. The holder's name was Daalyn."

"Laedica's husband. They're officially produce factors, and so is Geongyst. Their grandsires were smart enough to renounce being High Holders. The others were a stiff-necked bunch. They weren't used to reading the wind, and they got burned."

"Literally, from what we've seen. Have you ever seen any of the imagers who did that sort of work for the rex?"

The factor shook his head . . . then frowned. "I don't know as I saw them, or didn't. Years back, when Baernhem's hold was torched, the troopers who did it stayed in Yapres for a few days. There were men in uniform who didn't look like rankers or officers. They might have been imagers, or they might have been clerks who totaled up the value of the goods they returned to the rex. They might have been both."

"It seems to me that Rex Kharst was more inclined to deal with the factors than the High Holders."

"Wouldn't you be? The High Holders always want things their way. They never want to pay the market price of anything. Rex Kharst and his sire, their men would dicker, but they didn't demand. Of course, a few factors who cheated them ended up dead. For the most part, Kharst paid for value and got it."

"And because the factors proved more trustworthy, the factors' councils were used to gather, collect, and send tariffs to Variana?"

"Exactly!"

"Even the tariffs of the High Holders?"

"You wouldn't trust them to be honest if you were ruling Bovaria, Commander."

"Possibly not." Quaeryt had his doubts about the reputed honesty of the Bovarian factors, although he couldn't dispute the fact that the factors might well have been comparatively more honest than the High Holders. "That's also why the council oversees the town patrol and chooses the chief?"

"You get a good chief, and you don't have to oversee

much. You don't, and you can't do enough oversight. We've got a good chief, and that's one of the things that makes Yapres a good place to work and live."

"What about High Holder Caemren?"

"He's better than most. He's a practical type, and knows value. He and his family keep to themselves most times."

"Have you ever heard about a High Holder Fiancryt?"

"Not much. He got along with Rex Kharst, which shows common sense, but wasn't too close, I hear."

"What about Ryel?"

"Him?" Zoalon shook his head. "Everyone thought he was Kharst's spymaster. I had my doubts. How could anyone be an effective spymaster if everyone knows that's what you are? They say his wife saved his holding. She was wealthy, maybe from Khel or someplace. People don't ask questions when you've got gold and jewels."

Although Quaeryt talked to Zoalon for another two quints, he didn't learn anything significantly new after the factor's comments on Ryel.

When Quaeryt returned to the inn, he found Zhelan and Calkoran, and the three took a table in the corner of the public room.

A red-haired and freckled serving girl, probably younger than Elsior, thought Quaeryt, approached, looking tentatively at the officers.

"Pale lager, or whatever lager's the lightest, if you would," requested Quaeryt.

"Dark lager," added Calkoran.

"Ale," said Zhelan.

After the server hurried toward the kitchen, Quaeryt asked, "How are the dispatch riders?"

"They're still confused," replied Zhelan. "I just asked them what they thought might happen to them if someone was capturing and killing dispatch riders. I said we were making good time toward Rivages, and that they'd only be a day or two longer . . . and that they could blame you for the delay." The major grinned.

"Thank you."

"You're welcome, sir. Did you learn anything new from the factor?"

"A few things, but they all tend to confirm what we've been seeing all along. According to Zoalon, Kharst ended up relying on the factors because the High Holders were stiff-necked, uncooperative, and totally dishonest. Then, given how Kharst dealt with them, I can see why they might be perceived that way."

"They deserved each other," said Calkoran. "Bovarian High Holders value their power and privileges over everything. Bovarian factors value golds above everything."

Quaeryt smiled wryly, then frowned. There had been something like that . . . in *Rholan and the Nameless*. But he waited while the server set three beakers on the table, then handed her a silver. "The extra is for you."

Her mouth opened for a moment, then closed, before she finally said, "Thank you, sir," and hurried off, as if afraid Quaeryt would change his mind.

"You were about to say something, sir," reminded Zhelan.

"I was just recalling something Rholan was supposed to have said, something along the line that everyone thinks merchants and factors know the price of everything and the value of nothing, but that's not true. They know the value of every kind of good to the last part of a copper. . . ." Quaeryt paused. There was something else that had been there.

"Sir?"

"There was more. I can't remember it exactly, but it was about how factors don't value beliefs or understand what they mean to others."

"Does anyone who has power?" asked Calkoran sardonically.

"I believe Lord Bhayar understands the importance of at least some beliefs, and that others value their beliefs. But he has been forced to see more than most rulers. I don't think the same of most factors, especially not Bovarian factors. That's also why I think that factors should always advise, but never govern, because a land can't be governed just on the basis of golds."

"He was forced to see?" asked Calkoran. "Who forces a ruler?"

"In his case, his own father," replied Quaeryt.

"You said that Bhayar was actually a ranker in Tilbor?" said Zhelan.

"He was. His sire wanted him to understand what the men he commanded felt. That has been a tradition since the time his forbears were just Yaran warlords."

"He was on the field at Variana," Zhelan pointed out.

"Better than any other ruler in Lydar," conceded Calkoran.

"How long do you think it will take us to reach Rivages?" asked Quaeryt, not wanting to get into a detailed discussion about Bhayar, because, at times, he wondered if he truly knew the man who called him a friend.

"Looks to me like we're less than a hundred milles from Rivages," said Zhelan. "That's if the maps and what the locals say is right. If the roads don't get worse, four long days." He paused. "You just want to ride in?"

"I was thinking of sending out scouts, with one of

the imagers to give them concealment, just to see what they can find."

"That might be best." Calkoran nodded.

Zhelan nodded.

Quaeryt lifted his beaker and took a swallow of the pale lager. He'd had better, but he'd had much worse.

39

Quaeryt was up early on Vendrei, not that it mattered, because it had turned out that many more horses needed reshoeing than he had realized. Since that would take most of the day, he and the troopers would be spending an additional day in Yapres.

So much for making good time, he thought as he rode off to see Suelyr, on one of the spare mounts, as soon as he had finished meeting with the imagers—to whom he assigned specific exercises—and his senior officers. Since Suelyr was the wealthiest factor, Quaeryt suspected that he would find the man in his factorage, almost exactly as far south of the inn as Zoalan's factorage had been to the north. While Suelyr had one more warehouse than did Zoalan, he also had one less pier, and his study was located on the end of the smallest warehouse, rather than in an elaborate separate building.

Suelyr was also older, with iron-gray hair and a brush mustache, and he wore a plain white linen shirt above gray trousers. When Quaeryt entered the factor's study, escorted by a young clerk, Quaeryt also saw a gray jacket hanging on a wall peg behind the desk. The factor did not rise from a battered desk and gestured to the single chair before it. "Commander. I thought I might see you."

"Why might that be?" Quaeryt smiled easily as he sat down on the chair that was as battered and scratched as the desk.

"You have two companies of troopers. Troopers usually need supplies, especially provisions and grain, and you only have a single supply wagon." Suelyr's smile was not quite predatory. "You'll find that I'm most reasonable in my terms."

Quaeryt nodded, then said, "If we need provisions, I'm certain we'll reach terms." He gently projected absolute confidence and authority. "We'll talk of such later. I actually came as much to hear what you might have to say about the role of the factors here in Yapres as to talk about provisions."

After just the slightest hesitation, Suelyr replied, "The role of factors? We gather and transport goods so that others may purchase them. We turn trees into planks and timbers, wheat corn into flour, and pack it in barrels so that those in other places may have bread. We make a modest profit in doing so, and everyone benefits."

"Factors do indeed undertake all you have said, but you do far more than that, I understand. You gather tariffs for the rex and for the town. You pay the town patrollers and choose the patrol chief. In various ways, you and all the factors have enforced standards so that the streets, lanes, and alleys are clean, and so that low women do not solicit from dark alleys."

"We do have a hand in such." Suelyr paused. "And your point is . . . ?"

"I'm interested in what else factors do. Do you collect fees for those who use the River Aluse? Who pays for keeping the river road in good repair? And I must congratulate you for its condition."

"Thank you. All the factors and merchants of

Yapres—and some of the larger growers around the town—contribute to maintaining the roads, either coin or labor. We feel it is our duty."

"And it encourages people to come here and to trade . . . and patronize the gaming houses. Tell me. Which one do you own?"

"Sandina's," replied the factor calmly. "It's the best. I prefer to be the best at all I do."

"That's understandable. I assume you have your own guards, then?"

"Just for Sandina's and the warehouses at night. The town patrol is adequate for everything else."

"And river tariffs?"

"We keep the river north and south of Yapres free of debris and dredge out sandbars or mud bars that block the channels. We charge a modest fee for that, but only for those using the river for trade."

"Do not some High Holders do the same?"

"I think you know that few indeed are interested in providing services beyond their own lands. Have you seen otherwise?"

"Certainly not in Bovaria," admitted Quaeryt. "It is more common in Telaryn."

"What about provisions? Surely, you could use some."

"We could use some grain," Quaeryt admitted, "but it is not absolutely necessary."

From there, the negotiations proceeded, and in the end, Quaeryt managed to procure some replacement grain for a copper a barrel, not too dear a price, and given the small number of barrels, there was little to be gained by pressing for less, and far too much to be lost. Quaeryt saw that Suelyr understood that as well.

After leaving Suelyr, Quaeryt rode back to the inn with the four ranker escorts to meet the duty squad, also riding spare mounts, for the ride north to High Holder Caemren's estate.

Riding beside Squad Leader Paelort, Quaeryt asked, "What do you think of this part of Bovaria?"

"It's a mite bit cooler. The folks on the street and in the fields look to be the same, excepting that most of us can't understand more than a few words." Paelort paused, then asked, "Why do all the officers speak Bovarian as well as Telaryn?"

Quaeryt laughed. "Because Lord Bhayar's grandsire decided that everyone in his court would speak Bovarian in his presence. He'd learned it so that he could understand what Bovarian captives were saying when they tried to attack Extela. He wasn't exactly the most trusting of rulers. It's been said that he insisted on those around him speaking Bovarian to prove that speaking one language or another wasn't a mark of superiority, and that if the Rex of Bovaria only spoke one language, then everyone around him would speak two. He insisted that anyone who wanted to curry his favor had to have served as a ranker or officer and speak two languages. He couldn't force the High Holders to serve in his forces, although the younger sons of a number did, but he refused to talk to them and increased their tariffs by one part in ten if they didn't learn Bovarian. After he leveled three holdings, the other High Holders decided they'd learn Bovarian, or so the story goes. Then it became a point of pride, and . . . well, officers who wanted to advance beyond captain found they just didn't get promoted if they didn't have at least passable Bovarian. I learned it because the scholars insisted on it for the simple reason that the Lord of Telaryn wouldn't support them or favor them in the slightest way if they didn't address him in Bovarian."

"That's very strange, sir . . ."

"Is it? Many things have happened because of the whims of rulers. Anyway, that's the way it is."

Paelort was still shaking his head as they left Yapres behind and rode along the river road under a hazy sky that reminded Quaeryt of midsummer in Tilbora, but then, he supposed, Rivages was just about as far north as was Tilbora.

The road was surprisingly good, as the five milles into Yapres had been. He wondered whether the road would deteriorate after a point five milles north of Yapres when they left for Rivages, but after four milles, when the stone walls of Caemren's holding came into view on the left side of the road ahead, the road remained packed and level. The walls surrounding Caemren's hold weren't that high, about three yards, and they were designed for privacy and to keep out casual intruders, given that they were constructed of soft limestone, and showed some softening of what had once doubtless been crisp edges.

When Quaeryt reined up outside the entry gates, he could see that the iron gates were clearly sturdy enough to stop anything short of a military attack, and the guardhouse was inside the gates.

The single guard stood behind the gates, locked and chained, and possibly even blocked with an iron bar set in brackets. "High Holder Caemren's not receiving."

Quaeryt repressed a sigh. "Tell the High Holder that Commander Quaeryt is here to see him. I'm representing Lord Bhayar, who is now Rex of Bovaria. It might be best if we didn't have to destroy such beautiful iron-works." He smiled. "We'll wait for you to convey the message, but we won't wait too long."

The guard looked at Quaeryt and the trooper, and

then glanced at the long drive, a good half mille straight back to a white-stone mansion on a slight rise, presumably overlooking the River Aluse. He looked at Quaeryt again.

Quaeryt waited.

"Those are heavy gates," the guard said.

Quaeryt looked at the chains and concentrated.

With a dull clanging, the chains dropped to the stone drive.

The guard looked at the chains, then at Quaeryt before offering a resigned look. He walked to the middle of the gates and dragged the heavy chains to one side, then moved to the back side of the right gatepost, where he began turning a wheel. A slight grating accompanied his turning. Shortly, the guard walked back to where the gates joined and lifted a heavy latch, then slowly backed up, pulling the gate open. He watched, almost dolefully, as Quaeryt and the squad of troopers rode past and onto the stone-paved drive up to the main dwelling.

The house was not excessively large for a High Holder, just two levels, with a central square section, and a wing on each end. The central part was roughly thirty yards across, and each wing was twice that. The mansion walls were of the same limestone as the walls along the road, and the roof was of moderate pitch, finished in slate. A small, at least for a high holding, covered portico extended from the main entry, and Quaeryt led the squad into the shade under the portico.

Two men stood at the top of the three steps up from the paved area below the portico. One wore gray livery with white piping, the other maroon trousers and jacket with a bright green shirt. Quaeryt managed not to blink at the unusual attire of the man he thought might be the High Holder. He inclined his head politely and said, "High Holder Caemren, I'm Commander Quaeryt, here on the affairs of Lord Bhayar."

"How did you convince Whealyt to open the gates?" asked the white-haired man in maroon and green.

"We removed the chains, and suggested it would be better if we didn't have to ruin the gates. He wasn't pleased, but he did see our point."

"Well . . . you're here. You might as well dismount and come in." The High Holder turned and walked to the door. "Come on, Commander. Don't dawdle. I'm sure you've got others to visit. Tiresome business it must be, being at someone else's beck and call. Even at a distance."

Quaeryt suppressed a grin, dismounted, and handed his mount's reins to the ranker who had moved up beside the squad leader. "This might take a bit longer. You might let some of the squad stretch their legs."

"Yes, sir."

Caemren stood waiting as Quaeryt walked quickly toward him.

"You're young for a commander. Your sire a marshal or a High Holder?" He looked closely at Quaeryt. "No . . . wouldn't be that. Don't know of any Pharsi holders or marshals. I'd wager that you're the highest-ranking Pharsi officer in either Telaryn or Bovaria."

"That's probably true."

"No probability about it, Commander." Caemren turned and walked through the door, saying over his shoulder, "We'll sit on the north terrace. Coolest place around during the summer, and it might as well be, close as it is by the calendar."

The north terrace was roofed and off a small salon and occupied the northwest corner formed by the center square of the main section of the house and the north wing. Caemren gestured to a table set back from a small fountain, comprised of what was meant to be a stone seasprite with water spraying up from its blowhole. Quaeryt had only seen one of the shy creatures ever, but they didn't look much like the statue. He seated himself across the small circular table from the High Holder.

For a moment Caemren looked closely at Quaeryt, who had removed his visor cap and set it on the edge of the table. Then the High Holder nodded. "Lord Bhayar's said to be part Pharsi. You his tribute officer?"

"Hardly. I was a scholar before the war. I ended up directing troops in Tilbor during the hill holder revolt. I was appointed princeps after the fighting was over. What with one thing and another, when Kharst attacked Ferravyl, I ended up commanding a company, then a battalion, then a regiment."

"You ever lose a skirmish or a battle?"

"No. Except for the first skirmish, when I was just observing and took a crossbow bolt in the shoulder."

"You look like the Pharsi descriptions of a hand of Erion, and you limp. You paint your fingernails?"

"No. After the battle of Variana, they turned white. So did my hair."

Caemren nodded again. "What do you want?"

"Information."

"Fair enough. About what? Or who?"

"The High Holders around Rivages. Are there others besides Fiancryt and Ryel?"

"Two others. Paliast and Daefol."

"What about them?"

"I've nothing to say. They're non-entities who mean nothing and who will defer to anyone who has power in order to keep their lands and privileges."

"That's it?"

"What else is there to say? You must know the type."

Quaeryt couldn't contest that. So he went on. "Most towns in Bovaria only have one or two High Holders."

"Rivages is a city, not a town. It is a place unto itself. It was also the home of Caldor."

"The unifier of Bovaria."

"So-called unifier. The Yaran warlords who were your Lord Bhayar's forbears were paragons of virtue by comparison."

"And Rivages has not changed much since?"

"With High Holders such as Ryel and Fiancryt in power and indulging Kharst's every whim? How could it change?"

"I'd be interested to hear what you know about High Holder Fiancryt, the late High Holder, rather than his heir . . . if he has one."

"Ah, yes. Fiancryt. Interesting fellow. He kept to himself and his lands when he was in Rivages, but he was very social in Variana. He married twice, both wives to his advantage. He obtained additional lands from his first wife. Cytha was the sister of Ryel, the father of the Ryel who died when Lord Bhayar took Variana and destroyed the Chateau Regis. . . ."

Quaeryt didn't bother to correct Caemren, but continued to listen.

"The lands were thought to be worthless, but Fiancryt found coal there. Cytha supposedly died of a fever she caught from her eldest daughter, who also died. That left Fiancryt with a son. He was about ten. After Cytha conveniently died, Fiancryt wasted no time. His second wife is said to be beautiful, but in the way a good blade is beautiful. Never talked to her, and I don't care to. Myranda came from Variana. She was once a favorite of

Kharst's. Nameless knows how she survived, but Fiancryt's fortunes improved even more after he wed her. Of course, he was at Chateau Regis when it fell to the brother of all storms." Caemren looked guilelessly at Quaeryt. "It was either that, or a storm brought by the hand of Erion."

"It froze all of Kharst's troopers and anyone who was in or around the Chateau Regis," Quaeryt said evenly.

"That was your doing, wasn't it?"

"I had something to do with it."

"That's like saying winter has something to do with the cold."

"Myranda wasn't in Variana?" Quaeryt really didn't want to say more. For all of Caemren's gaudy finery, Quaeryt trusted the High Holder less than any he had met, if for reasons he couldn't voice.

Caemren laughed, a softly ironic sound. "She never set foot in Variana after she wed Fiancryt. It's been said that was one of the conditions. I don't know that it was her condition, either. Kharst was said to be wary of her after a time. I saw the way every eye turned to her when she entered a chamber in Variana."

"I thought you hadn't met her."

"I saw her. That was enough. Even most men who don't like women were caught by her presence."

And she's the one whose holding Myskyl is using as a base of his operations.

"What about Fiancryt's son? The heir?"

"He died this winter. Fell in the river on a hunt. He was with his stepmother and the Telaryn submarshal." Caemren's eyes, hard and intense green, focused on Quaeryt. "That's why you're asking all these questions, isn't it?"

"I'm just following Lord Bhayar's orders to see what

the situation is in Rivages. I take it that Myranda has a son by Fiancryt?"

"She has a son. He was born at Fiancryt."

Most likely by Kharst. That was the conclusion Quaeryt reached by the way Caemren had spoken. "What else should I know about Myranda and Fiancryt?"

"Does it matter?"

"It could."

"It wouldn't hurt if Lord Bhayar turned Fiancryt— without the lady—over to the most loyal and least corruptible officer he has."

"I'll pass that on." Quaeryt nodded. "What about Ryel?"

"He's dead. His widow is an outlander. She'll do fine . . . if Bhayar lets her."

"He already has," replied Quaeryt.

For the first time in their conversation, Caemren showed a brief flash of surprise. Then he smiled. "Your doing?"

"Yes. And Lady Vaelora's."

"You knew her . . . before?"

Quaeryt shook his head. "I knew who she was. I never met her until she came to Variana to petition Lord Bhayar to hold the lands for her children."

When Caemren did not speak, Quaeryt asked, "Who else might be able to tell me about what has happened in and around Rivages in the past two seasons?"

"Besides Lady Myranda, you mean?"

Quaeryt nodded.

"You might try Seliadyn. His hold is in Vaestora. That's some fifteen milles south of Rivages. He's . . . different. He's also one of the oldest High Holders, and he has ways of finding out things. That's if he'll talk to you."

"He'll talk to me." *One way or another.*

"You don't take no for an answer, I see." The High Holder smiled, then added, "Sometimes, it's better not even to ask."

Quaeryt thought about that and smiled. "That's a very good point."

"I thought so." Caemren stood. "You ought to be about your business, Commander."

Quaeryt didn't object. He just stood. "Thank you for the time and information. I do trust that you pledge allegiance—and tariffs—to Lord Bhayar."

"With men like you supporting him, how could I do otherwise?" Caemren gestured toward the open door from the salon, then turned and led the way.

"You might because it's the wisest course." Quaeryt followed the older man.

"Wisdom is always of the moment, Commander. That is something I've learned to my regret. When the moment changes, so does the wise course."

"I can't argue that, but I will say that Lord Bhayar generally chooses well for those who serve and support him." Quaeryt wanted to get the point across that Bhayar had chosen others of capability.

"A host of good and capable men can be brought low by one who is evil and excellent, especially one without principles."

"I've seen that."

"So have others, but most good men hesitate to act until it is too late."

But acting too soon is as much a danger as too late. "Timing is everything."

"So it is. So it is."

When they reached the portico, Caemren looked to Quaeryt. "A pleasure meeting you, Commander."

Quaeryt thought he actually meant it . . . although he wasn't totally certain about the reasons behind Caemren's statement. "And I you." He could feel those intense green eyes on his back as he walked down the steps, took his horse's reins from the waiting ranker, and mounted.

As Quaeryt rode down the paved drive, he thought over the meeting. One thing was certain. The more he learned about Bovaria, the more he realized that Bhayar would need the imagers far more than even Quaeryt himself had realized. Far more, but that was assuming he was successful in dealing with whatever schemes Myskyl and Deucalon had set in motion . . . and although he couldn't have said why, every conversation he had with either factors or High Holders made him more and more concerned about just what the relationship between Myskyl and Deucalon, and the Bovarian High Holders and factors might be.

40

By midday on Samedi, Quaeryt, riding with Calkoran's company, was some ten milles north of Yapres under a sun that seemed just short of blistering. The road remained as good, if not better than it had been coming into and leading into the town. Quaeryt couldn't help wondering if that was at least partly because the distance from Variana was great enough that Kharst wouldn't have known the condition was better? Or because he had seen little point in marching troopers hundreds of milles over bad roads to get to good ones?

As a matter of caution, he'd also instructed Zhelan and Calkoran, whenever they were in the rear, to maintain scouts a good half mille behind the squad acting as rear guard both to avoid any surprises, and in case Deucalon had sent another courier. He also instructed the scouts forward of the vanguard to pull back if they saw any Telaryn riders approaching so as to allow them closer to the lead squads. Quaeryt could only hope that would give his forces a chance to capture such dispatch riders or Telaryn scouts before they turned and galloped back to Rivages to report to Myskyl.

"The road's really good," said Zhelan. "It's like we're in another land."

At Zhelan's remarks, Quaeryt almost froze in the

saddle. *Another country? Maybe that's exactly what most of the High Holders here believe.* Was that another reason why Tyrena had traveled to Variana to petition Bhayar to hold on to control of her lands for her daughter? That certainly fit with what Quaeryt had learned from Laedica and Daalyn. *But Myskyl can't believe that Bhayar would let him set up his own land.*

Quaeryt shook his head. Myskyl didn't have to believe that. He only had to persuade the High Holders and factors of the north that their only chance for continuing their privileges and power was to back an overthrow of Bhayar—and Quaeryt and the imagers. *And you've played right into that by disciplining High Holders and factors for their high-handed ways—except those high-handed ways are exactly what they've always done and what they believe is their due.*

If that was what Myskyl and Deucalon were doing . . . he had to admire their strategy, but it raised even more questions about exactly what he could do to thwart it—and them—without destroying the regiments Bhayar needed to unite Lydar.

"What is it, sir?" asked Zhelan.

"I was just thinking. Your point about the north of Bovaria being a different land may be truer than you thought."

"Do you think that's because of the High Holders?"

"They're at least part of the problem. I doubt they're all of it, but they could be. We'll just have to see." And Quaeryt wasn't looking forward to that.

About a glass later, Quaeryt saw all three scouts heading back toward first company at a good pace—a moderate canter, he thought. "Trouble of some sort ahead . . . or dispatch couriers."

"It could be both," suggested Zhelan.

"You're cheerful," said Quaeryt sardonically.

"It is Bovaria, sir."

"You would remind me of that." Quaeryt laughed.

In less than half a quint, the lead scout had reined up—just after Quaeryt ordered a halt.

"Sir! Three Telaryn riders headed this way. We saw them as we came over that rise and pulled back. They didn't see us. They kept riding, anyway."

"Were there any riders behind them?" asked Quaeryt. "A squad? A company?"

"Didn't see any, sir. No road dust behind them, either."

"Good. Scouts, move back of the head of the column." Quaeryt turned in the saddle. "Undercaptains. Khalis! Raise a concealment shield across the road so that it looks empty. Elsior, stay and support Khalis. Lhandor, you come with me. Major, send a man back to request Subcommander Calkoran join you. I'll need five rankers to follow us. They'll have to stay behind us so the riders won't see them."

"Yes, sir."

Quaeryt gestured to Khalis, then raised his own concealment shield as he urged the gelding forward at a fast trot, in order to be as close to the rise in the road as possible, just in case the Telaryn riders from the north saw dust or something else that would cause them to turn once they rode over the low rise whose crest was still a good two hundred yards ahead. Five rankers from first company fell in behind Quaeryt and Lhandor.

"Do you think they'll try to ride away, sir?" asked Lhandor.

"Don't you?"

After a moment the undercaptain nodded. "They'll have been given some believable reason to avoid any other Telaryn forces. Just like the other courier."

Quaeryt and his small party had covered a little over a hundred yards when he caught sight of a rider in a Telaryn uniform, then another. "Off the road . . . on me," he ordered quietly, but firmly. "We'll try to let them pass, so that they're caught between us and first company." With that, Quaeryt guided the gelding off the road and turned him to face the road, his head about two yards from the outer edge of the shoulder. "A line along the road, even with me."

Once the five were lined up, Quaeryt turned to Lhandor. "You've practiced putting shields around others, right?"

"Yes, sir . . . if they're not too far away."

"I may need some help with that."

"I can do that, sir."

"Good. Quiet now."

Quaeryt and his men waited. In a sense, he could see that the scene would have looked surreal to an observer, at least one who could have seen through the concealment shields. Seven men in Telaryn uniforms lined up on the east side of the road, the woods at their backs, facing the river concealed largely by the high undergrowth on the west side of the road, while a courier and two escorts rode south, oblivious to those waiting and watching.

The dispatch courier frowned as he neared where Quaeryt and his men waited behind their concealment shields. Abruptly, less than five yards from Quaeryt, he reined up and studied the road. Then he shook his head. "I don't like this. There's something here. It looks like tracks on the road. Riders heading into the woods over there."

Somewhere, a horse made a whuffling sound, most likely one of the rankers' mounts, thought Quaeryt.

The dispatch rider glanced at his escorts, then started to turn his mount, gesturing toward the north. "Someone's waiting for us up ahead."

Quaeryt dropped the concealment shield. "We are."

"Ride!" called the courier.

Quaeryt imaged a shield barrier in front of the three retreating riders, anchoring the shields to the road itself. He winced as the three horses encountered the unseen barrier, but they were not moving that quickly. "You're not going anywhere."

The courier turned his mount back toward Quaeryt and simultaneously reached for his sabre.

Quaeryt clamped shields around the courier, still holding the shield barrier as well. "Lhandor, use shields to restrain the escorts. I've got the courier." He rode forward until he was beside the lead rider. "We're not interested in hurting you, but you're not going anywhere."

The man swallowed as he took in the gold crescent moon insignia on Quaeryt's uniform collar.

"By the way, I am Commander Quaeryt, and you will be accompanying us back to Rivages."

The man's brow furrowed, even as he tried to struggle against the unseen shields that held him. "Sir . . . I'm just a dispatch courier."

"I know that. I'm interested in the dispatches you're carrying." *And in your not letting anyone know who we are and where.* Quaeryt reached out and unfastened the dispatch pouches from behind the courier's saddle and slung them over the front of his own saddle. Then he eased the shields away from the man's sabre, which he lifted from its scabbard. He looked to Lhandor. "How are you doing?"

"It's easier than defending against Aliaro's imagers."

"Good." Quaeryt looked to the first company rankers. "If you'd come forward and restrain them so that they can't ride off."

"Yes, sir."

Quaeryt and Lhandor held the three riders until they were conventionally immobilized, with rope and tethers.

"Everyone back to the main body," ordered Quaeryt, releasing the confining shields, and turning the gelding back toward first company.

When they neared where Khalis and Zhelan had to be, Quaeryt called out, "You can release the concealment." He couldn't help but look back and see the surprise on the captives' faces, but he said nothing.

Once he reined up beside Zhelan and Calkoran, who had clearly just arrived, Quaeryt said, "Major, have these dispatch riders held with the others. The men can take a break for water for a quint."

When that had been accomplished, Quaeryt gestured, and the two senior officers joined him just off the shoulder of the road in the shade of an older oak. There Quaeryt opened the dispatch pouches. There were several personal missives in one of the pouches, which Quaeryt left, and a single sealed and official dispatch in the other, from which he removed the seal, by imaging, and began to read.

The first part of the document was the same as any Telaryn dispatch:

To: Deucalon Calonsyn, Marshal, Armies of Telaryn
From: Myskyl Sarronsyn, Submarshal, Northern Army
Date: 24 Avryl
Subject: Current Status

Tariff collections continue apace, and now exceed ten thousand golds, comprised of the token 100-gold levies required of High Holders, and to an equal degree, of the ten-gold factors' tariffs. Because of the uncertainty of transporting such a large amount of golds, we await your instructions on when to do so and with how many troopers. I would suggest a battalion.

Modifications of the Northern Army headquarters are largely complete, and we await further orders.

From there, another page of details about the training of various regiments, as well as suggested promotions, once senior officers eligible for stipends were released.

Quaeryt found the next section, especially in a larger context, disturbing.

The negotiations with the High Holders and the others have proceeded satisfactorily, and I believe the results will be all that could be desired in dealing with those who have usurped the powers of the marshal . . .

Yet, he had to admit that, by itself, it was proof of nothing other than the fact that Myskyl was meeting with High Holders and others, all of which was certainly within the scope of the duties assigned to him and, in fact, in accord with what Quaeryt himself had suggested two seasons before. *To keep Myskyl from making trouble in and around Variana.*

As he lowered the sheets of paper, Quaeryt wanted to shake his head. And to think he'd actually recommended Deucalon as a regional governor.

"Sir?"

Quaeryt handed the dispatch to Zhelan. "You might find this interesting. Let Calkoran read it after you do."

He waited as Zhelan and then Calkoran read the dispatch. When they finished, he asked, "What do you think?"

Zhelan nodded to Calkoran, clearly deferring to the older senior officer.

Calkoran's smile was wintry. "Are you certain that the submarshal is not related to the former Rex of Bovaria? Is there no loyalty there?"

Myskyl and Deucalon are most loyal to gaining power for themselves. Rather than comment on Calkoran's words, Quaeryt just addressed Zhelan. "Your thoughts?"

"Begging your pardon, sir, but I said it all smelled like overdead fish. I was wrong. The fish couldn't smell this bad."

"I'd like you both to think over ways to approach Rivages and the submarshal's forces this afternoon, and we'll talk after we settle the men in Ariviana."

"Yes, sir."

Quaeryt had his own ideas . . . and none of them were promising. He hoped the three of them could come up with something better.

41

By fifth glass of the afternoon on Samedi, the two companies were billeted, after a fashion, in and around the two inns in Ariviana, a town that wasn't quite that, but was too large to be called a hamlet. The larger inn, Traveler's Rest, had but ten rooms and a stable and a barn, although the public room was of a size more suited to a larger town, suggesting the locals also frequented it to a greater extent than might have been expected. The Copper Pot had eight small rooms, a public room, and a single combined barn and stables, but Calkoran professed himself satisfied with the arrangement. So did both innkeepers, which suggested to Quaeryt that given what he was willing to pay, travel was light, times were lean, and then some.

After everyone had been fed, Quaeryt, Calkoran, and Zhelan met at a circular table in the corner of the public room, somewhat too warm for Quaeryt, but when he'd earlier ventured onto the porch in the twilight, he'd been attacked immediately by hungry mosquitoes and even red flies. He decided on being uncomfortably warm rather than being a meal for the insects.

He was nursing his second lager, and it could not have been called pale by any stretch of the imagination, but thankfully at least it wasn't bitter, and the fare, prepared partly from Quaeryt's supplies, had been adequate, although the noodles were pasty, as he'd expected, since there hadn't really been enough time to make them properly, and the dried mutton chewy, if edible. The biscuits had been the best part of the meal.

"You've had some time to think over the dispatch from Myskyl to Deucalon," Quaeryt began. "What are your thoughts?"

"I can't say as I have much more to offer," began Zhelan, after Calkoran had nodded to him. "Submarshal Myskyl has to be preparing some sort of surprise for us. I can't see him attacking us, not with you and some imagers present."

"That suggests that he may plan to separate us from your companies, then," said Quaeryt mildly, not that he hadn't already considered that possibility.

"They won't attack you," replied Zhelan.

"Not with troopers," agreed Quaeryt.

"Then with poison or treachery," concluded Calkoran. "After that, we will be asked to surrender or be attacked as traitors." He paused. "That is sad, when they are the traitors."

"They'll only be the traitors if they fail," said Quaeryt, offering a sardonic smile, before taking the smallest sip of the now-warm lager, and then blotting his forehead.

"Why are the marshal and submarshal doing this?" asked Zhelan.

"Because Chayar—Bhayar's father—died unexpectedly young, and Bhayar became Lord of Telaryn when he was twenty-seven, a mere stripling. I'm guessing that they believe that they could do a better job of ruling." *And they don't much care for the fact that Bhayar trusts me and my judgment more than them . . . and the fact that I'm two years younger than Bhayar.*

"Do you believe he has been a good ruler?" asked Calkoran.

"I do. He could have done some things better. That's true of any ruler. It's easy to see mistakes in hindsight. There are also some things he managed as well as he could, but did not turn out well. His regional governors have often been corrupt and unfair, but until he was forced into war with Bovaria, Bhayar did not have enough troopers to deal effectively with either regional governors or High Holders."

"Will that not happen again after the wars are over?" pressed Calkoran.

Quaeryt could see a glimmer in the eyes of the older officer, but decided to answer the question. "That will depend on how long he keeps all the troopers under arms, and whether other things happen."

"Like your Collegium?" asked Zhelan.

"If Bhayar approves all the plans for the Collegium, he will be able to keep the High Holders and governors in line."

"That is only if you survive to make sure he keeps his word," said Calkoran.

"Bhayar has always kept his word," Quaeryt said.

"Perhaps he will, should something happen to you," rejoined Calkoran, "but he will be a better ruler if nothing befalls you. Khel will not easily accept terms from Bhayar without you at his shoulder."

"Nor will Lady Vaelora's influence be as powerful without you," added Zhelan.

Quaeryt grinned. "I think you two are trying to tell me something." He laughed, good-humoredly.

After a moment so did the other two.

42

At second glass of the afternoon on Mardi, Quaeryt spied one of the millestones that had become less and less frequent the farther north they had ridden from Variana: VAESTORA—5 M.

"Wasn't sure we'd see another town," said Zhelan. "It's almost like the old borders in the north between Telaryn and Bovaria. Just hamlets, and no real towns."

"You did say that it was like a different land in the north. Maybe these are the marches or the borderlands."

"Didn't you say one of the High Holders said the same thing, sir?"

"Caemren said that the High Holders in the north behaved like Rivages was a different land. That's true. He also said that because the unifier of Bovaria came from Rivages, they felt special." *And from what I've seen, people who think they're innately special are dangerous.* Quaeryt looked northward along the road, but nothing ahead looked any different from the cots and fields and woodlots they'd been riding past for the past three days.

More than a glass passed before Quaeryt caught sight of what he thought might be the outskirts of Vaestora. The first thing that struck him was that, at the clear boundary of the town, there was a street set at right angles to the river road, with the streets beyond, all paved in brick, laid out in a gridlike pattern, forming square blocks. The dwellings and shop were modest, but all had walls of either rough-cut native stone or brick, if not both, with roofs he had thought were dull slate. As he drew closer, he saw they were of a flat dark gray tile.

The second striking fact was that the river road led straight to a raised circular hill whose crest had been flattened, possibly centuries ago, on which stood a large walled keep, dominated by a tall square tower that rose behind the eastern walls. Quaeryt realized that Caemren definitely had not overstated matters when he'd told Quaeryt that Seliadyn's holding was in the middle of Vaestora. Both the hold and its rough-finished stone walls had to be ancient, and the town had clearly grown up around it, suggesting to Quaeryt that Seliadyn's lineage was long-standing—or that he or his forbears had taken over the holding from an ancient lineage.

When Quaeryt neared the edge of the square just below the open gates in the hold walls, he could also see that those walls enclosed a space larger than the town itself, although, properly speaking, Vaestora looked to be the size of a large hamlet. Yet he'd never seen a hamlet with paved streets. Nor had he seen a high holding or a keep with such a large tower, especially one that so dominated the dwellings over which it looked.

Various shops lined the north and south sides of the open paved square. The west side was bordered by the grassy slope leading up to the walls, with the paved road to the gate leading from the middle of the western edge of the square. On the eastern end of the square was a small inn that had no signboard or indicator of what it might be called.

As Quaeryt entered the square, he caught sight of a

pump and a watering trough in the northwest corner. "Water the horses here in the square, and have the men stand down. Given the smallness of the inn, I may see about prevailing upon Seliadyn's hospitality."

"If he has any."

"That's a possibility as well," replied Quaeryt. "But I might as well see. The mounts need water in any case."

While Zhelan and Calkoran arranged for the watering, Quaeryt and three rankers from first company rode from the square up the slight slope of the stone-paved road to the open gates. At first glance, the gates looked to be a formality, attached to the front of the walls, and barely blocking the opening. But the walls on each side and above the gates rose almost ten yards, and Quaeryt could see two sets of ironbound doors and the stone slots into which they could be moved. In the middle of the five yards between the war gates he could see the bottom of an iron portcullis.

Very interesting. Quaeryt nodded.

Just inside the very thick walls was a guardhouse, and standing in the shades of the overhanging roof were two guards in yellow and black uniforms. Quaeryt reined up short of them.

"Yes, sir?" inquired the taller guard.

"I'm Commander Quaeryt. I've been sent by Lord Bhayar to see High Holder Seliadyn."

The guard nodded. "If you'll follow Hiern, here, he'll show you the way."

"This way, sir!" offered the younger and shorter guard enthusiastically. "You can tie your horse right outside the tower." He turned and hurried at a fast walk back toward the square tower, set some fifty yards directly behind the gates.

Quaeryt followed, noting that the entire space inside

the east wall of the keep was paved, running from the north wall to the south wall, a distance of some four hundred yards. While many of the stone paving squares were clearly ancient, others were replacements, creating an intermittent pattern of lighter and darker squares. The pavement extended perhaps ten yards west of the rear of the tower, a structure fifty yards on a side. Farther to the east, there appeared to be several large outbuildings, one of which looked to be a stable and another a barracks, although all the windows and doors were covered with shutters.

Following the guard, holding full shields, Quaeryt looked up at the tower, counting the levels, using the windows as a guide. From what he could tell, there were at least eight levels, but it appeared that the lowest level—the one set at ground level—had no windows at all, and the second level offered only intermittent embrasures.

The guard stopped at the bottom of a stone staircase perhaps three yards wide that led up to the second level and a set of double doors. Quaeryt had the definite feeling that the staircase had been added later—much later. On each side of the steps were bronze hitching rails, and a long mounting block was set out from the bottommost step.

"You can tie your mount here." The guard rang a bell set in a bronze bracket on a bronze post by the foot of the staircase.

As Quaeryt dismounted, a figure in black and yellow livery stepped out of the doors at the top of the steps.

"A commander from Lord Bhayar to see the master!" called the young guard.

"He's expected." The functionary bowed slightly.

Quaeryt turned to the rankers. "Just wait here."

"Yes, sir."

Then he turned to the guard. "Thank you."

"My pleasure, sir."

Quaeryt made his way up the steps to the wide area outside the double doors.

"I'm Wereas, the steward, sir. How might I announce you, sir?"

"Commander Quaeryt."

"You're fortunate. He saw your forces enter the town. He's curious. He isn't always."

"Do you know why?"

"No, sir. He just said that there was something different, and that he was receiving."

Receiving?

"In his study. That's on the fourth level, facing the river. This way, if you would, sir." The steward held the polished and oiled heavy oak door, then closed it behind Quaeryt, and stepped ahead to lead Quaeryt through the square entry hall past an arch to another staircase, one of green marble that led up a level to a landing, with two smaller staircases, one at each end of the wide landing, and each leading back east and up another level. The staircase in effect created an atrium of sorts almost three levels high. After riding much of the day, Quaeryt was careful with his bad leg as he made his way up the grand staircase, with its green marble steps and its dark wooden paneled walls, graced in places with light green silk hangings.

"To the left, sir," suggested Wereas once they had reached the fourth level, "and all the way back."

Quaeryt only passed one door, and it was closed, before the steward stopped at the second door, also closed, and rapped on it once. "Commander Quaeryt, from Variana and Lord Bhayar."

"Have him come in."

Wereas opened the door.

Quaeryt stepped into the study, a chamber whose interior walls were entirely covered with floor-to-ceiling bookshelves, possibly one of the two or three largest collections he'd seen, certainly smaller than the collection of the Khanar in the Telaryn Palace, and possibly the same size as that of the scholarium in Solis. The exterior walls, except for the tall and narrow windows, were paneled in the same dark wood as the staircase. Each window was flanked by the pale green silk hangings. A thick carpet of a darker green, its border showing intertwined black and gold chains, covered most of the dark wooden floor except a half yard from the walls.

High Holder Seliadyn sat behind a wide table desk, empty except for two volumes, bound in green leather. As Quaeryt stepped toward the desk, Seliadyn stood.

Quaeryt hadn't been certain what to expect, given the way Caemren had described Seliadyn, but the High Holder was a tall man, at least a few digits taller than Quaeryt. He wore dark gray trousers and a matching jacket over a pale gray shirt. His boots were black and polished, and his silver-white hair was thick, but cut short. He gestured to the pair of wooden armchairs, upholstered in leather stained pale green to match the hangings.

Seliadyn asked politely, "Do you prefer lager, ale, or wine, Commander?"

"Pale lager, if possible."

"A fighting commander, but one with taste." The High Holder addressed the steward. "Two lagers, Wereas."

The steward nodded and stepped back, departing, but leaving the study door open.

Quaeryt moved to the chair closest to the window, but did not seat himself until Seliadyn began to do the same.

"Also familiar with court protocol," said the High Holder. "You brought two companies. That speaks of a man sent to investigate or to take over command. Even with that white hair, I have my doubts about your taking command of six regiments from a submarshal. Do you care to tell me the problem?"

"Let me just say that Lord Bhayar doesn't know if there is a problem, except in communications." Quaeryt smiled politely.

"Your uniform is a brownish green, but well cut. That doesn't suggest shoddy tailoring or cloth. Were you a scholar? Or are you?"

"Both, I suppose."

"You limp slightly, and there's something wrong with your hand. How many times have you been wounded?"

"Enough." Quaeryt almost laughed.

Seliadyn's eyes went to the door, and he motioned.

Wereas carried two beakers on a tray. Both held an extremely pale lager. He offered the tray to Quaeryt, who took the beaker slightly farther from him.

Seliadyn took the other beaker and lifted it, then took a small swallow before setting it on the table desk. "This isn't mine. My vineyards produce a good hearty red and a passable white, but I don't have the best grain lands. We do get a few barrels of a decent apple brandy once in a while." After the slightest pause, Seliadyn went on. "You're Pharsi, aren't you? Was your hair black or white-blond before it turned white?"

"White-blond," replied Quaeryt, before taking a small sip of the lager. "This is excellent."

"Thank you. I've always thought so. White-blond.

That makes you the dangerous kind. It also explains why Bhayar won."

"Why do you say that?"

"Even with his heritage, you wouldn't be a commander if you weren't good at something. Cowards or those who command from the rear—or cosseted staff officers—usually don't get wounded. If you're commanding from the front, you're good or you'd be dead."

"So why are you still alive?" asked Quaeryt.

Seliadyn nodded. "That's a perceptive question. I assume you noticed the real gates?"

"Two sets of ironbound war gates and a portcullis."

"That's part of the reason. The hold is close to self-sufficient. It's also almost three hundred milles from Variana, and I said little on the few occasions I was requested to attend Rex Kharst. I've always paid my people well for information, and whenever Kharst's assassins appeared nearby . . . well . . . they found matters difficult here. After I outwaited them several times, while giving no overt offense, Kharst decided other interests were less troublesome. That could not have continued, of course. My eldest daughter is twelve and is already showing signs of beauty. So I must admit that I'm grateful for Lord Bhayar's intervention. You are married?"

"Yes. Comparatively recently."

"Of course. Young and dashing commanders are much more appealing than scholars. But then, scholars are also often more ruthless."

"I wouldn't say I'm dashing."

"But you're well connected. For that reason, and for reasons of my own, you and your men are welcome to use the old barracks for the night. I can supply provisions, but your cooks will have to do the preparations.

The officers' quarters are spare but comfortable. The rankers' quarters are just spare. There is a small fenced pasture inside the walls which should hold your mounts." Seliadyn smiled. "That way, also, you won't have to impose on the people of Vaestora."

Quaeryt returned the smile. "I had hoped that your hospitality might be a possibility."

"I can be hospitable to those who are reasonable."

"Such hospitality is still much appreciated." Quaeryt lifted the beaker to the High Holder.

Seliadyn nodded, then said, "I assume you are headed to Rivages. You might be interested to know that the submarshal has stationed a regiment—I assume he is rotating them—some five milles south of Rivages proper."

"Is there a road along the west side of the Aluse?" asked Quaeryt.

"There is, but it's a poor excuse for one, except for the last four or five milles into Rivages. That's because Daefol has his holding off it. His great-great-grandsire built it on the top of the highest hill around. Rather, the highest hill with a spring. The present Daefol claims that was so that his forbear would always have water and never be flooded out." Seliadyn snorted. "It doesn't matter if you've got water and walls, if you're a fool."

"Would you care to explain his particular foolishness?"

"Agreeing with the late Fiancryt and his scheming wife."

"I heard she had some ties with Kharst."

"That's one way of putting it. Too bad she wasn't at Chateau Regis when Lord Bhayar's imagers froze it solid. Then, she's always been good at getting others to pay for her ambitions. Now . . . she's likely using her wiles on the submarshal or some senior commander."

"I'll have to keep that in mind . . . but that was why you told me, wasn't it?"

"Of course." Seliadyn smiled and took a sip from his beaker.

"Are there any bridges across the Aluse between here and Rivages?"

"Not except for the one in the middle of the city. Half of Rivages is one side, half on the other."

"What about High Holder Paliast?"

"He's mostly a High Holder by courtesy. He lost half his lands to Ryel. Rather, he lost them to Ryel's wife. She wouldn't leave the holding, but she ran it better than he ever could have. While he was spending golds in Variana, she was making them in Rivages. Paliast owed more than he or his son—I guess young Paliast is now High Holder, but he's no stronger than his sire was. . . ."

Quaeryt continued to take small sips of the excellent pale lager while he asked questions and listened to Seliadyn.

After another quint had passed, the older man smiled. "I've talked enough, and you need to get your men settled. The head ostler can show your captains where the grain for your mounts is. If you have any other questions, Wereas can answer them for you."

"Thank you." Quaeryt rose and inclined his head. "I do appreciate your kindness and hospitality . . . and the excellent lager."

"It's to my interest . . . and to yours, Commander." Seliadyn paused, then asked, "Are you as ruthless as they say?"

Although that was the first inclination that the High Holder had given that he might know Quaeryt, at least by reputation, Quaeryt couldn't say he was surprised. "I'd like to put it another way, High Holder.

Commanders don't make the choices of whether men get killed. Those choices are made by rulers like Rex Kharst and Lord Bhayar. Once those choices are made, my only choices are how what I do affects how few of my men die. I am likely ruthless in working to keep those numbers low . . . and that usually means that a greater number of my opponents die. When possible, I've tried to obtain advantages where few die. Those occasions have been few. I hope they become more frequent in the future."

"A very scholarly and very practical answer. I wouldn't have expected less." Seliadyn rose. "A good afternoon to you, Commander."

"And to you, sir." Quaeryt inclined his head, then eased away from the chair.

He wasn't surprised to see Wereas waiting in the hallway outside the study.

43

By the time Quaeryt conveyed Seliadyn's invitation to his officers and the two companies reached the barracks, all the shutters and doors had been opened, and a footman waited to show the officers through the quarters. An assistant ostler also helped with informing the squad leaders where they could find the hay and grain set asides for the companies' mounts, while an assistant cook helped with the preparation of rations for the men and officers.

The barracks were indeed spare, but there were enough bunks with pallets for all the rankers and every officer had a small chamber on the upper level. Quaeryt's was slightly larger and had a table desk and attached washroom and jakes. The spaces were clean, although there were some traces of dust, suggesting that they had been used sometime in the last year, or that they were cleaned and maintained regularly. Quaeryt also could see that there were three buildings on the south side of the hold, roughly matching the barracks in position, that looked to be in regular use. While not as large as the Telaryn Palace in Tilbora, Seliadyn's hold was the largest in extent of any belonging to a High Holder that Quaeryt had ever seen . . . and was definitely kept in good repair.

For the size of the high holding, there was a definite feeling, at least to Quaeryt, that the staff and occupants represented but a fraction of what the holding either could contain, or once had. Yet everything was in good repair, and there was no sign of neglect anywhere. And before Quaeryt retired, when he surveyed the tower, he saw the glimmer of but a few lamps.

The mattress pallet in his quarters was comfortable enough and better than many beds in the inns in which he had stayed, but his sleep was restless, and filled with unsettling dreams he could not remember when he woke early on Meredi. He was relieved that he had not imaged in his sleep, or not enough to have left any traces in the chamber, although he thought the air seemed cooler than it should have.

He was down in the mess early, but Zhelan and Ghaelyn immediately saw him and headed his way. Both looked concerned.

"What is it?" he asked as they approached.

"One of the couriers from Northern Army escaped, sir," reported Ghaelyn as he stopped and stiffened. "He slipped away sometime after midnight and before dawn. He rolled up a pallet to look like a sleeping man and pulled a blanket over the pallet."

"Did he take a mount?"

"No, sir. There were guards on duty."

"So he's on foot, unless he steals a horse . . . or someone miscounted."

"I talked to the High Holder's ostler," said Zhelan. "They aren't missing any horses, and our counts match the records. Do you think he's headed for the submarshal's forces?"

"At High Holder Fiancryt's?" replied Quaeryt. "It's hard to say. On foot, it's likely to take a good day, and he might not be well received. Then again, he might be. Or he could just be hoping to lie low and see what happens. And he still might have a mount. There's always the possibility that the mount totals didn't include the spare mounts of the first riders."

"Ah . . . I don't think they did," admitted Ghaelyn.

"Lying low might be hard, sir. Most rankers don't speak Bovarian," Zhelan said.

"Do we know if he did? Myskyl likely would have wanted either the courier or one of his escorts to speak Bovarian, I'd think."

"I'll see if his escorts know," volunteered Ghaelyn.

Quaeryt nodded for the undercaptain to leave.

"Even if he does have a mount, it will take him a good three glasses, most likely, if not more, to reach Rivages," said Zhelan.

"Which means he could already be there, if he left at first glass this morning." Quaeryt shook his head. "There's no help for it. We'll have to assume that Myskyl knows we're here, or that he'll know shortly. He'll also know that we've read one of his dispatches and one from Deucalon. But he won't know what Deucalon wrote. Whether that will make a difference . . ." He shrugged.

Quaeryt only had to wait a fraction of a quint before Ghaelyn returned.

"You were right, sir. Khend does speak Bovarian . . . and one of the couriers' spare mounts is missing."

"How soon can we move out?" Quaeryt asked Zhelan.

"A quint after the men finish eating. Say three quints. Could be sooner."

"Then we should. Give the orders to first company. I need to brief Subcommander Calkoran."

"Yes, sir."

Quaeryt found Calkoran near the east end of the fenced pasture, talking over something with Major Eslym, in Pharsi, while some of the rankers of his company were gathering and saddling their mounts.

Calkoran looked up. "Yes, Commander?"

"We need to move out in the next few quints . . . as soon as all your men finish eating. One of the dispatch riders escaped. We'll have to assume that he'll be making his way to report to the submarshal. He may not be, but I'd be surprised if it were otherwise."

"As would I." Calkoran snorted. "You should have chained him."

"For doing his duty under the command of a Telaryn submarshal? If this all turns out to be a misunderstanding, I could be the one ending up in chains. Or having to explain chaining one of our own men when we haven't chained Bovarian prisoners."

"That is the problem with treachery. It puts the honorable men in most difficult positions. That is something traitors seldom worry about."

Quaeryt smiled. "You're right about that. Will you have any problems being ready in three quints?"

"No, sir. Most have already eaten, except for the duty squad."

"Good." Quaeryt headed to grab a quick bite and his own gear.

Little more than a quint and a half later, as the companies were forming up in the paved area east of the barracks, Quaeryt rode to the tower to pay his respects and offer thanks to Seliadyn. He tied the gelding to one of the bronze hitching rails and had barely started up the stone steps to the second-level entry when Wereas appeared.

"Commander . . . the master is not yet awake, and is not receiving." The steward walked down the steps. "He thought you might be leaving early, and he left this for me to give to you if you should come to see him." The steward extended an envelope closed with a yellow and black wax seal.

"Thank you . . . and please convey my thanks and appreciation to the High Holder. We did our best to leave the barracks and quarters in good array."

"Even had you not, that would have been fine, but your care is appreciated."

"As is yours." Quaeryt paused. "I would not intrude, but the High Holder mentioned his daughter. . . . Yet . . . there are few signs. . . . Has he sent her elsewhere for her safety?"

Wereas smiled almost sadly. "She is with her aunt in the hill hunting lodge. Many of the master's retainers are there as well."

"Thank you. I just wondered."

"He would appreciate your concern, sir, but even short visits take their toll."

"If you would convey my concerns, as you see proper, Wereas."

"I will indeed, sir."

Quaeryt inclined his head, then turned, descended the steps, and mounted the black gelding. After riding to the head of the column, while he waited for the last of the squads to join the formation, he imaged the seal farther down the envelope, then opened it. Inside was a brief note, accompanied by a hand-drawn map of Rivages, showing the main roads and the location of the four high holdings, as well as a pointed arrow simply labeled "Regiment patrol." Fiancryt was on the west side of the river, Ryel and Paliast on the east. The west river road was also drawn in. He slipped the map into his uniform shirt, then began to read the brief missive.

Quaeryt Rytersyn, Commander and Envoy
Southern Army of Telaryn

My dear Commander,
Much as I would have enjoyed a longer visit, I am not the man I once was. None of us are, I suppose, even when we were. I trust you will allow me the indulgence of vanity, one of the few I can still enjoy, if in a limited fashion.

The map is as accurate as my hand and memory can make it. Trust none of the High Holders, except Lady Tyrena D'Ryel, and her only if she gives her word. Nothing at Fiancryt is what it seems, even when it appears obvious.

You may be the man others think you are. You may even be the Lost One of Pharsi legend. Yes, I know the legend, and you fit that description. But none of us are the man we think we are. Remember that.

With my highest regards.

Seliadyn D'Alte

Quaeryt read the short missive twice, then folded it and slipped it into his battered leather dispatch case. Especially after the map and missive, Quaeryt couldn't help but wonder about Seliadyn. Caemren had said Seliadyn had ways of knowing things, but Quaeryt hadn't expected all that the missive revealed. But then, there was the phrase about Tyrena. Had she stopped to see Seliadyn on her return to Rivages? It was possible, but going back and asking more questions of Wereas would change nothing and intrude too much on a man who was clearly trying to hold on to his faculties. For all of the High Holder's courtesy and assistance, Quaeryt had only seen Seliadyn for one brief period, and had not been invited to dine with him. Usually, such courtesy included a dinner with the High Holder, but the missive gave the impression that Seliadyn was not up to a long dinner or conversation . . . and so had Wereas's first comments. Yet the High Holder's concern for his people was palpable.

And what about his daughter? Was there something not quite right there? Wereas's expression had suggested something.

Quaeryt shook his head, then straightened in the saddle as Calkoran and Zhelan rode up to report.

"Ready to ride out, sir!"

Quaeryt nodded assent.

"Column! Forward!" ordered Zhelan.

As they rode out through the gates and past another pair of guards in yellow and black, Quaeryt was still wondering about Seliadyn. Had Caemren purposely intrigued Quaeryt into visiting the High Holder, or had Seliadyn—or even Tyrena—set it up? Or was it all coincidence? Or something even more devious?

Neither Quaeryt nor the scouts saw any tracks in the road once they had left Vaestora. That didn't mean anything, because a courier would know not to leave tracks.

After the first seven or eight milles, Quaeryt rode on the left side and kept studying the river, looking for a place suitable for a bridge across the Aluse, its waters now less than fifteen yards across in spots. Once or twice he could see what looked to be the west river road, and it was a dirt track, if one wide enough for the single donkey cart he did see.

Quaeryt rode another mille before he located what

appeared to be a likely spot, where the river in ages past had cut through higher ground, with a narrower channel below two bluffs. He turned in the saddle. "Call a halt here."

"Column! Halt!"

"Imager undercaptains! Forward!"

Once the three had gathered around him, he continued. "We're going to ride out to the end of that low bluff there. If it's suitable, we're going to image a bridge across there. Not a wide grand one, but a simple stone structure comfortably wide enough for one wagon or two mounts abreast. We'll also have to image causeways and enough of a paved road to join to the east river road here and the west river road there. We'll do it mainly piece by piece, because I don't want any of us too tired to image from here on. But we do need another way to get to Rivages, one by which we're less likely to be expected . . . and there aren't any bridges until we reach Rivages itself." As he finished speaking, he eased the gelding forward and then to the edge of the road.

From there, Quaeryt began by imaging a paved causeway from the river road to a point some ten yards from the edge of the bluff. The air was warm enough that only a faint white frost appeared on the gray stone, disappearing almost immediately. He was pleased that he didn't feel a touch of tiredness. Even so he took a healthy swallow of the watered lager in his bottle, and then chewed on a biscuit before leading the imagers westward along the gently sloping pavement. He reined up just short of where the pavement ended, then turned the gelding so that he could see both the three imagers and the River Aluse.

"We'll need a stone pier on each side, down to the bedrock and rising to the height of the bluff here. Remember . . . the bridge is only to be three yards wide. Lhandor, would you like to try imaging the one on the far side?"

"Yes, sir." Lhandor eased his mount forward and studied the river. After several moments, he concentrated. Mist wreathed the pier that rose from the edge of the water on the far side, then dispersed, leaving a smooth gray pier, an oblong whose top looked to be a yard wide and three long, the long side paralleling the river.

"Good. Khalis, if you would create a matching pier on this side."

"Yes, sir."

In moments, another mist-shrouded pier appeared.

"Now . . . drink something and eat a biscuit or two, both of you."

While Lhandor and Khalis refreshed themselves, Quaeryt imaged the span between the piers. He did feel a bit tired after his second imaging. He took out his water bottle again and ate another biscuit before addressing the third imager. "Elsior, image the paved causeway connecting the bridge to the road here."

"Yes, sir."

After that, the three undercaptains alternated in adding the stone side rails and pillars. Then they rode to the far end of the bridge, where Elsior added the approach causeway, and each of the three added five-yard sections of stone paving from the end of the causeway until they reached the rutted dirt track that passed for the west river road.

"Now . . . we'll take a break while the companies cross and then rest the men and water the mounts." Quaeryt signaled to Zhelan to have first company begin crossing the bridge, then waited for the major.

"That's a solid bridge, Commander," observed Zhelan when he reined up beside Quaeryt. "I'd wager that the locals will be using it in days."

"Most likely. We'll stand down here for two or three quints. Men can rest and water their mounts. They'll have to ride back south to get access to the river."

"You want the imagers rested, don't you, sir?"

"I'd rather be careful."

Zhelan nodded, then turned to Ghaelyn. "Have the men water their mounts. Stand down for two quints . . . and pass the word to the Khellans."

"Yes, sir."

Quaeryt rode south a good hundred yards and turned the gelding. Before heading down to the water, he looked back at the gray-stone bridge with its gentle arch over the River Aluse. *A solid workman-like structure, and none of us are noticeably exhausted.* And they were on the west side of the river, with Daefol likely only a few milles ahead. *And our real difficulties are just beginning.*

44

The second glass of the afternoon on Meredi came and went, and the west river road remained rutted and rough as Quaeryt and his force rode north, more slowly than he would have liked. The road was mostly shaded by tall trees that grew closer to the road than Quaeryt would have preferred. There were no cots or fields beyond the trees to the west, suggesting forest or woodlands belonging to Daefol, as opposed to fields tilled by tenant growers.

He studied the maps, both the large one and the hand-drawn one he'd received from Seliadyn, trying to determine just how to deal with the situation . . . or to explain to Daefol how he ended up at his gates, so to speak. Abruptly he shook his head. Fiancryt's holding was across the river bridge in Rivages and just north of the town.

He almost laughed, but ludicrous as the idea was, it just might work . . . and it might tell him something about what Myskyl was doing. He put the maps away and beckoned for Zhelan to move closer.

"Sir?"

"If I can, when we get to Daefol's hold, I'm going to act like a very stupid commander. I want to see how he reacts. So . . . try not to act as though I'm out of my mind."

A puzzled expression crossed the major's face.

"I'm going to insist that I was just following directions, the way Kharllon did when he wanted to make trouble, except I just want to confuse the High Holder and get enough men in position to take over the holding without anyone getting hurt. . . ." Quaeryt went on to explain what else he wanted Zhelan to do when the time came. Then he rode back and gave a similar explanation to Calkoran.

The senior Khellan officer snorted. "The High Holder . . . he will likely believe you. A commander who comes late to an area is often not the smartest."

"I hope he does. It will make matters simpler."

As Quaeryt rode back to the front of the column, he could hope that Seliadyn's description of Daefol as a fool was at least partly accurate. At the same time, he pondered over the mysterious older High Holder . . . and about what he had missed in observing him.

Another quint passed, and Quaeryt was beginning to wonder about the maps and the directions he had received when one of the scouts rode back and reined up—since Quaeryt had ordered a halt when he saw the scout returning.

"Sir, there's a walled holding ahead, west of the road."

"It's not on the river?"

"No, sir. It looks to be quite a ways back from the road, maybe a good half mille."

"Good. Did you see any scouts or troopers?"

"No, sir. The lane from the river road to the gates is empty. Much better than the road we're on. The river road north from where the hold road joins it is better as well."

Seliadyn had said it would be. That confirmation made Quaeryt feel somewhat less uneasy about relying on the white-haired High Holder's information. "I was told that, but it's good to know it's so."

"Much better. Leastwise, it looks so from a distance. You told us to stay out of eyeshot from the hold."

"I did . . . and thank you. From here to the hold, you're only to be a hundred yards in front, and let that decrease as we near the gates."

"Yes, sir."

Quaeryt turned to Zhelan. "We'll take a break here. A last watering for the horses." *And then I play the willfully stupid commander . . . and hope it works.*

While Zhelan dealt with the details of rest and watering, Quaeryt gathered the imager undercaptains under a large tree, not an oak but something equally large and impressive, if a species he didn't recognize.

"Once we get inside the hold, assuming we don't have to use force, we're going to need to find out as much as we can quickly. All three of you can hold personal concealments. I'd like each of you to slip into areas where you can under concealment outside the hold house itself and listen—"

"Ah . . . sir," interrupted Khalis, his tone one of embarrassment, "I can hold a concealment, but listening won't help. I don't know much Bovarian."

Quaeryt wanted to shake his head. He'd known that. He just hadn't thought about it. "Lhandor? You know some, don't you?"

"I can pick up some things. I'll miss some, but I can try."

"Elsior?"

The youngest undercaptain nodded.

"All right. Khalis, you stay close to Major Zhelan and

make certain nothing happens to him. Elsior and Lhandor, here's what I want you to do . . ." Quaeryt went on,
detailing the possibilities and what he wanted them to
look and listen for, and where to go.

Then he explained to Zhelan what would happen . . .
if all went well . . . and what they would do if it didn't.
Then he rode back to Calkoran and outlined what he
wanted from the subcommander and his men.

Less than two quints later, Quaeryt led his small force
out of the tree-concealed section of the west river road
past the meadow pasture area that fronted the hold and
toward the lane up to the gates. The rutted section of
the river road ended abruptly, exactly when the smooth
graveled lane heading westward to the walled hold began. Quaeryt could see that the gates were open . . . and
that they were simple, if tall, ironbound wooden gates
drawn back from gate buttresses that were part of the
reddish stone walls that surrounded the hold house and
its outbuildings. There was no stonework between the
buttresses, either. As he rode closer, Quaeryt could see
that the walls were not hard redstone, but sandstone.
That and the gate structure indicated that the hold
might withstand a short assault but not even a modest
siege—or a force with a single accomplished imager, not
that Quaeryt wanted to image his way through the gates.
The hold house or keep looked to be only three stories,
since a single level and a slate tile roof were all that
appeared above the walls.

There was a small flock of sheep grazing several hundred yards to the north, and the fact that the grass closer
to the road on the right was lower than on the left suggested that they were being used to keep the growth in
the meadows at a low level. Quaeryt could see some thin

trails of smoke from hold chimneys, most likely from the kitchens.

As they neared the gates, several guards hurried up, clearly nervous, but not a one of the three said a word, although they stood across the lane just outside the walls.

"Just move aside!" Quaeryt called out cheerfully. "We're expected." He image-projected warmth and assurance. "Just don't get in the way. It's been a long ride."

"But, sir," called a taller guard, trotting toward Quaeryt, "no one told us . . . there are no preparations!"

"We made good time," replied Quaeryt. "Now . . . just move aside." He kept riding, turning in the saddle and calling out, "Keep moving! We don't want to block the gates!"

The guards backed away, forced back by the press of first company.

Once through the gates, Quaeryt turned the column toward the hold house, trying to keep in character as a clueless commander. He glanced over his shoulder, but Calkoran had halted his company just inside the gates, in a way to keep anyone from leaving, just as Quaeryt had ordered.

Quaeryt reined up and halted first company short of the wide sandstone steps leading up to a small uncovered front terrace before the formal entry to the hold house, not quite a tower, nor exactly a mansion, but with red sandstone walls showing a certain amount of wear. Almost at that moment, a man several years younger than Quaeryt and possibly not that much older than Khalis or Lhandor emerged, flanked by two guards on each side. He sported a square-cut but short curly beard, above a white shirt, a crimson doublet or jacket of a style Quaeryt had never seen, and dark blue trousers. His polished boots were also dark blue, something Quaeryt hadn't seen before, either. The arrogant walk to the end of the terrace suggested that he was indeed Daefol.

Once at the end of the terrace, Daefol squared his shoulders and glared at Quaeryt. "You're not the submarshal. He's the only one with permission to ride in here unannounced." A heavy gold rope chain hung around his thick neck and above his slightly jowled jaw.

"Who are you?" asked Quaeryt. "Aren't you High Holder Fiancryt?"

"Do I look like Fiancryt? He's dead, by the way."

"Then why were we directed to Fiancryt?" asked Quaeryt. "And if this isn't Fiancryt, where are we? And who are you?"

"I'm Daefol D'Alte, and this is Folan. And why are you here, rather than where you should be?"

"According to my orders," Quaeryt hid a smile as he spoke, "I was told to stop at the first high holding I came to."

Daefol looked puzzled. "Folan is scarcely the first."

"We crossed the bridge and came up the west river road, and your holding is the first one," said Quaeryt, trying to look as confused as the High Holder did.

"You came up the west river road?" Daefol's voice contained astonishment and a little skepticism. "It only goes another five milles south before it becomes a path . . . or not even that."

"No, sir," insisted Quaeryt. "We were given directions to follow the east river road to the first bridge, and then cross the bridge and turn north until we came to the first high holding."

"But this isn't the first high holding," protested Daefol.

"It's the first we've come to, and it looks like a high holding, and you say that it is," replied Quaeryt.

"Besides," insisted Daefol in an exasperated tone, "there's no bridge south of here."

"But there is, sir," protested Quaeryt. "It looks new. Gray stone. It arches over the river between two bluffs. It's wide enough for two or three mounts, but probably wouldn't take two carts abreast." He turned to Zhelan. "Didn't it look new to you, Major?"

"Yes, sir." Zhelan did not quite roll his eyes.

"You see?" continued Quaeryt. "You can ask any of the troopers. We crossed the river south of here, I'd say three milles or so. Over that bridge."

Daefol, standing on the upper steps of the entry to the low tower, frowned. "I don't know . . ." Then he nodded. "I'd heard the submarshal had some imagers. That must be it . . . but he should have let me know."

"I wish they'd let us know." Quaeryt frowned. "I thought all the imagers were in Variana or somewhere in Khel. That's what the marshal said. He ought to know." Then he looked hard at Daefol. "How did you know the submarshal has imagers and we don't?"

"I must have overheard something,"

Quaeryt shook his head. "Here I am a commander, and I don't know what's happening in my own army." He paused, then said, "We'll have to stay here tonight. Then we'll be on our way tomorrow."

"It's not all that far to Fiancryt . . . maybe ten milles."

Quaeryt shook his head. "That's too far for this late in the afternoon."

"Commander, I must protest! Submarshal Myskyl said that I would not have to garrison any Telaryn troops. He said that if matters changed, I'd be the first to know."

"We'll be gone early in the morning," said Quaeryt cheerfully. "I'll also let the submarshal know how helpful you've been."

"And you want to take over the hold house as well—"

"Oh, no, sir," Quaeryt replied. "That wouldn't be right. Some of the outbuildings and the like, but not your dwelling. If Submarshal Myskyl thinks so highly of you that there's no garrison here, I wouldn't dream of intruding. But my men have had a long ride from Variana, and trying to push them and arriving late in a strange place, that wouldn't do."

"I'll send a messenger to the submarshal!"

"High Holder, sir . . . that won't do. It's ten milles there, you say, and ten milles back. That's a good four glasses on a fast mount."

Daefol opened his mouth, then shut it, and finally spoke. "Just the outbuildings. I'll have my steward show you."

"He can show the major here, sir. He takes care of all billeting arrangements."

"The major, then." Daefol did not quite snort before he turned and walked back toward the entrance, followed by the guards.

Quaeryt dismounted immediately and handed the gelding's reins to Khalis. "Hand him off to someone."

"Yes, sir."

Quaeryt then stepped back between the next set of mounts and raised a concealment before moving to the side and then walking along the edge of the terrace. A single guard remained outside the main doors, but he was positioned on the other side from where Quaeryt was when he reached the point where the terrace met the wall. As quietly as he could, Quaeryt levered himself

up onto the terrace, then flattened himself against the
wall beside the closed entry doors.

A good half quint passed before the door opened and
a stern-faced graying man in dark blue livery stepped
out through the door. Quaeryt slipped inside before the
guard could close it, almost hitting the footman who had
opened it and barely dodging away, again flattening himself against the side wall of the entry hall, not moving.

"What was that?" declared the surprised footman.

"What was what, Fontoy?" demanded the steward,
stopping and looking back.

"Like . . . someone was here, but they're not, sir."

"Don't go seeing things. We've got enough to worry
about. Don't say a word to the master unless you do
see something."

"Yes, sir."

The steward turned, and the door closed.

"Nameless knows there was something . . ." murmured the footman, drawing himself up and looking toward the closed main door.

Quaeryt slowly moved along the wall of the square
entry hall, trying to make certain his boots didn't click
on the polished gray marble floor, then eased out of the
entry hall into a larger circular space. Ahead of him was
a staircase and, to each side, long corridors.

After glancing around, Quaeryt took the hallway to
the right, beyond the square entry hall, also floored in
the polished gray marble, but with wainscot paneling
with off-white plaster walls above. Hung every half yard
or so was a portrait—except for where there were doors.
The first door on his right was a small parlor, the second what looked to be a family dining area, while across
the hall was a large formal dining area.

Shaking his head, Quaeryt retraced his steps, stopping and moving close to the wall as a maid of some sort hurried past him toward, he presumed, the kitchen. Then he continued past the entry hall and staircase. He passed a small sitting chamber on his left, then a large salon on the right, holding a clavecin at one end, followed by a lady's study on the left, and a large library on the right. All were vacant.

Quaeryt headed back to the staircase and started up, trying to be as careful and quiet as possible. At the top of the steps were two men in livery. Quaeryt listened as he neared them.

". . . avoid the master if you can . . . for a time . . ."

". . . heard him talking to himself about imagers . . . they with those Telaryns?"

". . . don't think so . . . the ones at Fiancryt . . ."

". . . better see if the salon is set up . . ."

The two parted, one coming down the steps past Quaeryt and the other heading south along the corridor.

From somewhere on the upper level, Quaeryt heard the voices of small children. When he reached the top of the staircase, he turned to his right, hoping he had better luck. The third door he came to was ajar. Even before he reached the doorway of the corner chamber, he could hear voices, one of which sounded like that of Daefol. The door was open just wide enough for him to slip into the room, which looked to be an upper-level private sitting room.

Daefol stood near the window, looking down at the rear courtyard, while talking. "It's intolerable, I tell you. Being forced to quarter two companies, even for a night." The High Holder looked to the visibly pregnant woman in the loose-fitting but still stylish pale blue linen dress, trimmed with lace.

"You could have told them no."

"With all those armed men? And with six regiments at Fiancryt or nearby?" Daefol winced at a peal of childish laughter that penetrated the sitting room. "They don't have to be that loud."

"They are children."

"I just can't believe that he rode in like that."

"The commander didn't commandeer the hold house, dear."

"Don't condescend to me, Elajara. It's still intolerable. Absolutely intolerable. If I'd had to talk to him another moment . . . He sounded just like one of Kharst's courtiers. . . ."

"He spoke Bovarian?"

"Most of the senior Telaryn officers do. Not as well as this one, and they're not as condescending. Or stupid."

"Tell me about the commander. Why did he upset you so much? Besides being condescending and stupid."

"He was so arrogant . . . You'd have thought he was Bhayar himself . . . and he couldn't even get his directions straight . . ."

"He couldn't get his directions right? And he's a commander?"

"He's likely a commander by grace. I think his major does all the thinking."

"But how could he end up here and think it was Fiancryt?"

"There's a new bridge across the Aluse south of here. That's what he said, and he's too stupid to lie about that. That's intolerable, too. That submarshal must have had his imagers create it, and they didn't even have the courtesy to let me know."

"I don't understand about the imagers, dear. I thought you said all of Bhayar's imagers were in the south."

"So did I, but Paliast claims that some of the three have thrown in with the submarshal. It makes sense. That way Bhayar gets more imagers, and they have a patron."

"What about the commander?"

"I just don't understand why he's here. He powders his hair to look older than he is."

"Do you think he might be a minion of that imager who married Bhayar's sister. The one you said has enthralled Bhayar with some sort of Pharsi spell?"

Quaeryt stiffened at those words, then smiled ruefully. That explanation made sense in light of Myskyl's and Deucalon's actions.

"The submarshal didn't say enthralled. He said that the imager has convinced Bhayar to pursue unwise policies with regard to High Holders here in Bovaria and also with regard to the larger factors."

"You've never been that enchanted with the factors, yourself."

"No . . . but they were a necessary buffer between Kharst and us. This imager . . . and he's apparently converted Bhayar's sister as well . . . well . . . he's already become the Minister of Administration for Bovaria, and he's personally destroyed high holds all over Bovaria."

"Why does Submarshal Myskyl care? He's from Telaryn. I know you've explained this before, but I didn't quite understand."

Quaeryt had the impression that Daefol's wife understood very much, and was trying to get the High Holder to think about matters more deeply, without being able to say so.

"He feels that, before long, the High Holders here and

in Telaryn will turn against Lord Bhayar, and that some will try to unseat him. That will mean fighting, and no one will benefit from that."

"Kharst destroyed the holds of anyone he felt was disloyal for years. No one did anything. Why would that change? Perhaps, dear, I'm missing something, but I really don't understand."

Quaeryt almost choked as he heard the sweet and seemingly guileless words from Elajara.

"You're right. You don't understand. Fiancryt and Ryel were close to Kharst. If anyone is vulnerable to charges of disloyalty, it would be the northern High Holders."

"I suppose that's true, but Fiancryt and Ryel are dead. I wouldn't think Lord Bhayar would have to worry about them. Myranda, perhaps, but from what you say, she's been most accommodating to the sub-marshal."

"You've never liked Myranda."

"Dear . . . I've never said a word. I've never acted in any way other than the most proper toward her. You know that's true."

Daefol snorted. "I'll be in my study." With that, he turned and headed toward the door.

Quaeryt quickly stepped away from the door, hoping that Daefol didn't slam it on the way out.

"Dear . . . please don't slam the door," added Elajara. "You know how that upsets the children."

Daefol did not reply, but he left the door wide open as he stormed out.

Quaeryt watched Elajara.

The young woman shook her head, then slowly stood and walked to the window.

After several moments Quaeryt, still holding his concealment, slipped from the chamber and walked slowly toward the stairs. He had heard more than enough . . . and doubted he could learn much more by staying.

45

~~~~~

For all his determination to make his way back to his forces, Quaeryt found that getting out of the hold house was more involved than getting in had been—at least getting out undetected, since there were two guards at the main entry. He also discovered that there were guards at side doors at the east and west ends of the long corridor, and that none of the chambers on the main floor had exits onto terraces or porches or verandahs. That left the serving and kitchen doors.

The main door from the side hall to the kitchen was closed, as was the one from the formal dining chamber. From the noise rising from behind those doors, Quaeryt was reluctant to open either, deciding to wait for someone else to open the one between the side hall and the kitchen. After what seemed a good two quints, but was probably less than half a quint, someone did, a footman who hurried out.

Quaeryt darted in, only to find himself in a small chamber filled with drawers and shelves, all of which seemed filled with platters, plates, serving pieces, goblets, and who knew what else. The chamber was empty.

But how were you to know?

The din came from the chamber beyond—and

below—a long stone-walled room filled with tables and ovens . . . and at least four cooks and several assistants.

". . . you send Deltryt packing?"

". . . he was just hanging around . . ."

Quaeryt decided that no one was moving toward the stone ramp leading up to the pantry. He made his way down along the wall, just to be careful. His concealment seemed to hold. At least no one looked his way by the time he was on the lower level . . . and sweating from the overpowering heat in the kitchen.

"Use the old dried mutton . . . sauce it up and put it over anything . . . troopers will eat it . . ."

That was certainly true enough, reflected Quaeryt.

". . . have to fix bread for all those troopers!"

". . . could be worse, dearie," cackled one of the older cooks.

". . . woulda been . . . Kharst's avengers at the door . . ."

". . . or the three . . ."

"Enough chatter!" snapped a tall woman with a narrow face. "Fire up the old ovens! They'll take twenty loaves each, and if you use all three . . ."

Quaeryt wondered how many retainers the hold had supported at one time if the kitchen could turn out sixty loaves at a time. Slowly, he eased along the side of the kitchen wall well back from the long battered preparation tables.

"What about the master's and mistress's dinner?"

"If you keep working it won't be late . . ."

With all the cacophony in the kitchen and his primary purpose that of leaving the hold house, Quaeryt only picked up a few scraps of conversation as he made his way to the rear door. That posed another problem, because, even with all the bustling around, no one was leaving. They were going down steps to the cellars below, out to side rooms and pantries and cubbyholes, but not leaving.

Quaeryt kept waiting, but no one still departed.

Finally, he edged toward the door, and lifted the heavy latch, then gave it the slightest of pushes, as if the latch had not been closed, as though a gust of wind or a breeze had caught it, then slipped through. Behind him, he heard one of the cooks shout, "Who didn't latch the door? Iliza! Close it, and make sure it's latched firm!"

Even as Quaeryt stepped out onto the back steps, he had to dodge around a guard in blue livery, not so much on duty as spending a few free moments waiting for someone.

The guard stepped back and looked around, puzzled, then grinned at the kitchen maid who hurried toward the door. "Best not let it get unlatched again, Iliza."

Iliza made a face and closed the door.

Quaeryt took his time walking across the courtyard toward the far buildings, looking around as he did. There was a fair amount of dust on the sandstone paving, but that was likely the result of wear on the soft stone as anything. At the same time, he had the feeling that as at several of the holdings he had seen or visited, the holding had once had many more servants and retainers than it did at present.

Kharst's tariffs? Inability to compete against the factors in growing grains and crops? Quaeryt shook his head. It could have been any of those, or just a decline in the ability of the High Holders. Certainly, Daefol didn't strike him as the brightest of High Holders, although his wife obviously had more perception than Daefol. *But that doesn't help if he doesn't listen.*

Quaeryt released the concealment inside one of the stables, where no one was looking, and then went to find Zhelan, who was in a dusty tack room at the end of the last and unused stable.

"Sir! I'm glad to see you."

"Are there any problems?"

"No, sir. Not so far." The major grinned. "I was very determined and very polite. I insisted on some rations for the men and some use of the kitchen for warm food. Elsior and Lhandor just drifted off, and no one noticed."

"Are they back?"

"Lhandor is, not Elsior . . ."

"Once Elsior gets back, we all need to meet, all the officers, including the undercaptains. In the meantime, I'll hear what Lhandor found out."

Sitting on a short stool in the dusty tack room, he had Lhandor brief him.

"I didn't find out that much, sir. I followed the stable hands and the assistant ostler. The old ostler talked about how the young ones should be thankful it wasn't like the days before Kharst died, when the old holder had two hundred men-at-arms. He went on about how dealing with two hundred mounts was normal . . . and what a shame it was that they'd all died at Variana. He said something about imagers. I didn't get it all, but it was something about imagers should be saved for dealing with rebels and disloyal High Holders, not for slaughtering honorable men following their master . . . One of the stable boys said his brother died there . . . another said it didn't make much difference how a man died. If he was dead, did it matter whether he was frozen by an imager or run through with a sabre . . . ?"

"Did they say anything about Bhayar or Myskyl or Daefol?"

"The only thing anyone said about Lord Bhayar was that no one could have been worse than Rex Kharst. No one disagreed with that. No one said anything about High Holder Daefol, and the only thing anyone said about the submarshal was that they wished he'd just march his troopers back to Variana."

Lhandor didn't have that much to report, and before long, Elsior arrived.

"Sir . . . it took a while . . ."

"That's fine. What did you discover?"

"I followed the guards, sir. They talk a lot, but they didn't say all that much."

Quaeryt nodded for him to continue.

"The guards don't like Daefol that much. They call him Master DaFool, but not when the guard captain is around. He's loyal to Daefol, I think."

Or at least not overly disloyal.

"Did they say anything about Myskyl or Bhayar?"

"Not much," admitted Elsior. "There was something about being more interested in rebuilding part of the hold house at Fiancryt than in patrolling anything except the east river road. One said that he didn't see much difference between the Telaryn regiments and the Bovarian ones. Neither fought, and both ate too much. Several guards said they were happy to stay here as long as the Telaryn troopers were anywhere close to Rivages."

"Anything else?"

"One of them did say that we were fighting troopers, not barracks boys. No one seemed to hear him. Or they didn't want to. Besides that, they talked about the serving girls and the nearest alehouse . . . other stuff like that."

Quaeryt nodded slowly. He hadn't expected to find out much, but he'd hoped. He turned to Zhelan. "Bring in the others."

"Yes, sir."

Quaeryt stood, but he had to wait only a fraction of a quint before Calkoran, Ghaelyn, and Khalis joined the others and he began to brief them. "I did manage to overhear some interesting conversation between High Holder Daefol and his wife. What Daefol said seems to support what I thought might be happening. Here's the problem we face. The submarshal appears to be telling the local High Holders that Lord Bhayar has been unduly influenced by an evil imager who has married and enchanted his sister. According to High Holder Daefol, this evil imager has also decided to reduce the power of the High Holders and factors and has already destroyed scores of holds and holders. Therefore . . . it is up to the submarshal and perhaps others to rescue Lord Bhayar. I'm fairly certain that at least some of the regimental commanders agree with that story. As I've told most of you before, we cannot afford to deal with this in a military fashion. Lord Bhayar needs those six regiments, but we also cannot allow the submarshal to control them and march them south, with the High Holders behind them." Quaeryt stopped and studied the faces of the officers, then waited.

Calkoran snorted. "He wishes to be the rex . . . or lord."

"Not in name. Only in fact," added Zhelan.

"Do they want to destroy all the imagers, sir?" asked Lhandor.

"Only those that would support Lord Bhayar," replied Quaeryt. "I think that the submarshal understands that if there is no unified body of imagers, Bhayar will have to pay much greater heed to the marshal and submarshal."

"So it's all a trap to kill you, sir," said Zhelan. "They

set it up so that you'd be sent. . . ." He paused, then frowned. "But how . . . ?"

"Do you remember what Daefol said when I mentioned the new bridge?" asked Quaeryt.

"He said that . . . the submarshal had imagers. Wouldn't you know about that?"

"If they were Telaryn imagers," agreed Quaeryt. "We never did find Kharst's imagers, the ones that survived."

"You think they've thrown in with the submarshal?"

"It's the only explanation I can think of."

"Sir, you can't just walk in there," protested Khalis. "It's a trap."

"Then we'll have to spring it without getting caught."

"You'll have to take first company," insisted Zhelan. "The men will be safer. Myskyl wouldn't have any compunction about killing a hundred Khellans."

"Eighty-nine, now," said Calkoran.

"We'll all leave here tomorrow . . . early," said Quaeryt. "Very early. Then we'll find a woodland or the like where most of the companies can wait, but be ready to move as necessary." *If necessary.*

Quaeryt went on to explain what he had in mind. He also hoped that whatever the kitchen fixed, it wouldn't be unpalatable. His stomach was growling.

46

After sleeping on a makeshift straw pallet on Meredi night, Quaeryt was up early on Jeudi morning and making certain that both companies were out of Folan well before seventh glass. As the scouts had reported the day before, the west river road north from the hold was far better and, in less than a glass and a half, they had covered a good six milles, when the scouts Quaeryt had sent out earlier, accompanied by Lhandor, riding a spare mount, to provide concealment when necessary, returned to report.

Quaeryt did not call an immediate halt until they reached what was either a large woodlot or a less than well-managed hunting park, most likely not part of Fiancryt, where the troopers would be hidden from casual view. Then he gathered the imagers and the officers so they could hear what the scouts had found.

"How did it go?" asked Quaeryt.

The squad leader smiled. "Just as you thought, sir. When we went through the town . . . well, the west part of Rivages, no one even looked at us. The edge of the city proper is less than a half mille ahead. You can see that most of the city is on the east side of the river. Barely a town on this side. Not all that prosperous on this side, either. We rode past the bridge. The High Holder's lands start, it looks like, another two milles north, and the gates are maybe a mille farther."

"Did you see any patrols? Did they see you?"

"We saw two patrols heading out, sir, but the under-captain did whatever hid us once we left the town proper area." The scout turned to Lhandor.

"Yes, sir. I thought we could run into troopers any-time. So when we went into a shaded place where the trees shadowed the road, I raised a concealment. That way, anyone who might be watching would just think they lost us in the shadows."

"Good thought. Tell us about Fiancryt."

"It's on the river. The road swings west a bit around the buildings and grounds. There's a low stone wall around the whole hold house and all the outbuildings. Some of the parts of the wall look new. There are two iron gates off the river road. One looks to be for most folks. The gates are open, but there's a full squad sta-tioned right at the gate. There's a trade gate, or maybe for supplies, south of the main gate. It's chained and locked, but there are some guards there, too."

"Is there a lane or road along the wall where it heads toward the river?" asked Quaeryt.

"More like a path, sir. We took it a ways. There aren't any gates there, not even posterns."

"Is there any other way into the grounds?"

"No, sir," answered the squad leader. "Leastwise not from the paths or roads, not without climbing the wall, or by boat from the river."

Quaeryt looked to Lhandor. "What do you think?"

"There are places, I think, where we could image a postern in place, one wide enough for a single mount and rider. Without too much effort. The wall is not that high or thick."

"I like that idea," replied Quaeryt with a laugh. After a moment he said, "You'd best get your own mount. We need to head out."

"I can't say as I like this, sir," said Zhelan.

"We've been over this already," replied Quaeryt. "I don't like it any better than you do, but anything else is worse."

"I know, sir. That's why Ghaelyn will be commanding the four rankers accompanying you."

"He's the undercaptain," said Quaeryt.

"He insists, sir. He says it has to be done right, and that means he wants to make sure it is. The only way that's possible is if he's there."

Ghaelyn nodded and added, "Yes, sir."

"Imager undercaptains," said Quaeryt, "I appreciate your willingness to accompany me, but I want you to understand that I cannot order you to come with me."

"You could, sir, and it would be within your rights and our duty," replied Khalis with a broad grin, "but you won't. That's why we're coming." He looked to Lhandor and Elsior.

Both nodded.

"Besides . . . even if we hadn't promised, we'd be coming," added Lhandor, "because you have to succeed . . . or we'll all end up dead or exiled."

"Or like in Antiago," added Elsior.

Quaeryt looked to Calkoran and Zhelan. "If we don't come back or if Ghaelyn and the rankers come back alone, then you know what to do."

"I don't much care for that, either, sir, begging your pardon," replied Zhelan.

"Neither do I," replied Quaeryt, "but Lord Bhayar and Lady Vaelora need to know."

"Yes, sir."

With a quick gesture to Ghaelyn, Quaeryt said, "Let's head out."

After waiting for a mule cart to pass and get a good hundred yards away, headed north toward Rivages, presumably to market for something, the eight riders moved out from cover and onto the road, slightly covered by a blurring concealment that Quaeryt dropped once they were all on the road.

"Sir?" ventured Khalis, from where he rode beside Quaeryt.

"Yes?"

"I know you think that if . . . well, if your plan doesn't work . . . that Lord Bhayar will need to deal with the marshal and submarshal in order to hold Lydar together. I don't see how that will work without the Collegium."

Quaeryt smiled wryly. "I don't either. But I've been wrong before, and I could be wrong now." *You likely just won't be around to see it this time if you are.* "And Lord Bhayar needs to know in order to have a chance to make it work. He can always disavow anything we do if we fail. After all, he didn't give us precise instructions. He just ordered me to find out why he wasn't getting any dispatches and see if we could do something about it, and send word back if we couldn't."

"You don't care much for the submarshal, do you, sir?"

"What I feel doesn't matter. What matters is whether he's loyal to Lord Bhayar." Quaeryt stopped talking as Ghaelyn led the small party of nine around the mule cart.

The man leading the mule glanced up, gave the smallest of headshakes, and resolutely looked at the road ahead.

So far as Quaeryt was concerned, that was just fine.

As he rode along the west river road toward Rivages, and Fiancryt, to the north, he went over his rough plans again. He had thought about entering Rivages and Fiancryt under the cover of darkness, but he'd dismissed that for a number of reasons, including the fact that it would have been much harder to find Myskyl and the others he sought.

In another quint, they were at the outskirts of the western part of Rivages, with neat brick and timber-plastered cots, some with thatch roofs, but most with fired flat tile roofs. The shutters were largely oiled, rather than painted. The road remained a graveled dirt way for another two hundred yards until they came to a square, paved in yellowish brick. A narrow timber bridge crossed the River Aluse, its causeway ending at the eastern edge of the square. A varied array of carts, small stalls, booths, tables, and peddlers were lined up around the edges of the square, except in front of the long and low inn on the west side.

As they rode past, Quaeryt ignored the efforts of those selling . . . and a few comments as well.

". . . early apples . . . better than potions for you know what . . ."

". . . cherries, fresh cherries . . ."

". . . just what we need . . . more Telaryn troopers around . . ."

". . . wonder where they've been . . . didn't come over the bridge . . ."

". . . coulda been delivering a message to DaFool . . ."

". . . careful . . . playing up to the high ones . . ."

". . . scarves for your woman, scarves for your lady . . ."

Once they had ridden through the square, the road narrowed into a street, largely fronted with shops for the next few blocks, then small dwellings . . . and then a few blocks of larger houses, before they rode past another block or so of smaller dwellings that dwindled into scattered cots. At that point, when he thought no one was looking Quaeryt raised a concealment shield. "I've raised a concealment. If any troopers ride toward us, they won't see us. So we'll need to move to the right shoulder of the road."

"Yes, sir."

After they had ridden another hundred yards or so, they came to a stretch of the road where there were no cots. On the west side of the road were tilled fields, filled with alternating crops, including beans, wheat corn, some maize. On the east side, there was what appeared to be a hunting park, with little undergrowth and trees with greater separation than in a natural forest. *Fiancryt lands*, thought Quaeryt.

Before long, Quaeryt saw riders in Telaryn green riding at what looked to be a fast trot, three of them, likely a dispatch rider and two escorts. Since they did not have spare mounts, they were most likely traveling a comparatively short distance, perhaps to the regiment patrolling south of Rivages on the east side of the river or to High Holder Paliast or, less likely, to Lady Tyrena D'Ryel-Alte. Quaeryt eased the gelding to the shoulder, and the others followed his example.

The three rode past as if Quaeryt's party did not exist, which was fine with Quaeryt.

After riding another mille, Quaeryt saw the stone wall of Fiancryt, and in another two quints, he turned the gelding onto the path along the south wall, occasionally standing in the stirrups to see over the wall in order to locate a place where trees or bushes blocked a direct view of that section of the wall from the hold house and its outbuildings. Roughly two hundred yards off the west river road, Quaeryt found such a spot, where a grove of some sort of ornamental topiary was flanked by two small flower gardens. From what he could determine, no one was in the gardens, and there were no sounds of voices, not that he would have expected such during the morning in a hold largely occupied by Telaryn troopers.

He gestured to the others and reined up. "First, we need to image a smooth opening in the wall, wide enough for a single mount and rider. Khalis?"

"Yes, sir." Khalis looked at the wall, and after a moment an opening appeared, with a faint hint of mist vanishing from the smooth stone on each side of the gap.

"Now we need a gate, hung on two sturdy iron gate hinges drilled into the stone. It should look old. Lhandor."

In moments, what looked like a postern gate filled the space.

Quaeryt smiled. "After we ride through, Elsior, we'll need a latch on the other side."

"Oh . . . I'm sorry, sir," said Lhandor.

"That's all right." Quaeryt looked to Ghaelyn. "Undercaptain, you and the men are to wait here among the trees until you have word . . . if you can, avoid detection. If you cannot, ride off and return later. If you have no word by fourth glass of the afternoon, you're to return to Major Zhelan and report that. Is that clear?"

"Yes, sir."

Quaeryt extended his shields enough that they pushed open the gate as he rode through it, still holding the concealment. He glanced around, surveying the area, but it was deserted and he moved forward to allow the other three to enter the hold grounds. He waited while Elsior imaged a proper latch with a heavy catch before he spoke.

"Now, what we'll do is ride as close as we can, under concealment. When I order it, most likely in a corner of a courtyard, hopefully near a stable, Khalis, you and Elsior raise personal concealments. You'll have to tie your mounts and walk away to follow us. Lhandor, you won't raise a concealment. I'll drop the overall concealment and immediately head for a junior officer. Lhandor, you're to accompany me until you get to a position where you can raise a concealment without much notice, but all three of you are to follow me, but at a distance, and under concealment. Follow me into the hold house, but do not enter any chamber I enter. They could be traps, and I might need help from outside."

"Yes, sir, but . . . ?" Lhandor looked puzzled.

"I'm a senior officer. I wouldn't show up without a junior officer. Appearing without an escort would make everyone suspicious. What will happen"—*You hope*—"is that everyone will see that I'm properly accompanied, and when you vanish from sight, that you've been told to wait somewhere."

All three undercaptains nodded.

As the four rode out from behind the topiary and across the meadow, largely clover, Quaeryt noted, toward the hold buildings, Quaeryt concentrated on trying to identify which buildings were likely what. The hold house itself was one of the larger ones Quaeryt had seen in Bovaria, built of the same gray stone as the wall and rising three stories. Unlike Seliadyn's hold, or that of Daefol, the hold house showed no signs of fortification or the like, with comparatively wide windows on all levels. The plan of the main house was simple, with a square central section and two wings extending from the main section, running roughly north-south, parallel to the River Aluse, some three hundred yards to the east. The main house was situated on a rise some twenty or twenty-five yards above the riverbank. There was a courtyard at the south end of the main house, almost directly ahead of Quaeryt, if several hundred yards away, but nothing directly behind it so as not to block the view of the river. While he could not be certain, it appeared as though there was also another courtyard on the north end. Several low buildings formed an arc away from the south wing of the hold house, possibly a guesthouse, two stables, and two barns, plus a low shed. There was also a small pier on the river with an adjoining pavilion. The pavilion was vacant.

Quaeryt rode slowly across the meadow angling the gelding toward the rear of the south courtyard, that section where troopers, and officers, were more likely to assume someone there had been there for a time. When they neared the rear of what was clearly a stable, Quaeryt said, "Keep your voices low if you have to speak."

Then he rode through the paved space between the stable and the barn to the east of it, reined up just short of the courtyard, and dismounted. "Lhandor, you dismount."

Lhandor nodded.

"Concealments, Khalis, Elsior."

The pair acknowledged his order by vanishing from his sight.

Quaeryt led the gelding around the corner and into the courtyard toward the nearest stable boy, noting that there was a hitching rail just a bit farther on.

"If you'd stable him," Quaeryt said with a smile, "somewhere you can find him in a glass."

The stable boy looked up at Quaeryt, took in the commander's insignia, and nodded. "Yes sir."

"Also, my undercaptain's mount, if you would?"

"I can do that, sir."

"Thank you." Quaeryt offered a pleasant smile and then began to walk toward the hold house, not rushing, but not being leisurely, either. After he'd walked a good ten yards, he glanced back, smiling as he saw Khalis's and Elsior's mounts tied to the railing.

Lhandor kept pace with Quaeryt, just at his shoulder, but a half step back.

When they reached the side entrance to the hold house, the trooper standing there glanced at Quaeryt's insignia, but said nothing as Quaeryt stepped through the doorway, followed by Lhandor, who paused as if brushing something from his eye and held the door for several moments before leaving it ajar and hurrying to catch up to Quaeryt, murmuring, "They're inside, sir."

"Good. Thank you," replied Quaeryt in a low voice as he looked down the long corridor, before spotting an undercaptain carrying a folder of papers. Quaeryt turned his steps toward the junior officer, catching up with him just outside an open doorway, through which Quaeryt could see several table desks and a number of rankers seated at them, some with ledgers.

"Undercaptain . . ."

The undercaptain turned, puzzled rather than surprised as he took in the gold crescent insignia, before looking at Lhandor and relaxing his expression slightly. "Yes, sir?"

"I'm looking for the submarshal."

"He's in the command study, sir."

"If you'd show me the way . . ." Quaeryt smiled

politely, but his tone conveyed the sense of an order, not a request.

"Yes, sir. This way, sir." The undercaptain turned and continued past the chamber holding the ranker clerks.

Quaeryt glanced around, trying not to be too obvious in doing so, and seeing no one near or looking at them, nodded to Lhandor.

Lhandor returned the nod and vanished from sight.

A younger captain whom Quaeryt neither knew nor recognized, not surprisingly, stood from behind a small table desk outside a set of double oak doors as Quaeryt and the undercaptain appeared. The captain frowned, clearly not recognizing a strange commander.

"Sir?"

"Just tell the submarshal that Commander Quaeryt is here to see him," said Quaeryt pleasantly, hoping that the three imagers stayed separated and well back from him, as he'd ordered.

The captain stiffened slightly, then swallowed. "Yes, sir." He walked over to the door and rapped, firmly, then announced, "Commander Quaeryt is here to see you, sir."

After a moment of silence, Myskyl replied, his voice clear even through the heavy door. "Show him in by all means."

The captain opened the door and inclined his head. "Commander."

"Thank you."

Even without looking back, as the captain closed the study door, Quaeryt could sense the looks of puzzlement exchanged by the two junior officers.

The study had likely been used by a younger member of the High Holder's family, or perhaps by guests, given its modest size, four yards by five, with a single bookcase on the inside wall to Quaeryt's right and a settee and a single upholstered reading chair set before the left wall. A table desk had been set before the single wide window, with three chairs before it and one behind it, from which the gray-haired Myskyl had risen, a smile upon his face and in his eyes, not that Quaeryt would have expected anything less.

"Quaeryt! What a pleasant surprise to see you." Myskyl frowned for a moment, then resumed smiling. "I hadn't heard that you had arrived."

"That's not surprising. We just got here."

"I hope you didn't divert too many troopers. We scarcely need any more."

"Oh, no. Only a few."

"I just got word that Skarpa was successful in conquering Antiago, and that he's acting governor."

"He was most successful. Unhappily, sometime after Vaelora and I left Antiago, he was assassinated. Commander Kharllon is currently acting governor, and all appears to be calm from his dispatches."

"Strange things often happen after you've left places," mused Myskyl.

"They have," agreed Quaeryt, "but as you know, I wouldn't have had anything happen to Skarpa. So it must have been someone else's strangeness."

"That's possible. I can't imagine who, though."

"There's always someone. I'm certain you've found some strangeness here. Several of the High Holders I spoke to on the ride north mentioned that Rivages was almost a different land."

"I wouldn't call it that," replied Myskyl. "A great deal more traditional, however."

"Traditional . . ." mused Quaeryt. "Yes . . . I suppose that would fit as well."

"We should go to the officers' salon. It's comfortable there, especially for you after such a long ride."

"You even have an officers' salon?" asked Quaeryt. *Since when has Myskyl ever been concerned for your comfort?*

"It's better than imposing on Lady Myranda too much." Myskyl gestured toward the study door.

"Then that might be for the best." Quaeryt offered an agreeable smile.

"Excellent."

Quaeryt let Myskyl lead the way.

As they left the study, Myskyl nodded to the captain at the small table desk outside and said, "If you'd have Commander Luchan and his assistants join us in the officers' salon."

"Yes, sir."

"Luchan is your second in command?" asked Quaeryt as the captain walked briskly away.

"He is. Very competent. He's devoted to the cause of Telaryn." Myskyl turned northward, toward the center of the hold house.

"As you and the marshal are, I'm certain."

"And as you are to Lord Bhayar," replied Myskyl genially.

"Obviously, Commander Luchan is here in the chateau," said Quaeryt. "Do the other commanders and subcommanders have studies here, or did you follow the marshal's example and house them in the outbuildings?"

"You still show great concern for others in the most peculiar of ways, Quaeryt." Myskyl stopped at the second door, leaving it open, and then entering through a deep archway almost a yard and a half long.

"I suppose I always have, but . . . I do try to learn from what I observe." Quaeryt followed the submarshal, taking in the chamber. There was one wide window set in the middle of the wall, with plain dark wood paneling on each side, as well as around the room. The window casements looked slightly deeper than those in Myskyl's study. A circular wooden table, with chairs for eight, sat before one window, while a settee, flanked by comfortable leather upholstered chairs, was set against the left inside wall. Brass corner tables held unlit lamps.

Myskyl took the chair facing the window and gestured to the one facing him.

Quaeryt took it, not without some trepidation, strengthening his shields. The "salon" bothered him, although he couldn't have explained why.

"The regimental commanders have studies in one of the guesthouses," replied Myskyl. "Might I ask why you're inquiring?"

"As a scholar, I try to observe what works and why people do things. You obviously have learned much from Deucalon, and he, I daresay, much from you."

"We do work well together, as do you and Lord Bhayar."

"How did you come to such an accommodation with Fiancryt's widow?"

Myskyl shrugged. "There was no accommodation. We needed a base of operations. Fiancryt died, and he'd been a close supporter of Kharst."

"So was Ryel."

Myskyl shook his head. "Ryel has a much smaller hold house and fewer outbuildings. Fiancryt was far more suitable, and it even has a wall that makes it secure . . . in a limited way, as you must have seen on your way in."

"I didn't observe any breaks in the wall, and both entrances were gated and guarded. There is, of course, the river. . . ."

At the rap on the salon door, Quaeryt paused.

"Yes?" asked Myskyl.

The young captain opened the door slightly, peering in. "I beg your pardon, sir, but Commander Luchan has an urgent question, sir. He needs to send word before he joins you."

Myskyl sighed and stood. "It's always something."

Quaeryt stood as well when the submarshal rose. "It is, indeed."

"Just sit down, Quaeryt. I'll likely only be a few moments."

Quaeryt tried not to stiffen as Myskyl walked toward the salon door, but he did not seat himself, instead strengthening his shields.

The submarshal half turned, as if to say something, when he stepped into the doorway, the door but half open. Abruptly he stopped, as if somehow blocked from moving. Behind Myskyl, Quaeryt could see the young captain, reaching for something, when he suddenly froze in place. The slightest rumbling alerted Quaeryt, and he clamped shields around Myskyl. Then, what looked to be a solid iron shutter descended from the upper window casement, and the salon dimmed into total darkness except for the sliver of light from the half-open salon door, partly blocked by Myskyl's shield-frozen figure.

A massive concentration of force slammed into Quaeryt's shields, and he could barely remain standing.

Kharst's imagers.

Quaeryt tried to move against the forces—or shields that pressed against him—then stopped as a shower of silver flared into the salon. Silver rain cascaded toward him from the iron shutter that had covered the salon window. In instants, it became clear that the rain was melting away those heavy shutters even as silver fragments floated toward him.

Myskyl stood frozen in the doorway, and three shadowy figures appeared as the rain also melted away a false wall beside the half-open salon door, then formed into chains of light that pinned the shadowy figures against the metal wall behind them. The silver rain flared in intensity. Yet, even as its pattering died into silence, the silver formed a glittering and gleaming archway where the iron shutter and window had been, with a reddish silver road beyond it leading upward into a brilliant star-filled night sky, for all that Quaeryt *knew*, outside the chateau, it was a bright midmorning.

Fascinated, Quaeryt could only watch as a figure strode down that reddish silver road, then walked through the archway and halted. Erion, for it could only be he, stood there for a moment, then looked at Myskyl.

In the light that poured from and around and behind the silver-haired man, Quaeryt could see Myskyl's eyes widen and an expression of disbelief infuse his face. His mouth opened soundlessly, and an expression of fear and shock appeared. The same expression was duplicated on the face of the captain behind him.

As before, Erion held a dagger with a blade of brilliant light, and he pointed the dagger at Myskyl. Across Erion's back was the mighty bow, and in his other hand was a small golden yet leatherbound book.

"There is blood on this dagger," said Erion. "Were it up to you, this land would flow with blood once more. But that will not be." In a single fluid motion he threw the long dagger, and like lightning it struck Myskyl squarely in the breastbone, buried to its hilt and pinning him to the heavy oak door.

The silver-haired figure then turned, looking to Quaeryt's left at the three shadowy figures, held in chains of silver light, and saying, "You have seen treachery, and you have supported it. You have seen evil, and you would again replicate it. There is always treachery, especially by those like you who are powerful, but for whom no amount of wealth and position will suffice, for you know your failings and will not see them. Instead, you seek forgetfulness in the elixir of power. You will have eternal forgetfulness." Erion gestured, and three lightnings flared, and the three figures blackened, and crumpled. Erion turned back to Quaeryt. "You, my son, will never know forgetfulness of your failings. Nor should you. Ever."

For all that he had heard words like that once before, Quaeryt could believe them, more than ever in the cold certainty of Erion's voice.

The silver-haired figure nodded, offered an enigmatic smile, then turned and walked back up the red-silver road through the archway in what had been a window covered by an iron shutter. But when the silver radiance faded, the archway remained, an archway of fused stone and metals combined, and the brilliant sunshine of midday in summer flowed through the opening.

The shields that had imprisoned Quaeryt were gone. Myskyl's body hung from the long silvery dagger, and three charred and dead imagers lay facedown on the charred wood of the false bookcase behind which they had waited.

Quaeryt shook himself, then took one step, and then another.

"Sir! Are you all right?" called Khalis, wrenching the door full open, and ignoring the dead submarshal. "Get out of there now!"

Quaeryt didn't hesitate. He ran, if still holding full shields, through the salon and into the corridor to see the three imager undercaptains, as well as an ashen young captain, immobile. Quaeryt looked to the imagers.

"The other wall, the one on the other side of the salon from where the imagers were—it's got a small cannon filled with balls and aimed at where you were. Lhandor stopped the commander from triggering it."

Quaeryt glanced at the open door to a concealed alcove. Inside, a body lay facedown below what did appear to be a small cannon or a huge blunderbuss.

"The imagers were trying to block me. I had to kill him," explained Lhandor. "Khalis managed to slow down the submarshal so he couldn't get out of the salon so quickly. Elsior's holding the captain. Elsior also told us where the imagers were. That helped. He also said we couldn't let the door close."

Couldn't let the door close? For a moment that puzzled Quaeryt. Then he nodded and said to Elsior, "You can release the captain. But you can kill him if he makes a single wrong move."

"Yes, sir."

The captain stood there shaking. "That . . . That was Erion . . ." Then he fainted.

"It was Erion, wasn't it, sir?" asked Khalis.

Once again, Quaeryt had to question whether it had been Erion, or his own creation of the great hunter. *Will you ever know? For certain? Most likely not.* "I don't know. I don't suppose we'll ever know."

The three exchanged dubious glances.

Quaeryt squared his shoulders. "How are you all with fire?"

"Fire, sir?"

"The one that started when we were fighting the evil imagers."

"But, sir . . ." Khalis broke off his protest, clearly belatedly understanding.

"Of course, the fire started when we fought them, after the submarshal escaped their control of his mind and they killed him and Commander Luchan," Quaeryt added.

"Yes, sir."

Besides which, this holding isn't going to revert to heirs, not after all that it's been used for. Quaeryt sent a fireball into the paneled wall, beside the salon doorway. "Wake up the captain there and tell him the hold house is on fire."

"Yes, sir."

Quaeryt imaged fireballs to various points along the corridor that stretched northward to the main section of the hold house. So did Khalis, and then Lhandor. Then he turned and began to hurry toward the courtyard entrance, calling, "Fire! Everyone out! Fire!"

When they hurried into the courtyard, Quaeryt imaged fire into the upper rooms he could see, as well as sending fireballs to the north wing.

"Fire! The entire hold house is on fire!"

Men appeared from everywhere, some running from the outbuildings, and some from the hold house. Almost in moments, or so it seemed, flames were shooting from the hold house in dozens of spots.

Quaeryt hoped most people could get out of the hold house, but with the numbers that were appearing in the courtyard, he thought there might not be many casualties. *And a lot fewer than if Myskyl's and Deucalon's plans hadn't been thwarted.* Except . . . he knew that the business of thwarting them wasn't quite finished. *Not yet.*

"Elsior . . . you go find Ghaelyn," ordered Quaeryt. "You and he and the rankers ride back and tell Zhelan and Calkoran what happened, then have them ride here to join us. Be ready to provide shields. I don't think you'll have to, but it's possible."

"Yes, sir."

Abruptly Quaeryt found that his legs were shaking, and flashes of light flared across his vision.

Something exhausted you. "I think I need to rest."

"We'll get you away from here, sir, and find something to eat and drink," said Khalis.

"So you're ready to deal with the other commanders after the fire," added Lhandor.

That was fine with Quaeryt, even though he wasn't looking forward to such a meeting or what would follow.

47

The hold house fire did not erupt quite so quickly as it seemed to Quaeryt at the time he hurried out into the courtyard, but it spread fast enough and burned long enough that it was well past the third glass of the afternoon before all that remained was a pile of smoldering ashes and charred stone and brick walls. The various regimental commanders had managed enough men and buckets to keep the fire from spreading to the outbuildings, although that was helped greatly by the fact that the courtyards were wide enough that, with almost no wind, few sparks and embers traveled that far. In the upheaval and firefighting, Zhelan and Calkoran had little difficulty in entering the hold grounds.

Quaeryt did take the precaution of putting the shaken captain under guard and protection of the imagers, since he was the only witness besides the imager undercaptains. He also had a guard posted around the area of the south wing of the hold house where the officers' salon had been. Once the fire was no longer a threat, slightly before fourth glass, Quaeryt summoned the remaining two full commanders—Justanan and Nieron—to a meeting in what had been Luchan's study in the large guesthouse.

By the time both commanders entered the study, Quaeryt had eaten and rested somewhat, and he stood beside the table desk that had been Luchan's. He gestured to the chairs before the table desk. Nieron had thick black hair, wide blue eyes, and an open face, the kind most people trusted on sight. Justanan was narrow-faced, with deep-set watery green eyes and fine and thinning blond hair. His forehead was lined, as if he'd worried his entire life.

After a moment both sat. Quaeryt settled into the chair behind the table desk.

"You asked us to join you, Commander?" asked Nieron. "Should that not have been Commander Justanan's prerogative, since he is senior?"

"Commander Justanan is indeed senior, but there are a few matters to discuss, Commander," replied Quaeryt coldly. "Lord Bhayar sent me to determine why he had received no reply from Submarshal Myskyl, despite a number of dispatches and inquiries. When I tried to ask the submarshal about that, he turned three of Kharst's former imagers on me, and attempted to use a blunderbuss on me. The failure of the Bovarian imagers resulted in a fire and an explosion that killed the imagers, the submarshal, and Commander Luchan."

"We have only your word for that."

"Actually, that's not true. Captain Whandyn, the submarshal's personal aide, was a witness to the entire disaster, and we managed to rescue him from the fire. So were two of my undercaptains. Shortly, I'll let the captain tell you his version. Once we return to Variana, Lord Bhayar will make a final judgment, but at present, given the fact that Submarshal Myskyl appeared to have been compromised, or somehow had his judgment or loyalties altered by the Bovarian imagers, and perhaps Lady Myranda . . ." Quaeryt paused, then asked, "By the way, has anyone seen the lady?"

"She rode off during the fire, we think," replied Justanan.

"There will likely be a price on her head," replied Quaeryt, "but that will be up to Lord Bhayar."

"Don't you speak for Lord Bhayar?" asked Nieron sardonically. "In anything that matters?"

"Only when he's told me what to say," replied Quaeryt quietly. "Only then. That's something that Submarshal Myskyl never understood."

"You were saying," prompted Nieron.

"At present, under Lord Bhayar's authority and as Minister of Administration for Bovaria, I will be acting as senior officer."

"The other officers will have something to say about that."

"No," said Quaeryt. "As you pointed out, Commander Justanan is senior. If, after he hears all that has occurred, he has reservations, then, and only then, will we discuss that. First, you need to hear some background. Then you need to read a dispatch. After that, you will hear Captain Whandyn, and if necessary, my undercaptains. And . . . once the fire has cooled enough, we will examine the so-called officers' salon in the ruins of the hold house."

"What exactly will that tell us?" said Nieron.

"Oh, I imagine that the iron of the blunderbuss mounted in a hidden alcove will be largely untouched, as will the iron shutter in the wall, and the iron backing of a false bookcase . . . as well as a few other items."

At that, Nieron frowned, but did not speak.

"For you to understand what happened and why,

there's one set of facts you have to keep in mind. For the entire campaign up the River Aluse, and even at the battle of Variana, Lord Bhayar and Marshal Deucalon were greatly concerned about Rex Kharst's imagers. Yet neither those imagers nor their bodies were ever found. They were known as 'the three.' There were in fact more than three. How many we may never know. What I do know is that several of them contacted Submarshal Myskyl, most likely through the most attractive and charming widow of High Holder Fiancryt."

Quaeryt looked at Nieron and image-projected a compulsion to tell the truth as he asked, "Were you aware they were here?"

For a long moment, the commander was silent. Finally, he said, "I knew the submarshal was meeting with men who had served Rex Kharst."

Justanan cleared his throat and looked at Nieron.

"We all thought they might be imagers," added Nieron quickly.

"Why did you think he was talking to them?"

"It wasn't my place to ask," replied Nieron.

"And what did Myskyl say about them?"

"He only said they might be helpful in restoring full power to Lord Bhayar."

"I see. And did he mention why Lord Bhayar might not have full power?"

Nieron did not quite meet Quaeryt's eyes.

"Did he?"

After a silence, Quaeryt went on. "We'll come back to that presently. Myskyl met with the three. What they said I don't know. What I do know is this. For more than three months, the submarshal has sent no messages or dispatches to Lord Bhayar. He has sent no tariffs to Lord Bhayar, and he responded to none of Lord Bhayar's requests. Now, I have known the submarshal since he was a commander in Tilbor. He was always a faithful and responsible officer, one whose efforts were always in service of Lord Bhayar. Yet, sometime after the three contacted this devoted officer, he changed. He sent no tariffs. He pretended to send dispatches, but they never arrived. He began to talk to High Holders, expressing worry that Lord Bhayar was the one who changed . . ."

"He said you changed Lord Bhayar," said Commander Nieron.

"That I was the one who usurped Lord Bhayar's power?"

"He never quite said that," interjected Justanan. "It was always implied."

Quaeryt laughed softly. "If I were such a schemer, why was I always at the front of the battles? Why have I been the one wounded three times? I came here with two companies, and I entered Fiancryt nearly alone, with two junior undercaptains. If I were a schemer, why would I leave my regiments, leave Variana and Lord Bhayar, and spend a month traveling to find out why Lord Bhayar received no dispatches? I didn't agree with Kharst's imagers to build an iron-walled room to trap another officer. I didn't withhold tariffs, but sent everything I collected in southern Bovaria. . . . Oh, and by the way, Submarshal Skarpa didn't just squat in a high holding in southern Bovaria. When the High Holders there revolted, he put down the revolt, discovered they were allies of the Autarch, and went on and conquered Antiago and turned it over to Lord Bhayar. He didn't let himself be turned against Lord Bhayar by Aliaro's imagers." Quaeryt smiled coldly at Nieron. "Now . . . Submarshal Myskyl was once an honorable officer. He was turned from his duty by the evil three. Who knows? Perhaps those imagers of Kharst's were the reason why Kharst was so depraved."

Quaeryt couldn't help but notice that Justanan nodded thoughtfully.

Nieron worried his lower lip.

Quaeryt lifted the dispatch from Myskyl from the folder on the table desk and extended it to Justanan. "We intercepted this several days ago. You may find it somewhat interesting."

The worried-looking officer took the dispatch and began to read. His expression became more worried as he continued. Abruptly he looked up and shook his head. "By themselves, his words are merely worrisome, but knowing what we know . . ." He handed the dispatch to Nieron.

The black-haired commander began to read. When he finished, he said, "He's only talking about not wanting the powers of the marshal to be usurped . . ."

"Are you an idiot?" asked Justanan. "He's admitting he delayed sending tariffs, which is an act against Bhayar. He's plotting against another officer appointed by Bhayar. Lord Bhayar is the one who decides how much power an officer under his direct authority has. Commander Quaeryt was not under the command of either the marshal or the submarshal. And as Commander Quaeryt pointed out, as you must be aware, he's talking about an officer who has laid his life on the line in battle time after time. If there is a blunderbuss in that ruin, and I suspect there is, what other proof do you want?"

Nieron swallowed. "But why?"

"I think," said Justanan, "Commander Quaeryt has the right of it. We know Kharst was corrupt. We know he did not hazard his imagers in battle. Every single one of Bhayar's imagers has fought, and several have died. Does that not tell you something?"

Nieron shook his head. "Why would he turn . . . give up everything?"

"Perhaps they convinced him that he should be ruler and not Lord Bhayar, who is, as the submarshal did say, young to be a ruler over all of Lydar."

"Could we hear from the captain?" asked Nieron.

"Of course." Quaeryt stood and walked to the study door, opening it and asking the ranker stationed there— from first company, "Have Major Zhelan escort Captain Whandyn here, please."

"Yes, sir."

Quaeryt left the study door ajar and walked back to the table desk. "The captain should be here momentarily."

When Whandyn entered the study, he looked to Quaeryt. "Sir?"

"Please sit down, Captain." Quaeryt motioned to the remaining chair and waited until the junior officer was seated.

Whandyn was clearly ill at ease, sitting only on the front half of the chair, his eyes flicking from Quaeryt to the other commanders and back to Quaeryt.

"Captain," began Quaeryt, "the commanders would like to hear what you heard and saw earlier today, beginning after you escorted me into the submarshal's study. If you would tell them . . ."

"Yes, sir." Whandyn moistened his lips. "I announced Commander Quaeryt and Submarshal Myskyl told me to show him in by all means. I closed the door. They must have talked for a while. Then the door opened, and the submarshal came out. Commander Quaeryt followed him. The submarshal stopped and told me to get

Commander Luchan and his assistants and have them join him in the officers' salon."

"His assistants?" asked Nieron.

"What assistants?" inquired Justanan almost simultaneously.

"The commander was supposed to bring the Bovarian imagers. That's all I knew, sir." Whandyn trembled.

"You knew that was what the submarshal meant?" asked Justanan.

"Yes, sir. He'd told me they were always to be called his assistants."

"Go on."

"The submarshal and Commander Quaeryt went into the salon. It wasn't long because Commander Luchan and the imagers came almost immediately. The imagers went into the little room with the peepholes into the salon. . . ."

Quaeryt could see Nieron's eyes widen.

". . . and then Commander Luchan told me to knock on the door and tell the submarshal that he—Commander Luchan, I mean—had an urgent question for the submarshal. I did that. The submarshal hurried toward the door, and then he stopped . . . like he couldn't move . . ."

"Pardon me, Commander," said Nieron, turning to Quaeryt, "but there is one question I do need to ask." He looked back to Whandyn. "At any time, did Commander Quaeryt threaten or use force against the submarshal?"

"Oh, no, sir! Not that I heard, sir . . . He just stood there when it all happened. The others . . . Erion and the imagers, they did everything. Well, and Commander Luchan. He tried to trigger the blunderbuss, but the imagers did something to stop him, I guess, because he fell down, but Commander Quaeryt couldn't even have seen that. He was inside the salon."

"Erion?" asked Nieron. "Erion?"

"Well . . . there was a figure that appeared. He looked like Erion. He said something, and then there were lightnings and flame everywhere. Then he was gone, and the Bovarian imagers were all burned up."

"What about the submarshal?"

"Erion threw lightning or something at him."

"Erion? How did you know it was Erion?"

"He gleamed all silver and he came down a path from the moon, and there was a huge bow across his back, and he melted an archway in the iron shutter."

"Oh?"

"Sir . . . it sounds strange, but that's what happened. It really did."

"And Commander Quaeryt had nothing to do with this?"

"No, sir! It was Erion. Commander Quaeryt couldn't do anything, either."

"And Commander Quaeryt did nothing?" repeated Nieron.

"No, sir. It was like the submarshal and he were caught. I didn't see how, but they couldn't move."

"I see." Nieron looked to Justanan.

Justanan shook his head.

"Do you have any more questions of the captain?" asked Quaeryt.

"No," said Nieron, a clear tone of discouragement in his voice. "That is sufficient."

"Likely more than sufficient," added Justanan.

"Captain, you may go. Please report back to Major Zhelan," said Quaeryt quietly.

"Yes, sir."

After the door closed behind the departing captain, Quaeryt asked, "Do you want to hear from my under-captains?"

Nieron shook his head. He looked at Quaeryt. "How did you manage it?"

"I didn't manage what happened in the officers' salon," Quaeryt replied. "I honestly have no idea how that happened. I am an imager, and I was holding full shields to protect myself, but something had clamped around me, and I couldn't move. I thought that was something done by Myskyl's imagers. I had a good idea that he would use them against me, and I was prepared to defend myself. I'd thought that would prove he was disloyal." Quaeryt shrugged. "How all that happened after that . . . I don't know." *Not precisely, anyway, and it's better left like that.*

"The captain's story is very hard to believe," stated Nieron.

"That's most likely why he did see what he did," said Justanan. "Do you honestly think any officer could invent that? Especially one that has never even met Commander Quaeryt before?" Justanan looked to Quaeryt. "Begging your pardon, Commander."

"No offense taken," replied Quaeryt. "I didn't believe what I saw, either."

"It may be better just to tell the other officers that the fire and explosion caused by the Bovarian imagers' attack on Commander Quaeryt created the fire and killed Myskyl and Luchan."

Nieron nodded slowly. "It's so hard to believe." Suddenly he looked at Quaeryt. "If we agree that you're in command, what are your plans?"

"To leave one regiment here, and ride with the others back to Variana," said Quaeryt. "One regiment here is enough. One has proved sufficient in the west, at Laaryn, and two companies are at Kephria, holding southern Bovaria at the moment."

Justanan nodded.

"Who would you suggest . . . ?"

"One of the subcommanders," suggested Quaeryt. "With the death of Commander Luchan and the sub-marshal, you two are among the most senior officers remaining, and the marshal and Lord Bhayar may have need of you."

"That makes sense," said Justanan.

More than you know. But Quaeryt did not voice that as he watched Nieron.

After a moment Nieron nodded. "When would we leave?"

"As soon as possible. Within a day or so." Quaeryt paused. "I'd suggest we plan to inspect the hold house first thing in the morning, at seventh glass. I've posted guards to keep men away from the building. It could be dangerous, and we don't want anyone tempted to try to loot."

"The tariff golds aren't there, anyway," said Justanan. "They're in the strong room below."

"That's good to know. Will you take responsibility for guarding and transporting them?"

The balding blond officer smiled wryly. "The submarshal already gave me that duty."

"Good." Quaeryt returned the smile. "I'd also suggest that Commander Justanan and I address the senior officers tomorrow after we inspect the hold house and meet among ourselves. Perhaps at ninth glass?"

"That would be good," said Justanan.

Nieron nodded.

"Is there anything else we need to discuss before then?"

The two exchanged glances. Then both shook their heads.

"Then I suggest we meet outside the hold house, or what remains of it, at seventh glass tomorrow morning." Quaeryt rose.

So did the other two.

Once they had left, Quaeryt sent word that he needed to speak to the imager undercaptains. Then he sat back down behind the table desk and took a deep breath, wondering what else he had forgotten or overlooked, but at that moment could think of nothing else. *Because you're too tired?*

Elsior entered the study first, followed immediately by Lhandor and Khalis.

Quaeryt waited until the door was closed and all three were seated before he spoke. "I haven't had a chance until now to tell you three how much I appreciated your help in dealing with the Bovarian imagers. If you hadn't done what you did, I doubt I'd be here at the moment."

"Begging your pardon, sir," replied Khalis, "if you hadn't done what you did, we wouldn't be here, and the other imagers wouldn't have much to look forward to."

"That might be so, but it took all of us, just as it did at Liantiago, and just as it likely will in the years to come, if in a slightly different way. I did want you to know that I understand that and that I am grateful for all that you did."

"Sir . . ." ventured Elsior, "how did you manage Erion?"

"Manage Erion?" asked Quaeryt, trying to keep his voice matter-of-fact.

The other two looked at Elsior.

"I can sense shields. You know that. Everything was linked between you and Erion. How did you do it?"

Quaeryt laughed ruefully. "I don't know. I honestly don't. After you three stopped Myskyl, I tried to put shields around him, but that was all I could do. Then Erion appeared. At first, I thought I was imagining things, but it was too real for that."

"It was real," affirmed Lhandor. "Terribly real."

"But it was you," insisted Elsior.

"My dreams, thoughts of Erion? That could be, but I didn't image him into being, not that I felt then or recall now."

"Whatever you did, it worked out," said Khalis. "We're all glad of that."

"So am I," replied Quaeryt. *So am I.* "And I'll say one more time that it wouldn't have happened without you three. Thank you." He smiled. "That's all I had to say."

"Thank you, sir." Elsior paused, then added, "I'm glad you saved me in Liantiago. I never had an imager maître there say 'thank you' or much like it. I'm not saying that just because of today, either." He looked down, as if embarrassed.

"We all feel that way," added Khalis.

The other two nodded.

"I'm glad you do." Quaeryt paused, then said, "We're all tired. Let's get something to eat and see what we can do about quarters."

48

On Jeudi evening Quaeryt took over Luchan's personal quarters in the guesthouse, but only after making certain that both his own companies were fed, with the other regiments, from a kitchen in one of the outbuildings. The men were quartered together in one of the converted barns. While the spaces were tight, both Zhelan and Calkoran professed themselves satisfied. The fact that only Myskyl—and apparently the three imagers—had been actually quartered in the hold house added weight to Quaeryt's beliefs about the submarshal, not that he was about to use that fact except to Bhayar and Vaelora.

Quaeryt slept heavily, but not all that well, waking up at dawn out of disturbing dreams he could not recall. He washed and dressed and went to find Zhelan . . . who was awake and waiting for him.

"No one tried to enter the hold house."

"Good. Has it cooled enough for inspection?"

The major nodded.

"Did you hear anything last night?"

"Most of the majors didn't want to say much. A couple of captains I knew years back did."

"And?"

"They weren't feeling all that bereaved. Some of them

said that it wasn't right the way Myskyl was acting more like a High Holder than a submarshal." Zhelan paused. "Most of the majors are scared shitless of you, sir. Probably the commanders, too. I did hear one major say that Myskyl was an idiot to do anything against you."

Quaeryt smiled. "If he'd been successful, they'd have said I was an idiot to do anything against him."

"That might be, but it didn't happen that way."

"No, it didn't, but it could have." *And might well have if the three undercaptains hadn't been there.* "I'm just glad it didn't."

"Yes, sir."

With a smile, Quaeryt headed for the officers' mess, a small chamber at the end of the converted stable that had become a mess hall for the rankers and squad leaders. He was among the first there, although Calkoran was sitting at the end of one of the two tables. Quaeryt joined the former Khellan marshal, and a mess server immediately set a beaker of lager before him.

"Thank you."

"I'll have something for you right away, sir." The server hurried off.

He knew I'd want lager. Quaeryt turned to Calkoran. "Did you tell him I'd want lager?"

"Of course."

"Did everything go well last night?"

"Yes, sir. No one gave us any trouble. They wouldn't." Calkoran paused. "I talked to Elsior. He said Erion appeared and melted a hole in solid iron and pinned Myskyl to an oak door with a long silver dagger."

Quaeryt took a swallow from the lager before replying. "That was what I saw as well." He shook his head. "I still doubt the existence of either the Nameless or Erion. But that was what I saw."

"Lhandor and Khalis saw it as well. And you doubt?"

"I don't doubt what I saw. I'm not certain . . ." Quaeryt shook his head. "It seemed real and unreal at the same time."

Calkoran laughed. "Never have I known a man who fought for what he believed in so much who also fought the idea that he was different that much."

"I am different. I'm an imager. I was a scholar. I suppose I still am. But I could die just like other men. I almost have. I love like other men. I make mistakes like other men."

"All that is true," said Calkoran. "You know you are a man. You know you have limits. All that is good. But . . . you are blessed, and that is both gift and curse. You understand the curse. I have seen that. Accept that there is a gift as well. Does it matter from where it came?"

Quaeryt started to reply, then stopped. *Does it? What if it came from the Namer . . . something you also doubt?* He smiled. Ironically. *Then you're beholden to do what is right.* He didn't feel like debating internally at that moment the question of what might be right. "Only insofar as I do my best to do what is right."

"As any man should," replied Calkoran.

At that moment the server set a platter of egg toast, ham rashers, and several biscuits before Quaeryt. "Would you like anything else, sir?"

"No, thank you."

Quaeryt ate methodically, mostly listening to Calkoran. He did notice that no other officers sat anywhere close to the two of them.

At a quint before seventh glass, under hazy skies that suggested a hot day to come, Quaeryt walked over to the charred ruins of the south wing of the hold house.

A squad from Calkoran's company was waiting, along with Major Eslym.

"The subcommander thought you'd need men to clear away stuff to get into that mess, sir."

"He's very right. I appreciate it. I should have thought of that."

"You've thought of plenty, sir." Eslym smiled happily.

Before long, Justanan walked toward Quaeryt. "Good morning."

"Good morning to you. How are the regimental commanders this morning?"

Justanan offered a crooked smile. "Worried. Some of them didn't realize who you were. It will do them good."

Quaeryt glanced around, then asked, "Nieron?"

"He's still upset. Not so much at you. He can't believe it. He'll be looking closely."

"There's nothing to hide."

"Interestingly enough, that was one of the few things that Myskyl said about you. He said that you had no secrets, that you did everything in the open, and that men like that were dangerous."

Quaeryt laughed softly. "I learned that from watching him . . . and others." *Except you do have secrets, and some you've even kept from yourself.*

Quaeryt turned to Eslym, who had stepped back to allow the commanders space. "If you'd have the men clear the end entryway and start up the main corridor."

"Yes, sir."

"If there are any bodies, leave them where they are, and leave all weapons or personal articles alone." According to the musters of the night before, the only casualties from Northern Army were Luchan and Myskyl . . . but there was no way of telling how many or who from the hold staff might have perished, not with Lady Myranda and her personal retainers missing.

"Yes, sir."

"You think others might have perished?" asked Justanan.

"It's possible. It's also possible that the only casualties were the three, Luchan, and Myskyl. I just want them to be careful."

"That would be good," said Nieron, who had clearly heard the interchange, as he joined Quaeryt and Justanan.

The three commanders moved to the entry and watched as the rankers began to clear away debris. Nearly a glass passed before the nearly thirty yards from the entry to near the officers' salon was passable. Even so, Quaeryt and the other two commanders had to step over and around massive charred timbers and stone and masonry that had fallen in from the upper level. Finally, they reached the area outside the chamber that had been the officers' salon.

"You can see the blunderbuss from here, or what's left of it," observed Justanan, stopping a good five yards from where the doorway to the salon had been. "It looks like it was loaded and the fire set off the charge."

Nieron moved forward, stepping around a large section of what had to have been the tile flooring of the upper level, until he was within several yards. "That's a gun port as well." He shook his head. Then he looked down. "There are bones here. Parts of them."

"That was where Commander Luchan fell," said Quaeryt.

"You didn't try to drag him out?"

"He was dead, and with everything on fire and

exploding around me, I wasn't exactly feeling charitable," replied Quaeryt.

"I suppose not."

"We did drag out Captain Whandyn, you might recall."

Nieron moved to his left, bending down and moving aside a large piece of thin iron, frowning as he did so. "This looks like it was fastened inside a door, but there's a hole in the middle. Like it had been pierced by a blade." He moved a few more chunks of tile, then stopped. "Something shiny . . ."

Slowly he pulled something out from under a small pile of rubble and held it up, his mouth open. In his hand was a silvery blade, totally unmarked, except for fragments of soot that flaked away. Even the hilt and grip were silvery. The polished blade itself looked to be a little more than half a yard long.

"Erion's dagger?" asked Justanan.

Nieron said nothing. Instead, he turned and bent, extending the blade toward the discolored iron sheet he had earlier set aside.

"It looks like the door was lined with iron and that silver dagger went through Myskyl and the iron and pinned him to the door," observed Justanan. "Are there any bones there, or insignia?"

Nieron turned and looked down. "There's one melted star and crescent here. It looks like that's what it was."

"Are you satisfied?" asked Justanan, his voice kinder than Quaeryt had heard before.

Nieron straightened, still holding the silver dagger. Wordlessly, he nodded, then handed the dagger to Justanan. "You should keep this for now."

"For now," agreed Justanan, although he glanced to

Quaeryt for a moment. "It looks like there was another chamber, opposite where the blunderbuss is."

Nieron turned and nodded, almost despondently.

Justanan then pointed toward what remained of the outer wall. "There's also that."

Nieron followed the worried-looking commander's gesture. Where the window and iron shutter had been was an archway, with stone and metal fused all the way around the edges. Nieron turned and looked at Quaeryt. Then he shook his head. "I've seen more than enough. Myskyl was a fool."

Quaeryt spoke for the first time. "I think we might return to the study and discuss what should be said at the senior officers' meeting. We all should agree on that."

"Might be best," agreed Nieron.

Justanan nodded.

The three retraced their steps back out from the burned ruin. As they stepped away from the south entry Quaeryt heard murmured words from someone among Calkoran's rankers.

"Erion's dagger . . ."

Another legend to live down . . . or outlive. If you can . . . Quaeryt kept walking.

Just before ninth glass, Quaeryt, Justanan, and Nieron stepped into the officers' mess room off the south courtyard. Every waiting officer stood.

Justanan nodded to Quaeryt.

"As you were," Quaeryt commanded, infusing the words with a touch of image-projected authority. "Please be seated."

The three commanders remained standing, with Quaeryt in the center, Justanan to his right, and Nieron to his left.

Quaeryt looked out at the three subcommanders and at the more than twenty majors seated at the two long tables. "I'm Commander Quaeryt. Some of you may know who I am. Some won't. It doesn't matter. What matters is that you've all been led astray." Quaeryt image-projected the sense of absolute assurance and truth. That wasn't hard, since most of what he was going to say was indeed the truth, with one slight amendment.

"For you to understand what happened and why, there's one set of facts you have to keep in mind. For the entire campaign up the River Aluse, and even at the battle of Variana, Lord Bhayar and Marshal Deucalon were greatly concerned about Rex Kharst's imagers. . . ." Quaeryt went on to give the simplified and shortened version of what he'd told Justanan and Nieron the afternoon before, with the changes that they had suggested. Then he added, "I'd like Commander Justanan, as the senior commander here, to add whatever he would like to say."

Justanan stepped forward and cleared his throat. "Difficult as what Commander Quaeryt has said may be to believe, it appears to be absolutely true. When Commander Quaeryt met with the submarshal yesterday, the submarshal, Commander Luchan, and three imagers who had served Kharst attempted to kill Commander Quaeryt, both with imaging and with a special blunderbuss actually built into the wall of the officers' salon. The commander's defenses held, and the blacklash from the imaging created the explosions and fire that gutted the hold house. During the fire, the Lady Myranda and her personal retainers fled, suggesting that she may have had something to do with matters. Commander Nieron and I physically investigated the hold house this morning, once the embers and ashes had

cooled enough for us to do so. We found the blunderbuss. We also found a secret room with access to the
salon with the bones of the Bovarian imagers. There are
dispatches which reveal that the submarshal was requested to send the tariffs he collected to Lord Bhayar
and that he never did. I feel that we are most fortunate
that Commander Quaeryt merely defended himself in
this deplorable situation. The three of us have met several times, and in accord with Lord Bhayar's orders, we
will be leaving one regiment here in Rivages to keep
order in the area. That regiment will be Sixteenth Regiment, under Subcommander Moravan. The rest of us
will be leaving on Mardi morning to return to Variana."
He looked to Quaeryt.

"Are there any questions?" asked Quaeryt.

"Do you have any idea where we'll be assigned once
we return to Variana?" asked one of the subcommanders, Ostlyn, Quaeryt thought.

"That will be up to the marshal and Lord Bhayar. It's
likely that several regiments will return to Solis fairly
soon, but that had not been decided when I left Variana." Quaeryt glanced around the mess.

"Will we have to fight in Khel?"

"Lord Bhayar sent envoys to ask the High Council
of Khel to consider terms. The Council is considering
those terms. Lord Bhayar is hopeful that an invasion will
not be necessary, but that depends on the High Council. Any other questions?"

There were no more questions.

"That will be all, then," Quaeryt finally said, after a
long silence.

Quaeryt followed Justanan and Nieron from the
mess. Once outside, he looked to the older blond officer. "You handled that well."

Justanan shook his head. "You handled it well. I picked up the pieces as well as I could." He paused. "Do you think Lord Bhayar will wish to replace Moravan?"

"I doubt it. He said that he trusted Moravan more than any regimental subcommander in Northern Army. When he goes on his own instincts, and not out of loyalty to those who served his father, his judgment of people is usually accurate."

"What did his father think of you? Did he know you? Or say anything?"

"He said something, according to Bhayar, along the lines that I'd be a loyal friend and that it would be best were I not an enemy."

"I can see that," said Justanan slowly, then looked at Quaeryt directly. "You've risked more for Bhayar than any senior officer. Why?"

"Because he is a friend and because he has been fair and because he offers the only hope for imagers in all of Lydar."

Justanan nodded.

Even Nieron nodded, if reluctantly.

49

By midmorning on Samedi, Quaeryt, Justanan, Nieron, and Quaeryt had completed the general outlines and plans of the withdrawal from Rivages, as well as laid out the parameters of the duties assigned to the remaining regiment. For the most part, Quaeryt had deferred to the other two commanders, partly because he agreed with their proposals and partly because they had more experience than he did in planning such evolutions. Once they were agreed, he and two squads, third squad from first company and fourth squad from the Khellan company, rode out so that he could pay a visit to High Holder Paliast, whose holding was east of Rivages, perhaps even slightly southeast.

Once Quaeryt and the two squads crossed the timber bridge over the River Aluse, and passed the east river road, which continued northward along the water, Quaeryt paid even more attention to the buildings and people. The bridge joined two squares, but the structures on the eastern square were larger and taller, all of them at least two stories, and several were three, including the all-brick River Inn. Not for the first time, Quaeryt wondered how many River Inns there were across all of Lydar. The main streets were paved, and the dwellings were mainly brick and extended a good mille along the east road before giving way to cots and small fields and woodlots. At that point, the paving ended, and the road became packed clay. After another mille, the small-holder plots vanished, and they rode past larger fields with unmortared stone walls.

Ahead, Quaeryt made out a modest hold house on the north side of the road, with only a handful of build-ings, none of them excessively large, all of which called to mind Seliadyn's observation that Paliast's sire had lost many of his lands to Ryel—or Tyrena. The gates were unguarded, drawn open, and attached to two natural stone pillars, roughly three yards high and mortared, un-like the yard-and-a-half-high walls that flanked them.

Quaeryt rode between the gate pillars and onto the lane, both companies following. The lane itself was unpaved, but graveled. It showed ruts that had only been partly smoothed out, and some of the gravel had been sprayed onto the grassy shoulder by mounts or carriage wheels. The pastures on each side of the lane looked to be clover. Some parts, Quaeryt thought, ap-peared to have been overgrazed, although he saw no sheep or cattle nearby.

Less than a half mille from the gates was the hold house, set facing south. All the outbuildings were to the west, below a rise. As he rode toward the graveled area around the entry, Quaeryt couldn't help but wonder why the house had not been set there, as were most hold houses. When he reined up at the foot of the steps down from the modest receiving rotunda, he saw a function-ary who stood under the edge of the roof.

The man, in peach and white livery, looked to Quae-ryt, studying him, and then asking, "Who might I say is calling, sir?"

"Commander Quaeryt, on direct behalf of Lord Bhayar."

Quaeryt dismounted, without waiting for an invitation, and walked up the steps toward the man. "You're the steward?"

"Baankyt, the assistant steward, sir. Maalan is the steward." He inclined his head. "If you would come this way, sir. High Holder Paliast is in his study."

Quaeryt followed Baankyt through the square brick archway that led to the brassbound double doors and then through a square foyer and straight back along a corridor floored in pale peach and black tiles.

The assistant steward stopped at the second door. "Commander Quaeryt on behalf of Lord Bhayar, sir." Baankyt did not wait for an acknowledgment, but gestured for Quaeryt to enter the study.

Quaeryt stepped into the study, some six yards by four, with a brick hearth at the left end of the room and an ancient desk whose oak had darkened to a deep golden brown at the right end. Two leather armchairs were set before the hearth, angled so that whoever sat there could observe the other chair . . . or the fire, although the hearth was dark, and covered with an ornate brass screen.

Paliast stood and walked from behind the desk toward Quaeryt. He looked to be younger than Quaeryt, mostly likely close to Vaelora's age. His unlined and round face was boyish, but his eyes were deep-set, with a quizzical expression.

"Are you one of the submarshal's commanders?"

"No. I'm the one who replaced the late Submarshal Myskyl . . . and the late Commander Luchan as well."

Paliast stiffened, just for a moment, then said, "I do

suppose these things happen in and after a war. Might I ask why you are here? We have paid all that Lord Bhayar has requested."

"I'm here to meet with you, of course." Quaeryt looked toward the chairs.

Paliast ignored the look. "You're here. What do you want?"

Quaeryt smiled. "Why don't you take a seat? You'll likely be more comfortable."

"I suppose that would be the thing to do." Paliast took the leather chair farthest from the door.

Quaeryt turned the other one so that it faced the High Holder directly, and then settled into it. "You recently became the High Holder, I understand."

"In Ianus."

"Had you met Submarshal Myskyl before then?"

"I can't say that I had. My sire had little desire to meet him and only did so when required."

"How many times did you meet with the submarshal?"

"Does it matter?"

"It does if you wish to remain High Holder," replied Quaeryt mildly. He was already getting weary of young Paliast.

"Isn't that Lord Bhayar's decision?"

"He appointed me Minister of Administration for Bovaria and delegated that authority to me. Now . . . how many times did you meet with Myskyl?"

"Three . . . as I recall."

"Did you go there?"

Paliast laughed. "With Lady Myranda acting as High Holder? She barely deigned to see Father when Fian-cryt was alive. No . . . he came here."

"Alone, or did he bring the three?"

"He came alone. He had a whole company with him, and we had to feed them all each time."

"What did he want?"

"The first time he wanted to meet me and tell me that I was obligated to meet the obligations of a High Holder to the ruler of Bovaria."

"Did he say it that way?"

"That's what I recall."

"Did he ever mention Lord Bhayar by name?"

Paliast frowned. "I don't think so."

"What about the other two times?"

"The second time . . . he told me to expect a major and to sell the Northern Army some grain and flour at the prevailing price. Maalan took care of that. The third time he said that a second 'token' tariff might be due in late Mayas. Do you know anything about that?"

"At the moment, Lord Bhayar has not decided. Did you know that Submarshal Myskyl had come under the influence of the three?" asked Quaeryt.

"Should I have known that?" replied the High Holder almost insolently.

Quaeryt imaged absolute authority and contempt at the bearishly rotund High Holder, powerful enough that Paliast jolted back in his chair and paled. "I did ask you a question. I would appreciate an answer." Quaeryt kept his voice mild and pleasant.

"You're the one, aren't you?"

"The one what?" asked Quaeryt, curious to know what Paliast had been told.

"The one Lady Tyrena mentioned. She met a commander in Variana, and he made certain she could hold her lands until Iryena is married. She said . . ."

"Yes?"

"That you were the most dangerous man in Lydar." Paliast did not quite meet Quaeryt's eyes.

"That's Lord Bhayar. I merely serve him."

Paliast looked as if he might dispute that, but did not speak.

"About the three?"

"I heard rumors . . . Maalan did, really, that some of Kharst's imagers had met with the submarshal. I didn't ask him about them. No High Holder in his right mind would want to be anywhere around them. . . ."

Although Quaeryt spent almost another glass talking to Paliast, he learned little more . . . except that he doubted the young man would be able to hang on to his holding unless he or matters changed greatly.

Quaeryt and his squads did not reach Ryel until close to second glass, since they had to ride partway back toward Rivages and then take another road that led northeast. The hold house and its immediate buildings were located on a flattened hilltop, with the rear of the expansive dwelling overlooking a small valley through which a stream flowed.

The footman immediately conveyed Quaeryt's presence to Tyrena, and she hurried down a massive silver and black marble staircase to meet him in the main entry hall.

"Commander, I never expected you to come to Rivages. To what do I owe this visit, if I might ask?" Her Bovarian still held the faintest trace of a Tilboran accent.

"For you, it is a courtesy. For Daefol and Paliast, it is a necessity, although I can't say I expected to be here under present circumstances."

Her blond eyebrows lifted. "Present circumstances?"

"It will take some explaining."

"Then we should go to the terrace. It's pleasant there, and there's enough of a breeze that there won't be any red flies or mosquitoes there."

Quaeryt wondered about the need for that, given that the hold house was well above the stream.

As if reading his thoughts, Tyrena smiled and said, "The Khanar's Palace had few, especially in the winter, and anything that flies and bites seeks me out."

"The terrace, by all means," replied Quaeryt with a laugh.

Neither spoke as Quaeryt followed the former Khanara along a side hallway and then to the left and almost to the end of the second hallway, where she turned into a spacious salon and through it and the double doors. The terrace was roofed and looked down over a formal garden with a low wall to the stream valley below.

Tyrena gestured to a small circular table with three chairs. The place without a chair was the one that would have faced away from the garden.

Quaeryt took one of the end chairs, and Tyrena sat in the one opposite him. As soon as they were seated, a red-haired serving maid in black livery appeared.

"Would you like something to drink? I have the stewards providing some refreshments for your men."

"A pale lager, if you have it."

"That, we can do." Tyrena nodded to the serving maid, who slipped away, then addressed Quaeryt. "Just courtesy?"

"To provide information and courtesy. You may already know, but apparently Submarshal Myskyl had fallen under the influence of the three."

"After I returned from Variana, I heard rumors of such."

"When I arrived, they attempted to kill me. In the events that followed, they and the submarshal and Commander Luchan perished. The main hold house at Fiancryt burned to charred walls. It is likely that the holding will revert to Lord Bhayar. Oh . . . and Lady Myranda rode off with her personal retainers while the hold house was still burning."

Tyrena looked unsurprised.

"You already knew, didn't you?"

"I knew the hold house had burned and that Myranda had fled. I did not know what had happened to cause the fire." Tyrena paused. "Are you certain that the three perished?"

"I know that three imagers died and their bodies were burned to ash and bone. I understood that the term 'the three' was not precisely accurate, at least not in terms of numbering the imagers who served Kharst."

"That was correct, but it's likely that there were only three left. I did receive a letter before the battle at Variana that hinted that some were present at the Chateau Regis, as some always were when there were High Holders there. There were never more than a handful and one or two more."

"Ryel worried about them?"

"Everyone worried about them. Anyone with any sense." Tyrena looked up as the serving maid reappeared, carrying a tray on which there were two silvery glass beakers with black glass bases. The beakers both held pale lager.

The server offered the tray, allowing Quaeryt to choose. He took the closest beaker.

Tyrena smiled. "Most would take the far one."

"I know, and I know that you knew I would. I trust you in this."

She laughed lightly. "Because my fate rests not just with you, but with your wife."

Quaeryt nodded, then waited for Tyrena to take the second beaker. Then he raised his beaker slightly. "To trust."

"To trust," she replied.

They drank.

"Why did you tell young Paliast that I was the most dangerous man in Lydar?"

"Besides the fact that you are?" Tyrena smiled. "Because he is young and arrogant and has less in the way of brains than does a toad. And so that when he complains about what will happen to him, he will have no excuses. He will make them anyway, and Daefol will likely listen."

"And Seliadyn?"

Tyrena shook her head sadly. "He still thinks his daughter is alive."

"And that she is twelve? How long ago was that?"

"Five years ago."

"Kharst?"

"No. She was headstrong and took a boat into the river during the spring high waters. There was a sudden flood, and her mother drowned trying to save her. Seliadyn was in Variana, at Kharst's command. He was much older than Maereth, but he loved them both deeply. Maereth almost died having Seliatha, I was told, and she could never have children after that."

"And who will inherit Vaestora?"

"That will be up to Lord Bhayar, I imagine. Seliadyn had no brothers or even cousins."

Quaeryt nodded. *Perhaps Calkoran. He would do well there.*

"You might recommend someone who would fit and be loyal."

"I likely will, but Lord Bhayar will decide. He often follows my recommendations . . . but far from always."

"And you do not press him?"

Quaeryt smiled. "If I cannot convince him by my words, it is as he says."

"What did you do to convince him in my case?"

"I told him the facts."

"Including who I once was?"

"Eventually." That was true enough.

"He did not change his mind?"

"I pointed out that you were to be trusted far more than any man in being loyal, for you had everything to lose. Vaelora agreed. So did Bhayar."

"I said you were the most dangerous man in Lydar."

Quaeryt shrugged. "Tell me what Bhayar and I should know about Rivages and the north."

"The land is everything to the High Holders, and golds are everything to the factors. . . ."

Quaeryt listened, asking a few questions, for well over a glass, before he finally took his leave and began the ride back to Fiancryt.

50

On Solayi, Quaeryt took another two squads and rode south to Folan, arriving just before midday on a cloudless day where the sun beat down mercilessly. Once more, Daefol charged out of the tower-like hold house, if with but a single guard, instead of two. He wore a brilliant blue jacket over dark blue trousers, possibly the same pair he had worn the first time Quaeryt had entered the hold.

"Commander! I thought we had seen the last of you, especially after the hold house fire at Fiancryt."

"Shortly . . . shortly." Quaeryt dismounted and walked up onto the raised terrace. "I'd appreciate it if you and your wife would spend a quint or so with me."

"Appreciate it? You aren't the submarshal."

Quaeryt shook his head. "No . . . I'm Commander Quaeryt, merely the acting submarshal, I suppose, and I'm that imager married to Lord Bhayar's sister—as you told your wife last Meredi . . . when she tried to suggest to you that Submarshal Myskyl might not be trusted." Quaeryt smiled. "Now . . . shall we go in and meet your wife?"

For several moments Daefol's mouth moved. Finally, he nodded.

Quaeryt could sense the consternation and the anger,

possibly because Daefol knew full well he'd made a fool of himself before the guard who had accompanied him. So Quaeryt looked squarely at the guard. "Your master isn't the first to assume the wrong things, and he won't be the last. So have more than a few armsmen and guards. It might be best if you said nothing." With his last sentence, Quaeryt image-projected overwhelming power and authority.

"Yes . . . sir," stammered the guard.

"And you can help arrange for water and shade for my men and their mounts." Quaeryt turned to Daefol and said again, "Shall we go?"

"Yes, sir." Daefol's voice was subdued.

Once inside the entry hall, Quaeryt asked, "Is Elajara upstairs in her sitting room . . . or elsewhere?"

Daefol glanced sideways at Quaeryt, then replied, "She's in the sitting room. She says that it's the most comfortable in this warm weather."

"When is she due?"

"Did you come from Variana when you said you did?" countered Daefol.

"I did. And did you have someone check on the new bridge?"

The High Holder nodded, then started up the marble steps. Quaeryt kept pace with him.

At the top, Daefol turned to the right and walked to the last door on the left, pausing before entering and then saying, "Elajara, we have a visitor. This is Commander Quaeryt, the one who was here earlier. He is now the acting submarshal. He is also the imager who married Lord Bhayar's sister."

Quaeryt entered the corner room, followed by the High Holder.

The brunette in another loose-fitting linen dress, this one of pale peach, also with white lace trimming, did not rise from the chair, but laid the embroidery hoop on the side table and inclined her head. "You're kind to visit us again. Will you be staying the evening?"

Quaeryt offered an amused smile. "No, Lady Daefol. This is both a courtesy visit and one to provide some information."

"Do sit down, Commander. I am to the point where standing for a time tires me, and I feel uncomfortable with you standing."

Quaeryt took the straight chair closest to Elajara, leaving the other armchair for Daefol, who also seated himself.

"You are kind to include me," added Elajara.

"No, I am not kind. I hope I am being wise. Now that I am married, I have become much more aware that those men of power whom I respect almost always include their wives in their confidence, and the ones who generally make the best decisions listen and consider what their wives have to say."

"Still," replied Elajara, "few women, if any, have real power."

"Lord Bhayar has granted Lady Tyrena the power to manage the holding until her daughter is of marriage-able age. He has also appointed his sister as envoy to Khel, and upon her return named her as joint Minister of Administration for Bovaria with me."

"He is kind to them."

Quaeryt shook his head. "Wise. They are both strong and intelligent . . . as I suspect you are."

"What is this information you wish to convey?" asked Daefol.

"First, it appears that Submarshal Myskyl was suborned by the surviving members of the three, as was Lady Myranda. In the confrontation I had with the submarshal and the three, all four of them perished when the efforts of the imagers did not work as they intended. In the fire that ensued, Lady Myranda fled. It is likely that her life and holding will be forfeit once Lord Bhayar hears of her role. Second, you will be pleased, I trust, to learn that five of the six regiments currently at Fiancryt will be departing this Mardi, assuming the weather holds. Subcommander Moravan, greatly trusted by Lord Bhayar, and his regiment will remain to assure that matters remain calm."

Daefol nodded slowly.

Elajara studied Quaeryt. "You don't powder your hair or paint your nails, do you?"

"No."

"You're Pharsi, are you not?"

"I am, but I did not know it until about two years ago. I was orphaned as a young child and raised by the scholars of Solis."

"He knew much of what we said when he was first here," added Daefol.

Elajara nodded. "Are you a lost one?"

"Many have declared that I am. I cannot say that. I don't know. How did you know about the legends of the lost ones?"

"When Daefol described you, I went to the library. There was nothing there. Then I began to ask my maids and others. One of the cook's helpers knew an old Pharsi woman, and she said that the lost ones had white-blond hair and dark eyes, and they often limped. The greatest sometimes had their hair and nails turn white. When we heard that Kharst had been bested at Variana, the word was that most of the destruction had been wrought by a Pharsi imager who was a commander. You were that imager, were you not?"

"I was the imager in charge of all those who created the destruction," Quaeryt admitted.

"And you defeated the three by yourself. That makes you most powerful."

"No. I did not defeat them by myself. Facing them alone would have been idiocy. I brought several other imagers with me."

"There were no old and powerful imagers among your men. Or were they hidden?"

"No. Those who helped me were young."

"Did you not train them?"

"Yes." *All but one.* "You are rather perceptive, Lady."

"No. I am trying to be logical."

"Your logic is largely accurate. You must be of great assistance to your husband." Quaeryt could see exactly where the conversation was going and what Elajara wanted, and he was happy to do what he could, because she was far more likely to be reasonable and practical and Daefol would be far more rational for listening to his wife. "Or you could be." Quaeryt turned to Daefol. "If you let her be."

"She is not interested—"

"She is not interested in angering you. She is very interested in your making the right decisions because those decisions affect her and your children. I would strongly suggest that you give her views and opinions careful consideration. Lord Bhayar has always considered the views of his wife, and of his sisters. It's a good example to follow, especially since he is now lord and Rex of Bovaria."

"He does not seem terribly interested in maintaining the traditions of Bovaria," murmured Daefol.

"Oh . . . he's happy to allow those that work. But ignoring the intelligence of half the people isn't exactly wise, and it apparently didn't work too well for Rex Kharst. It didn't work very well for Tilbor, either, when the northern High Holders there decided they wanted an inept male ruler rather than a competent woman."

"How often do you listen to your wife?" asked Daefol slyly.

"Enough that her advice has saved my life at least three times." Quaeryt smiled. "That kind of example tends to make one a believer." He rose, then inclined his head to Elajara. "I'm pleased to meet you, Lady, and wish you well." Then he turned to Daefol. "I've said what I needed to say, and I trust you'll find the information useful." He paused for a moment, and when the High Holder did not speak, he said, "Shall we go?"

Daefol nodded and led the way from the chamber.

Quaeryt did not shake his head, although he felt like doing so.

51

Early on Mardi morning Quaeryt met with Subcommander Moravan, reviewing his responsibilities, then met with all the other regimental commanders to review the order of departure. While Quaeryt let Justanan do most of the talking, he and the senior commander had already worked out that order, largely by seniority, with the exceptions that the regiment formerly commanded by Luchan would follow Justanan's regiment and that first company would serve as vanguard and Calkoran would provide the rear guard. Quaeryt didn't want any dispatches that he and Justanan did not know about leaving Northern Army. In addition, because there were now two bridges over the Aluse, the army was split into two groups, with the first two regiments and first company to use the new bridge and the other three regiments to use the old one in Rivages.

By seventh glass Northern Army had largely departed Fiancryt, and Quaeryt rode at the head of first company, with Zhelan beside him and the three imagers directly behind him heading south along the west river road.

"Have you heard anything of interest in the last few days?" asked Quaeryt.

"Most of the junior officers are happy we're heading back to Variana. So are the men. Rivages is . . . well . . ."

"Somewhat limited in terms of entertainment?" suggested Quaeryt.

"More limited than that, sir. The submarshal didn't allow the men or the officers to leave Fiancryt except on patrols or maneuvers."

"For more than four months?"

"Yes, sir."

That was something Quaeryt hadn't known, but then he hadn't asked, because that sort of restriction hadn't occurred to him. Skarpa had never enforced anything that stringent. Nor had he, except in Khel. "Anything else?"

"The hold house was off-limits to everyone but Myskyl's assistants and the senior officers. No one but Myskyl had a study in the hold house."

"Has anyone said anything about the imagers and the fire?"

"They wouldn't say anything to me," replied Zhelan. "I had Ghaelyn ask some of the men to keep their ears open. The only thing that's clear to pretty much everyone is that it's dangerous to do anything against you . . . and that captain has told a number of the junior officers that Erion came to your aid. He even took some of them into the ruins and showed them that section of the iron shutter with the archway melted into it."

Quaeryt couldn't help smiling slightly. "You looked, too, didn't you?"

"Of course. I wanted to see for myself." Zhelan paused. "Was Erion really there?"

Quaeryt managed a shrug. "I don't know. Something or someone that looked like Erion was there and threw thunderbolts at the three imagers and flung that silvery dagger at Myskyl."

"Eslym still has it. He says it is the dagger of Erion. It's lighter than iron, but feels stronger."

"Has Calkoran said anything to you?"

"Not very much. He did say that if you weren't the lost one and the son of Erion, there was no difference between you and him . . . and that was good enough for him. I think most of the Khellans would follow you anywhere. Even into the gates of death."

"Let's hope we're done with that." Quaeryt offered a rueful laugh, then looked at the houses ahead that marked the northern edge of the western part of Rivages.

Ahead, a woman hanging laundry on a line at the side of a small cot scurried toward the back door and disappeared. Quaeryt couldn't fault her caution, but hoped that would change over the coming years.

Before long first company was riding into the western part of the city and toward the square and the old timber bridge. The center of the square cleared quickly as the column approached, but the peddlers and crafters and those in the square to shop all watched as the troopers rode past. Quaeryt saw neither resentment nor joy, just a mixture of curiosity and almost indifference as the riders passed.

Once first company had passed through Rivages, Quaeryt rode back to the head of Justanan's regiment, easing in beside the senior commander.

"How do your officers and men feel about leaving Fiancryt and Rivages?"

"Most are happy to go. They didn't see much of Rivages and too much of Fiancryt."

"I understand that access to the hold house was limited," offered Quaeryt.

"With almost ten thousand men in the area, it had to be," replied Justanan.

"I can see that." Quaeryt paused. "Did you ever meet Lady Myranda?"

"I wouldn't have called any of the times I encountered her a meeting," said Justanan dryly. "There was one reception at which she appeared and spoke a few words briefly to each of the regimental commanders. She was warm and apparently charming without saying much of anything, and before any of us knew it she had vanished. Beautiful woman, but the kind you always wonder about how deep that apparent warmth might be."

Quaeryt nodded. "I've met some like that. Was there anything strange that happened around her?"

"Besides having five or six regiments around all the time?"

"She was Fiancryt's second wife, and the first died rather suddenly, from what I heard."

"Oh . . . that business about Fiancryt's son drowning? He was a headstrong boy, and he rode off from his mother and the submarshal and apparently tried to jump a creek. The horse threw him, and he hit his head on a rock or something and drowned in the creek before they found him. That's all we were ever told. The hold house was draped in black for a month. . . ."

"Was that before or after you knew that the three imagers were here?"

"We didn't know that they were imagers. Not then. I suspected there was something not right about them. I told you that. The submarshal said that their knowledge would be most useful to Lord Bhayar in time."

"That's hard to argue against," said Quaeryt. *And it suggests that one of the imagers had something to do with the boy's death*. Again, it was another thing that would be hard to prove. *Just like so many over the past two years.* "Especially to a submarshal who's the favorite of the marshal. Was that obvious to all the regimental commanders?"

"Nieron knew and flattered both Luchan and Myskyl. I doubt that's any surprise to you," said Justanan dryly.

"No. What about Tibaron and Ostlyn?"

"They never gave much indication one way or the other, as befit intelligent junior subcommanders."

"And Moravan?"

"He never said anything, but once in a while when he didn't think anyone was watching, he rolled his eyes. At first. I cautioned him against that, because Myskyl had very good senses."

"He did, indeed," said Quaeryt.

"You were never included in the meetings after Ferravyl," offered Justanan.

"Not after they were changed from meetings of senior officers to meetings of the regimental commanders," replied Quaeryt.

"I wondered about that."

"Until after Variana, the only senior officers who weren't regimental commanders were Subcommander Ernyld and me. After Variana, when I became a commander with regiments under me, I was detached and reported to either Submarshal Skarpa or Lord Bhayar."

"But Ernyld was there."

"To record the proceedings, doubtless," replied Quaeryt.

"Is Skarpa still in Liantiago?"

At that moment Quaeryt realized that he'd never mentioned Skarpa's assassination. "No. I should have mentioned this. He was assassinated by the heir of a rebel High Holder. The High Holder was killed fighting for Aliaro. The assassination happened after Commander Kharllon insisted that the imagers I left to protect Skarpa not be allowed close to the senior officers' meetings in Liantiago."

"Kharllon?"

Quaeryt nodded.

"That doesn't surprise me. Do you know what happened after that?"

"When I left Variana, the latest dispatches we had indicated that Commander Kharllon was acting governor of Liantiago, except for Westisle, which was being held for Lord Bhayar by the imagers and my Nineteenth Regiment, until they received orders to the contrary, since my command reported directly to Bhayar."

"What did Lord Bhayar do, or did he tell you?"

"He said he would promote acting imager Captain Voltyr to major and confirm the separate jurisdictions for a time until he had time to reconsider."

"That was what you recommended, wasn't it?"

"It was. Kharllon will be loyal to Bhayar, but he doesn't know how to handle or use imagers. His own report of Skarpa's assassination confirmed that."

"Do you intend to become marshal of the armies?"

"That's the last thing I want, and the last thing the armies and Bhayar need. I'm working to create a collegium of imagers, where imagers and their families from all over Lydar can live and where their children can be educated and those that are imagers properly trained to serve Lord Bhayar. Lord Bhayar agrees with the idea and the plans he's seen so far."

"You could be marshal and still do that."

"No. It wouldn't work. The High Holders, the factors, the senior officers, even the people would rebel against an imager in control of the armies. Especially since Bhayar is part Pharsi."

"You've thought this out."

"I've had to. When you're married to Bhayar's sister . . ."

"That makes sense. You give the imagers safety, and they support the ruler, and that keeps High Holders and ambitious marshals in line."

"And the Collegium removes the imagers from seeming to threaten people, so that Bhayar can point out that the Collegium protects both the imagers and the people. He's agreed that the Collegium will be on that isle in the Aluse, the one that had all the piers."

Justanan nodded thoughtfully, then said, "It's too bad more officers don't understand their limitations."

Quaeryt noted the tense the senior commander used, but merely said, "Power can be very tempting."

"It can indeed," replied Justanan with a laugh. "How long do you think it will take us to reach Variana?"

"My thought is roughly three weeks. What do you think?"

"I wouldn't disagree . . . unless we get rain."

From then on, the two talked about details of the journey ahead.

52

By midafternoon on Meredi, the regiments were approaching Vaestora in good order, and Quaeryt rode out with a squad from first company to request permission from Seliadyn to allow the regiments to stay overnight at the high holding. Even though the spacious barracks would not accommodate all the troopers, except in the most crowded of conditions, Quaeryt did not wish to impose Northern Army on any town as small as Vaestora and such a force would create a certain amount of destruction on any lands where they camped.

As he and fourth squad entered Vaestora from the north, he was again impressed by the order and cleanliness of the town, not to mention the imposing presence of the keep tower of Seliadyn. When he reached the square and rode toward the open gates in the ancient wall, both guards stepped out and waited. He reined up short of them.

"You're the commander who was here last week or so, aren't you?" asked the shorter guard.

"That I am. I'd like to see the High Holder."

"He's not been well, sir, but it'd be best that you talk with the steward."

"That's Wereas, isn't it?"

"Yes, sir."

Quaeryt and the squad followed the guard at a walk from the gates and across the stone-paved front courtyard to the base of the stone up to the second level and a set of double doors. He reined up, dismounted, and tied the gelding to the nearest bronze hitching rail, while the guard rang the bell on the bronze post.

Wereas, in his black and yellow livery, emerged from the doors at the top of the steps when Quaeryt was halfway up the steps. "Greetings, Wereas."

"Commander." The steward inclined his head.

"I was hoping to see the High Holder. I'm returning the Northern Army to Variana and would prefer to camp in the courtyard and barracks for the night." Quaeryt walked the rest of the way up the steps to the entry.

"He's not well, sir, but he did leave instructions to admit you when you returned. If you would come with me, sir." Wereas stepped back through the still-open heavy oak door, then closed it behind Quaeryt.

As Quaeryt followed the steward through the square entry hall to the interior staircase, and then up the green marble steps, he gained the feeling that the entire tower was hushed, almost as if holding its breath. Quaeryt almost caught the heel of his boot on his bad leg twice on the last set of steps, up to the third interior level, one below that where he had met Seliadyn in his study.

"He's in his sitting room, sir, to the right," offered Wereas.

As with the study, the sitting room was at the rear of the tower on the north side.

The steward did not knock, but eased the door open. "Commander Quaeryt has returned and is here to see you."

"Good. Afraid he might not make it."

Wereas gestured, and Quaeryt entered the sitting room.

The walls were paneled in the same dark wood as the study had been, and the tall and narrow windows held the same pale green silk hangings. The carpet was of a pale green. While there was a small table desk, on which were several folders, Seliadyn sat in a green leather armchair, a dark green blanket across his legs. He wore a sleeveless gray vest over a gray shirt, and his silver hair seemed yellowed from the last time Quaeryt had seen him.

Seliadyn looked to the steward. "A lager for the commander, Wereas."

The steward nodded, then turned, leaving the door open.

Quaeryt moved to the chair that matched the one in which Seliadyn sat and seated himself, waiting.

"I was not totally truthful with you, Commander. You've likely discovered that. I have no heirs. Not even distant ones. I won't go into my reasons . . . or the history. My sources tell me that you destroyed the hold house at Fiancryt as well as the submarshal and the last of Kharst's imagers. Is that true?"

"Three imagers died in the fire that resulted from their actions. So did the submarshal and his senior commander. Lady Myranda fled."

"Good riddance." Seliadyn smothered a cough with a black handkerchief. "You're taking the army back to Variana?"

"All but one regiment."

"They can stay here tonight. That was what you wanted, wasn't it?"

"Partly. I also did wish to see you and thank you for

the information you provided the last time. It was most helpful."

"That was the idea."

"I know," replied Quaeryt, "but it still merits thanks."

"I want a favor."

"I will do what I can."

"According to the laws of both Bovaria and Telaryn, Lord Bhayar will appoint my successor . . . or take my lands as his own. What influence do you have on his choice?"

"I can recommend. At times, he does heed my thoughts."

"More than at times, I suspect." Seliadyn coughed again, more violently.

Quaeryt waited.

"I may recover from this flux. I may not. At my age, you never know." He lowered the handkerchief, then waited as Wereas returned with a tray, on which were two lagers.

The steward tendered the tray to Quaeryt first. Quaeryt took the nearer beaker. Then Wereas extended the tray to Seliadyn.

"All right. I'll drink it. It can't hurt, I suppose." Seliadyn took the beaker, then lifted it and took a small swallow.

After Quaeryt took a swallow of the lager, as good as he remembered, he noted the smallest nod of approval from the steward once Seliadyn had drunk. Then Wereas slipped out of the sitting room, but the door remained ajar, and Quaeryt had no doubt that the steward remained close.

"As I was saying," the High Holder went on, "I have no heirs. I would not wish that Vaestora become just a source of golds for whoever receives the hold. It is also a hold that can withstand a moderate siege, perhaps more, with the proper High Holder, and that might be valuable to a ruler still consolidating his power." Seliadyn looked intently at Quaeryt.

"You would like me to prevail upon Lord Bhayar to bestow Vaestora upon someone who would respect the hold and the people of the town as well, someone who would appreciate its history and its capabilities, and someone who would be loyal to him."

"I thought you would understand. I would hope that it would not go to the younger son of some Telaryn High Holder who would ruin it in years. It is most productive, but that production comes as much from the loyalty of the people as from the lands themselves. Most High Holders take anywhere from one part in three to one in two from their tenants. I have taken but three in twenty and at times as little as one part in ten, and over time I have been richly repaid."

"I have seen few towns as orderly and as clean as Vaestora," Quaeryt said.

"You have seen many, have you not?"

"More than I ever wished," Quaeryt admitted.

Seliadyn started to laugh, but the laugh became a painful and extended bout of coughing. When he finally lowered the handkerchief, he said, "I should not talk more. Will you do what you can for my lands and my people?"

"I will."

"Good. You had best go. I will put my wishes in a petition as well, to be delivered to Lord Bhayar when it is time." Seliadyn gestured toward the door.

Quaeryt rose. "Like your steward, I would suggest you drink more of the lager. That might help assure that

I do not have to carry out your wishes for some years yet."

Seliadyn lifted the beaker, but Quaeryt could see that the old man's hand trembled as he did.

"I will do that, but it will not be years, Commander. I wish you well." The High Holder took a small swallow and lowered the beaker.

Quaeryt inclined his head, then slipped from the sitting room, still wondering about the history Seliadyn had declined to relate.

53

As before, Quaeryt did not see Seliadyn again on Meredi evening, or on Jeudi morning, when Northern Army left Vaestora. He did inquire of Wereas about Seliadyn's health, and the steward replied that the High Holder was no better, but neither was he worse, and that he would prefer not to meet with Quaeryt unless the matter was urgent. While not encouraging, that news was better than it could have been . . . and Quaeryt had nothing of urgency to impart.

Despite skies that became increasingly cloudy, over the next three days, they made good time, and on Solayi evening, Northern Army camped on the grounds of a long-deserted high holding some fifteen milles south of Ariviana. Less than two days later, by midafternoon, Northern Army had settled into the inns and the buildings around them in Yapres, with Quaeryt again at the Copper Tankard.

When he and Justanan had taken care of the necessities, Quaeryt asked Calkoran to provide a squad and to accompany him on another visit to High Holder Caemren. Less than a glass later, they reined up outside the entry gates.

Once more, there was a single guard standing behind the iron gates and in front of the small guardhouse.

While the guard wasn't the same one who had challenged Quaeryt earlier, he looked at the commander, then offered a resigned look.

"I suppose you want to see the High Holder." Without waiting for an answer, the guard walked to the middle of the gate, unlocked the chains, and then pulled the gate open.

Quaeryt, Calkoran, and the troopers rode up the stone-paved drive and reined up before the small covered receiving portico. A single functionary stood there, wearing the gray livery with white piping.

"If you'd announce me to High Holder Caemren. I'm Commander Quaeryt."

In only a few moments, the footman returned with Caemren. Quaeryt was moderately surprised to see the High Holder in just a white shirt and gray trousers, rather than the colorful outfit he had been wearing on Quaeryt's first visit.

"The word is that you seem to be in charge of the army of the north and that you're leading the regiments back to Variana. Is that true?" asked the white-haired High Holder.

"You got the word rather swiftly," replied Quaeryt.

"Since you're here—again—you might as well come in." Caemren turned and walked to the door, where he waited.

Quaeryt shook his head, dismounted, and handed his mount's reins to the ranker who had moved up to take them. He motioned to Calkoran and the two officers walked to the entry.

"This is Subcommander Calkoran. High Holder Caemren."

Caemren nodded. "Pleased to meet you, Subcommander." He turned.

The two followed him to the terrace off the small salon on the northwest corner of the main section of the dwelling. All three sat down around the small circular table.

"You're Pharsi, too, aren't you, Subcommander?" asked Caemren.

"Khellan," replied Calkoran.

Caemren nodded and turned to Quaeryt. "What do you want this time?"

"I thought you'd like to know what happened, but you apparently already know some if not all that occurred."

"I understand that those of Kharst's imagers who survived persuaded the submarshal to take you on. There's a rumor that Erion arrived and destroyed them."

"Let's just say that their imaging was turned against them and the submarshal and that the hold house burned to the ground."

"What about Lady Myranda?"

"She escaped. If she ever turns up, I imagine Lord Bhayar will have her executed."

"That would be too merciful," replied Caemren, his voice coldly sardonic.

"I wouldn't know. I never met her. The events around her were less than favorable."

"They seldom have been."

"Tell me more about Seliadyn. About what happened to his family."

"He has never spoken about them. His daughter and his wife died in a boating accident. They were both good swimmers."

"Kharst's imagers?"

"That was the supposition. He did not remarry. After his daughter died, he was . . . different."

"His people seem very loyal to him," observed Quaeryt.

"He is known for treating with them fairly. Anyone who succeeds him will need great experience. Seliadyn takes a lower tithe than most High Holders."

"But if they produce more . . ."

Caemren smiled. "That blade has more than two edges, Commander, and all of them are sharp."

"What do you know about Magiian?"

"You think I would know about him?"

"I think you would know about any person of power within fifty or even a hundred milles of Yapres. You could tell me the annual income of the Copper Tankard, I expect, and the wealth of the largest factors in Yapres."

"I suppose I could come close."

"Magiian," prompted Quaeryt.

"He has extensive lands. Except for crops to supply the holding, his tenants plant oilseeds. Most of his flax is for linseed oil, but some goes to a small linen mill. He avoided Kharst. Kharst never paid much attention to him. Magiian cultivated the impression of being the descendant of a grower who stumbled into being a High Holder."

"And he's anything but, with the best mills and crop yields?"

Caemren nodded.

"How old is he?"

"Younger than I. We've met but a handful of times. I've never been to his place. I understand it's modest."

"Heirs?"

"He has two sons and two daughters. His wife always pled that she was carrying a child when she was invited to Variana. Since she did have a few, Kharst never pressed."

Even after asking more questions, Quaeryt still hadn't learned that much, and he finally asked, "What about you? You've avoided talking about your holdings and family."

"There's little enough to say. The holding has enough land to provide timber to Yapres, and we've got a clay quarry and brick kilns, and the east lands are wet and flat enough for maize. A little of this and that, but not enough of any one thing. Two sons, no daughters. One handles the brick-making and timber, the other the crops and tenants. My wife died ten years ago." Caemren shrugged, as if to indicate there was little left to say.

Quaeryt didn't feel like pushing. Instead, he stood. Caemren and Calkoran did as well, although a quick look of puzzlement crossed the High Holder's face. Caemren gestured toward the door from the terrace to the salon, then led the way back to the main entry. Quaeryt could not help but notice how quiet the house was, as if inhabited only by Caemren and a few servants.

When they reached the portico, Caemren looked to Calkoran. "A pleasure meeting you, Subcommander." His eyes flicked to Quaeryt. "And to see you and learn your mission was successful, Commander. I'd have been surprised if it hadn't been."

"I appreciate your confidence," replied Quaeryt.

"Not confidence, just knowledge." Caemren watched as the two officers mounted and then led the squad down the paved drive toward the gates.

Quaeryt thought over the brief meeting, which had only reinforced his feelings, about both Caemren and the High Holders of Bovaria.

"What did you think of the High Holder?" Quaeryt asked Calkoran.

"He is smart, and he will not cross you. He will only

do what he must, but he will do it promptly. That is so he does not call attention to himself."

"And he's one of the better holders."

"That surprises you?"

"No," replied Quaeryt wryly, "but I could hope."

Calkoran laughed.

After a moment so did Quaeryt.

54

Quaeryt and first company left Yapres before fifth glass on Solayi morning, taking the east road to Choelan to reach Magiian's hold by seventh glass. Quaeryt didn't want to spend an extra day on the road just to visit Magiian, and Justanan could certainly handle Northern Army, since officially he was in command, no matter how much he deferred to Quaeryt. He did detail Calkoran's company as vanguard . . . and to make sure no "couriers" rode out.

While the road east was not that good, after the first three milles out of Yapres, which wound through low hills, the land was flat and the way largely straight. Without pushing the mounts, Quaeryt reached the holding a quint before seventh glass. The only indication that they might be at a hold was the single name—MAGIIAN—chiseled into a stone plaque on the left brick gatepost. The iron filigree gates, painted white, were open. There were no guards, and no guardhouse, no walls or hedgerows, just a long graveled drive that ran straight back through fields filled with green plants a yard high. Ahead was a reddish brick building about the size of Caemren's hold house with white pillars framing an entry portico. Scattered lines of trees flanked the edges of some fields, but with the exception of a small woods or woodlot perhaps a mille and a half to the east, Quaeryt could see no other stands of trees.

As he rode toward the dwelling a good mille back from the road, Quaeryt looked for the blue flowers that indicated the plants were flax, but decided it was too early in the summer for them to be blooming . . . at least from what he'd read.

"The High Holder doesn't seem to be worried about anyone attacking," observed Zhelan.

Quaeryt had to agree. He'd never seen a hold with fewer defenses. Without the plaque on the gatepost, he wouldn't even have considered the dwelling a hold house. Then, as they neared the main dwelling, set on a man-made rise less than two yards above the surrounding fields, he saw the extensive outbuildings—six large barnlike structures, two long stables, a score of small cots, and ten or eleven sheds of various sizes. All were built of the reddish brick.

The red brick house itself was of two stories and extended some eighty yards, end to end. The upper level had wide windows, and most were open, although Quaeryt thought he saw fine mesh netting inside, covering the opening. All the trim and the pillars supporting the portico roof were painted white. The drive joined a circle that ran up to the portico.

As Quaeryt reined up at the foot of the three wide steps leading from the drive up to the portico, a graying man dressed in brown shuffled from the wide single door toward the end of the portico, then straightened when he reached it. He looked at Quaeryt, but said nothing.

"I'm Commander Quaeryt. Lord Bhayar sent me. I'm here to see High Holder Magiian. If you would tell him I'm here."

The man nodded. "Yes, sir. I'll tell him." He shuffled back toward the hold house.

Only a few moments later the door opened. The man who stepped out onto the red brick pavement of the small roofed portico wore rough brown trousers with a collarless brown shirt and scuffed boots. The crown of his head was bald and tanned, and short and wispy brown hair circled his pate. He was perhaps ten years older than Quaeryt.

"High Holder Magiian?" asked Quaeryt.

"That's who you asked for. That's who I am," the man replied with a mischievous smile. "What do you require of me? Or what does Lord Bhayar require?"

"He requires your allegiance and your tariffs. I just need a glass of your time."

Magiian's eyes ran over the company. "That's all? And on a Solayi morning?"

"Water for the mounts would be appreciated. We're actually on our way back to Variana. I didn't have time to stop on the way to Rivages. This is the only time I have to meet you." Quaeryt dismounted and handed the gelding's reins to a ranker.

"If your men will ride back to the water troughs, I'll have my people expecting them."

"Thank you." Quaeryt looked to Zhelan. "Hold the company for a bit to give them time."

"Yes, sir."

Quaeryt walked up the steps to meet the High Holder.

Magiian studied Quaeryt for a moment, then nodded. "It's early, but the study is still neat." He turned and walked toward the door.

Quaeryt followed, noting that, despite the simplicity of the hold house, everything looked to be in perfect repair, the brick paving even and well pointed, the paint on the trim and shutters and on wooden-faced and fluted pillars smooth and unweathered. The plain but brassbound single front door was also painted white. Inside, the hold was cool, but Quaeryt suspected it would be uncomfortably warm by late afternoon. He also heard voices.

"... all those troopers ..."

"... an officer to see your father ..."

"... don't like—"

"Kylan!"

The last was clearly a forceful mother's tone, and Quaeryt wondered what the youngster had been about to say. Instead, he said, "I take it I interrupted a family breakfast."

"We were close to finishing."

"I apologize, but I'm trying to see as many High Holders as possible, and that's not always convenient."

The study was moderate in size, perhaps four yards by six, with table desks at each end and a pair of leather armchairs set at a slight angle to each other before a wide window, arranged so that whoever sat there could read with late afternoon light or talk to another person.

Magiian gestured to the chairs, and they both sat.

"What do you want to know, Commander? I assume you didn't come all the way from Variana merely to make my acquaintance?"

"I went to Rivages to resolve a situation for Lord Bhayar. One of his submarshals was compromised by Lady Myranda of Fiancryt and by the surviving imagers of Rex Kharst. I've met with as many High Holders as I could on the way out, and I'm doing so on the way back."

"I presume you removed the submarshal and the imagers."

Quaeryt didn't answer the question, but merely raised his eyebrows.

"Every High Holder in Bovaria knows that a white-haired and young-faced commander who is likely an imager himself destroyed Kharst's army to almost the last man and then was involved in the campaign to subdue Antiago. There cannot be many such, and you are returning from Rivages. Had you not been successful, you would not be heading out of your way to meet with one of the less renowned High Holders."

"The matter was resolved, with the exception of Lady Myranda, who escaped." Before Magiian could reply, Quaeryt added, "I was a little surprised when I saw your hold."

"Why?" asked Magiian with a smile.

"There aren't any walls, no hedgerows. . . ."

"No defenses," admitted the High Holder. "What would be the point? There aren't any towns near here, not even hamlets. To build anything to withstand an attack would be prohibitively costly, and paying the guards to man it more so. The land holds the value, and there are enough men with skill at arms here to deal with common bandits and raiders."

"I see no signs of older fortifications. One of your forbears came to that conclusion?"

"My great-great-grandsire. He also had a knack of convincing others. Most of those, and their descendants in this part of Bovaria, look at matters in much the same way as we do."

"Concentrating on the land and leaving the politics to others?"

Magiian laughed softly. "I can't see that getting closely involved with a rex has ever benefited a High Holder's children, and certainly not his grandchildren."

Quaeryt offered a wry smile in return. "There's much to be said for just paying your tariffs and not plotting or scheming. Lord Bhayar has already tried to make it clear that he has little intention of disinheriting those who have followed that path."

"I would hope that would be the case."

"It has been so far. He may take a holding from a holder who dies without a widow or heirs. Do you have a dwelling in Variana?"

"Yes. It's also rather modest. None of us—except me—have visited in years. I traveled there as little as possible, and at times when few others would."

"In the depth of winter? Or the height of summer before harvest?"

"Something like that."

"High Holder Caemren said that you deal largely in oilseeds, and somewhat in flax. Do you ship the linen to Variana by the Aluse?"

"When we produce more than the weavers in Choelan need."

After that Quaeryt asked a number of questions, but from all that he could tell Magiian was what he purported to be—a High Holder more actively involved in his lands than most and one totally uninterested in much else . . . except as other matters might impact his holding.

Less than two quints later, Quaeryt and first company were riding back toward the River Aluse. While his visit revealed almost nothing new, in another way it was strangely reassuring to learn there might be significant numbers of High Holders who would pose no problems at all.

But then, you would be more likely to run across those who would cause trouble. The ones like Magiian would keep their heads down and pay their tariffs.

He nodded and looked at the flatness of the road. He had no doubt that it would take most of the day to catch up to Northern Army, and he almost wondered why he'd taken the time to ride all that way to visit with yet another politely self-centered High Holder. On the other hand, in addition to what he had learned, he had also conveyed the unspoken message that time and distance would not be a barrier to oversight or action by Bhayar . . . or his subordinates.

55

Unfortunately, the good weather that had favored Northern Army for the first part of the journey toward Variana did not last. By midafternoon on Mardi, the rain began to fall, heavily enough that the river road was soon a quagmire. That slowed the army so that it took three glasses to cover the last few milles into Roleon, and it was well after eighth glass before the men and mounts were settled . . . as well as possible. The rain did not let up until late Meredi. Finally, at eighth glass on Vendrei, Northern Army plodded out of Roleon.

The road had largely dried, but the worst part of riding, from Quaeryt's point of view, was that the moisture and the summer sun had combined so that he felt as though they were riding through a steam bath populated with hordes of mosquitoes and red flies, both of which were far too small for him to use shields against.

By the time the army reached Caanara on the following Mardi evening, Quaeryt had insect bites in more places than he wanted to count, despite the fact that he'd worn his visor cap and a long-sleeved uniform shirt the entire time. He felt he'd seen and experienced more mosquitoes and red flies over the past two days than he had on the entire campaign the previous summer, a fact he mentioned to Justanan as the two of them sat at a corner table in the public room of the best inn in Caanara, the Red Bear, which, in Quaeryt's mind, barely merited being termed an inn. Each had a beaker of lager before them, supposedly pale, but more like amber.

"I'd have to agree," said the older officer. "They weren't near as thick there, especially the red flies. Well . . . maybe in a few places, but not for days straight, even when it rained."

"I wondered if I was the only one who thought that way."

"Nieron has more bites than you do, I think, from the way he talks."

"How do you think he feels about Myskyl, now that he's had a chance to think it over?"

"He hasn't said much. We were never close, you know. He did say that it was obvious that your loyalty was to Lord Bhayar." Justanan paused. "You meant what you said about not being marshal, didn't you?"

"Absolutely. That would not be good for Bhayar or for Lydar."

"You'd be good at it."

"That doesn't mean that I should be. I'd be seen as having too much power. It's one thing to be an imager and one commander among many. . . ." Quaeryt let the words hang.

The older commander nodded. "You prefer to remain less visible."

"It's not just that. Lord Bhayar needed the imagers after Kharst attacked, but imagers should not be a part of the armies on a permanent basis. They should be separate, and they should provide other benefits and services, and they should report directly to the ruler. They also need to be better organized and structured."

"You're working on that?"

"Lord Bhayar has agreed to establish a collegium of imagers, located on the isle of piers in the River Aluse. Initially, they'll be supported by fifth battalion and my regiments, but that will only be for a few years, until more imagers are trained. That way, the imagers will have a place to be schooled, trained, and supervised."

Justanan laughed softly. "They'll balance the power of the armies . . . and whoever is marshal. That's what you have in mind, isn't it?"

"Partly. But only partly. Imagers need a safe place to learn and grow. There are so few that they'll never be a danger to the people, but if they're scattered, the people are a danger to them. They can protect a ruler, and he can protect them."

"What will keep them in check after you're gone?"

"The fact that a ruler can dissolve the Collegium and return them to persecution. Most imagers aren't as powerful as the ones you've seen. They're the survivors and the best . . . and there are only ten of them in all of Lydar. Even if there are ten times as many as that who are that able—which I doubt—that number could not survive without protection or without continuing to hide. Even a number of those in my forces died, and I've been wounded three times."

"Will you remain a commander?"

"Only so long as necessary. I'd prefer to be the maître of the Collegium."

Justanan took a swallow from the beaker of lager before him, then set it down and looked at Quaeryt. "I'd tell you not to coddle the younger ones, but I have the feeling you won't."

"I intend to make the standards for imagers far

tougher than for troopers or officers, and the punishments for transgressions far harder. There has to be a price for protection."

"Do you really think that it will outlast you?"

Quaeryt smiled and shrugged. "I'd like to think so, but that will depend on how well we educate and train those who succeed us." He paused. "Isn't that true in everything?"

Justanan laughed again. "It is indeed." He lifted the beaker. "To those who follow. May we train them well."

With a smile, Quaeryt lifted his own beaker and took a healthy swallow.

When he set the beaker down, the smile was gone. "I'm going to take my two companies and leave very early tomorrow morning."

Justanan offered a faint smile. "I thought you would."

"I'd suggest that you not press, either. It's possible that you may receive additional orders before you reach headquarters in Variana. Then, again, you may not."

"That depends on Lord Bhayar, I assume. What will you tell the marshal?"

"Nothing. I'll report to Lord Bhayar, as he ordered. He'll decide what happens after that."

"You will certainly recommend something."

"My only recommendation will be that Deucalon not remain as marshal. He either had no idea what Myskyl was doing, or he was part of it. Given the fact that Bhayar requested information and was effectively denied that information . . ." Quaeryt looked to Justanan.

"Deucalon was either negligent or complicit," finished the older commander.

"Were you reporting to Lord Bhayar, what would you recommend?"

"The same as you will . . . but I'm glad you're the one

who has to." Justanan offered a rueful expression. "We just may take a rather leisurely approach to Variana."

"Not too leisurely," suggested Quaeryt.

"You don't expect . . ."

"I don't, but I've been surprised before."

"When was the last time? When you were born?"

Quaeryt had to smile at Justanan's cheerful sardonicism. "I think it was a bit after that."

"Not much."

Quaeryt shook his head and took a small swallow of the amber lager.

56

Quaeryt and first company reached the circle road around the Chateau Regis slightly after first glass on Jeudi. They had made better time covering the distance from Caanara to Variana than they had in leaving the capital weeks earlier, despite encountering some rain north of Talyon, largely because the road was in better condition as a result of the earlier imaging work . . . and because they didn't stop to make additional road repairs. Variana itself appeared unchanged, with people coming and going and most giving but a passing glance at the troopers.

As first company started up the paved side road to the rear courtyard of the chateau, Quaeryt glanced to Calkoran on his left and then to Zhelan on his right. "We talked this over last night, but I want to make it clear. No troopers or officers are to be allowed to leave the Chateau Regis except by my order or that of Lord Bhayar personally. All troopers and officers riding in from anywhere are to be detained." He looked past the two senior officers to the imager undercaptains. "You three are to support the major and subcommander until I return."

"Yes, sir."

"How much trouble do you think there will be?" asked Zhelan.

"None, I trust, but I want to make this as smooth as practicable." *And I want Deucalon having as little notice as possible.*

The rear courtyard held only the duty squad assigned to the chateau, and the squad leader looked up with interest, but not concern, as first company approached.

Quaeryt rode to the hitching rail nearest the rear door and dismounted. He eased his leather dispatch case from his saddlebag and walked swiftly to the door. Behind him, the troopers were taking control of the rear courtyard. The two guards at the door stepped aside. Then Quaeryt was astounded to see Vaelora opening the door from inside, since no one had even announced him and he and his troopers had ridden in as quietly as possible.

She motioned for him to come into the chateau.

"Were you watching for me?"

"I've had a man stationed on the upper level for the past week with orders to report to me the moment any large bodies of troopers arrive. I've also had a courier by the front door to summon your imagers from the Collegium, if necessary."

"Is it that bad?"

"Not if you're back. What about Myskyl?"

"He was planning what we thought, and he had three of Kharst's imagers. He's dead and so is his senior commander. I left one regiment with a subcommander Bhayar trusted, and the rest of Northern Army is a day behind. They're under the Commander Justanan, whom he trusts . . . and so do I."

"Good. You need to read this before you see Bhayar." Vaelora extended a dispatch.

"It's that urgent?"

"More than that." She gave him a quick hug and a quicker kiss before stepping back.

Quaeryt extracted the two sheets from the already opened envelope and began to read as they walked toward the center of the chateau.

Commander Quaeryt—

It is my unfortunate duty to inform you that both Commander Kharllon and Subcommander Dulaek passed away due to various mishaps over the past week. The first of these mishaps occurred after the governor had suggested that the orders governing Southern Army came through the chain of command from the marshal of the armies, or his successor, and that, henceforth, Southern Army would report directly to the marshal, rather than to the Lord of Telaryn. Commander Kharllon apparently suffered a seizure in his sleep the night after declaring that, since his guards reported that no one had entered or left his quarters. Then Subcommander Dulaek tripped and fell off a balcony on a late night visit to Subcommander Paedn who, as senior commander of Southern Army after the death of acting governor Kharllon, had assumed the role of acting governor. Dulaek was carrying a sabre smeared with an unusual substance. . . .

Quaeryt read the remainder of the dispatch quickly, which assured Quaeryt that Voltyr and Paedn were working together, because the imagers had provided services for the new acting governor, although they remained based in Westisle, where they were converting naval barracks into quarters for the imagers and Nineteenth Regiment.

After finishing the dispatch, he looked to Vaelora. "What are your thoughts?"

"Myskyl had enlisted Kharllon from the beginning, and either Kharllon or Myskyl had suborned Dulaek."

"I'd always thought that Kharllon was a possibility. Did Bhayar have a fit at what Voltyr did?"

"He wasn't happy. I did point out that it was possible that the imagers acted to stop a rebellion in Antiago before it could take place."

"He still wasn't happy, I suspect."

"You need to see him now."

"That's where I'm headed. You should come with me."

"I intend to."

Even if Quaeryt had thought she should not have come, he wouldn't have argued with the iron behind her words.

"This way," she said. "The back staircase that comes up close to his study is quicker, and fewer people in the chateau will see you. What else should I know?"

"I'd be surprised if there's any more trouble in the north, but Bhayar is also going to be unhappy because he's going to have to realize that the land he rules is too big for him to control it just by personal maneuvering and intrigue."

"You're right. I've been saying things along those lines, and he's been close to dismissive."

"Have we heard anything from the Khellan High Council?"

"Not a thing, but it might be another month . . . if they have to consult with all the local councils."

That requirement had skipped Quaeryt's mind, but another thought struck him after Vaelora nodded to the guard at the base of the narrow circular staircase and he followed her up the steps. "How did you get that dispatch?"

"Major Voltyr sent it with instructions that if you were not present, it was to go to me, and if I were not present, to Bhayar directly. It arrived last Lundi. The one you read is a copy. I even forged Voltyr's signature. After reading the original, I made the copy and gave the original to Bhayar. Otherwise, he might have been misled by reports that were sent to Deucalon. He is still less than pleased."

"Do you know what he told the marshal?"

"No. He said that matters would remain as they were until he had a report from you. He did say that Deucalon agreed that was for the best."

"Deucalon is trying to maintain a position where he hasn't committed himself."

The eyes of the guard outside Bhayar's study widened when he saw both Vaelora and Quaeryt as they walked from the top of the staircase toward the half-open study door.

"If you'd announce us," suggested Quaeryt, removing his sweaty visor cap and tucking it under his arm.

"Yes, sir, Lady . . ." The guard turned. "Commander Quaeryt and Lady Vaelora, Lord Bhayar."

"Send them in and close the door."

Once more, the dark-haired Lord of Telaryn and Rex of Bovaria was standing by the open window. Even from across the study Quaeryt could see the dark circles under his eyes. Bhayar did not speak until the door clicked shut.

"You could have sent a dispatch." His words were flat.

Quaeryt recognized the anger behind that flatness. "Not without risking your life and rule. And that is something I would not do."

"You could have sent it with a full squad."

"Against all of Deucalon's regiments? I came ahead of Northern Army with my two companies. I doubt that a squad could have traveled that much faster." Quaeryt gestured to the conference table. "I suggest we sit. I need to tell you what happened and show you some dispatches of interest."

"Before we sit . . . what was Myskyl doing . . . if anything?"

"Plotting with Lady Myranda of Fiancryt, three imagers who served Kharst, and Marshal Deucalon to remove me and turn you into their puppet, if not to replace you completely. Shall we sit?"

"It might be best, brother dear," said Vaelora. "I doubt that the story and all the details can be conveyed all that briefly."

Bhayar's face remained impassive as he walked toward the table.

Once the three were seated, Quaeryt began. "I'm going to relate events as they happened. Not the mundane business of what the companies did each day, but the events relating to what Myskyl and Deucalon, and others, did and were planning."

"Should I summon Deucalon to hear this? It appears you are making a charge against him, and he has served Telaryn long and faithfully."

"I think you need to hear and see what evidence I have. If you have questions about my recollection, you can question any of my troopers, imagers, or officers."

Bhayar nodded. "Go on, then."

"We left Variana on the seventeenth of Avryl. Nothing untoward occurred until the twenty-second of Avryl. We were some fifteen milles south of a town called Roleon when the rear guard intercepted a courier from Marshal Deucalon. This is the dispatch he carried." Quaeryt eased the dispatch from the case and passed it to Bhayar, then waited as he read the dispatch.

"It only gives the date when you left Variana," said Bhayar, laying the sheet on the table.

"It also points out that Deucalon has 'obvious reasons' for not asking about my destination, and states that Myskyl would find the information useful. Later on in the dispatch, you will note that Deucalon states that he agrees with Myskyl's suggestion that when speaking to High Holders they should always refer to the power of Telaryn and its forces and never mention any individual by name or position. That way, he writes, their allegiance is to Telaryn and not to any individual."

"Your point is?" asked Bhayar.

Quaeryt wondered if Bhayar were baiting him or being deliberately obtuse. "My point is that Rescalyn never mentioned you by name or position when addressing his officers in the entire time I was in Tilbor. I don't think that is coincidence, not when Myskyl was Rescalyn's deputy and was also submarshal under Deucalon."

"Go on," said Bhayar.

Can he really not see what was happening? Quaeryt cleared his throat. "When we questioned the dispatch riders, they informed us that they were ordered to avoid our forces and that more than three dispatch riders had arrived from Northern Army in the month before we set out. The courier knew them by name. Yet, according to what you told me, Deucalon said he had received no word from Myskyl since winter."

Bhayar nodded again, and Quaeryt continued, detailing the information he had received from various sources and High Holders along the way.

"... about fifteen milles north of Yapres, on the twenty-eighth of Avryl, we encountered and had to restrain with imaging another courier. He and his trooper escorts had been dispatched from the high holding of Fiancryt north and west of Rivages by Submarshal Myskyl. They were given specific orders to avoid at all costs any Telaryn troopers." Quaeryt extended the second dispatch, again waiting for Bhayar to read it.

This time, he did see a hint of a frown, perhaps when Bhayar reached the part that mentioned that Myskyl was effectively holding on to ten thousand golds in tariffs from the factors and High Holders of the north.

"He seems preoccupied with the safety of the golds. By the way, what happened to them?" asked Bhayar.

"They are safe, being transported and guarded by Commander Justanan's forces. They should arrive here in a day or two. I strongly suggested that he deliver them here."

"Strongly suggested?"

"He does outrank me," Quaeryt pointed out

"Who are the others with whom Myskyl was negotiating?"

"Most likely the three remaining imagers who served Kharst, based on what occurred later. All the commanders of Northern Army knew Myskyl was meeting with men they suspected were imagers." Quaeryt paused, then added, "You might also note the line about 'those who have usurped the powers of the marshal.'"

"I can read, Quaeryt. Continue."

Quaeryt did so.

Surprisingly, Bhayar did not interrupt as Quaeryt relayed what had happened on the approach to Rivages, including an entire regiment being deployed to detain or capture him and his troopers, and then how Myskyl had attempted to murder him with the imagers and the metal-lined room and the oversized blunderbuss, ending with, ". . . After the hold house burned, I met with the two surviving senior commanders, Justanan and Nieron. Once the fire had died to ashes we inspected the remnants of the house, and they verified that there was indeed a blunderbuss mounted in the wall and that the so-called officers' salon was metal-lined to keep me from imaging—"

"Why didn't that work?"

"It would have if my imagers hadn't kept Myskyl from closing the door. . . ." Quaeryt did not mention the appearance of Erion, only that the interplay of imaging forces had resulted in lightnings and flame that killed Myskyl and the Bovarian imagers, and that the imager undercaptains' efforts to keep Luchan from using the blunderbuss had resulted in his death. He did mention Lady Myranda's escape.

"You couldn't stop her?"

"We were rather occupied," said Quaeryt mildly. "It takes some effort to infiltrate five regiments and deal with the three strongest Bovarian imagers." He glanced to Vaelora. That quick look told him that she appeared ready to strike her brother dead.

Bhayar took a long deep breath, then looked at his sister. "Don't glare at me."

"Then stop acting like a clueless idiot," she snapped back.

"That's exactly the way many senior commanders would see it," he returned. "Deucalon and Myskyl have served long and faithfully."

"Until now," said Quaeryt. "Even Nieron, who was predisposed to support Myskyl, is now convinced that Myskyl was plotting to destroy me and to increase the power of the marshal."

"What exactly do you suggest I do with the high holding of Fiancryt, now that you turned it into a ruin?"

For a moment, Quaeryt couldn't believe Bhayar's question. Then, abruptly, he realized that Bhayar was having great difficulty in dealing with the magnitude of the treachery that had almost engulfed him. So he was focusing on something far smaller. *Because Deucalon and Myskyl had served his father so faithfully that he cannot believe they would turn against him? Or does he believe that Myskyl and Deucalon betrayed him because he has turned to me? Or perhaps both?*

"Only the hold house," replied Quaeryt after a moment of silence. "All the other structures are in good repair. I'd suggest that you grant the lands to Tyrena D'Ryel and her daughter."

"What?"

"Can you think of anyone more likely to be loyal? In addition, it reduces the number of High Holders in Rivages, which has always been a trouble spot for the rulers of Bovaria."

"Why does so much of what you do create consternation," asked Bhayar, "when so much of it makes sense?"

"Because, sir, you wish to be respected for your sense of fairness, justice, and practicality, while most who have or seek power respect only power and its exercise and fear justice." *And I have exercised power you do not wield, except through me, on your behalf.*

"Why her?"

"Why not? She would have worked out terms with your father, I suspect, had she been allowed to be Khanara. She's intelligent, and she owes you. She understands that the lands are hers on sufferance. It will also make the point that appointing Vaelora as Minister of Administration is not just a gesture . . . and she should have that position alone, once I officially become maître of the Collegium."

"I'm beginning to think that cannot happen soon enough," said Bhayar dryly, "especially after that business in Antiago."

"What business?" asked Quaeryt guilelessly.

"You already know, I'm sure." Bhayar handed an envelope and a dispatch to Quaeryt. "It's a dispatch from Subcommander Paedn."

Based on the dispatch from Voltyr, Quaeryt had few doubts about what the dispatch contained.

"I don't know why I bother. You doubtless know what it contains." Bhayar looked hard at his sister.

"I know what Major Voltyr said," replied Quaeryt. "I don't imagine that there's much difference in the dispatch from Paedn."

"Why not?"

"Because, unlike some, Paedn is both honest and loyal, and a decent commander."

"Read it."

Quaeryt did. The only difference in Voltyr's dispatch and that of Paedn was a single section, and even it was not that much different.

... The night after Commander Kharllon declared that he would report directly to the marshal and not to Lord Bhayar he suffered some sort of seizure in his sleep and died suddenly. His personal guards were quite clear that no one entered or left his quarters that night.

Quaeryt had no doubts about what had happened. He looked up and returned the dispatch to Bhayar.

"What do you have to say?"

"Obviously, the commander had a guilty conscience about what he was doing, so much so that it triggered that seizure."

Bhayar snorted. "The same things are happening with Major Voltyr as have happened around you, and I won't have it!"

Quaeryt looked directly at Bhayar. "If you wish to remain Rex Regis of Solidar, you will have it. You cannot ever afford another senior officer who either attempts to take unnecessary power or who wants to destroy imagers and the Collegium."

"*You* are telling me? Are you planning to be the next Rex Regis?"

"No. I don't want to be rex. I don't even want to be a marshal or a submarshal. Why do you think I took the extra risk of not bringing all the imagers with me to Rivages? Why do you think I left two imagers to support Meinyt, and two in Antiago? Why did I leave two here, working on rebuilding an anomen and building a Collegium? Why is Vaelora struggling with ledgers and gathering tariff rolls and information on factors and High Holders?" Quaeryt realized that his voice was getting louder and louder. He swallowed and lowered it before continuing. "Anytime an imager has tried to take power in the history of Lydar, the result has been a disaster. Even the High Council of Khel only has one imager out of five councilors, and most local councils have none. The people all across Solidar would rise in revolt if I even were named marshal, or submarshal, let alone considered as rex. Unlike Rescalyn and Myskyl . . . and Deucalon, I have no delusions about what I can accomplish. I can make your rule more secure, and I can assure that the imagers survive and support you. If you do not let me, in the end, we will both perish . . . and so will Aelina, Vaelora, and Clayar . . ."

"You think so?"

"So do I," said Vaelora coldly. With her words came an image of bloody bodies strewn across the very study in which they stood, and one of those bodies was that of a graying Bhayar, another that of a young man that might have been Clayar in another ten years.

Bhayar paled, if only for a moment.

Quaeryt waited, then sighed. Loudly. "Rescalyn, Myskyl, and Deucalon all tried. So did Lady Myranda and the three imagers of Kharst. Do you know who will emerge to try again in five years . . . or ten? If you maintain a mighty army, how will you afford it? Even if you can, how well will you trust the marshal after Justanan?"

"I haven't even named him as marshal."

"You could name Pulaskyr. He would support you. After those two . . . then whom?"

Bhayar paused, then abruptly shook his head. "You two alone will stand up to me and tell me what I do not wish to hear."

"No. Not alone. Aelina will, and before long, so will Voltyr."

"Voltyr?"

"He'll be in charge of the part of the Collegium in

Westisle. That will make it far harder for anyone to contemplate attacking the Collegium here."

"Two collegiums?"

"One Collegium . . . two locations."

Bhayar's sigh was short and explosive—the one that signaled true anger.

"Brother dear . . ." said Vaelora gently. "It does not become you to be so angered when Quaeryt has likely saved both your rule and your life."

"Without even asking me . . ."

Neither Quaeryt nor Vaelora spoke, letting the silence draw out.

Finally, Bhayar sighed again, this time a drawn-out exhalation. "The more pressing question is how do you suggest I handle Deucalon?"

"Summon him here to meet with you at fifth glass. What you decide to do will depend on how he handles himself."

"Unless he's a fool, and he's not, he won't say anything, and there won't be a single piece of paper or dispatch that will incriminate him."

"The ones on the table are indicative," replied Quaeryt. "And I may be able to persuade him to reveal more. The very fact that he has been receiving dispatches from Myskyl, while lying to you, is treason in and of itself. There are scores of witnesses to confirm that. The withholding of ten thousand golds is also a form of treason. So is colluding in the attempted murder of a commander acting under your direct orders. And so is ordering a commander—Kharllon—to disregard your direct orders in favor of the marshal's. That is more than enough to order an execution."

"You understand that. Will all the men who served?"

"Give Vaelora and me a glass or so. We might have a

better solution. One that doesn't involve 'accidents' or death."

Sister and brother looked at him quizzically.

Quaeryt just smiled.

"Fifth glass, then, but I want to know your proposed solution by fourth glass."

"We'll see what we can do."

Bhayar started to reply, then shook his head, finally saying, "Fourth glass." Then he rose and walked toward the window.

Quaeryt and Vaelora left the study silently.

57

"What now?" asked Vaelora once they were well away from Bhayar's study and approaching the grand staircase down to the main level.

"First, I have to tell Zhelan and Calkoran to allow a messenger to leave to summon Deucalon. I ordered them not to allow any troopers or officers to leave Chateau Regis."

"You didn't want Deucalon storming in until you briefed Bhayar?"

"Exactly, and I didn't know if Bhayar would even be here or if he would be busy meeting with someone." Quaeryt started down the grand staircase.

"He would have met with you."

"And while we were meeting, some junior officer would have been riding off to warn the marshal. I wasn't sure how Bhayar would take it. You saw how he didn't want to believe it of Deucalon."

"I did. But brother dear can be most implacable when he feels he has been betrayed."

"Does he feel that way about Deucalon?"

Vaelora frowned. "He's angry. He doesn't like being deceived, and he doesn't like it when he's shown that he made a mistake. And he hates being wrong."

"Don't we all?" asked Quaeryt wryly. "While I'm

giving orders to Zhelan and Calkoran, would you see about assembling what records you have about vacant high holdings, including any that Kharst bestowed in Khel?"

"Khel? You have a nasty turn of thought, dearest."

"You mentioned sending word to Baelthm and Horan. Are they quartered on Imagisle now?"

"Since last week."

"Then we'll need to call them in, and have Khaern ready to bring in Eleventh Regiment."

"Do you think that will be necessary?"

"I doubt it, but we'd both be neglecting our duty to Bhayar if it turns out to be required."

"Do you need anything else?" she asked.

"You," he replied with a warm smile.

"That, dearest, will have to wait."

They separated at the foot of the staircase.

Quaeryt turned and walked half the width of the chateau to the rear door to the courtyard. When he stepped out into a stiff breeze under the high gray clouds, he saw Zhelan walking toward him. With the major was an undercaptain, and from the junior officer's impassive expression, he was less than happy.

"Undercaptain Culean has a problem with your orders, Commander," said Zhelan, offering a predatory smile.

"What is your difficulty, Undercaptain?" asked Quaeryt.

"The marshal himself ordered me to report when any companies or officers returned to the Chateau Regis. Your officers refused to let me do so."

"They refused to let you do so because I ordered them not to. Since I report directly to Lord Bhayar, and since Lord Bhayar is the marshal's superior, they were right to do so, since they are not in your chain of command. They also outrank you." Quaeryt smiled. "Shortly, I understand, Lord Bhayar will be sending a courier to the marshal. You—and you alone from your command—may accompany that trooper and report to the marshal."

"Yes, sir."

Ignoring the combination of fear and anger almost but not quite suppressed from appearing on the undercaptain's face, Quaeryt turned to Zhelan. "See that he does not leave until Bhayar's courier departs."

"Yes, sir."

"Where is Subcommander Calkoran?"

"He and his men are deployed in the front of the Chateau Regis."

"Thank you. I need to give him some instructions." He turned to the waiting imager undercaptains, all standing beside their mounts. "Lhandor, if you'd join Subcommander Calkoran. Khalis, Elsior, you're to support Major Zhelan."

"Yes, sir."

Quaeryt hurried back into the chateau, crossing to the front entrance, where he found Calkoran at the base of the steps up to the entry and there conveyed his orders for the messages to the imagers and Subcommander Khaern. Then he made his way back to Vaelora's study.

She looked up from a ledger. "It will be a quint or so before the clerks have what we need about the high holdings in Bovaria. There weren't many granted in Khel. I can only find six, and all were near port cities."

"How did you find that out?"

"The tariff records kept by the Bovarian factors' councils. I assume you're thinking about giving Deucalon a high holding in the northwest of Khel."

"I am. One as far away as possible—Eshtora or Moryn."

"Khel hasn't even agreed to terms."

"They will. Bhayar can tell him that he will not only be stipended with honor, but he will be named as High Holder once Bhayar has determined a large and appropriate holding, and that it will not be that long. If Khel doesn't come to terms, we'll find the most isolated large high holding we can and bestow that on him."

"It's too bad we can't just have him executed," said Vaelora.

"It's better that Myskyl be thought the villain. Besides, he is the greater villain. We can spread the word that Deucalon wasn't himself in the last part of the war and that Myskyl took advantage of that . . . and that Bhayar felt his previous service merited recognition. That way, if Deucalon does try to stir up trouble, then Bhayar will have reason to act more harshly."

"Brother dear might like the honorable stipend approach better."

"Much as I dislike Deucalon, it makes more sense. That way, Deucalon becomes an officer who served well, but just too long, and it buries the fact that the two top-ranking officers were conspiring against Bhayar."

"There were more than two, if you count Kharllon."

"He just had a seizure after being faced with an impossible situation," said Quaeryt dryly. He said nothing more as Vaelora continued to look through the ledger.

Finally, she looked up. "There are several vacant high holdings in Khel, all of them, in fact. The one that meets your criteria best is Khunthan. It's one of the largest in Lydar. It's located northeast of Eshtora, and it was bestowed on one Elizaran. According to the tariff records, the last tariffs were not paid because Elizaran and his family vanished and are possibly dead. That's true of all six of the holdings Kharst created."

"All we have to do is insist on a few high holdings when Khel comes to seek terms," said Quaeryt.

"Will they?"

"You're better at seeing what will be. What do you think?"

"The High Council isn't stupid. Khel now stands alone. They don't have anything to lose by suggesting the most favorable terms they can."

"We both know that. What do you feel? Or farsee?"

"I haven't had farsight flashes, not since the one . . ." She frowned. "You've never said . . ."

"You were right. The officers' salon was pitch-dark from where I stood when Myskyl ordered the iron shutters dropped. We can talk about that later, but your telling me about the farsight made me aware that I would be facing some sort of trap."

"I'm glad it helped."

"We don't have that much time," Quaeryt said. "Would you mind seeing what the clerks have come up with?"

She smiled and headed for the door to the adjoining study.

In the end, even with the incomplete records that Vaelora and the clerks had been able to piece together, Quaeryt and Vaelora found three possible high holdings in Bovaria that could be granted to Deucalon, assuming that Bhayar agreed with their "solution."

Promptly at fourth glass, Quaeryt and Vaelora entered Bhayar's study.

Bhayar was already seated at the conference table. He did not rise, but gestured for them to sit, waiting to speak until they were seated. "The more I think about this, the angrier I become. At first, I couldn't believe it was possible, but then . . ." He shook his head. "How could he do this? Why?"

"Because Myskyl was very persuasive, obviously," replied Quaeryt. "I was wrong, you know? I thought that Myskyl was merely a loyal follower of Rescalyn, when it had to have been the other way around."

"How did you know? And when?" asked Bhayar.

"I didn't, not for certain. But when Skarpa and Southern Army were always detailed to attacks and positions designed so that we took the greatest risk . . . and then when Deucalon changed who was to attend senior officers' meetings, it became clearer and clearer that one of them, if not both, wanted me dead in a way that couldn't be traced to them, as well as isolated from the other commanders. Looking back, I can see that Myskyl feared that the imagers would undermine his and Deucalon's power and influence. I suspect, but there's no proof, that Kharllon was part of it. If he'd been allowed to remain as acting governor of Antiago, and Myskyl controlled Northern Army, and Deucalon the regiments remaining near Variana . . ."

"I'd have had a hard time not doing what they wanted if they'd been able to remove you," concluded Bhayar.

Vaelora nodded.

"So what solution do you have—besides the execution he deserves?"

"The execution is exactly what he deserves," began Quaeryt, "but that will not serve you all that well. The proof we have of what he did is more than sufficient to prove his guilt, but not the sort that is easily explained to troopers and officers—or to many others. We were thinking about a gilded prison of sorts—rewarding him with a high holding in a locale where he could not make trouble . . . and where, if he did, an accident would not be all that unusual . . . or noticed . . ." Quaeryt went on to explain his thoughts. When he finished, he waited.

Bhayar fingered his chin. Then he frowned. He shifted his weight in his chair and frowned again. Finally, he shook his head. "I don't like the idea of his getting away with this. I don't."

"He won't," said Vaelora. "Keep him here until you decide on which high holding. Make him a guest."

"But forbid him any contact with other officers, beginning right after you tell him of his good fortune."

"He won't see it as good fortune," said Bhayar.

"He will if you point out that his acts could be seen as treason," said Quaeryt, "and that you have evidence and witnesses."

"We'll have to see, won't we?" replied Bhayar.

For the next quint, the three discussed how they would proceed.

Then Vaelora stood. "If this is a matter for officers, I should not be present."

Bhayar nodded, but did not speak, as his sister slipped from the study.

Less than half a quint passed before the guard announced, "Marshal Deucalon."

"Have him enter."

Quaeryt stood. Bhayar did not.

"Sir," offered Deucalon, bowing his head slightly to Bhayar as he stepped into the study. Almost as an afterthought, he added, "Commander."

"Marshal," returned Quaeryt, without offering the usual head bow to a superior officer. *It might be petty, but Deucalon doesn't deserve it.*

Bhayar gestured to the seat at his left.

Deucalon offered the hint of a frown, but seated himself. Quaeryt took the seat to Bhayar's right.

Bhayar did not immediately speak, but studied Deucalon almost as if he had never met the marshal before. Finally, he began. "Deucalon, you served my father long and loyally and well. And for several years you did the same for me."

"I have always served you and the interests of Telaryn to the best of my ability."

"If you believe that," said Bhayar quietly, "then you and I have quite different ideas about what my interests and those of Telaryn are. For the past three months, I have inquired, time after time, about the activities of Northern Army. You have insisted that you have heard no word from Submarshal Myskyl. I dispatched Commander Quaeryt to see what might be the difficulty. Not only did he discover that the late submarshal was plotting a rebellion with the assistance of Bovarian High Holders and three imagers who had served Rex Kharst, he also intercepted dispatches proving that you lied about not receiving word from the submarshal."

"That is only his word, sir, and if I might say so, his interests are not yours."

"It is not just his word. One of those dispatches has your signature on it, and its content indicates that you had received dispatches from the submarshal during the time when you insisted there were none. There are also scores of troopers and doubtless several officers who can name the couriers who rode from your headquarters and returned. There are two senior commanders who know that as well."

"Their ambition will justify their perjury."

Quaeryt had to admire Deucalon's air of injured outrage, not that he believed in Deucalon's innocence for a moment.

"The couriers have no reason to lie, either about their dispatches or about the fact that they were ordered to avoid Commander Quaeryt's forces. Any reasonable interpretation of your acts would suggest either incompetence or treason," replied Bhayar.

"No one will believe your charges, sir. They have been fabricated by this . . ."

"Commander Quaeryt has risked his life time and time again over the past years. I allowed you to order attacks that put him and his troopers in danger in battle after battle because I trusted you. I even let you change the attendance for senior officers' meetings to exclude him. That was wrong on my part, and even more so on yours."

"If there was any treason, it was on the part of the submarshal. I have served you loyally, with your best interests at heart."

"That may be, but you recommended that Myskyl be made a submarshal and you failed to exercise adequate supervision."

"My conscience is clear, sir. I did what I thought best, but I had no idea . . ." Deucalon stopped abruptly.

"No idea of what?" asked Bhayar mildly.

"About whatever it was that Submarshal Myskyl was doing."

"You certainly knew that he had collected significant tariffs from the High Holders and factors, but those never reached me. Ignoring orders and keeping tariff revenues from your ruler . . ." Bhayar shook his head. "Those are not the acts of a loyal marshal."

"I acted in your interests, sir." Deucalon looked pointedly at Quaeryt.

"No . . . you decided that Commander Quaeryt was acting against what you thought were your interests, and you decided that your interests were mine. It doesn't work that way, Deucalon. My interests are yours, not the other way around."

"And his are not yours, either."

"Actually, they are. He wants a land where imagers and those suspected of imaging are not hounded and killed. Where the Pharsi are treated fairly as well. So do I. He wants a land where wars do not occur between neighbors every generation. So do I. And he wants a land where the ruler does not have to look over his shoulder at those who serve him, wondering who will try to betray him next. That . . . that, I definitely want." Bhayar's voice softened as he asked, "What do you want, Deucalon?" His dark blue eyes fastened on the marshal.

After a moment Deucalon replied, "A fair hearing, not a trumped-up judgment."

Bhayar shook his head. "No, you don't. If I give you a fair hearing, I'll have to order your execution. I already have enough evidence to justify that." Again he looked hard at Deucalon.

After a long time the marshal looked down.

"On the other hand," Bhayar continued, "you have rendered long and diligent service to both my father and me. It may be that this service has created too great a burden on you. For this reason, I will be appointing a new marshal. I am also allowing you to leave my service with a full and honorable stipend. . . ."

Deucalon's face hardened, and Quaeryt could see the suppressed anger.

". . . and further, in recognition of your devoted service, especially to my father, you will be granted a large and prosperous high holding. Because of the speed of recent events, I have not had a chance to review all of the holdings available and suitable, but I will decide shortly. In the meantime, you will be my guest here at the Chateau Regis."

"Your prisoner," suggested Deucalon.

"No. You can come and go as you wish, with one exception. You have been relieved of command, and you are not to meet or communicate with any officers except Commander Quaeryt. Should you do so, you will find that I will be far less generous. Far less." Bhayar's voice turned cold with the last words.

Deucalon looked to Quaeryt.

Quaeryt image-projected authority and cold certainty.

Abruptly Deucalon seemed to sag, looking older and tired. "I will do my best to be a loyal High Holder."

"You may send for your family, if you so desire," added Bhayar. "The holding you receive will not be in Telaryn, and they may wish to accompany you to it."

"You are most kind."

"All your personal items will be brought here," added Quaeryt.

"You are most thoughtful, Commander."

Quaeryt could hear the faint irony in Deucalon's words and replied, "I have always attempted to think through everything in a fashion that serves Lord Bhayar most effectively."

"He is most fortunate to have your loyalty."

"No. I am most fortunate to serve a ruler who acts beyond his anger and looks beyond the moment." After the slightest pause, Quaeryt added, "So are you."

"You may go, Deucalon." Bhayar turned to Quaeryt. "Commander, you may escort High Holder Deucalon to his quarters. They are the ones two doors down from yours."

Quaeryt inclined his head, then gestured toward the door, following the former marshal out into the north corridor. Once outside, he said, "This way, sir."

They walked several yards before Deucalon spoke. "You think you saved my life, don't you?"

"Lord Bhayar made that decision, based on your long service," replied Quaeryt.

"I've seen his anger, Commander. And I've seen his father's. Did you recommend my fate to humiliate me?"

"No. I think you were misled, as was Rescalyn, and it would have served no purpose to have you executed. You will be given, I understand, a good high holding, if one that is somewhat isolated, but prosperous enough that you will be able to live in great comfort."

"You and the imagers will be my gaolers."

Quaeryt shook his head. "The Collegium will serve, if you will, as patrollers of the High Holders and the army command, doing nothing unless a High Holder or a senior officer proves disloyal or commits a heinous crime. There are too few imagers, as you well know, to do otherwise. We can destroy individuals or bodies of troopers, but we cannot follow small crimes or pettiness."

"You've thought it all out, haven't you . . . from the beginning?"

"Not everything, but most of it. Myskyl and Rescalyn made it necessary if Vaelora and I were to survive."

"And when will you become rex?"

"Never," said Quaeryt. "Never. That is not my position, nor would that be good for anyone, especially for any children we might have."

"You really believe that, don't you?"

"No. I *know* it." Quaeryt halted outside the half-open door. "Your quarters, sir."

The former marshal looked at Quaeryt for a long time, then said, "You're the one who will be looking over your shoulder the rest of your life."

"I know that, too," replied Quaeryt. *I already have, and what is to come is a small part of the prices yet to pay.*

Abruptly Deucalon turned and pushed the door wide open, walking into the apartments and away from Quaeryt.

Quaeryt turned and walked toward the grand staircase, leaving the door open.

58

Once Quaeryt had seen Deucalon to his quarters, he confirmed with Vaelora that the quarters on Imagisle were complete, if rudimentary in some aspects, and then conferred with Calkoran and Zhelan about billeting. They also settled on having a squad remaining at Chateau Regis to supplement the single squad from Eleventh Regiment that had been providing guards.

Bhayar did not invite Quaeryt and Vaelora to eat with him on Jeudi evening, as he had on every other night that Quaeryt had returned from missions or assignments, but took his meals in his apartments. He also sent a note saying that he would meet with Quaeryt at seventh glass on Vendrei morning. Quaeryt and Vaelora ate in the family dining quarters, by themselves, and Vaelora made certain that meals were sent up to Deucalon. Quaeryt wondered if Deucalon would eat them or reject them, fearing poison, although poisoning Deucalon in the Chateau Regis would have defeated the entire purpose of sparing his life.

Deucalon apparently came to the same conclusion, because the server reported that he had eaten most of what had been sent up—although he had questioned her and seemed pleased to have learned he was eating exactly what Quaeryt and Vaelora were—pork cutlets with fried and seasoned apples and lace potatoes.

Vaelora and Quaeryt finished eating and repaired to their apartments.

Much later that evening, Vaelora drew the sheet around her and looked across her pillow at Quaeryt. "You didn't tell the entire story about what happened at Rivages."

"No . . . I didn't . . . but I will . . . to you, and only you . . . although the three imagers saw some of it." With that, Quaeryt related exactly what had happened from the time Myskyl had tried to leave the officers' salon through what his inspection of the ruins had revealed the following morning. He even pointed out that Elsior had seen the linkage between him and Erion.

Vaelora asked no questions during his recollection of events.

When Quaeryt finished, he looked to her and added, "I can't explain how it happened, but that is what occurred, and I wouldn't have been able to do a thing against Myskyl and the renegade imagers without Khalis, Lhandor, and Elsior." He shook his head.

"You expected treachery from Myskyl. You didn't expect the imagers."

"I should have. We talked about the missing imagers. It made perfect sense that Myskyl would recruit them for his scheme. And I have to believe that Myskyl was the greater traitor, not Rescalyn or Deucalon. Myskyl set both of them up as his stalking horses. I should have seen that much earlier."

"That's in hindsight, dearest. In hindsight." Vaelora smiled. "And you did . . . in your dream."

Quaeryt shook his head. "My own dreams were telling me, and I still didn't see it."

"You couldn't believe it."

"Maybe I didn't want to. That would have meant that I killed the wrong man."

"No, dearest. You killed the right men. Rescalyn had to have known what he was doing and why. He was as guilty as Myskyl, if only because he went along with what Myskyl laid out for him, just as Deucalon has."

"There was very little hard proof in dealing with Deucalon. Very little compared to the extent of his and Myskyl's treachery, and he is the marshal that all too many troopers and officers believe led them to victory over the Bovarians. Some of them have never served under any other marshal. I still don't like the fact that he won't have to pay . . ." Quaeryt shook his head again. "Given who he is, it could be that he will pay more in some ways . . ."

"Rholan had something to say about that . . ." ventured Vaelora with a smile between mischievous and sad.

"You're still reading and rereading it?"

"It's interesting, and there's more there than meets the eye in a first reading. Just as there is with you, dearest."

"So what did Rholan say?"

"You know. You've read the book."

"I'm tired. It's been a very long day. You tell me."

"I'll read it. The writer—or Rholan—says it better than I could." Keeping the sheet about her, she reached for the bedside table and retrieved the small leather-bound volume, opening it and paging through it. Finally, she reached the page for which she searched and began to read.

"Rholan said nothing about whether the spirit of a man or even a woman endured after death. What he did say, more than once, was that death was too quick an end for the great Namers and villains. Far greater is the punishment of living and seeing their name die before they do, of never hearing a word about their past greatness. If they die at the height of their villainy, or Naming, for they are opposing sides of the same coin, they die believing in the delusions of their greatness. All greatness fades, some sooner, some later, and for those who pursue Naming and the glory of their accomplishments, and not the accomplishments themselves, a long and lonely life, accomplishments long since forgotten, is far less merciful than a quick death. . . ."

Vaelora lowered the book. "You see?"

"It's a good thing I've already learned that," said Quaeryt dryly. "That's just another reason not to want to be a marshal or a submarshal."

"You have more important tasks ahead," said Vaelora.

"Making the Collegium strong enough to survive and prosper, among other things." He looked not quite lecherously at his wife.

"Dearest . . . you don't have to make up for absences all at once."

"I'll try to restrain myself."

"For a little while, at least." Her smile was warm. "Besides, what happened at Rivages and the other places while you were there has already proved you were right."

Quaeryt suspected he knew what she might say, but he only raised his eyebrows and waited.

"Voltyr acted as you would have, without instructions, and already your Collegium is bigger than you. I haven't had a chance to tell you, but Gauswn now has another five students."

"In addition to the four he brought?"

Vaelora nodded. "There will be others, as word spreads that young imagers have powerful protectors in you and Bhayar."

"Mostly Bhayar, right now."

"Dearest . . . that is false modesty, and it doesn't become you. All Bovaria knows who you are and of what you are capable."

"That's not necessarily good."

"If you step away from direct power, as you plan, that will make Bhayar seem more powerful in time. It will also reassure people. At the moment, though, all Lydar needs to know of your power."

"And, just say, what happens if some ill chance befalls me?"

"If anything happened to you, Bhayar would have to continue the Collegium." Her eyes flashed. "That doesn't mean you can go off and do something stupid. I won't have you courting ill fate to prove you are what you are. It's time for others to do that."

"I think I've done enough foolish things for a lifetime." *Except life always has surprises. We just don't need any more at the moment.*

"We both have." Vaelora looked at him shyly. "I'm going to need to be more careful . . . as well."

"You are?"

"She'll be a girl. I'm certain."

As he leaned forward and wrapped his arms around Vaelora—gently—Quaeryt wasn't about to dispute that.

59

Slightly before seventh glass on Vendrei morning, Quaeryt approached the half-open door to Bhayar's study, half wondering with what sort of mood the ruler of Telaryn, Bovaria, and Antiago might greet him.

When Quaeryt stepped into the study and shut the door behind himself, Bhayar stood from behind the table desk and smiled warmly. "Good morning, Quaeryt."

"Good morning."

Bhayar gestured to the conference table. "Did you sleep well?"

"I did. It's good to be back."

"Vaelora worried about you." Bhayar slipped into his chair.

Quaeryt took the chair on the other side of the circular table from Bhayar. He could see that Bhayar looked less worried, and that the circles under his eyes were much less pronounced. "I worried about me, too. I'm just glad matters worked out."

Bhayar laughed softly. "You usually find a way to work them out . . . if not always in the fashion I might have originally preferred. I've gotten used to that . . . mostly. I already sent off a dispatch to Subcommander Ernyld announcing that with the success of the campaigns in Bovaria and Antiago, Marshal Deucalon has stepped down to a full stipend and will be shortly awarded a high holding for his long and devoted service, and that a new marshal of the armies will be determined within the next week. I also wrote that in order to assure a proper transition High Holder Deucalon will not be dealing with any issues of the armies, and that all inquiries will be handled by his chief of staff."

"That leaves Ernyld in charge."

"No. I also said that he was to refer any decisions to me until the new marshal is appointed. Now . . . yesterday, you recommended Commander Justanan as the successor to Deucalon as marshal. Why? I'd like to hear more about that."

"There are several reasons. First, because he is the senior commander of Northern Army, and he'll keep its commanders in line in a quiet way . . . and you need quiet. He also knows more about Bovaria than Pulaskyr, and you need Pulaskyr as the governor of Telaryn." Quaeryt grinned. "You won't be able to keep Aelina and Clayar and your other children in Solis all that much longer."

"Did Vaelora tell you that?"

"No. I guessed that from what she's said before."

"I've gotten several letters along those lines. That's another reason why I need to decide the marshal's position."

"You should talk to Commander Justanan by yourself . . . and then decide on whether he or Pulaskyr would make a better marshal . . . or if there is a better commander for the post."

"You'd do a better job at it." Before Quaeryt could say anything, Bhayar held up his hand to stop Quaeryt from replying. "I know. Appointing you would work for a while and then cause more and more problems."

"Either of the two would do well."

"Especially since they know you'd be looking over their shoulders." Bhayar offered a smile. "But then, any marshal would know you'd be watching, and for now that's probably just as well. What else?"

"Whoever you send back to Solis, though, should go with three regiments, perhaps four. That will reduce the strain on quarters and golds here and give the governor of Telaryn a little additional power."

Bhayar nodded. "In time, we will need to reduce the size of the armies. But not yet. I know you want to devote more of your time to being maître or whatever you want to title yourself as head of your imagers' Collegium, but until we hear from the Khellans, I need you as a commander."

"I can do both. Vaelora's obviously able to handle being Minister of Administration for Bovaria."

"She's managed to set up courier stations on the Aluse River road between Ferravyl and Variana, and along the Great Canal to Laaryn. She says that the stations between Eluthyn and Kephria will be operating by the end of Juyn."

While Vaelora had not mentioned the courier stations, her progress didn't surprise Quaeryt in the slightest. Nor did her decision to use the older but shorter route. *We'll need to use imaging to improve the road even more once things settle down, though.* "In time, she ought to be Minister of Administration for all of Solidar."

"It would be best not to use that name until all of Lydar is under one rule," said Bhayar. "Do you think the Khellans will really accept terms?"

"They'll try for the best they can get, but I think they will."

"So long as you're around."

"No. There are five or six imagers now, who can wreak a fair amount of destruction." Quaeryt paused. "I hope it doesn't come to that."

"It would be better if it doesn't, but I intend to keep the armies ready until it's clear that they've accepted terms and are complying."

Quaeryt nodded.

"When do you think Justanan and Northern Army will arrive?"

"Unless there's a heavy rain, I'd judge it will be tomorrow afternoon."

"Then I'll have a courier waiting for him." After the slightest pause, Bhayar added, "By the way, the three of us should have dinner this evening, and you can fill in all the other things you learned on your way to and from Rivages."

"Sixth glass?"

"That will give you plenty of time," replied Bhayar with a nod. "What do you plan for the rest of the day?"

"To ride to Imagisle and see how Baelthm, Horan, and Khaern have done in getting the place in shape. We also may have to plan for more imager students, Vaelora tells me."

"She did say something about that." Bhayar stood. "I won't keep you. Until tonight."

Quaeryt rose as well. "I look forward to dinner."

"So do I."

As he walked down toward Vaelora's ministry study, Quaeryt couldn't help but wonder what had changed Bhayar's attitude so much. Just time and a good night's sleep?

When he walked into the study, Vaelora looked up from her table desk. "How was brother dear this morning?"

"Very warm and cheerful. He asked us to dinner with him tonight. We talked about Justanan and Pulaskyr . . . and you. He said that you'd almost finished arranging for courier stations to Kephria and that we now have dispatch service to Laaryn, thanks to your efforts."

"We do." She paused. "Actually, we received a dispatch last night from Eluthyn. No one wanted to disturb us. So I didn't see it until this morning. A squad from Calkoran's second company have been escorting the Khellan envoy and his party to Variana from Kephria. The envoy will likely arrive next Mardi or Meredi."

"Were there any details?"

"No. You can read it for yourself." She reached down and handed the single sheet to Quaeryt. "I'll have one of the clerks copy it and then take it up to Bhayar."

Quaeryt scanned the sheet, but it said little more than what Vaelora had already told him. He handed it back to her. "I need to go and see what's happened at Imagisle."

"You'll be surprised . . . and pleased, I think."

"You won't tell me?"

"No. You'll picture what I tell you the way you want to—"

"Just as with a farsight," he finished with a smile.

"Dearest . . . that is close to being disrespectful." Her smile was wide and happy.

"I'll be even more disrespectful, then." He wrapped his arms around her, and their lips met.

For a time they remained locked together. Then Vaelora disengaged herself, gently but firmly. "You need to see Imagisle, and I need to get this copied."

"Yes, dear." Quaeryt grinned.

"You're still impossible."

"At times."

She shook her head.

After another long look at his wife, Quaeryt turned and left the study, walking quickly to the rear courtyard door. As he stepped out into the already warm morning, with a clear but hazy sky promising a blistering summer day, Calkoran walked toward him.

"I didn't expect to see you here this morning," offered Quaeryt.

"I knew you would want to see all that has happened at the isle. So I brought a squad to escort you."

"A full squad?"

"It seemed . . . prudent, once we heard that Marshal Deucalon had been relieved and stipended."

"Does everyone know that?"

"Some things cannot be kept quiet for long, sir." Calkoran smiled. "Especially when they show that Lord Bhayar did what was right."

Quaeryt waited to see if the Khellan officer said more. Calkoran did not. So Quaeryt went on. "I hoped that he would, after I reported on what happened, but the decision was entirely his . . . as it should have been."

"You will not be marshal, then?"

"No. That would be a mistake, both for me and for Lord Bhayar."

Calkoran nodded. "For a son of Erion, it would doom you."

"Even for an imager who might not be a son of Erion, it would doom me."

"You will see others make mistakes you would not, and you will think that you could have done better," said Calkoran.

"Any man who is good, intelligent, and hardworking will see that in others, but no man can do everything, and one who tries will do all of what he tries poorly. What I can do best is guide the imagers. So that is what I should do." Before Calkoran could say more, he added, "Even if there is no glory and my name will be lost to those who follow." He grinned. "Ride with me. We can trade platitudes on the way to Imagisle."

Calkoran smiled.

One of the rankers led Quaeryt's gelding, already saddled, toward him, and he realized, as he had not for a time, how that signified how much matters had changed over the past two years. *From an impoverished scholar too poor to purchase a mount to a commander living in a palace married to a ruler's sister with others grooming and saddling a fine mount for you.* And yet, at that moment, all he could say was, "Thank you," and mean it.

He took the reins and mounted, then rode to join Calkoran. "Was this your idea or Zhelan's?" he asked with a smile.

"We both had the same idea. I told him that since I outranked him, I would take charge of the first duty. He insisted that we alternate until we are most certain that all is safe." Calkoran paused, then added, "We know that you can protect yourself, sir, and even those close to you, but it would be best that no attacks even be attempted."

Quaeryt couldn't disagree with that. "What do you think of what the imagers have accomplished on the isle?"

"They have done much, but the question is what you think?"

"You're not saying what they've done, then."

"No, sir. As you have indicated by all your acts, the deeds should first speak for themselves."

Quaeryt laughed softly. *Trapped by your own words and acts.* "Ready to head out?"

"Yes, sir." Calkoran flicked the reins of his mount and ordered, "Column! Forward!"

Once the squad was on the road to the Nord Bridge, where they would turn south on the west river road, Quaeryt asked, "Did Subcommander Khaern say anything about the marshal's being stipended off?"

"He said that it was too bad that Deucalon had changed from a good commander to one more concerned with preserving his own power."

Quaeryt nodded. "And the submarshal?"

Calkoran snorted. "No officer with brains would mourn him."

Unfortunately, there are some senior officers who would, and Justanan or Pulaskyr—or whoever else Bhayar chooses—will have to deal with them.

Once the squad was on the west river road, Quaeryt kept looking toward Imagisle, but not until they were almost abreast of the northern tip of the isle did he begin to distinguish additional changes, most notably that Horan had clearly finished the gray granite river walls that now appeared to completely protect the isle.

Then, when they approached the bridge, he saw that the shoulders of the causeway had been cleared and reshaped on both ends.

"This way, sir," said Calkoran as they rode off the end of the bridge and turned to the north along a paved way that Quaeryt did not recall. To the east, if west of the rebuilt barracks and some other new structures he could not make out clearly, he could see the old anomen, totally restored, if not rebuilt and better than it ever could have been.

Then they rode east before turning south. Some hundred yards east of the river wall stood four barracks, two on the east side and two on the west side of an area that had been planted with grass and flowers—vegetation that was admittedly struggling—and bordered by solid paved roads. Not only that, but to the south of the green area was another smaller and single-story building. Even farther to the south of the complex were two other long buildings, apparently stables. All the buildings were of gray stone and roofed with slate tiles. To say that Quaeryt was astonished was an understatement. He looked to Calkoran. "It's amazing . . ."

"Horan and Baelthm said that they had to earn their keep."

Quaeryt also noted a long cottage-like building adjoining the anomen, and he suspected that it might well be for the students. He didn't see buildings that looked like the cottages Lhandor had provided plans for, but that was more than understandable, given all the two had done.

They rode past the barracks toward the small building to the south of the barracks and facing north onto the area with the struggling vegetation that eventually would be a green.

"That's the new administration building for the Collegium," said Calkoran, pointing to where the other officers under Quaeryt's command—five imager undercaptains, Khaern, Zhelan, Eslym, and Ghaelyn—stood in two ranks on the steps. To their right stood nine boys, dressed in gray trousers and shirts, with Gauswn, in his chorister's garb, standing beside them.

Quaeryt reined up before them. For several moments, he struggled with what he felt and what he should say. After a time, he finally said, "I want to tell all of you that, without all that each one of you has done, and that includes those who are not here, we would not have this chance at a future for you, for those you love, and for those who will follow us. Without what Khalis, Lhandor, and Elsior did in Rivages, I would not be here. Without what Horan and Baelthm have accomplished while we were in the north we would have no place to which we could return . . . and I am truly astounded at what you two have done—"

"Begging your pardon, sir," interjected Baelthm, with a slight smile, "we didn't do it alone. All of the student imagers helped as they could. We just followed the example you set for teaching them . . . excepting that we tried to have them strengthen their imaging in building . . . hoping you don't mind that."

"Not at all! We'll be needing to do more of that in the weeks and years ahead." Quaeryt shook his head.

"Some of the buildings aren't finished on the inside like they should be," added Horan. "We really missed Lhandor in that."

Quaeryt couldn't help but shake his head in wonderment. "Truly amazing . . ." After several moments, he went on. "Lord Bhayar has agreed to the Collegium, and that means that before very long those of you who have wives or children can send for them . . . if they wish to come. There are some details we need to work out, and it may be a week or so before I know those . . ." He grinned. "We will need to build some cottages . . . but I doubt that will be much of a problem for you."

That brought smiles to most faces.

"I'll be meeting with each of you either today or over the next few days. Oh . . . I know some of you are interested, but Lord Bhayar has not yet informed me of his choice for marshal. That may be a few days because he will be meeting with various senior commanders once Northern Army returns to Variana.

"And now . . . I think we'll ride to those new stables . . . they are stables, aren't they?"

"Yes, sir!" Horan called out.

As Quaeryt urged the gelding toward the stables, Calkoran cleared his throat.

"Yes?"

"I wondered, sir . . . will you and Lady Vaelora be living in the Chateau Regis . . . for long, that is?"

"For now. Once I'm no longer needed as a commander and am just the maître of the Collegium, then we'll worry about quarters here. Right now, it's more important to make sure the quarters for the imagers and men are finished."

Calkoran merely nodded.

Once Quaeryt had stabled the gelding, he had Baelthm and Horan give him a tour of all that the two—and the student imagers—had accomplished. That took more than two glasses, and Quaeryt was impressed with the quality of the work—despite the concerns that Baelthm had expressed.

When the tour was over, and the three stood on the steps of the small building, which they had informed Quaeryt was the headquarters of the Collegium, complete with a room for a modest library and several private studies as well as a spacious conference room, Quaeryt looked to Horan and Baelthm. "Did you two ever sleep?"

"We slept well, sir, and we didn't have to worry about anything except building the Collegium. Subcommander Khaern and the chorister took care of everything else."

"Some of the students must have talent with imaging."

"They all do," replied Baelthm. "Some are better at small detailed imaging, and some look to be strong like Horan."

"I can't tell you how much I appreciate all you've done."

Horan looked at Quaeryt. "Sir . . . you let me do what I could. You didn't press me to do what would have hurt me more than you know. How could we not?"

"That is the idea of the Collegium," Quaeryt admitted, "but you've put it into practice."

The two smiled.

After that, Quaeryt met with all the officers. The meeting was short, and he simply told them what he knew, including the fact that there was an envoy from Khel and that no one knew exactly what that meant. When he finished informing the officers, he walked to the anomen to find Gauswn.

The young chorister was giving lessons to the student imagers, but excused himself, and the two walked to the small study that held a table desk and two chairs. All three were plain, but appeared sturdy.

"Chartyn and Doalak imaged those for me," said Gauswn. "They've also managed bed frames and tables for the other students."

"I can't believe all that everyone has managed."

"All of them would likely die for you, sir."

Quaeryt wasn't so sure that Threkhyl would, but he was likely to be Voltyr's problem for some time to come. *If not for as long as the Westisle part of the Collegium exists.* "That may be an exaggeration."

Gauswn shook his head. "You've risked your life time after time for them."

"I risked it so that Lord Bhayar would succeed,

because that is the only way imagers can have a chance at a better life. And I've asked them to risk their lives time after time, and some of them died following me."

"You've given them pride and hope . . . and a sense of being able to control their own future. No one has ever done that for imagers."

Except perhaps the Naedarans . . . and that might be doubtful. "What else could I have done?"

"What Myskyl and Deucalon tried . . . to seek power and fill your wallet. You didn't." Gauswn smiled, almost ironically, yet gently. "In turning from that kind of power, you may have become the most powerful man in Lydar, simply by refraining from excesses . . . from Naming."

"I didn't have a choice," said Quaeryt quietly.

"How many men would recognize that?"

"There must be some."

Gauswn shook his head again. "Calkoran talked to me last night. The Khellans believe that you're the son of Erion. So do some of the imager undercaptains. I hope you won't disappoint them."

Someone else had said similar words. After a moment Quaeryt realized who it had been . . . and that recalled what Skarpa had said about Gauswn. In turn, that reminded Quaeryt all too clearly of how a single failure to correct a misconception had led to Skarpa's assassination . . . all because Quaeryt had failed to do the littlest thing. With that jumbled recollection, Quaeryt found his eyes burning,

"What is it?" asked Gauswn gently.

For a moment Quaeryt could say nothing. Then he shook his head. "You never escape the past . . . and within us, it's never really totally past." *And Erion told you that would be so.*

Gauswn smiled, sadly. "No . . . it is only never past for those who understand."

"You may be right about that." Quaeryt forced a smile. "I did say you'd be a good chorister, and I think you're also going to be a good head of studies for the young imagers. . . ." Even as he forced himself to concentrate on what he needed to tell Gauswn, Quaeryt still found himself thinking of Skarpa . . . and wondering why Gauswn's words, echoing those of Phargos, another chorister, had brought on such strong and bittersweet memories.

60

Promptly at sixth glass on Vendrei evening, Quaeryt and Vaelora met Bhayar outside the family dining room of the chateau.

Bhayar smiled warmly at them. "I always like seeing you two. You belong together."

"We do," said Vaelora, "and you can be proud that it was your idea."

Quaeryt managed not to smile, knowing that it had been Vaelora's idea at a time when Quaeryt wouldn't have dreamed of it and Bhayar wouldn't even have considered it.

"I suspect you had a few ideas along that line, sister dear, but I will take credit for allowing it to happen." He gestured toward the dining room.

Once they were seated—Bhayar at the head of the table, Vaelora on his right, and Quaeryt across from her and on Bhayar's left—the serving girl, a change from the troopers who had served at the time when Quaeryt had left for Rivages, set two crystal carafes of wine before Bhayar, one of a white with the slightest hint of yellow and the other deep red.

Bhayar looked to his sister.

"The white, please."

Bhayar filled her goblet with the white and his own with the red.

Quaeryt took white.

"To your safe return and to health." Bhayar lifted his goblet.

Quaeryt and Vaelora lifted theirs. Then they drank.

"Ten thousand golds, you say, arriving with Justanan?" asked Bhayar.

"Slightly more. We also left three hundred with Subcommander Moravan for anything in the way of supplies and provisions he could not obtain from the holding."

"We can use them. It's still months before the regular tariffs are due," said Vaelora.

"Spoken like the Minister of Administration and Supply," replied Bhayar, pausing and taking another sip of wine as the two servers set three platters and a covered dish on the table.

None of the three spoke while they served themselves in turn, beginning with Bhayar, with thin slices of beef covered in a wine reduction, tarragon lace potatoes in cream butter, early beans almandine, hot fried peach slices, and fluffy brown bread rolls.

"Just a simple family dinner, but good," said Bhayar with a glint in his eye.

"No family dinners are ever simple," replied Vaelora sweetly.

"Do you have any later word on the progress of the Khellan envoy?" asked Bhayar.

"Only the first message," replied Vaelora.

"Will this envoy actually be empowered to consider and agree to terms, do you think, or will his—or her—presence merely be a way to stall for time while the

Khellans try to rebuild their land?" Bhayar looked to his sister and then to Quaeryt.

Quaeryt glanced at his wife.

Vaelora took a sip of her wine before answering. "Either is possible. From what we saw, it will be years before Khel recovers. The High Council is aware of that. They also fear Quaeryt and his imagers. If they are as wise as I hope they are, they will press for the best terms they think they can obtain."

"I cannot be too generous," said Bhayar.

"You cannot afford to *appear* too generous," suggested Quaeryt.

"How do you propose I accomplish that?" Bhayar's tone seemed genuinely curious.

"You insist on language whereby the High Council and people of Khel agree to be part of the great land of Solidar and to acknowledge you as the sole sovereign. You insist on a total of annual tariffs based on the accounting of the Ministry of Administration and Supply, not to be less than a certain amount that we'll have to calculate, but raising roughly the same revenue per person as you receive in Telaryn, except the terms won't put it that way—"

"Why . . . oh . . . because they don't have any High Holders . . . and not that many factors?" replied Bhayar.

Quaeryt nodded. "We might need some language making raising those tariffs the responsibility of the local councils, with, of course, the oversight of the governor and his princeps. Oh, and you will have to insist on having at least a few high holdings, including most of those already established by Kharst." *So we can place a few people here and there, including Deucalon.*

"What else?"

"Ports obviously open to all Solidaran ships, with standard tariffs on all outside merchanters. . . ."

The talk about the terms continued through the main course.

Then, as the servers were clearing away the dishes, Bhayar cleared his throat.

Both Vaelora and Quaeryt looked up.

"There is one other matter I wanted to bring up," said Bhayar. "I've received a letter from a High Holder Ensoel. Several in fact. They concern you, Quaeryt." His face remained pleasantly bland.

"I don't recall that name," replied Quaeryt. Although he was fairly sure he had never met the High Holder, there was always the possibility that he had passed the man's lands or that some of his forces might have . . . and even damaged something. *But several letters?*

"You wouldn't." Bhayar smiled. "In his first letter, he inquired about a rumor that I was establishing a school for imagers and wished to know if that might be true. I replied that construction of the school, the Collegium, was under way and that a number of students were already receiving instruction in both the usual subjects, as well as training in proper imaging." Bhayar looked to Quaeryt. "I trust that is correct."

"It is," replied Quaeryt.

"Good. Because he sent a second letter saying that he has a daughter who he believes is an imager, and that renders her . . . unsuited . . . to the usual life of a High Holder's daughter. He also wished to know if the Collegium would be suitable for a young woman of her background."

"What he means is that no son of a High Holder would ever consider marrying a woman who is more powerful than he is," said Vaelora.

"Quite possibly," admitted Bhayar.

"There aren't many women imagers," ventured Quaeryt, looking to Vaelora and continuing, "although I think you might be one, or close to it, and your great-great-grandmere likely was."

Bhayar frowned, but did not speak.

"I think we can make it suitable without much trouble," said Quaeryt. "We might need a separate cottage—"

"No," interjected Vaelora. "Just make one end of the student quarters totally separate from the one for the boys, with a separate room for bathing. If necessary, she can stay here while the changes are being made."

"They shouldn't take that long. I think Horan and Baelthm could probably just add that section to the end of the student quarters. That might actually be easier."

"You'll need some women there," added Vaelora. "It wouldn't hurt to have some cooks and a few other women to help." She looked to her brother. "You will have to pay for this for a time."

"I hadn't thought otherwise," replied Bhayar dryly.

From there the conversation continued on various aspects of the Collegium and what else might be required, for which Quaeryt was thankful.

61

Quaeryt was working with Vaelora in her ministry study on Samedi morning when one of the clerks brought in a dispatch from Justanan, indicating that Northern Army would be arriving at headquarters slightly before noon. Quaeryt carried the message up to Bhayar, who read it and said, "I'll have a message ready in less than half a quint, commending him on his speed and politely requesting that he deliver the tariff golds here and then meet with me. The rest of Northern Army can return to the headquarters holding."

"I'll have a trooper standing by to carry it back with the courier."

Bhayar nodded and sat down at his desk.

Three glasses later, Justanan and a full company of troopers—and two armored wagons—arrived in the rear courtyard of the Chateau Regis. Vaelora took charge of having the golds—in locked chests—transferred to the underground vaults, while Quaeryt escorted Justanan from the courtyard and up the grand staircase.

The older commander studied the staircase and the walls. "You and your imagers rebuilt this, didn't you?"

"No." Quaeryt smiled. "They did it all. I was still recovering." *And out of my mind amid the whiteness of ice and death.*

"I didn't know that."

"Many people don't. The two imagers I left on Imagisle have done wonders there already." After the slightest pause, Quaeryt asked, "How is Commander Nieron?"

"He's in good spirits now. What happened at Fiancryt unsettled him, but after he saw the bridge your imagers built, and all the improvements to the roads, I think he understands just what a boon the imagers could be."

And that he wants me heading them and not the armies. But Quaeryt just nodded, rather than voice that thought.

"Do you know what Lord Bhayar wants?"

"To talk to you," replied Quaeryt. "He only told me that he wanted to meet you immediately upon your return. I did tell him that I thought you could handle a position of greater authority well, but that was only my recommendation."

"Only your recommendation? Do you make many, Commander?"

"More than Lord Bhayar would like at times," said Quaeryt wryly. "Did you encounter any unforeseen difficulties after we departed?"

Justanan shook his head. "Everything went as expected."

When they reached the closed door to Bhayar's study, Quaeryt looked to the guard. "I'll announce us."

"Yes, sir."

Quaeryt eased the door open just slightly. "Commander Justanan is here, as you requested, sir. So are the tariff golds. Lady Vaelora is overseeing their transfer to the vaults."

"Have the commander come in, Quaeryt. I'd appreciate it if you'd wait outside until summoned."

"Yes, sir." Quaeryt turned to Justanan and gestured for him to enter, then stepped back.

A quint passed, then two, and then three, before the bell rang and the guard at the study door opened it. He listened, then motioned for Quaeryt to enter the study.

Quaeryt did so.

Bhayar rose from behind his desk, not the conference table, and Justanan quickly stood from one of the chairs before the desk.

"Commander Quaeryt," said Bhayar formally, "I have offered the position of marshal of the armies and Commander Justanan has accepted."

"Congratulations, Marshal," offered Quaeryt. "You have my support and loyalty."

"As he should," said Bhayar, adding after a pause, "There will be a meeting of all available senior officers, major and above, in the upper great hall at fifth glass. I will make the announcement at that time. Until then, you are not to mention the appointment."

"Yes, sir," replied both Quaeryt and Justanan.

"I will see you both a quint before fifth glass. I realize you both have much to do, but I do not wish to leave the marshal's post vacant any longer than necessary." Bhayar offered a wry smile. "You may both go."

Once they were outside Bhayar's study and well away from the guard, Justanan looked to Quaeryt. "Being marshal is not something that I ever sought."

"That's likely one of the reasons you are receiving the position."

"I know what you have said about it not being wise for you to be promoted. . . ."

"I'm too young in the eyes of many, too close personally to Bhayar, and I'm an imager. Bhayar and the senior officers need a trusted and trustworthy officer of proven experience. You recall how Nieron reacted to the idea that I might take over command of Northern Army."

"Still . . ." pressed Justanan.

"It should not happen, and I should never be more than a commander." Quaeryt smiled. "And you have much to do before fifth glass."

Justanan chuckled. "I suspect that's all the answer I'll get."

"That's because it's the right answer and right for the officers and men."

Once Quaeryt had seen Justanan off, he returned to Vaelora's study to try to get caught up on more of what Vaelora had handled in dealing with various matters of administration while he had been gone.

He kept at that until a quint before fifth glass, when he met Justanan. The two walked up to Bhayar's study. When they entered, both were surprised to see Deucalon, in full uniform, standing somewhat stiffly by the conference table.

"Both Marshal Deucalon and I thought that a formal transfer of position would be the most suitable way to commemorate his service and to begin Marshal Justanan's responsibilities as marshal of the armies," said Bhayar pleasantly.

Deucalon nodded stiffly, and Quaeryt half wondered just what Bhayar had said to him.

"Commander Quaeryt," Bhayar continued, "you will enter first and call the officers to attention. Then you will join the other officers. The marshals and I will deal with the rest of the ceremony. You should leave shortly, and send a guard to inform us when all officers are present."

"Yes, sir." Quaeryt understood perfectly what Bhayar was doing, and he appreciated its necessity. He inclined his head, then turned and left the study. Once he reached the area outside the double doors to the upper great hall of the chateau, he took his position and waited.

The first officers to arrive were, unsurprisingly, Zhelan, Calkoran, Eslym, and Khaern. And Khaern's four battalion majors. All eight stopped short of Quaeryt.

"Can you tell us what the meeting is about, sir?" asked Khaern.

"I can only say that Lord Bhayar has requested that all senior officers gather so that he can address them. I wouldn't wish to say more, since I don't know exactly what he wants to say, only the general subject, and he's requested that I say nothing yet."

Calkoran and Zhelan exchanged quick glances. Khaern smiled faintly. "I understand, sir."

Quaeryt smiled in return. "I'm certain you do, but I'd appreciate your keeping any speculations to yourselves."

"Yes, sir."

The next officers were several subcommanders Quaeryt did not recognize, although he possibly knew their names from various dispatches, along with their senior majors.

Then came Commander Pulaskyr, who stopped and addressed Quaeryt. "Commander, any word on what Lord Bhayar will be saying?"

"I don't know what he'll say, only the general subject, and he's requested that I not divulge that so that he can address it in his own way."

Pulaskyr nodded and smiled. "Thank you."

Shortly after Pulaskyr entered the hall, Subcommander Ernyld stopped and looked at Quaeryt. "Commander . . . I find myself at a loss. I'm the chief of staff to the marshal of the armies, and I have no idea about the subject of this meeting. It seems most . . . irregular."

"A number of things have been rather . . . irregular lately, Subcommander," replied Quaeryt, his tone mild. "This meeting was called by Lord Bhayar to restore a certain . . . regularity to the activities of the armies. I'm certain he will make that perfectly clear."

"I would hope so, Commander."

"Whatever he says or does, Subcommander, he is the head of the armies, and the one to whom all officers and men, whether rankers, undercaptains, or marshals, owe their allegiance and loyalty. And that is how it should be." Quaeryt smiled.

Ernyld swallowed just slightly.

"Everything will be fine," Quaeryt added. "You'll see."

"Thank you." Ernyld did not sound convinced.

That's another problem Justanan will have to address . . . but in his own way.

It was almost fifth glass before Quaeryt felt that all the officers were present, slightly less than seventy in all, and sent word to Bhayar. The ruler of most of Lydar and the two marshals appeared almost within moments. When Bhayar approached, he nodded to Quaeryt, who stepped inside the great hall and to one side.

Deucalon was the first one through the door, and at that instant Quaeryt announced, boosting his voice slightly with image-projecting, "Lord Bhayar!"

All the officers stiffened.

Deucalon led the way to a place before the assembled

officers, followed by Justanan, and then Bhayar, who took a position just forward of the two, with Justanan to his right and Deucalon to his left.

"Commanders, Subcommanders, and Majors," began Bhayar, "I appreciate all that you have done in our efforts to unite Lydar into a single land. Without you and your men, what we have accomplished would not have been possible. One whose knowledge and experience in this has been most noteworthy is Marshal Deucalon. He served my father loyally and faithfully, and in leading you and in serving me, he always put foremost his beliefs of what was best for Telaryn. He is stepping down after a long and distinguished time as a senior officer, and I have appointed him as a High Holder. Which high holding he will receive will be announced within the next week or so, once I finish determining which of those who have no heirs as a result of the war will be most suitable." Bhahar smiled broadly and warmly. "I am sure that you all can appreciate that such long service should be rewarded."

From where he stood at the side of the great hall, Quaeryt could see that most officers were nodding, although Khaern, Zhelan, and Calkoran were understandably not among them.

"The new marshal of the armies of Telaryn is former Senior Commander Justanan, who has most recently commanded Northern Army and who has been most effective in assuring that northern Bovaria is completely loyal." Bhayar turned to Justanan and nodded.

The new marshal smiled, almost shyly, then said, "Most of you know this is a position I did not seek and did not expect. One thing I have learned, especially from others, is that demanding anything as due or owed is usually the road to disaster. Doing one's duty as well and as faithfully as possible is not merely a goal for an officer. It is a necessity. I have attempted to follow that precept all my life, and I intend to continue following it as marshal. I also expect the same of you." He smiled again. "I'll probably have more to say later, perhaps too much." He turned back to Bhayar.

Bhayar glanced to Quaeryt.

"Attention!" Quaeryt amplified his voice with image-projection.

Bhayar followed the two marshals from the great hall.

Once they were well clear and on their way back to Bhayar's study, Quaeryt made the last announcement. "As you were."

Within moments, Quaeryt was joined by Pulaskyr.

"You handled that rather well, Commander."

"I just announced people," replied Quaeryt blandly.

"That you did, but it was better this way. A pity about Myskyl, though." Pulaskyr's voice was so matter-of-fact that it was clear he felt no sympathy whatsoever.

"It is," Quaeryt replied.

"It's said that you don't plan to remain a commander."

"Only so long as necessary. I'll likely become head of the imagers' Collegium. Lydar needs a place where imagers can be schooled and where they can feel safe and be productive supporters of Lord Bhayar and his heirs . . . and their heirs."

"That's also likely for the best," replied Pulaskyr. "I don't know if I'll be seeing you again."

"Oh?"

"Bhayar has asked me to serve as regional governor of Solis and acting governor of Telaryn during the transition . . . and to arrange for Lady Aelina and the children to come to Variana. I'll be taking several regiments, of course."

"I wish you well."

"And I you." Pulaskyr smiled, then turned.

Bhayar had definitely been busy, Quaeryt reflected. *And that's good.*

62

By Mardi morning, Quaeryt was beginning to feel as though he had at least a basic grasp of what Vaelora had dealt with and accomplished while he'd been involved in thwarting Myskyl's and Deucalon's scheming. Although Bhayar had not indicated whether he intended to accept Quaeryt's recommendation for the eventual disposition of the lands belonging to the late High Holder Fiancryt, he had issued a proclamation declaring Lady Myranda guilty of treason and her life forfeit.

Quaeryt had also arranged for Calkoran to ride out to meet whomever the High Council of Khel had sent as envoy once word was received that the envoy was within a glass or so of the chateau. That left him free to deal with the other matters that seemed to appear from everywhere, including yet another letter about repairs of the Anomen D'Variana and an inquiry from the sole scholarium, the one north of Variana, asking for consideration and support.

Quaeryt had almost, but not quite, mentally pushed aside the issue of Khel and the arriving envoy when a trooper hurried into Vaelora's study slightly after midday and announced, "The Khellan envoy is riding up to the front of the Chateau Regis."

"We should greet him, then," said Vaelora calmly, "even though no one greeted us properly in Saendeol."

Quaeryt couldn't help smiling, thinking, *She may forgive, but she never forgets.* He'd learned that quickly. "Him?"

"Bhayar sent me. The High Council will send a man, most likely Councilor Khaliost."

"Because he's the only man on the High Council and the oldest, so that he can be replaced when he commits Khel to terms that the others don't like?"

Vaelora shook her head. "They'll keep him on the Council for a time so that everyone can demand of him the reasons why he gave away so much."

"Bhayar won't—"

"Bhayar might," she said. "We won't. Let's go see if I'm right."

Quaeryt would have been surprised if she'd been wrong.

"We need to let the kitchen know to send up the refreshments to the lower receiving parlor," added Vaelora.

Before that morning, Quaeryt hadn't even known there was such a parlor, let alone where it was, not that he was surprised to find one existed, given the size of the Chateau Regis.

After sending instructions to the kitchen, the two left the study and headed for the front entry. They had only been waiting at the top of the white-stone steps for about a third of a quint when the squad from Major Zhael's second company reined up. A second squad was behind the first, led by Major Eslym. Quaeryt frowned, then realized that Calkoran was at the front of the group, and beside him was the white-haired Khaliost, and beside and behind him several others in Khellan garb.

Calkoran dismounted immediately and walked half-way up the steps, then turned to face Quaeryt. "Lady and Minister Vaelora, Commander Quaeryt, might I present the envoy of the High Council of Khel, Councilor Khaliost?"

"We look forward to receiving the councilor and his party," replied Quaeryt.

At that, Khaliost immediately dismounted and walked up the steps. He still wore the tan tunic and red chorister-like scarf. He also carried a leather folder. Behind him was a black-haired older woman, if not so old as Khaliost. She wore dark leathers, despite the warmth of summer, and the red leather gloves and belt of a Khellan Eleni.

Quaeryt knew he had seen her before.

"The Hall of Heaven," murmured Vaelora.

The Eleni who tested us.

Quaeryt waited until the two reached the top of the steps and stood opposite them, then offered the sole Pharsi greeting he knew, and then in Bovarian, "Welcome to the Chateau Regis, Councilor and honored Eleni."

Vaelora added a few words in Pharsi.

Khaliost inclined his head. "Your men have treated us well, Son of Erion and Daughter of the Greater Moon, but we are glad to be here."

"We have refreshments for you inside," said Vaelora, stepping back.

The Eleni studied the chateau, then looked to Quaeryt. "Your imagers are skilled."

"Some of them. Others are just powerful."

She merely nodded thoughtfully.

Once the four of them were seated in the receiving parlor, and Khaliost and Vaelora had sipped some of the white wine, and the Eleni and Quaeryt had tried the pale lager, Khaliost looked across the circular table.

"I stopped to talk to the Khellan officers and troopers in Kephria," said the white-haired councilor.

"What did you discover?" asked Vaelora.

"That Liantiago belongs to Lord Bhayar. We knew that. The High Council would not have sent me otherwise. I wished to know how that had happened. They told me." Khaliost turned slightly to address Quaeryt directly. "They also told me that there are at least four other imagers of great power, although you are more than a great imager, and far more than a mere commander." His eyes shifted to Vaelora. "And you see more than any woman, even any *Eherelani* or Eleni, should see. The majors told me you lost your daughter protecting them."

"I did lose her at Kephria."

"You expect another," said the Eleni flatly.

"I do," admitted Vaelora.

"She will be an imager. I do not know if she will have your sight. That comes later."

"Thank you."

"I would not wish thanks for that, Lady. A woman who is an imager . . . she will face great trials, even with the protections you and your consort can provide."

After another sip of the wine, Khaliost went on. "I took the liberty of also talking to Marshal Calkoran after he came to escort us. He insisted that I meet with Major Eslym. The major presented me with a dagger. He insists it is the dagger that Erion threw to protect you against the remaining imagers of Rex Kharst when you faced them while trapped in a chamber lined with lead and iron." The older man smiled cheerfully. "Is it?"

"It was thrown by a figure that looked like Erion," Quaeryt admitted.

"It is stronger than iron and lighter, and the edge is sharp enough to shave a man or behead him. The major says that it also pierced an iron-lined door."

"That is true. It pinned Submarshal Myskyl to the door."

Khaliost nodded. So did the Eleni.

For several moments, there was silence.

Then Quaeryt asked, "Are you empowered to agree to the final terms you work out, and will the Council be bound by those terms? Or will we work out something only to discover that the Council will reject it, and then we'll have to invade Bovaria?"

"That is why Chiana is here. Whatever terms we agree on, the High Council will accept." Khaliost sighed. "I hope we can agree, because I cannot agree to what would amount to a complete surrender of who and what Khel is."

"Lord Bhayar is generally reasonable."

"The Council knows that of you. We hope that of him."

"Might I inquire as to what instructions the High Council gave you?"

"To obtain the best terms possible, and to obtain assurance from you that you will support those terms." Khaliost paused, then opened the leather folder and extracted several sheets, which he handed to Quaeryt. "Here is an outline of what the High Council would suggest for terms, based on what you said in Saendeol. Chiana and I realize that these are what the High Council wishes, but the more that Bhayar wants beyond these, the more unhappy the Council and the people of Khel will be."

"I can only promise that Vaelora and I will go over the suggestions first before presenting them to Lord Bhayar. Although we will have to read your proposed terms, there will doubtless be some provisions that will need to be added."

"Such as?" inquired Khaliost.

"I would not wish to prejudge what the Council has proposed," replied Quaeryt. "I'm only stating that such additional provisions may be necessary."

Khaliost nodded, then asked, "Might I ask what laws will govern Khel if Khel agrees to terms?"

"Lord Bhayar is considering a new legal codex that will merge the past laws of Bovaria with those of Telaryn, with certain additional changes to provide some protections . . . and possibly some limitations on . . . certain individuals. He intends that, in general, all laws and tariffs across Lydar be the same, with no special provisions for traders or factors from one part or another."

"There are differences in customs . . ."

"We know," replied Quaeryt.

More than two quints later, Quaeryt and Vaelora exchanged glances.

"There are quarters for you . . ." Quaeryt looked to Chiana.

Khaliost laughed softly. "She is my cousin."

"We have more than enough rooms for your party," said Vaelora. "We don't have the chateau fully restored, and the smaller dining chamber is rather bare. Its sparseness is not a lack of respect, but a lack of time and golds to complete the refurbishing of the chateau."

After another quint of discussing arrangements, Vaelora had one of the maids, essentially serving as a footman, escort the two to their quarters, while one of the administration clerks dealt with the six guards that had accompanied them.

Then Vaelora and Quaeryt retreated to her ministry study and began to read through the terms proposed by the High Council.

Two quints later, they looked at each other.

"Bhayar will never agree to all of this," said Quaeryt.

"They know that," replied Vaelora, "and we know that they know that."

"So what do we do? Separate out the provisions into groups—those that are acceptable, those that are unacceptable under any conditions, those that we can soften to acceptability, and those Bhayar needs that they haven't addressed and we need to add?"

Vaelora smiled. "That's a start."

Quaeryt had the feeling that long days and nights lay ahead of them.

63

Neither Quaeryt nor Vaelora felt comfortable bringing the terms of the agreement with the High Council of Khel to Bhayar until midafternoon on Meredi, when they had finally considered all the provisions and then written out their recommendations for changes to those provisions that they thought were unacceptable or needed improvement.

The terms suggested by the Khellan High Council only comprised three pages, the actual terms consisting of little more than a page and a half, but when Quaeryt and Vaelora entered Bhayar's study, both carried leather folders filled with other papers, ranging from tariff reports to the proposed legal code Bhayar was considering . . . as well as other calculations that Vaelora and the clerks had worked out.

Bhayar walked from the window and sat down at the conference table. "Before I read it, tell me what you think their terms mean."

Quaeryt settled into the chair on Bhayar's left, and Vaelora on her brother's right.

"They accept your sovereignty and protection on both land and sea," began Quaeryt, "but will not pay any reparations, since they have done no damage to either Bovaria or Telaryn. They agree to the same tariffs as levied, by category, on merchants, factors, holders, and growers in Telaryn, and paid at the same times and collected by local councils. They agree to your building military establishments as necessary in Khel, provided the land or other property is purchased at a fair price. They wish you to agree that the ruler of Lydar will not use his position to require any specific form of belief or worship. . . ."

Bhayar nodded. "So far . . . so good."

"Those are the provisions that we thought you would generally agree with. There are others, however . . ." Quaeryt cleared his throat. "The Council agrees that all Khellan troopers and officers who served you may now return to Khel if they wish, but that they must not be compelled to do so. There is one exception. Former Marshal of Khel Calkoran must never set foot on the lands of Khel for the rest of his life."

"What?"

"He disobeyed the Council's orders in dealing with the Bovarian invasion. Rather than break his army into smaller units and fight scattered battles against the Bovarians, he massed his forces at Khelgror. He was defeated and lost most of his command—except for those he brought to Telaryn. But in doing so, he also almost won and killed nine out of ten Bovarians—one reason why Kharst couldn't hang on to Khel once you attacked."

"They feel strongly about this?"

"Yes," said Vaelora.

"I suggest that you give him a small high holding, sir."

"You have one in mind?"

"Vaestora. High Holder Seliadyn is failing, and he requested that I intercede with you to find a proper successor. It is not that large, but prosperous and well managed. It has a walled keep whose gates are never closed, and Seliadyn tariffs his underholders less than other High Holders . . . and that will likely be necessary for his successor."

"I suppose . . ." mused Bhayar.

"You can point out that it's a small recompense for a man who lost his homeland in opposing Rex Kharst and essentially made it possible for you to unite Solidar."

"I'll think about that. Go on."

"They do not want Khellan lands confiscated for high holdings . . ."

"I can't agree to that!"

"You can . . . in a way," suggested Quaeryt. "Kharst already confiscated lands and established six large high holdings. You can agree to not confiscating any more lands, but on maintaining those six . . . and on recognizing any landholder or factor whose success in creating a holding that meets the standards of a high holding can be recognized as such in the future. That way, any future additional high holdings would be established in the same way that many already have been."

"What else?"

"They want to maintain their own laws."

"So?"

"You don't want that. We need to come up with a way of combining their laws with the code you're already working on. Maybe put in a provision that the laws of Solidar will take full force in five years or some such."

"Which laws? The ones you sent me?"

"Exactly." Quaeryt grinned. "Vaelora and I worked on the codex, and you changed it, and we sent it back to you. Most important, it was based on both the

Telaryn codex issued by your grandsire and what reasonable Bovarian laws there were. It also creates more controls over the factors. If you've lost your copy . . ." He took the sheaf of papers from the leather folder and laid it on the conference table.

Bhayar shook his head. "I have what you sent me. You two did take some liberties with the codex."

"Very few. We did add a section on imagers, saying that, while they were subject to the laws of Solidar, they could not be executed or imprisoned for more than two seasons for violations of the code without the express written consent of the Rex Regis, and that the Collegium Imago had the right to investigate any death or injury to an imager. We also simplified the sections on tariffs, and made misuse of tariff revenues by a regional governor a crime with penalties ranging from fines to death, depending on the severity of the abuse, and we spelled out each level of abuse. We also allowed High Holders to retain the right of low justice, but high justice must be meted out by regional justicers appointed by the Rex Regis—"

"Enough! After we work out the terms with Khel, I'll sign it, and the Ministry of Administration and Supply can send copies to everyone, and you'll spend the next year explaining it to all the High Holders and factors. Here and in Khel." Bhayar paused. "What about governing?"

"They want the High Council to govern on your behalf."

"No. Absolutely not."

"We suggested that you appoint a regional governor and that he have two princeps, rather than the usual one. One would be for logistics, and the second would be to advise the governor, and would be the head councilor of the High Council—or, alternatively, an appointee of the High Council."

"That might work. Who would you suggest as regional governor for Khel?"

"Subcommander Meinyt. Promote him to Commander and make it clear to both Meinyt and the Council that the governor's role is gentle oversight, the collection of tariffs, and that, so long as the Council maintains order under the code of laws you've promulgated. . . ." Quaeryt offered both a smile and a shrug.

"I'll have to think about that." Bhayar squared his shoulders. "We might as well go over the terms line by line."

Quaeryt did not sigh, much as he felt like it.

64

As Quaeryt had feared, the next two days were long, and while not exactly unpleasant, he found them tiring in first explaining to Khaliost and Chiana why some of the High Council's proposals would not work or could not be accepted, and conversely, pointing out to Bhayar how the accommodations suggested by either the Khellans or Vaelora and Quaeryt would not measurably affect his rule and power. The largest sticking point was the issue of governance, but in the end, Khaliost and Bhayar agreed on the point that the High Council would appoint the princeps of Khel, while an assistant princeps, not a second princeps, largely for logistics and supply, would be appointed by the Rex Regis.

On Vendrei morning, at eighth glass, two glasses before the final agreement was to be signed, Quaeryt and Vaelora met once more with Bhayar in his study.

Quaeryt handed a single-page document to Bhayar.

"What is this?"

"It's the proclamation you'll issue after signing the terms with Khel. It declares that the united lands of Lydar, comprising the former lands of Tilbor, Telaryn, Bovaria, Antiago, and Khel, are henceforth united and to be known as Solidar, and that the capital city, formerly known as Variana, is now L'Excelsis, and that your title as ruler is also henceforth Rex Regis."

"L'Excelsis?" Bhayar frowned, as he had for much of the week.

"Just let it be, brother dear, and sign it," snapped Vaelora.

"Don't get snippy with me . . ."

"Who else dares to be honest with you?" she said quietly.

"Your husband, but he's more politely insistent."

"That's because he didn't grow up with you."

Bhayar shook his head and looked to Quaeryt. "I am glad she married you . . . and I'm looking forward to the time when you're maître of the Collegium."

"Even when that happens, and we have quarters there," replied Vaelora, "I'll still be your Minister for Administration."

Bhayar mock-groaned. "I know. I know." Then he picked up the document and read through it. After a moment he reached for the pen in the holder, dipped it in the inkwell, and signed the proclamation. "There!"

"Good," said Vaelora. "I'll have the clerks make copies and we'll send them out everywhere."

Quaeryt eased the proclamation away from Bhayar and slipped another one before him. "Here's the other document you requested—the assignment of the high holding of Khunthan, one of the largest in Solidar, to Deucalon."

"Given its size, he shouldn't complain," said Bhayar, "even if it is just about as far from . . . L'Excelsis . . . as possible."

"Eshtora's not close," admitted Quaeryt, "and we will convey to Deucalon that the regional governor and princeps will be watching closely to see how he handles those lands. Meinyt will be perfect for that."

"You're sure he'll accept being regional governor of Khel?"

"He's done well so far as acting regional governor of the west of Bovaria, and you can always hint that other possibilities exist in time if he does well in Khel." Quaeryt paused. "He will, though. He's tough and practical, yet reasonable, and that's what you need to deal with the High Council, especially when they're collecting the tariffs." *And Meinyt won't put up with any foolishness . . . from either the Council or Deucalon.*

65

~⁓~

As they dressed for the comparatively small formal dinner on Samedi evening to celebrate the signing of the terms between Khel and Solidar, Quaeryt stood behind Vaelora as she sat peering into the mirror and studying her reflection, an image with which Quaeryt could find no fault . . . although he suspected she would discover some way to improve it.

"You have that distant expression on your face," she said abruptly after glancing up at him. "Are you still thinking about how everything happened?"

"I wasn't . . . but I have on and off. It's hard not to. I couldn't have done it without you . . . and Khalis and Lhandor . . . and Elsior." *Elsior was the one who knew the dangers of metal-lined rooms.* "I should have thought about the metal rooms and darkness after your flash. . . ."

"How could you have known . . . ?"

"You were the one who told me about how Aliaro kept his imagers in metal-lined rooms . . . but I didn't even think about Myskyl and his imagers . . ." Quaeryt shook his head.

"That's one of the things I like about you," Vaelora said warmly.

"What?"

"You're not like Deucalon, or Myskyl . . . or even

Rholan. You know a great deal, but you don't think you have the answers for everything."

"That's because I have you, with me and behind me . . . and sometimes very much in front of me," Quaeryt replied playfully. "You remind me just enough that I know I don't have all the answers. Rholan likely didn't, either. He just didn't have someone like you."

Vaelora's mouth opened. "That's it."

"What's it?"

Without answering, Vaelora jumped up from the dressing table and hurried into the bedchamber. She returned holding the leatherbound volume of *Rholan and the Nameless*, leafing through it as she did. "Remember that part when the writer talks about Rholan not knowing the importance of a woman's appearance and how it is a source of her power?"

"Yes," replied Quaeryt warily.

"Here's another section . . . when the writer is talking about Rholan's feelings about factors." She began to read . . .

". . . they know the value of every kind of good to the last part of a copper. What they cannot value are the ideals of the people that make those values possible. Among those values are the beliefs that a good reputation is to be more valued than golds in one's wallet or that a man should be paid honestly for his work. Of course, he never mentioned that the same should be true of women. . . ."

"It's the only thing that makes sense."

Quaeryt began to grin. "Go on."

She turned to the last page of the small leatherbound book. "Here . . . look." She pointed to the last letters.

Quaeryt looked over her shoulder at them. "The End."

"They're not a fancy way of writing 'The End,'" said Vaelora. "They're initials."

Quaeryt looked more closely, seeing what she meant—the curled letters, studied closely, actually read "TN&D."

Abruptly he understood fully. "Thieryesa of Niasaen and Douvyt . . . *She* wrote the book. He did have a woman behind him all the time, even if he never acknowledged her." *And she did get the last word . . . in her own way. But then, so did Vaelora.*

He smiled.

"What are you thinking?" Vaelora asked as she closed the book.

"That it's time for us to make an appearance." He grinned, taking in her still-slender figure and her beauty in the pale green gown with the brown sleeveless silk vest that highlighted her eyes.

"You were not."

"You're right. I'll tell you later."

"You'd better."

"I always do."

"In your own good time."

"But I tell you." *Always.* He reached out and took her hand.

They walked down the grand staircase arm in arm.

EPILOGUE

Quaeryt, Vaelora, and Calkoran rode down the west river road. To their left was Imagisle, and ahead was the bridge over the River Aluse.

"I don't see why I have to come to Imagisle in order to see the changes the imagers made to the student quarters for young women," said Vaelora. "High Holder Ensoel's daughter could certainly live with whatever changes they made. I've accommodated myself to a range of housing over the past years."

"I know," replied Quaeryt. "Calkoran insists that it's also so that we can inspect the family cottages as well. Neither of us has been here in weeks with all the other details your brother has piled on us. All the imagers are male, and not many have wives—or daughters. The wives of the few that do have them have been sent for, but they haven't arrived yet. According to both Gauswn and Horan—even Zhelan—the imagers worry that they may have overlooked something."

From where he rode on Vaelora's right, Calkoran cleared his throat. "I would not feel comfortable, Lady Vaelora, if the imagers were building a house for the families of my men . . ."

"When are you leaving for Vaestora?" asked Vaelora

gently, the softness of her words conveying her understanding of the mixed feelings behind Calkoran's words.

"The day after tomorrow, Lady. The last of my companies left for Khel yesterday to support Governor Meinyt."

Escorting Deucalon as well. Quaeryt nodded at that.

"You don't have to call me 'Lady,' " replied Vaelora, "now that you're a High Holder."

"Only through the kindness of your brother and husband," replied the former marshal and subcommander.

"You earned that holding," replied Quaeryt. "Both in Khel and in Bovaria. And you'll take care of it."

"I have no heirs," Calkoran said.

"You're still young enough to have them," replied Vaelora, "and a distinguished commander and marshal who's handsome and now a High Holder won't have any lack of interested young women."

"There are likely some daughters of wealthy Pharsi who would be very interested," added Quaeryt with a grin.

The gray-haired officer actually blushed, then gestured for them to guide their mounts onto the bridge.

"They've done so much." As she reached the middle of the bridge, Vaelora gestured to the anomen. "It's so beautiful now."

When they reached the green, Quaeryt pointed toward the building at the south end. "That's the administration or headquarters building. There's even a study there for me when I become the full-time maître . . . whenever that happens."

"It won't be that long now," said Vaelora. "Things are settling down."

"That's true. Justanan has a firm grip, and so do you."

"To the north of the green," said Calkoran. "That is where the family cottages are."

Quaeryt and Vaelora turned north and took the left side of the paved boulevard. There were five houses on the east side, then the paved lane, a narrow green, another paved lane, and five more dwellings on the west side. Each was solidly constructed of a gray brick, with a roof of slate tiles. Each dwelling had white shutters and matching trim, with brassbound oak doors set in the middle of wide covered front porches.

"They left space behind each one for more lanes and houses," said Calkoran.

Quaeryt looked up. A large structure stood at the north end of the parkway. Before it was a wide paved area. A lane led to a small structure that had to be a stable set to the rear of the dwelling and to the west. Unlike the family dwellings, the larger building was of two stories, its walls of gray granite. It extended a good forty yards across the front and was completely surrounded by a covered porch. Broad stone steps led up to the porch, and the shutters and trim were painted a luminous light greenish brown that somehow avoided being garish. Wide windows graced both floors.

Flanking the short walk to the steps were the imager undercaptains, with Zhelan standing slightly to one side.

Quaeryt looked to Vaelora, but she appeared as stunned as he felt. Then Quaeryt looked to Calkoran. "That wasn't here the last time I was here."

"No, sir." Calkoran smiled. "Why don't you let the major explain?"

Quaeryt kept studying the large dwelling as he and Vaelora rode toward it, taking in the brassbound front doors with the elaborate etched glass whose pattern he could not quite make out, what looked to be stone tiling on the porch floor, and the stone pillars supporting the porch.

When they reined up, Zhelan stepped forward, followed by the imager undercaptains. "Commander and Lady . . . your future home."

"It is not finished yet, inside," declared Baelthm. "We would not do that, Lady, without your guidance."

"We all knew you wouldn't ever ask for what you deserve, sir and Lady," said Khalis, with a broad smile. "So we did our best to build it before you could object. Lhandor did the plans."

Quaeryt just kept looking at the magnificent dwelling, not a palace, but certainly a small mansion. He could feel his eyes burning.

Vaelora reached across the gap between their mounts and took his hand. "You deserve this."

He shook his head. "Not without you."

"We deserve it, then." Vaelora smiled warmly at him.

Quaeryt didn't object. Not so long as she was beside him.